The Florios of Sicily

The Florios of Sicily

a novel

Stefania Auci

Translated by Katherine Gregor

HARPERVIA

An Imprint of HarperCollins*Publishers*

This book is a work of fiction. References to real people, events, establishments, organizations, or locales are intended only to provide a sense of authenticity, and are used fictitiously. All other characters, and all incidents and dialogue, are drawn from the author's imagination and are not to be construed as real.

HarperCollins books may be purchased for educational, business, or sales promotional use. For information, please email the Special Markets Department at SPsales@harpercollins.com.

Originally published as *I leoni di Sicilia* in Italy in 2019 by Nord.

Translated from the Italian by Katherine Gregor.

FIRST EDITION

Designed by SBI Book Arts, LLC
Map illustraion on p. xiii by Beehive Mapping

Library of Congress Cataloging-in-Publication Data

Names: Auci, Stefania, author. | Gregor, Katherine, translator.
Title: The Florios of Sicily : a novel / Stefania Auci ; translated by Katherine Gregor.
Other titles: Leoni di Sicilia. English
Description: First edition. | New York, NY : HarperVia, [2019] | "Originally published as I leoni di Sicilia in Italy in 2019 by Nord"—Title page verso.
Identifiers: LCCN 2019030861 (print) | LCCN 2019030862 (ebook) | ISBN 9780062931672 (hardcover) | ISBN 9780062931696 (ebook)
Subjects: LCSH: Sicily (Italy)—Fiction.
Classification: LCC PQ4901.U28 L4613 2019 (print) | LCC PQ4901.U28 (ebook) | DDC 853/.92—dc23
LC record available at https://lccn.loc.gov/2019030861
LC ebook record available at https://lccn.loc.gov/2019030862

ISBN 978-0-06-293167-2
ISBN 978-0-06-303013-8 (Int'l)

20 21 22 23 24 LSC 10 9 8 7 6 5 4 3 2 1

To Federico and Eleonora:

to the courage, recklessness, and folly

we have shared over days

that were lost and found again.

What though the field be lost?
All is not lost—the unconquerable will,
And study of revenge, immortal hate,
And courage never to submit or yield:
And what is else not to be overcome?

—JOHN MILTON, *PARADISE LOST*

CONTENTS

THE FLORIO FAMILY TREE 1723–1868

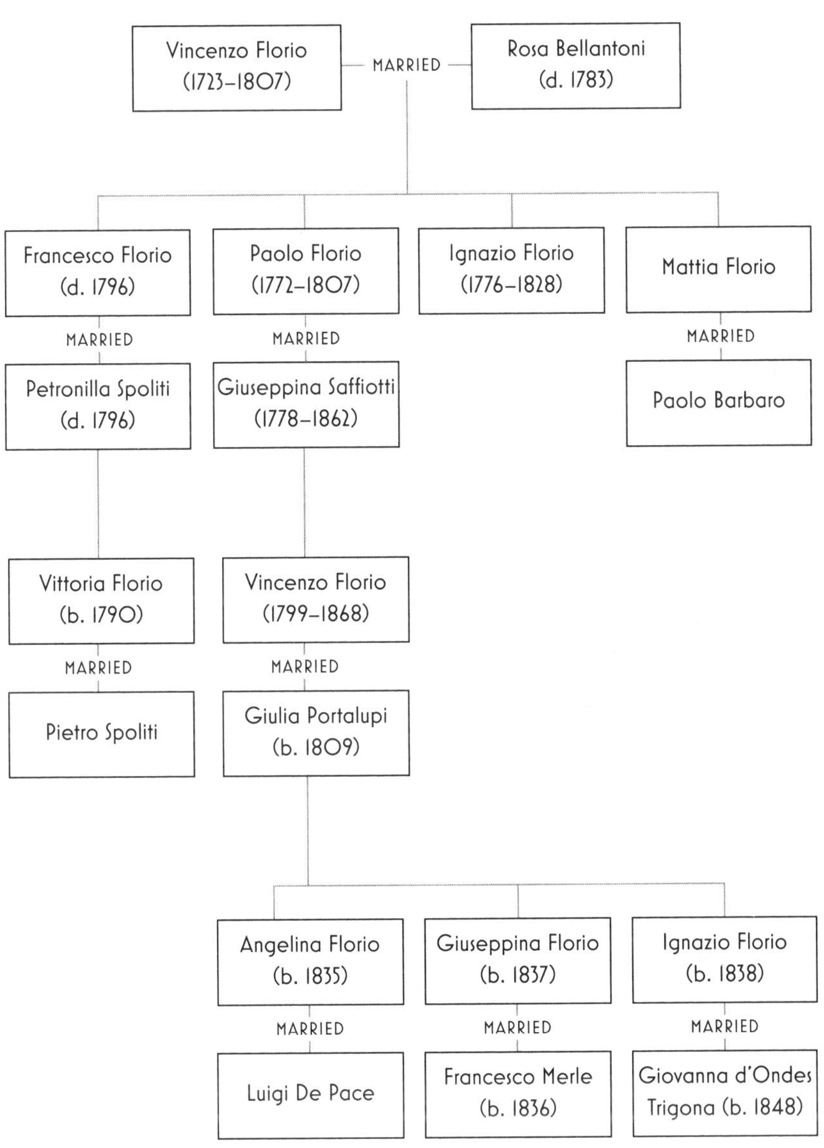

AUSTRIA-HUNGARY
KINGDOM OF
LOMBARDY-VENETIA
Venice
KINGDOM OF
SARDINIA
Parma
Modena
Ferrara
Genoa
OTTOMAN
EMPIRE
Lucca
Florence
Adriatic Sea
GRAND DUCHY
OF TUSCANY
PAPAL
STATES
Corsica
(France)
Rome
Naples
Brindisi
Tyrrhenian Sea
Sardinia
KINGDOM OF THE TWO SICILIES
Bagnara
Mediterranean Sea
Palermo
Messina
Marsala
Sicily
ITALY, 1815

The Florios of Sicily

Prologue

Bagnara Calabra, October 16, 1799

Cu nesci, arrinesci.

Those who leave, succeed.

—SICILIAN PROVERB

THE EARTHQUAKE IS A HISS that starts in the sea and wedges itself into the night. It swells, grows, then becomes a roar that tears through the silence.

In the houses, people are asleep. Some are awoken by the clinking of pots and pans, others by slamming doors. By the time the walls begin to shake, however, everybody is up.

Cattle lowing, dogs barking, praying, and cursing. The mountains shrug off rocks and mud, and the world turns upside down.

The tremor reaches the Pietraliscia district, grabs a house by its foundations, and shakes it violently.

Ignazio opens his eyes, snatched from his sleep by this tremor sending cracks running through the walls. Above, the low ceiling seems to be falling down on him.

It's not a dream. It's reality at its worst.

In front of him, Vittoria's—his niece's—bed is swaying between the wall and the middle of the room. On the bench, the metal casket wobbles and falls to the floor, along with the comb and the razor.

A woman's screams echo through the house. "Help! Help! Earthquake!"

The yelling makes Ignazio bounce to his feet but he doesn't run away. He must first make sure Vittoria is safe. She's only nine and so frightened. He drags her under the bed to shelter her from the rubble.

"Stay here until I come back for you—you hear me?" he says. "Don't move."

She nods, too terrified even to speak.

Paolo. Vincenzo. Giuseppina.

Ignazio runs out of the room. The corridor seems endless, even though it's only a few steps. He can feel the wall pulling away from his hand, tries to touch it again but it moves, like a living thing.

He reaches his brother Paolo's bedroom. A beam of light is filtering through the shutters. His sister-in-law Giuseppina has leaped out of bed. Her maternal instinct has woken her up to warn her that Vincenzo, her son, just a few months old, is in danger. She tries to pick up the baby, who's sleeping in a cradle suspended from the beams of the ceiling, but the wicker basket is prey to the seismic tremors. The woman weeps in despair and reaches out as the cradle frantically sways.

Her shawl slips off, exposing her bare shoulders. "My baby! Holy Mother of God, help us!"

Giuseppina manages to grab the child. Vincenzo's eyes open wide and he starts crying. In the chaos, Ignazio sees a shadow. His brother Paolo. He jumps off the mattress and pushes his wife into the corridor. "Out!"

Ignazio goes back. "Wait, Vittoria!" he shouts. He finds her in the pitch blackness under the bed, curled up, her hands on her head. He lifts her and runs. Pieces of plaster come off the walls as the howl of the earthquake persists.

He can feel the little girl seeking shelter, clutching so hard at his shirt she's practically wringing the fabric. She's so scared, she's scratching him.

Paolo pushes them over the threshold and down the stairs. "Here, come."

They run to the middle of the courtyard as the tremor reaches its climax. They huddle together, heads touching, eyes shut tight. There are five of them. Everybody's here.

Ignazio prays, trembles, hopes. It's coming to an end. It has to end.

Time splinters into seconds.

Then, just as it began, the roar calms down and finally stops completely.

For a moment, there is only the night.

But Ignazio knows that this tranquility is deceptive. The earthquake is a lesson he had to learn very early on.

He looks up. He feels Vittoria's panic through his shirt, her fingernails digging into his skin, her trembling.

He sees the fear in his sister-in-law's face, the relief in his brother's; he notices Giuseppina's hand searching for her husband's arm and Paolo breaking away to get close to the building. "Thank God the house is still standing. Tomorrow, in the daylight, we'll see the damage and—"

Vincenzo picks this very moment to burst into tears. "Shh . . . quiet, dear heart, quiet." Giuseppina rocks and comforts him as she walks up to Ignazio and Vittoria. Giuseppina is still terrified. Ignazio can tell by her quick breathing and the smell of her sweat. Fear mixed with the scent of soap on her nightgown.

"What about you, Vittoria? Are you all right?" he asks.

His niece nods but refuses to let go of his shirt. Ignazio pulls her hand off forcibly. He understands her fear. The little girl is an orphan, his brother Francesco's daughter. He and his wife died a few years ago, leaving the child to the care of Paolo and Giuseppina, the only people able to give her a family and a roof over her head.

"Don't worry, I'm here."

Vittoria stares at him, silent, then clings to Giuseppina just as she did to him a moment earlier, like a castaway.

Vittoria has been living with Giuseppina and Paolo since they got married, just under three years ago. She takes after her uncle Paolo: taciturn, proud, reserved. And yet right now she's just a frightened child.

But fear wears many masks. Ignazio knows that his brother, for example, will never just stand there, crying. Hands on his hips, grim, he's already looking around the courtyard and at thc mountains that enclose the valley. "Holy Mother of God—how long did it last?"

His question sinks into the silence. Then Ignazio replies, "I don't know. Long enough." He's trying to steady the shuddering inside him. His face is tense, the stubble of a fair beard on his jaw, his hands slender and nervous. He's younger than Paolo, who actually looks older than he is.

The tension melts into a kind of exhaustion, giving way to physical sensations: humidity, nausea, stones digging into the soles of their feet. Ignazio is barefoot, in his nightshirt, practically naked. He brushes his hair off his face and looks at his brother, then at his sister-in-law.

It takes him only a second to decide.

He walks to the house. Paolo rushes after him and grabs him by the arm. "Where do you think you're going?"

Ignazio indicates with his head Vittoria, and Giuseppina, who's rocking the baby. "They need blankets," he says. "Stay with your wife. I'll go."

He doesn't wait for an answer. Quickly but cautiously, he climbs the stairs and pauses in the hallway to let his eyes grow accustomed to the darkness.

Plates, ornaments, chairs—everything has tumbled on the ground. Next to the dresser, a cloud of flour is still hovering over the floor.

He feels a pang in his heart: this is the house Giuseppina brought his brother Paolo as her dowry. It's their house, true, but also a cozy place where he feels welcome. Seeing it like this upsets him.

He hesitates. He knows what could happen if there is another tremor.

But only for a few seconds. He goes in and snatches the blankets from the beds.

He goes into his room, finds the knapsack where he keeps his work tools, and picks it up. Finally, he finds the iron casket and opens it. His mother's wedding ring shining in the dark seems to want to comfort him.

He puts the box into his knapsack.

In the corridor, he sees Giuseppina's shawl on the floor. She must have dropped it as she ran out. She never parts with it. She's been wearing it since the day she became a part of their family.

He grabs the shawl, returns to the front door, and crosses himself before the crucifix on the jamb. A second later, the earth starts to quake again.

"Thank God, this one wasn't as long." Ignazio shares the blankets with his brother and gives one to Vittoria. Then the shawl.

When he returns it to Giuseppina, she feels her nightgown and finds her skin, naked. "But—"

"I found it on the floor," Ignazio says, casting down his eyes.

She mutters a thank-you and wraps herself in the fabric, eager for something comforting to take away this anomalous cold. She shudders with anxiety and memories.

"No point staying out in the open." Paolo throws open the cowshed door. The cow makes a weak sound of protest as he drags her by the halter and ties her to the opposite wall. Then he uses flint to light a lantern and stacks heaps of hay against the walls. "Vittoria, Giuseppina, come and sit down."

It's a caring act, Ignazio knows, but the tone is that of an order. The women, wild-eyed, stare at the sky and the road. They would stay in the courtyard all night if someone didn't tell them what to do. And that's the task of the head of the family. To be strong, to protect: that's what a man does, especially a man like Paolo.

Vittoria and Giuseppina let themselves collapse on a heap of straw. The little girl curls up, her fists clenched in front of her face.

Giuseppina looks at her. She looks at her and tries not to remember but memory is a sneaky bastard that creeps up inside her, grabs her by the throat, and sucks her back into the past.

Her childhood. Her parents. Dead.

She scrunches up her eyelids and pushes the thought away with a deep breath. Or at least she tries. She holds Vincenzo tight, pulls down the top of her nightgown, and the child immediately clings to her nipple. His little hands grab the delicate skin, his fingernails scratching the areola.

She's alive. Her son's alive. He won't be orphaned.

Ignazio is standing still on the threshold. He's studying the profile of the house. Although it's dark, he's looking for signs of subsidence, a crack or a chipped wall, but can't find anything. He cannot believe it, and almost doesn't dare hope that nothing is going to happen *this time*.

His mother's memory is a gust of wind in the night. His mother laughing, reaching out with her arms, and he, a child, running toward her. All of a sudden, the box in his knapsack feels very heavy. Ignazio gets it and takes out the wrought-gold ring, which he clasps, his hand over his heart. "Mamma."

He says it in a whisper. It's a prayer, perhaps a search for solace, for a hug he's missed since he was seven years old. Since his mother, Rosa, died. It was 1783, the year of the Lord's vengeance, when the earth trembled until there was nothing left of Bagnara but rubble. That devastating earthquake that struck Calabria and Sicily, killing thousands, and swept away dozens of people in one night in Bagnara alone.

Even back then he and Giuseppina were close.

Ignazio remembers her well: a pale, skinny little girl, wedged between her brother and sister, staring at two mounds of soil marked with a single cross: her parents, killed in their sleep, crushed by the rubble of their bedroom.

He was next to his father and sister; Paolo stood a little farther back, fists clenched and a dark expression on his adolescent face. In those days, nobody mourned just their own: the funeral of Giuseppina's parents, Giovanna and Vincenzo Saffiotti, took place on the same day as that of his mother, Rosa Bellantoni, and many other Bagnara residents. It was always the same surnames: Barbaro, Spoliti, Di Maio, Sergi, Florio.

Ignazio looks at his sister-in-law. As soon as she lifts her head and her eyes meet his, he knows that she, too, is haunted by memories.

They speak the same language, inhabit the same pain, and carry around the same solitude.

Ignazio indicates the hill beyond the village of Bagnara. "We should go and see what happened to the others." In the darkness, lights signal the presence of houses and people. "Don't you want to know if Mattia and Paolo Barbaro are all right?"

There's a slight hesitation in his voice. At twenty-three, he's a fully grown man and yet his gestures remind Paolo of the child who used to hide behind the family house, past their father's forge, whenever their real mother would chide him. Later, with *that other one*—his father's new wife—Ignazio did not cry anymore. He would just stare at her with deep resentment and say nothing.

Paolo shrugs. "No need. If their houses are still standing, it means nothing's happened to them. It's still night and dark, and Pagliara is a long way away."

But Ignazio keeps glancing nervously at the road and, beyond, at the high ground surrounding the village. "No. I'm going to check what's happened." He takes the path leading to the center of Bagnara, while his brother curses in his wake.

"Come back!" he shouts, but Ignazio raises his hand as a sign that no, he'll keep walking.

He's barefoot, in his nightshirt, but he doesn't care: he wants to check on his sister. He goes down the high ground where Pietraliscia is located and reaches the village in a few minutes. There's rubble here and there, chunks of roof, broken tiles.

He sees a man running, a gash on his head. The blood shines in the torchlight with which he illuminates the alley. Ignazio walks past the square and turns into the narrow streets blocked by hens, goats, and escaped dogs. There's a lot of chaos.

In the courtyards, women and children are reciting the rosary or calling out to one another, asking for news. The men, on the other hand, are looking for spades and hoes, and picking up knapsacks with tools, the only things that can guarantee their livelihood, more precious than food or clothes.

He clambers up the path to the Granaro area, where the Barbaros live.

There, on the side of the road, are shacks made of stone and timber.

Once upon a time, there were real houses there: he was a child but he remembers them clearly. Then the 1783 earthquake destroyed them. Those who were able to rebuilt them as best they could with whatever they had managed to salvage. Others used the ruins to build larger, wealthy houses, like his brother-in-law, Paolo Barbaro, his sister Mattia Florio's husband.

As a matter of fact, she's the first person he sees: Mattia, sitting on a bench, barefoot. Her eyes are dark, her expression stern, her daughter, Anna, clinging to her nightgown and Raffaele asleep in her arms.

At that moment, Ignazio sees his mother in her, with her dark coloring. He goes to her and puts his arms around her without saying a word. The anxiety stops biting at his heart.

"How are you? Paolo? Vincenzo? And Vittoria?" She takes his face between her hands and kisses his eyelids. There's a tearful note in her voice. "How's Giuseppina?" She hugs her brother again, and he can smell bread and fruit, a scent of home, of tenderness.

"All safe and sound, thank God. Paolo's put her and the children in the cowshed. I came here to see how you—how you all are."

Paolo Barbaro appears from behind the house. He's leading a donkey by the halter.

Mattia tenses up and Ignazio lets go of her.

"Oh, good. I was about to come and get you and your brother." He ties the animal to the cart. "We have to go to the harbor and check on the boat. Never mind if it's just you."

Ignazio opens his arms and drops the blanket. "Like this? But I'm half-naked."

"So what? Are you embarrassed?"

Paolo is short and stocky, while his brother-in-law is lean, with a young, sinewy body.

Mattia comes forward, struggling with the children, who are clinging to her. "There are some clothes in the chest. He could wear—"

Her husband silences her. "Who asked you? Why are you always butting in? As for you, hurry up, get on. With all that's happened, nobody'll care what he's wearing."

"Mattia was only trying to help me," Ignazio says, trying to defend her. He can't bear to see his sister with her head down, her cheeks burning with humiliation.

His brother-in-law jumps on the cart. "My wife always talks too much. Now let's go."

Ignazio is about to answer back but Mattia stops him with a pleading look. He knows only too well that Barbaro has no respect for anyone.

The sea is viscous, the color of ink, and blends into the night. Ignazio jumps off the cart as soon as they reach the harbor.

Before him is the windswept bay, enclosed by a wall of cliffs and sand, shielded by a sharp mass of mountains and Cape Marturano.

Around the boats, men are shouting, checking the cargo, tightening ropes.

There's such a bustle, one would think it's midday.

"Let's go." Barbaro heads toward King Roger's tower, where the sea is deep. That's where the larger boats are moored.

They come to a boat with a flat keel. It's the *San Francesco di Paola*, the skiff that belongs to the Florios and Barbaro. The mainmast is swaying to the rhythm of the waves, and the bowsprit stretches out to sea. The sails are folded and the rigging is in place.

A shaft of light is shining through the hatch. Barbaro leans forward and listens to the creaking with a mixture of surprise and annoyance. "Brother-in-law, is that you?"

Paolo Florio's head pops out through the hatch. "Who else?"

"How should I know? With all that's happened tonight . . ."

But Paolo Florio isn't listening to him anymore. He's now looking at Ignazio. "And you! Not a word. Just took off and disappeared. Now come on, get up here."

Then he vanishes into the belly of the boat and his brother also jumps aboard. Their brother-in-law stays on the deck to check the left side, which slammed against the dock.

Ignazio slots into the hold, amid the boxes and cloth sacks that will go from Calabria to Palermo.

This is their work: trading, especially by sea. There were serious upheavals in the Kingdom of Naples a few months ago: the king was ousted and the rebels founded the Neapolitan Republic. A group of noblemen and intellectuals spread notions of democracy and freedom, just as had happened in France during the Revolution, which cost Louis XVI and Marie-Antoinette their heads. Ferdinand and Maria Carolina had been more alert and escaped in time, with those in the army who were still loyal to the British, France's longtime enemies, before the *lazzari*, the common people, could run them over with their anger.

But only the final wave of this revolution arrived here, over the Calabrian mountains. There were murders, the soldiers no longer knew whom to take orders from, and the brigands who've always infested the mountains also started looting the tradesmen on the coast. Between brigands and revolutionaries, the streets became dangerous, and although the sea has no churches or taverns, it certainly offered more safety than the streets of the Bourbon kingdom.

It's stifling inside the small hold. Cedar in wicker baskets, required by perfume makers; fish, stockfish especially, and salted herring. Farther in, bolts of leather, ready to be taken to Messina.

Paolo inspects the sacks of merchandise. The smell of salted fish spreads through the hold, as does the slightly sour odor of leather.

The spices are not in the hold, however. They keep those at home until they leave. The sea humidity and salt could damage them, so they are stored with care. They have exotic names that bring tastes to the tongue and summon pictures of sun and heat: pepper, sandalwood, cloves, tormentil, cinnamon. They are the true wealth.

Ignazio suddenly realizes that Paolo is anxious. He can tell by his movements, hears it in his words, muffled by the lapping against the planking. "What's the matter?" he asks. He's worried he might have argued with Giuseppina. His sister-in-law is far from subservient as a wife should be. At least the right kind of wife for Paolo. But that's not what's troubling him, he feels. "What's the matter?" he repeats.

"I want to leave Bagnara."

His words fall in the fleeting pause between waves.

Ignazio hopes he's misheard, but he knows Paolo has expressed this wish on other occasions. "Where to?" he asks, hurt more than surprised. He's afraid. It's a sudden, primeval fear, an animal with the sour breath of abandonment.

Mattia and Paolo have always supported him. Now Mattia has a family of her own and her brother wants to go away. To leave him alone.

His brother drops his voice. It's almost a whisper. "Actually, I've been thinking about it for a long time and after tonight's earthquake I am ever more convinced that it's the right thing to do. I don't want Vincenzo to grow up here, with the danger of the house falling on top of him. And also . . ." He looks at him. "I want more than this, Ignazio. This village isn't enough for me anymore. This life isn't enough for me. I want to go to Palermo."

Ignazio opens his mouth and closes it again. He's disoriented, he feels his words turn to ash.

Of course, Palermo is an obvious choice. Barbaro and Florio, as they call them in Bagnara, have a *putìa*, a spice store, over there.

Ignazio remembers. It all began a couple of years earlier with a warehouse, a small *fondaco* for storing the goods they acquired along the coast to then sell on the island. In the beginning, it had been a necessity, but soon afterward his brother Paolo realized it could be turned into a profitable venture: they could increase their sales in Palermo, one of the Mediterranean's major ports at the time. And so their warehouse became an emporium. *Moreover, there's a large community of people from Bagnara in Palermo*, Ignazio thinks. It's a lively, wealthy place full of opportunities, especially since the arrival of Bourbons fleeing the revolution.

He makes a sign with his head to indicate the bridge above him, where they can hear their brother-in-law's footsteps.

No, Barbaro doesn't know yet. Paolo signals at him to keep quiet.

Solitude is squeezing Ignazio's throat.

They are silent on the way home. Bagnara is trapped in limbo, awaiting daylight. When the two brothers reach Pietraliscia, they go into the stable. Vittoria is asleep and so is Vincenzo. Giuseppina, however, is awake.

Paolo sits next to her. Giuseppina remains tense, on alert.

Ignazio looks for a spot on the hay and finds one by curling up next to Vittoria. The little girl emits a sigh. He instinctively puts his arm around her but can't sleep.

The news is hard to accept. How will he manage alone, when he's never been alone?

Dawn pierces the darkness through the gaps in the door. A golden light that heralds imminent autumn. Ignazio is shivering from the cold: his back and neck are stiff, his hair full of thistles. He gently shakes Vittoria.

Paolo is already up. He huffs while Giuseppina is rocking the baby, who has started to protest again.

"We have to go into the house," she says aggressively. "Vincenzo needs changing and I can't remain like this. It's not proper."

Paolo huffs again and opens the door: the sun pours into the cowshed. The house is still standing and now, by the light of dawn, they can see some flaking plaster and broken roof tiles. But no cracks, no damage. She mutters a blessing. They can go home.

Ignazio follows Paolo into the house. Giuseppina is right behind them. He hears her hesitating footsteps and waits, ready to help her.

They walk over the threshold. The kitchen is full of broken ornaments.

"Holy Mother of God, what a mess," Giuseppina says, holding tight the baby, who is now wailing uncontrollably. He smells of soured milk. "Vittoria, help me. Tidy up. I can't do everything on my own. Hurry up." The little girl, who has stayed behind, comes in. She tries to meet her aunt's eyes but can't find them. Tight-lipped, she leans down and starts to pick up pieces of crockery. She's not going to cry. She mustn't.

Giuseppina goes into the corridor that leads to the bedrooms. Every step she takes is a lament, a pang in the heart. Her house, her pride, is full of rubble and broken objects. It will take days to tidy everything up.

When she comes to the bedroom, the first thing she does is wash Vincenzo. She puts him down on the bed so she can also clean herself. The baby kicks his legs, tries to grab his little foot, and gives a shrill laugh.

"My love," she says, "my life."

Vincenzo is her *puddara*, her "North Star." She loves him more than anybody else. She finally puts on her housedress and her shawl, which she pins behind her back.

As she lays the child back into his cradle, Paolo comes in.

He throws open the window. The October air penetrates the room, along with the rustling of the beeches, which have started to turn red in the mountains. A magpie is chattering away not far from the vegetable patch Giuseppina takes care of personally. "We can't stay in Pietraliscia."

Her hands freeze on the pillow she has been plumping up. "Why not? Is there any damage? Where?"

"The roof is crumbling but, no, there's no damage. We're just leaving. Getting away from Bagnara."

Giuseppina can't believe it. She drops the pillow. "Why?"

"Because that's the way it is." His voice leaves no room for doubt: there's an irrevocable decision behind this announcement.

She stares at him. "What do you mean? Leave my house?"

"Our house."

Ours? she wants to ask. She faces him, jaw clenched. *My house*, she thinks resentfully. *Mine. The house I brought as my dowry because you and your father wanted more and more money and were never satisfied . . .* Because Giuseppina remembers very clearly all the going back and forth to obtain the dowry the Florios wanted, and what it took to finally please them while she didn't actually want to get married. And now he wants to leave? Why?

On second thought, she doesn't want to know. She runs out of the room, away from the argument.

Paolo goes after her. "There are cracks on the inside walls, a few roof tiles have fallen off. Next time there's an earthquake, it'll all come down on our heads."

They go to the kitchen. Ignazio understands immediately. He knows the signs of a storm and they're all here. He gestures at Vittoria to leave and she vanishes toward the stairs, outside. He moves back toward the corridor but remains just beyond the threshold: he fears Paolo's reaction and his sister-in-law's anger.

No good will come from this quarrel. Nothing good has ever come between them.

She grabs the broom to sweep the flour off the floor. "Fix it: you're the head of the family. Or else call in the roofers."

"I can't stay here to keep an eye on roofers and I don't have the time to do it myself. If I don't leave, we'll have no food on the table. I keep sailing from Naples to Palermo but I don't want to be a Bagnara man anymore. I want more for myself and my son."

She responds with a mixture of contempt and a guffaw. "You'll always be a Bagnara man even if you go to the Bourbon court. A man can't erase what he is, no matter how much he bathes in the fragrance of money. And you're a man who sells stuff on a skiff he bought in partnership with a brother-in-law who still treats him like a servant." Giuseppina busies herself with pans in the sink.

Ignazio hears the sound of dishes clattering and pictures her impatient gestures. He glimpses her back moving jerkily, bent over the tub.

He knows how she must be feeling: angry, confused, frightened. Anxious.

Just as he has been feeling since last night.

"We'll be leaving in the next few days. So you'd better tell your grandmother that—"

A plate flies to the floor. "I'm not leaving my house, so forget it!"

"Your house!" Paolo barely refrains from swearing. "Your house! You've been throwing it back in my face ever since we got married. You and your relatives, and your money! I'm the one who makes it possible for you to live here, with my work."

"Yes, it's mine. It's what my parents left me. You'd have a house like this only in your dreams. You used to live in your brother-in-law's hayloft, remember? You got my father and uncle's ducats and now you want to leave?" She grabs a copper pan and throws it violently on the floor. "I'm not leaving! This is my house! The roof is broken? So it can be fixed. You're never here anyway, you go away every month. Get out, go wherever you please. My child and I aren't budging from Bagnara."

"No, you're my wife. It's my child. You'll do as I tell you." Paolo is icy.

The color drains from Giuseppina.

She covers her face with her apron and starts punching her forehead, raw anger begging to burst out.

Ignazio wishes he could intervene, calm both her and his brother, but he can't and he has to look away to stop himself.

"Damn you. Do you really want to take everything away from me?" Giuseppina sobs. "Here I have my aunt, my grandmother, my mother's and father's graves. And you, just for the sake of money, you want me to abandon everything. What kind of a husband are you?"

"Stop it!"

She isn't even listening. "No? You're saying no? And where do you want to go, damn it?"

Paolo looks at the fragments of the terra-cotta dish and pushes one away with the tip of his shoe. He waits a moment for her sobs to die down, then replies, "To Palermo, where Barbaro and I opened the *aromateria*. For now it's a very wealthy city, not like Bagnara." He approaches and strokes her arm. A clumsy, rough gesture but one that means to be kind. "Besides, there are people from Bagnara living in the harbor, so you wouldn't be alone."

Giuseppina shakes off his hand. "No," she snarls. "I'm not coming."

Paolo's pale eyes harden. "*I'm* telling you no. I'm your husband and you'll come with me to Palermo, even if I have to drag you by the hair all the way to King Roger's tower. Start packing. We're leaving by the end of next week."

PART ONE

Spices

November 1799 to May 1807

Cu manìa 'un pinìa.

Those who roll up their sleeves don't endure.

—SICILIAN PROVERB

Since as early as 1796, the winds of revolution have been blowing over Italy, carried by troops led by an ambitious young general: Napoleon Bonaparte.

In 1799, the Jacobins of the Kingdom of Naples rebel against the Bourbon monarchy and establish the Neapolitan Republic. Ferdinand IV of Naples and Maria Carolina of Austria are forced to take refuge in Palermo. They return to Naples only in 1802; the republican experience ends in fierce repression.

In 1798, to hinder the growing French presence, various countries, including Great Britain, Austria, Russia, and the Kingdom of Naples, form an anti-French coalition. However, as early as following the defeat at Marengo (June 14, 1800), the Austrians sign the Treaty of Lunéville (February 9, 1801), and, a year later, Great Britain, too, makes peace with the French through the Treaty of Amiens (March 25, 1802), thereby succeeding in safeguarding its own colonial possessions if nothing else. This way, the Royal Navy strengthens its presence in the Mediterranean, especially in Sicily.

On December 2, 1804, Napoleon proclaims himself emperor of the French and, after a crucial victory at Austerlitz (December 2, 1805), he declares the end of the Bourbon dynasty and sends General André Masséna to Naples with the task of placing Napoleon's own brother Joseph on the throne, which makes the latter king of Naples. Ferdinand is once again forced to flee to Palermo under British protection, even though he continues to reign over Sicily.

CINNAMON, PEPPER, cumin, aniseed, coriander, saffron, sumac, cassia . . .

No, spices aren't just for cooking. They're medicines, they're cosmetics, they're poisons and memories of faraway lands few people have seen.

Before reaching a sales counter, a cinnamon stick or a gingerroot has to go through dozens of hands, travel on the back of a mule or a camel in long caravans, cross the ocean, and reach European ports.

Naturally, the costs rise with every leg of the journey.

Rich are those who can buy them, and rich those who manage to sell them. Spices for cooking—and much more so those for medicinal use—are for the select few.

Venice built her wealth on the spice trade and customs duties. Now, at the beginning of the nineteenth century, it's the British and French that sell them. Ships arrive from their colonies overseas loaded not only with medicinal herbs but also with sugar, tea, coffee, and chocolate.

The prices drop, the market diversifies, the harbors open, the amount of spices increases. It's not just in Naples, Livorno, and Genoa. In Palermo, the *aromatari* set up a guild. They even have their own church, Sant'Andrea degli Amalfitani.

And the number of those who can afford to sell them also rises.

Ignazio holds his breath.

It's always the same.

Whenever the skiff arrives within sight of Palermo's harbor, he feels a pang in his stomach, just like a man in love. He smiles, squeezes Paolo's arm, and Paolo reciprocates.

No, he didn't leave him in Bagnara. He wanted him to come with him.

"Happy?" he asks. Ignazio nods, his eyes shining and his chest flooded with the beauty of the city. He clings to the ropes and stretches toward the bowsprit.

He left Calabria and his family, or what was left of it. But now his eyes are filled with sky and sea, he no longer fears the future. The terror of solitude is just a ghost.

His breath catches in his chest before the different overlapping shades of blue against which the walls enclosing the harbor stand out, in the middle of the afternoon. His eyes glued to the mountains, Ignazio strokes his mother's wedding band on his right ring finger. He's put it on so he wouldn't risk ever losing it. In actual fact, whenever he touches it, he feels as though his mother is still close to him, as though he can hear her voice. She would call him, and listen to him.

The city unfolds, and takes shape before him.

Majolica domes, crenellated towers, roof tiles. There's La Cala, the port, crammed with feluccas, brigs, and schooners, a heart-shaped cove between two strips of land. Through the forest of ship masts, you can make out the gates set inside buildings erected literally on top of them: Porta Doganella, Porta Calcina, Porta Carbone. Houses clinging one on top of another, bundled together as though trying to push through to get a glimpse of the sea. On the left, partly hidden by the rooftops, there's the belfry of the church of Santa Maria di Porto Salvo; a little farther, you notice the church of San Massimiliano and the narrow tower of the church of the Annunziata, and then, practically behind the walls, the octagonal dome of San Giorgio dei Genovesi. To the right, another short, squat church, Santa Maria di Piedigrotta, and the imposing form of Castello a Mare, surrounded by a moat; a little farther, on a strip of land jutting into the sea, there's the leper hospital, for the quarantine of sick sailors.

Monte Pellegrino towers over all of this. Behind it, a belt of forest-covered mountains.

A fragrance wafts from the ground and hovers over the water: a blend of salt, fruit, burned wood, algae, and sand. Paolo says it's the smell of dry land. But Ignazio thinks it's the perfume of this city.

They can hear the sounds of a harbor in full activity. The scent of the sea is replaced by an acrid stench: dung, sweat, and pitch, mixed with stagnant water.

Neither Paolo nor Ignazio notices that Giuseppina's eyes are still fixed on the open sea, as though she can still see Bagnara.

They don't know that she remembers Mattia's hug. Mattia, the woman who is more than a sister-in-law to her, but her friend, her rock, the voice who guided her during the difficult first months of her marriage to Paolo.

Giuseppina had initially hoped that Barbaro and Mattia would follow them to Palermo, a hope soon stifled. Paolo Barbaro declared that he would stay in Bagnara, and go back and forth to Palermo, so he could trade with the north and have another safe harbor. And that he needed a woman to look after his house and children. Giuseppina suspected that, in actual fact, he wanted to keep his wife away from her brothers. He didn't like their proximity very much, especially the bond between Mattia and Ignazio.

A solitary tear runs down her cheek and drops on her shawl. She remembers the rustling of the trees that come almost all the way down to the sea, and running down Bagnara streets to King Roger's tower, with the sun refracting on the water and pebbles on the beach.

There, on the pier beneath the tower, Mattia kissed her on the cheek. "Don't think you're all alone. I'll ask the scribe to send you letters and you'll do the same. Now please stop crying."

Giuseppina clenched her fists. "It's not fair! I don't want to!"

Mattia hugged her. "It's the way things are, *cori meu*, dear heart. We're our husbands' property, we have no power. You must be strong."

Giuseppina shook her head because for her it was impossible to be uprooted from her land like this. Yes, women were their husbands' property, the men were in charge. But often husbands had no idea how to treat their wives.

That was the case for her and Paolo.

Then Mattia's face changed expression. She let go of Giuseppina and went up to Ignazio. "I knew this day would come. It was just a matter of time." She kissed him on the forehead. "God be with you and may the Blessed Virgin watch over you all," she said, blessing him.

"Amen," he replied.

Mattia reached out with her hand and held Giuseppina and Ignazio in a single embrace. "Mind our brother Paolo," she said. "He's too hard on everybody, especially on her. Tell him to be more patient. You can do it because you're his brother and a man. He won't listen to me." Remembering it all, Giuseppina feels a knot in her stomach. She stifled her tears of love on her sister-in-law's shoulder, rubbing her face against the coarse fabric of her cloak.

"Thank you, my dearest heart."

The response to this was a caress.

Hearing these words, Ignazio's face darkened. He turned to look at Paolo Barbaro. "What about your husband, Mattia? Is your husband patient? Does he respect you? You've no idea how much it upsets me to leave you here alone with him," he then added with a soft huff.

She cast down her eyes. "He's the way he is. He behaves the way he behaves." Just these words. A hiss, like burning straw.

And Giuseppina read in that expression what she already knew. That Barbaro was rough with her, that he treated her harshly. Their marriage had been arranged by their families for money, just like her and Paolo's.

The men can't possibly understand that what the two of them have in common is a broken heart.

Vittoria calls her. "Look, Auntie, we're nearly there!"

She is happy, excited. The prospect of a new city, far away from Bagnara, has filled her with joy from the very beginning. "It's going to be beautiful, Auntie," Vittoria said the day before they left.

Giuseppina responded with a grimace. "You're too young to understand. It's not like here in the village . . ."

"Exactly," Vittoria replied, refusing to be discouraged. "A city, a real city."

Giuseppina shook her head while grief, resentment, and anger were gnawing at her stomach.

The little girl leaps up and points at something. Paolo nods and Ignazio starts waving his arms.

A launch breaks away from the cluster of ships and guides them to the dock. By the time they land, a small crowd of onlookers has gathered. Barbaro stretches an arm to grab the rope and secure it to the bitt. A man comes forward to welcome them.

"Emiddio!"

Paolo and Barbaro jump off the boat and greet him with familiarity and respect. Ignazio sees them talking as he pulls out the gangplank to help his sister-in-law disembark. Giuseppina stands motionlessly on the deck, holding the baby tight, as though trying to protect him from a threat. So he gently guides her down and explains, "That's Emiddio Barbaro, Paolo's cousin. He's the one who helped us buy the *aromateria*."

Vittoria jumps off and runs to Paolo. He harshly motions at her to be quiet.

Giuseppina sees a strange tension in her husband's face. Like a deep vibration, a crack in that self-confident attitude that so often makes her stifle a cry of rage. But it's just a second, and Paolo's face resumes its hardness. He looks tough, wary. If he's afraid then he conceals it well.

She shrugs. She doesn't care. She turns to Ignazio again and, softly so no one will hear them, says, "I know him. He used to come to Bagnara until two years ago, while his mother was still alive." Then her tone becomes gentler. "Thank you," she mutters, cocking her head, granting him a glimpse of skin between her throat and her collarbone.

Ignazio slows down, then follows her.

He sets foot on the stone quay.

Palermo goes from his eyes to his stomach.

He's *in* the city now.

It's a feeling of wonder and warmth that slides into him, and which he will remember with longing when, just a few years later, he really gets to know her.

Paolo calls Ignazio so he can help him unload their things on the cart Emiddio Barbaro has brought.

"I've found you a place next to many other folks from Bagnara who live here in Palermo. You'll like it."

"Is it a large house?" Paolo throws a wicker basket full of crockery on the cart. A crashing sound heralds the destruction of at least one dish. Immediately afterward, two porters load the *corriola*, the trunk with Giuseppina's trousseau.

He grimaces. "Three ground-floor rooms. Of course, they're not as large as the ones in your house in Calabria. A fellow Calabrian told me about it after his cousin went back to Scilla. More important, it's just a few steps from your *putìa*."

All Giuseppina can do is stare at the stones of the quay and keep silent.

It has all been decided.

Her rage rises and roars inside her. It sticks to her fragmented heart and haphazardly glues it back together, so shards stick into her ribs and throat, hurting her.

She wishes she were anywhere. Even in hell. Just not here.

Paolo and Barbaro stay behind to unload their merchandise on the pier. Emiddio leads her and Ignazio through Porta Calcina.

Along the way, she is attacked by the city voices. They sound brutal, ungainly.

The air is rotten here. The whole city is dirty; she took just one look and saw it. Palermo is a wretched place.

Ahead, her niece is laughing uproariously and doing a pirouette.

What's she got to be so happy about? she thinks grudgingly as she drags her feet on the muddy cobbles. *Fair enough: she had nothing so she's lost nothing. Vittoria can only stand to gain something from this.*

As a matter of fact, the little girl is picturing her future and dreaming, dreaming of no longer being just an orphan taken in out of charity. She pictures having a little money, and perhaps a husband who isn't a relative. More freedom than what awaited her in that village squeezed between the mountains and the sea.

Giuseppina, on the other hand, feels destitute and crazy.

Past the city gate, the street runs between stores and warehouses that lead to alleys, side by side with houses like hovels. She recognizes a few faces but does not return their greetings.

She feels shame.

She knows these people, she knows them well. People who left Bagnara years ago. "Beggars," her grandmother called them. "Wretches who didn't want to stay in the village," her uncle added, who chose to live by their wits in a foreign land, or to force their wives to be scullery maids in other people's houses. Because Sicily is another land, a world apart that has nothing whatsoever to do with the mainland.

And her rage increases because she, Giuseppina Saffiotti, is not a wretch who has to emigrate for a loaf of bread. She owns land, she has a trousseau, she has a dowry.

The narrower the street gets, the heavier her heart. She can't keep up with the others. She doesn't want to.

They arrive at a widening. On the left there's a church with a portico enclosed by pillars. "This is Santa Maria la Nova," Emiddio says to Giuseppina. "While that one is San Giacomo. You'll have no shortage of places of worship," he adds, conciliatory.

She thanks him, crosses herself, but it's not prayers that are on her mind right now. Instead, she remembers what she was forced to leave behind. She looks at the flagstones where leftover fruit and vegetables are drowning in muddy puddles. There's no wind to blow away the smell of death and dung.

Finally, they stop on one side of the square. Some people slow down and steal glances at the newly arrived, while others, more impudent, greet Emiddio while eyeing their belongings, assessing clothes and bearing, prying into their lives.

Giuseppina wishes she could scream, *Get away, all of you! Get lost!*

"Here we are," Emiddio announces.

A wooden door. Baskets of fruit, vegetables, and potatoes stand against the shutters. Emiddio approaches and kicks one of the containers. He puts his hands on his hips and speaks in the tone of someone making an announcement. "Master Filippo, aren't you going to remove all these? The new tenants from Bagnara are here."

The seller is a hunched-over old man with a watery eye. He comes up from the back of the warehouse, holding on to the walls. "All right, all right, I'm coming." He looks up and reveals another eye, much more alert, which immediately studies Ignazio and lingers on Giuseppina.

"At last!" Emiddio says. "I've been telling you to remove this stuff since this morning."

The old man shuffles to the baskets and takes one down. Ignazio is about to help him but Emiddio puts a hand on his arm. "Master Filippo is stronger than you and me put together."

But there's another meaning to these words.

This is the first lesson Ignazio learns: that in Palermo, half a sentence can be worth an entire speech.

Huffing and puffing, the seller clears the passageway. He leaves behind leaves and orange peel.

It only takes a glance from Emiddio for them to be picked up.

They can finally go in.

Giuseppina looks around. She immediately senses that the place has been vacant for at least two months. The hearth for cooking is here, right by the door. The chimney flue is faulty: the wall is blackened, the tiles are chipped and covered in soot. There's just a table; no chairs, only a stool, a few cupboards wedged in the walls, closed with swollen, cracked wooden doors. The beams are covered with spiderwebs, and there are silverfish on the ground. The floor creaks under her feet.

It's dark.

Dark.

Anger turns into revulsion, rises to her stomach, and turns to bile. It's so overpowering that Giuseppina retches.

A home—this? My *home?*

She walks into the bedroom, where Emiddio and Ignazio are. It's a narrow room, almost a corridor: a sickly light comes in through a window, with bars, that looks out on the inner courtyard. She can hear the roar of a fountain outside.

There are two other rooms that are little more than closets. No doors, only curtains.

Giuseppina holds Vincenzo tight to her chest and keeps looking around, still unable to believe her eyes. And yet it's all real. The filth. The poverty.

Vincenzo wakes up. He's hungry.

She goes back into the kitchen. She's alone now: Ignazio and Emiddio are outside, beyond the threshold. She feels her legs give way and sinks onto the stool before collapsing on the floor.

The sun is setting and darkness will soon fall over Palermo and this hovel, and turn it into a grave.

That's how Ignazio finds her when he returns. Overwhelmed, with the child whining.

He busies himself with the luggage. "Shall I help you?" he asks. "Paolo will be back soon with the other baskets and the *corriola*."

He wants to erase Giuseppina's look of horror. He wants to distract her. He wants to . . .

"Stop." Her voice is broken. She lifts her head. "Couldn't we afford anything better than this wretched place?" she asks in one breath, without anger, without strength.

"Not here in Palermo. The city is . . . Well, it's a city. It's expensive.

Not a village like ours," Ignazio tries to explain but realizes that his words will never suffice.

Her eyes are blank. "This is a hovel. A pigsty. Where has your brother brought me?"

It's dawn. Piano San Giacomo, the square Florio and Barbaro's *putìa* looks out on, is almost deserted.

The store door creaks. Paolo goes in. He's attacked by the stench of mold.

Behind him, Ignazio lets out a breathless sigh. The counter is swollen from the damp. There are odd bottles and jars lying around.

Discouragement travels from one to the other, wraps around them, and settles between their chests and throats.

The store boy who's just handed them the keys tries to explain. "Nobody told me you were coming here. And then Don Bottari is ill, you know . . . He's been in bed for weeks."

Ignazio thinks that it's not so much that Bottari is ill, as the fact that he's completely lost interest in the store. This desolation isn't just a few days old.

Paolo doesn't comment. "Give me the broom," he says, instead. "Go get some pails of water." He grabs the broom and starts sweeping the floor. He does it with controlled anger. This is not what the *putìa* looked like last time he was in Palermo.

Ignazio hesitates, then heads to the room he glimpses behind a curtain.

Dirt. Mess. Papers piled up all over the place. Old chairs. Chipped pestles.

The feeling of having gotten it all wrong, of having gambled and lost, grabs hold of him. The rhythmic sound of the broom tells him that Paolo is feeling the same way.

Whoosh. Whoosh.

Every sweep is a slap. Nothing has gone the way they expected. Nothing.

He starts to pick up the papers, empties a jute sack to collect the trash. A large cockroach lands on his feet.

Whoosh. Whoosh.

His heart is a small pebble he could squeeze with his fingers.

He kicks the insect away.

~

By the time midday rings, they have finished cleaning. On the threshold, Paolo—barefoot, his shirtsleeves rolled up—wipes his flushed face.

Now the *aromateria* smells of soap. The store boy is dusting the glass bottles and jars and arranging them according to Paolo's instructions.

"Ah, so it's true. He's reopened the store."

Paolo turns around.

The voice is that of a middle-aged man with eyes of a blue so pale it looks washed out. A receding hairline forms a light patch on his forehead. He wears clothes made of thick cloth and a plastron with a gold tie clip.

Behind him, a girl in a lace-trimmed cape and pearl earrings, on the arm of a young man.

"What's happened to Domenico Bottari?" the second man asks. "Has he rented it out?"

Paolo's eyes drift to him. He's younger than the other one, with a strong voice and accent, and a face covered in freckles. "I'm the owner, with my brother and brother-in-law." He wipes his hand on his damp trousers turned up at the ankles and proffers his hand as a greeting.

"Are you the owner?" The young man's face scrunches up in a laugh. "What kind of an owner can't get someone else to wash the floor?"

"Another Calabrian!" the girl exclaims. "Honestly, how many are there? When these people speak, it's like they sing."

"So what are you going to do? Still trade in spices?" The older man has ignored the girl's quip. Maybe she's his daughter. Paolo thinks it's possible, since she looks very much like him.

The other man approaches and looks at him attentively. "Or are you also going to buy and sell other things? Where will you get your supplies from?"

"You must be in contact with other Calabrians and with Neapolitans. Are they going to sell you the spices?" the older man also asks.

"I . . . We . . ." Paolo would like to stop this volley of questions. He stretches out his hands, looking for Ignazio, but the latter has gone to the carpenter's to look for timber to repair shelves and rickety chairs.

He sees the store boy on a corner, not far from the store. He's holding a pail and watching the two men with reverence. He motions at him to approach but realizes the boy won't come.

The older man comes to the door. "May I?" He walks into the store without waiting for an answer. "Bottari did good business with this store but now it's been a while since . . ." A glance is all he needs. "You're going to have to work very hard before you can sell something without being embarrassed." He rubs his hands. "If you don't know from whom to buy and how to sell, you'll end up being open just from Christmas to Saint Stephen's Day."

Paolo leans the broom against the wall and rolls down his sleeves. His voice is no longer cordial. "True, but we have resources and goodwill."

"You'll also need a lot of luck." The younger man has followed the older. He's evaluating the shelves, counting the jars, reading the labels on the bottles. It's as though he's putting a price on everything he sees. "You won't get far with this stuff. You're not in Calabria anymore. You're in Palermo, the capital of Sicily, and this is no place for wretches." He picks up a bottle and follows a crack with his finger. "You're not thinking of getting ahead with cracked containers, are you?"

"We have people to sell us the goods. We're spice merchants and we have our own skiff. My brother-in-law will bring us the merchandise every month. We just need time to settle down and then we'll sort out everything else." Paolo is on the defensive, even though he doesn't want to be, but this man is provoking him, laughing at him, putting him on the spot.

"Oh, then you're sellers. Not *aromatari*."

The young man elbows the older one. He doesn't even take the trouble to speak softly. "What did I tell you? I thought it seemed odd . . . There's been no application made to the College of Aromatari, or even the Apothecaries. They're storekeepers."

The other man replies, "Yes, you're right."

Paolo wants to throw them out: they've come to stick their noses in his business, they've sized him up, and now they're even mocking him . . . "Now, if you don't mind, I need to carry on working." He indicates the door. "Good day."

The older man rocks on his heels, gives him a look of contempt, then clicks his heels, as though obeying an instruction, and leaves the store without saying goodbye.

The other man, however, lingers to look at the shelves. "I give you two months before you're out begging on the streets," he says. "Two months before you close down."

When Ignazio comes back, he finds Paolo looking drawn, his hands trembling. He's moving jars and bottles, looking at them, shaking his head. "What happened?" Ignazio asks. He knows something must have happened. His brother is upset.

"Three people came by a little while ago. Two men and a woman. They were asking me all these questions. Who are you, what do you do, how do you trade . . ."

Ignazio lifts some of the beams he got from the ship carpenter to repair the chairs and the shelves. "Nosey people." He takes a nail, pushes it in, and starts to hammer it. "So what did they want?"

"It's not just about what they wanted but who they were."

Ignazio pauses. The annoyance in his brother's voice isn't just dislike: it's unease, maybe even fear. He frowns. "Who were they, Paolo? What did they want from us?"

"The boy Bottari sent us told me. He was so scared he didn't even want to come close." He puts a hand on his brother's shoulder. "It was Canzoneri. Canzoneri and his son-in-law, Carmelo Saguto—you should have seen how he behaved."

Ignazio puts the hammer down on the counter. "*The* Canzoneri? The spice wholesaler who also sells to the Royal Army?"

"And to all the aristocracy, that's right."

"So what did he want here?"

Paolo indicates the *aromateria*. The void between his open arms is filled with the afternoon half-light of this weary autumn. "To tell us we won't get very far." The discouragement and resignation in his voice touch Ignazio to the quick. He can't bear it.

He picks up the hammer and grabs a nail. "Let him talk."

He slams down the hammer.

And, as though he is giving him back the thought he shared with him in Bagnara, when his brother told him he wanted to leave, "Let them all talk, Paolo. We haven't come here to starve or run back to Calabria in the middle of the night like beggars." His voice is harsh. It doesn't conceal anger, indignation, or pride. Another nail, another blow. "We've come here and we're staying."

After Canzoneri, other *aromatari* come to nose about. They loiter outside the store, peep through the windows, send their store boys to take a look.

Their faces are hostile, contemptuous, or commiserating. One of them, a certain Gulì, comes to tell them, all friendly, not to feel too clever, because Palermo is a "ruthless" place.

Palermo is studying the Florios. Studying them closely. And she makes no allowances.

There are just a few customers.

And to think that now they have the spices, and top-quality ones, too.

Therefore, when, a few weeks later, they hear the door creak, they almost can't believe their eyes.

A woman. She wears a scarf over her head and an apron around her hips. She's holding a piece of paper in her hand. She hands it to Paolo, who's nearest to her. "I don't know what it says here," she explains. "My husband has a stomachache and a high fever. They told me to buy these things but I don't have much money so I can't go to the apothecary. I went to Gulì's but he said that what I have won't buy anything. Can you folks sell them to me?"

The brothers exchange a glance.

Paolo reads, "'Medicines for constipation.' Let's see what we can do." He lists the herbs. "Rue, mallow flowers . . ."

Ignazio climbs to the shelves and brings down the jars. The herbs end up in the mortar while Paolo listens to the woman.

"My husband's been in pain for four days and can't get out of bed." She casts sidelong glances at Ignazio, who's crushing the herbs with the pestle. "Will these cure him? Because I have nowhere to go. I had to pawn my earrings to call the physicians because the barber didn't understand anything."

Paolo rubs his chin. "Is it a high fever?"

"He's taken to his bed and hasn't gotten up."

"He can't get comfortable, poor man . . . Of course, if the fever's high . . ."

Ignazio indicates a large jar behind him. Paolo understands.

A spoonful of dark bark ends up in the mortar.

She looks at Ignazio with suspicion. "What's that?"

"It's bark," Paolo explains patiently. "It comes from a tree in Peru, the cinchona, and it helps bring down the fever."

Still, the woman is worried, and puts her hands in her pockets. Ignazio hears the jangling of coins as she counts them.

"You don't have to pay this time, don't worry."

She almost can't believe it. She takes the money and puts it on the counter. "But the others . . ."

Paolo puts a hand on her arm. "The others are the way they are and do what they like. We're the Florios."

And that's how it all begins.

The weeks go by, one after the other. Christmas is approaching.

One day, Giuseppina comes to see them shortly after the bells have tolled midday. She finds her husband and brother-in-law putting aside jars and scales. "I've brought your lunch," she says. She is carrying a basket of bread, cheese, and olives. Ignazio gives her a chair but she shakes her head. "I must go. Vittoria is on her own with Vincenzo."

Paolo takes her by the wrist. "I wish you wouldn't always rush off."

He says it with an odd tenderness. So, cautiously, she comes back to her husband and he hands her a slice of bread soaked in oil.

"I've already eaten."

He squeezes her hand. "So? A little something more?"

Giuseppina accepts but keeps her eyes downcast.

Ignazio chews slowly, watching them.

They're teasing. Or rather, Paolo is the one teasing. Giuseppina accepts the morsels he gives her but her brow is still furrowed.

Someone knocks.

"Can't we have some peace and quiet?" Paolo wipes his mouth on his sleeve. He goes into the store while Ignazio swallows the last piece of cheese and is back on his feet.

Giuseppina grabs him by the sleeve. "Ignazio." Her tone is harsh, almost like his brother's.

"What's the matter?"

"I need your help. I . . ." There's a sound of clinking bottles in the next room. "I wanted to send Mattia a letter. Could you write it?"

Ignazio turns back. "Can't Paolo help you?"

"I did ask him." Giuseppina's hand is on the table. She clenches her fist and stretches until it touches him. "He says he hasn't got time and I shouldn't make him waste any more. The truth is he doesn't want to, I know it, and when I told him he lost his temper. Mattia doesn't know how we are, if we've settled in . . . Before, we'd see each other every day in church. Now I don't even know if she's alive, and I want to at least write to her . . ."

Ignazio sighs. These two are like water and oil: they can be in the same bowl but they'll never mix.

She drops her voice. She touches him and squeezes his hand. "I don't know who to ask. I'm not close to anybody here yet and I don't want to tell my business to a stranger. At least *you* help me . . ."

Ignazio keeps silent and thinks. *No*, he tells himself. *She should ask a scribe.* He doesn't want to know why Giuseppina looks so unhappy or why Paolo tries to approach her, knowing he will be rejected.

But it's pointless: he sees them and listens to them every day, even if they don't argue out loud. Because there are things you can feel with your soul and your instinct. He loves them both, and he's caught in the middle.

That's when he, the meek brother, the one who's generous and kind, feels a hidden little snake, a venomous grass snake, rear up its head. Ignazio has learned to throw stones at it, because it has no right to slither out. He can't tell Paolo what to do with his wife.

Giuseppina is now practically speaking in his face. "I beg you."

Ignazio knows he shouldn't butt in. He should go, he should tell her to ask Paolo again.

That's when he realizes that their fingers are interlaced.

He comes away abruptly, and says, with his back to her, "All right. Now go."

ન

When Paolo asks him why he's brought paper and ink home, he tells him. He sees his brother's face darken. "Suit yourself. I don't want to put up with her complaints also in a letter."

They say little over dinner; they help themselves to morsels from a single dish on the table. Afterward, there are grapes and a little dried fruit. Vittoria is walking up and down the room with Vincenzo in her arms. She is singing.

Look at this little boy of mine
This lovely little child
Sleep, yes, sleep
Sleep peaceful and mild
For now is the hour, now is the time
Come, sleep, come take this little boy of mine

Giuseppina dries her hands on her apron, goes to Vittoria and kisses her. "Go to bed, you two. I have business with your uncle." She slumps onto the bench and brushes her hair away from her face. "So?"

"I'll get the paper."

Ignazio goes into the bedroom he shares with Vittoria to fetch the ink. He listens to what is happening in the kitchen.

"Why didn't you ask me?" Paolo says.

"You told me you didn't have time." Giuseppina's voice is full of bitterness.

"That's right." A chair creaks. "In that case I'm going to bed."

Ignazio rushes in, blocking his brother's exit. "Here it is, Paolo, come, why don't you dictate a few words of greeting, too?"

Giuseppina is now looking at her husband. *Stay,* she seems to be saying.

So Paolo stays.

He sits back down, and writes. He has a difficult temper, but it couldn't be otherwise, given how he grew up. And he's proud, like all Florios.

Then he returns the paper to Ignazio, who grabs the pen and encourages Giuseppina to start.

"Dear Mattia . . ." She pauses and takes a breath. Then she starts and it's as though she can't stop. "The child is growing and doing well, your brothers work from morning till night . . .

"The house is small but close to the *aromateria* . . .

"They don't have here the green vegetables we used to pick together in the mountains . . .

"Palermo is very big and I only know the streets that lead to the harbor . . ."

Ignazio is concentrating.

He feels what Giuseppina is really trying to say.

Vincenzo, at least, makes me happy, while Paolo and Ignazio leave me alone all day and I'm losing my mind in this hole. That's right, because the house is little more than a warehouse at the service of the store and I spend my days alone, wretchedly alone, with my son and Vittoria, and there's no room for me in this huge city, you're not here, and I'm getting lost among these walls, the mud, and the nothingness.

In the end, Giuseppina falls silent.

Paolo approaches his wife and gives her shoulder a squeeze. "I'll send the letter tomorrow," he says. He strokes her hair. It's a very long caress, made up of regret, tenderness, and fear. He opens his mouth to speak but doesn't, and walks out of the room before his wife's bewildered eyes.

And yet he should do it, Ignazio thinks. *He should talk to her. Listen to her. Isn't that what marriage is about? Isn't it about bearing life's burdens together?*

Isn't that what he would do?

"Thanks again, Don Florio, good day to you."

"Always here to help. Goodbye."

Christmas 1799 went by quickly. Another year has gone by and the *aromateria* has grown. They, the Florio brothers—after much struggling—have become known. For a long time they were crushed by the mistrust of Palermo residents and by the rumors circulated by Saguto, Canzoneri's son-in-law. Partly through fear and partly not to upset Canzoneri, the other *aromatari* kept away from their store. Paolo still remembers the days he spent on the doorstep, waiting for a customer to come in, or another seller to reserve a supply of spices. Above all, they had to tolerate the looks Saguto gave them whenever he walked past the store, almost gloating at seeing it deserted. Paolo swore to himself that he'd wipe that superior smirk off his face.

The new year, 1800, has brought a wave of frost and rain. The door closes with the usual, now familiar squeak. For a moment, the sound of rain enters the store, along with the winter wind and the smell of burned wood.

Paolo looks around, and puts away the bottles left on the work counter.

At the end of last year, there was a violent fever epidemic. Christmas carols alternated with lamentations of many funerals.

The provisions of bark almost ran out. The larger *aromaterie*, like Canzoneri's, were selling it literally at the price of gold and so many people needed it.

Then Barbaro unexpectedly brought a load of spices. He came with the new year: with chests full of spices that had filled the store. And the news spread overnight. There's a rule of fate in life, *u' risu cammina nzemmula cu li vai*: "What makes one man laugh makes another man cry." That's what happened: the day after, the store was crowded, and not just with wretched people needing medicinal herbs.

Aromatari. Small apothecaries. A few physicians.

There they were outside the door, hats off and money in their pockets, begging to buy the bark they couldn't find anywhere else.

Paolo still remembers the time Carmelo Saguto, walking past Piano San Giacomo, stopped to look, incredulous, at the comings and goings of spice sellers who had come to these Calabrians nobody used to trust. He rushed into the store, pushing the other customers out of his way, and asked Paolo to show him the bark, because it couldn't be true, he shouted, they were taking people for a ride . . .

Paolo grabbed a handful and poured it on the counter. "Peruvian bark. Just arrived and already sold out. Eat your heart out, Saguto."

The man had taken a few steps back, surrounded by the embarrassed looks of other *aromatari* and physicians. His face was swollen, twisted by a sneer. He stood still, then spat and said, "Mud of the earth."

The next day, Canzoneri spread the word that he had other spices, had dropped his prices, and that he'd give special deals to loyal customers. But the damage was done.

"Never mind who dies, as long as you're alive," Paolo said.

Now he realizes that's how it works.

The moment he stopped being a simple man from Bagnara and became *Don* Paolo Florio.

And now this name is written on exchange bills, documents, and countersigned on the contracts by storekeepers who sampled the quality of their goods and have returned to buy from them.

Paolo puts the last jar away on the shelf.

True: that load of bark was a stroke of luck. But what happened next was not by chance.

Outside the windows, Michele, their store boy, is running. He is clutching a box covered in oilskin to his chest. He enters and shakes off the rain. "It's really coming down," he says, placing the box on the counter. "Here it is: nutmeg and cumin. I've also brought some fraxinella because I noticed we're running low."

"What's it like in the warehouse?"

"It's cold. There's damp but not much we can do about it with all this rain."

"Damp ruins the fragrance," Paolo huffs. "Later on, you and Domenico go and store all the bags high up and put paper in the gaps in the doors."

The boy nods, then vanishes to the back room. They have replaced the curtain with a door and painted the shutters.

This is not the only change to their business.

The store is no longer big enough.

Paolo and Ignazio have rented a warehouse in Via dei Materassai, in the Castellammare district. There they can store the merchandise that arrives from the entire Mediterranean. A step up in quality is essential since they've started wholesaling to other merchants.

He calls Michele.

"Yes, Don Paolo."

"I'm going out. Ignazio's late, I hope there are no problems at customs. Mind the store."

The roar of rain that greets him sends a shiver through him. He walks across Piano San Giacomo and looks at his house: there's light filtering through the shutters. Giuseppina must be cooking.

And Vincenzo . . .

Vincenzo is an intelligent child. In the evenings, Paolo watches him play with Vittoria or sees Ignazio trying to teach his nephew and niece the letters of the alphabet.

But shortly afterward, his wife comes out to pour out a basin of dirty water. She's seen him, of that he is sure, but nothing, not even a wave.

He draws his head into his shoulders and picks up the pace toward Palazzo Chiaramonte. Giuseppina does not love him. He knows that and it has never bothered him: he has his work. He often travels across the sea, and the spice store fills his days.

Only sometimes, he longs for an embrace, so that he can fall asleep feeling warm and loved.

Giuseppina slams the door shut. Paolo was out there.

She wonders where he's going.

She feels something heavy sitting on her chest.

My heart is dark, they would say in Bagnara.

Her heart is black. She hates this house. She hates this city and this damp weather. With the winter and the rain, she has to keep the windows shut and the lamps lit.

On top of that, she's not having a good day. She's not feeling well and had to stay in bed for a while, getting Vittoria to help her with the house chores.

She's pregnant.

She's been certain of it for a few days now. She's skipped her cycle and her breasts are sore.

As if she didn't have enough on her plate: to expect a child here, in Palermo, in this house with no light.

I should tell Paolo, she thinks. But she hasn't yet found a way or the right time.

The truth? She doesn't know if she wants it.

She doesn't trust Paolo, not at all. She is wary of him, sometimes even afraid. At other times, the deferential respect a woman should feel for her husband turns into burning hatred, a knife that twists in her belly. And now his child? Another one?

She's ashamed even to think it, but this child doesn't have to be born.

She throws a shawl over her head and puts on her shoes. She goes out, follows the perimeter of Piano San Giacomo and goes down to the harbor. There, in one of the hovels behind the walls, lives Mariuccia Colosimo, the Bagnara midwife. A smell of soap and laundry wafts through the door. She hesitates. "Donna Mariuccia!" she suddenly calls. "Are you in?"

The woman looks out. Her face looks chiseled from volcanic rock and her lips are thin. Her skin is sweaty. "Donna Giuseppina . . . I was making lye. What can I do for you?" she asks, drying her red hands with her apron.

For a moment, Giuseppina hesitates. What she wants to do is not right, it's a sin. Her grandmother used to say that the Blessed Virgin turns away when a woman throws away her child.

And yet.

Giuseppina comes closer and almost whispers into her ear. "Can I come and see you one of these days?"

The woman bends her head a little. She has a primeval smell, of hay and milk. "Whenever you like. What is it—an egg in the nest?"

Giuseppina nods. "My husband doesn't know yet," she whispers again.

The midwife straightens up. She asks no questions, and just opens her hands. She understands. She understands everything and knows that the things women cannot say are more than men could ever understand. "You know where I am. I'll be expecting you."

Giuseppina nods and the midwife disappears behind the door.

She slowly walks back home. The rain has soaked through her shawl and is now seeping through her bodice. Fat, heavy drops that make it difficult to walk. Once she's in Piano San Giacomo, she glances at the *aromateria*. She glimpses forms through the windows, customers perhaps.

She sighs. If her grandmother had chosen Ignazio to be her husband, maybe everything would have been different.

She remembers when, years ago, they buried their relatives after the earthquake that destroyed Bagnara. She recalls the face of that boy with gentle eyes and an angular face all red from crying, staring at the heap of soil under which his mother, Rosa, had been buried. And she, who had lost both her parents, was little more than a dried, crooked branch with fists clenched against her dress, angry with the whole world for having taken away her mamma and papà. She approached and gave him a handkerchief to wipe away the snot dripping from his nose.

She told him off. "Don't cry. Boys don't cry." But she said it grudgingly, perhaps because she envied those tears of freedom, because she had no more tears left herself. He looked at her and sniffed. He did not reply.

~

She comes back home. The hem of her skirt is soaked, and her shawl needs wringing. Vittoria's eyes question her. "You're all wet, Auntie! Are you all right?"

"Yes, yes . . . I had to go and ask Auntie Mariuccia something."

Vincenzo distracts her, pulling at her skirt. "Mamma, pick me up."

Giuseppina holds him tight and smells the warm scent in the crook of his neck. Her child is the only good thing her husband ever gave her. And he is enough for her, she doesn't want another, the one that's growing in her belly and making her feel tired and breathless. He could turn out to be like her husband . . .

The hatred toward her husband flares up again. It's an old resentment, one she harbors lovingly in her chest, right under her heart. She did want a husband and children, but if she'd known that this is what marriage was like, she would have run away to the mountains.

Of course, Paolo is respectful. There are only ever two things on his mind: work and money. Even on Christmas Day he went to the *aromateria* to check the packages, leaving her and Vittoria alone, eating chestnuts and staring at each other.

He isn't like Ignazio.

~

The rain is heavier. It's almost midday by the time Paolo goes through the carriage entrance, the one on the customs side inside Palazzo Steri: a cube perforated with slender mullioned windows, a fortress within the city, built as the house of the Chiaramonte family, then used as a jail by the Inquisition, then as a barracks, a silent witness to the city's history. He shelters in the passage between the two courtyards of Palazzo Steri, with other men, porters and traders.

He's still there when he sees, in the square courtyard, Ignazio following a man and arguing with him. He recognizes him. "Paolo! Ignazio!"

They can't hear him. Barbaro gives Ignazio a shove and the young man opens his arms.

Paolo rushes out of his shelter. "What's wrong with you two? What's happened?"

Barbaro comes at him. "You, too! I nurtured a viper in my bosom, that's what's wrong. Is this the thanks I get after sharing my bread with you when you were starving? You go and rent things without saying a word to me? And even sign with your own names?"

Paolo doesn't understand. "What do you mean?" He looks at his brother-in-law, then at Ignazio. "What's this about?"

Ignazio tries to explain. "One of Canzoneri's workers told him we rented the warehouse and he thinks we're trying to cheat him—"

"Well, isn't that the case?" Barbaro retorts. "I have to hear it from strangers that you do things without telling me? We're business partners and relatives, damn it. Is this how you screw me? Don't you forget who's putting up the money for this! If I want, I can take everything away from you and you'll end up belly-up."

Paolo snaps. "And what do you do? Who are the ones working here, you or us? We're the ones who fixed the store and relaunched it. When we were in Bagnara, you told us everything was all right but it was a room with silverfish and damp inside. And now people come, we're making money, and instead of thanking us, you want us to justify everything? You try to come and work here, and then you'll see for yourself if we were right to rent a warehouse. What are you shouting at us for?"

"Listen, you, you should have told me first."

"Why? To ask your permission?"

Barbaro gives Paolo's chest a shove. Ignazio stands between them before his brother can retaliate. "Now stop it, both of you," he says. "Everyone's looking at us."

Dozens of anger-hungry eyes are upon them.

"Let's go home. Better talk there."

They walk away. Barbaro walks ahead, followed by Paolo and Ignazio. At a distance. Side by side.

~

Carmelo Saguto watches the scene from the portico. He doesn't gloat or show the slightest pleasure.

Apparently, at least.

After the Florios have left Palazzo Steri, Don Canzoneri comes up to him. "Did you see the row the Calabrian gave them? Any minute now, they were going to club each other."

His father-in-law nods. "Nothing to do with you, is it?"

Carmelo opens his arms. His expression is one of innocence laced with poison. "Me? I didn't do anything. It was Leonardo, the longshoreman, who spoke loudly." He does not add that it was he who prompted him to speak like that, and that he's the one spreading rumors among customs workers that the Florios have fallen out among themselves and are piling up debts. He does not say that his favorite weapon is gossip, but his father-in-law knows this. That's why he keeps him close, even closer than his own children.

They laugh.

"*Jamuninni.*" Canzoneri indicates the carriage. "Let's go home." Then he turns to look at his son-in-law. "See what happens when you do business with relatives? You have to mind how you behave and learn your place."

Saguto's laugh stops abruptly. "Do you mean I don't? Have I ever been disrespectful toward you or my brothers-in-law?"

"Exactly. I'm telling you so things don't turn sour." He gives a tap on the roof and the carriage starts. "You're clever enough to know how to behave. You're a dog who knows his master. Right?"

He says yes and swallows bile. Because that's precisely what he is: a guard dog. He knows it, repeats it to himself every day when he sees his reflection in the mirror. He's not free like those two Calabrians who aren't afraid of anything and don't need anybody. And that's why he hates the Florios so much: because they are what he will never be.

That night, Paolo Barbaro doesn't spend the night at the Florios', like he usually does when he's in Palermo. The argument—heated and at times violent—lasted a long time. At one point, Paolo got up and left the store, slamming the door, tired of hearing over and over again that he'd tried to cheat him. Ignazio stayed behind and carried on trying to explain. Patiently. Calmly.

In the end, Barbaro said goodbye to Giuseppina. "Tell your husband to be reasonable," he said on the doorstep, "or else it'll end belly-up because there's no way I'm having anything to do with a man who cheats me."

Giuseppina did not reply because a housewife doesn't respond. But one thing she does know: Paolo and Ignazio are honest. Her husband is more devoted to his work than to his family. And Ignazio wouldn't be able to cheat anyone if he tried.

They eat late, when Paolo comes back. Nobody mentions the argument.

Ignazio looks tired, feverish. He doesn't even finish his food and goes to bed practically without saying good night. Vittoria and Vincenzo follow his example.

Paolo and Giuseppina are left alone.

Paolo clasps a terra-cotta cup. "Shall we go to bed?"

She carries on clearing up. She doesn't answer.

He puts the cup down. He lays his hands on her hips. Giuseppina knows what he wants.

"Leave me alone."

He presses harder. "You're always saying no. Why not?"

"I'm tired."

Paolo squeezes her hips harder. "What am I supposed to do? Beg for a little of what I'm entitled to? What's so strange about what I'm asking you?" There truly is a hint of supplication in his voice. He's practically crushing her between the stove and his body; Giuseppina thinks for a moment that he wants to take her here and now, at the risk of the others hearing everything. His hand has lifted her skirt, and she pushes it away, disengaging herself.

And yet she feels a quiver, yielding on the part of her traitor sex that cannot keep desire at bay. "No. I've told you, leave me alone!"

He stops. He doesn't know whether to shout, slap her, or leave the house, slamming the door, and find the first available woman so he can let off steam. Because that's what he needs: a little comforting. That's all he wants.

He takes her by the wrist and leads her to the bedroom. He undresses her. She keeps her eyes shut while her husband searches for love inside her and she has to give it to him.

In the next room, behind the curtain that acts as a door, Ignazio has woken up because of the cold. He stares into the darkness and listens.

The morning after, Giuseppina gets up while it's still dark and gets dressed in a hurry. Her husband is asleep. She doesn't look at him.

She opens the door. Winter is attacking Palermo ruthlessly.

Except for a few passersby heading for La Cala, Piano San Giacomo is deserted. She lights a lamp for a little light, and prepares slices of bread and honey. She takes a pan with pieces of cheese from a shelf and puts it on the table. Vittoria appears in the doorway, mutters good morning, then goes to get dressed.

A sharp pain makes Giuseppina freeze, her hand on her belly.

She's been taught that children are sent by God and that refusing them is a mortal sin. She believes that. She knows the Lord giveth and the Lord taketh away, and that He will punish her if she harms this child in any way. But what is she supposed to do if she doesn't feel this child is hers? It's not like Vincenzo, who clung to her flesh even before he was born. This creature is alien to her . . .

But maybe it's just a matter of time, she keeps thinking, trying to convince herself. She must get used to it, let nature take its course and teach her once again how to be a mother.

Or maybe she's committing a sin just by wishing not to be a mother anymore.

She will carry this thought within her for all the years to come. Whenever she remembers this thought, a nail will dig deep inside her.

Another cramp. She has to sit down and breathe deeply. Vittoria joins her soon afterward. "Auntie?"

"Women's pains."

Vittoria isn't fully grown yet but she already knows what this is. "You stay there. I'll get everything ready," she says. She's intelligent and alert. She also understood the night before, when she heard the noises coming from her uncle and aunt's room. One thing Vittoria does know: she doesn't want a man who orders her about like her uncle. She wants a husband who respects her, who lets her speak out, never mind her aunt telling her that's not the way things are.

Shortly afterward, the entire family is gathered around the table. A freezing cold draft comes in through the door, lowering the room temperature.

They eat quickly, heads buried in their shoulders. Ignazio and Paolo put on their cloaks and go out, one heading for customs, the other to the *aromateria*.

Paolo, however, stops and turns back. He approaches his wife and gives her a caress.

Giuseppina does not react, then watches him walk away.

Floors to sweep, beds to make, vegetables to prepare, pans to scrub. Vittoria comes in with buckets of water from the fountain, her hands pale from the cold. Vincenzo protests, he wants to go out. Giuseppina's tiredness grows by the minute, as do the pangs in her belly. She wishes she could rest but she can't: there's washing to be done, lye to boil. Sweat is running down her back and between her breasts.

Vittoria suddenly freezes. "Auntie," she whispers, her hand over her mouth. "What's happening to you?"

Giuseppina looks down. There are dark stains on her skirt. "What . . ."

She suddenly realizes that the heat between her legs is not sweat but blood. Her confusion turns to terror. She barely has time to mutter that the midwife should be called before she collapses on the floor.

Barefoot on the flagstones shiny from the rain, Vittoria runs toward San Sebastiano. She slips and gets back up. She looks for Mariuccia, the Bagnara midwife. Paolo told her women and girls often go to her for herbs.

The little girl finds the address. "Auntie Mariuccia, my aunt's bleeding!" she screams, frightened that the last shred of family she has left will also be snatched away. "She's fainted. Come, come!"

A face framed by a head scarf looks out the window. "Who is it? Who?"

"Donna Giuseppina, Don Florio's wife. Come!"

"Oh, sweet Saint Anne!"

The woman disappears inside. Noisy footsteps come down the stairs and a few seconds later Mariuccia is in front of Vittoria, holding a basket. "Calm down. Tell me what happened."

"We were about to do the washing when I noticed stains on her skirt."

At that moment, a voice makes her stop. "Vittoria! What are you doing here?"

"Uncle Ignazio!" The little girl throws herself into his arms and bursts into tears.

"What happened?"

Vittoria tells him and he turns pale. "But . . . was she pregnant?"

She shakes her head. "I don't know anything, Uncle."

He grabs his niece and pulls her under his cloak to shelter her. "Michele, take the goods to the warehouse and tell Paolo to come home. Let's go!" They all run to Piano San Giacomo.

Mariuccia has gotten there before them.

She's kneeling next to Giuseppina, who is awake and crying softly, her skirt pulled up to her hips. From the next room, they can hear Vincenzo screaming. There's a pool of blood on the floor.

"Go and calm Vincenzo down," Giuseppina murmurs to Vittoria.

The girl obeys, her eyes fixed on the blood. The little boy immediately stops screaming.

Mariuccia looks up. "Is it just you here?"

"I'm her brother-in-law. I must—"

She waves a hand. "Never mind. Come on, even if you're a man. Help me, we have to get her to bed."

But Ignazio doesn't move. "Was she really pregnant?"

The midwife nods. She takes a cloth from the basket and starts to wipe Giuseppina, who gives a moan of embarrassment and hides her face in the crook of Mariuccia's arm.

"That's right. She shouldn't have worn herself out like this. There's nothing to be done now."

Ignazio throws off his cloak and lifts Giuseppina. "You go ahead," he tells Mariuccia in a tone that bears no refusal. "I'll carry her."

"You'll get your clothes dirty." Giuseppina moans. "It's always you who's there for me," she adds, clinging to his shirt. "You and not him."

She says it softly, so softly that he thinks he's misheard. But it's not the case, and that adds to his sorrow.

Mariuccia puts sheets and towels on the bed to avoid staining the mattress, because she now has to end what nature has begun.

"Didn't Paolo know?" Ignazio whispers.

She shakes her head. She keeps crying, and all he can do is murmur an apology into her hair, damp with sweat. He helps her lie on the bed and is about to leave but turns back, takes her hand and kisses the palm. Then he walks away before the midwife notices the hell he carries inside him.

When Paolo comes home, Vittoria is on her knees, cleaning the floor.

"Auntie's next door," she says softly. She plunges her hands in the red-stained water, wrings the rag, and wipes the floor again.

Paolo goes up to her. "You shouldn't be doing this kind of thing . . ."

"And who's going to do this if I don't?" she says harshly, a hint of reproach in her voice.

He suddenly realizes how much she's grown, almost a woman now. But she doesn't let him continue. "She's been unwell for days. Vomiting, always tired. Didn't you notice?" She is serious, severe.

Paolo stutters, shakes his head. A feeling of guilt clumps around his heart, squeezing it like a fist. Only now does he understand many things. Like her rebelling the night before.

Vittoria watches him without saying a word. She gets up and throws the dirty water out the door. But there's no more blame in her dark, calm eyes. Sorrow, yes. Compassion. Maybe even understanding.

"Where's Ignazio? And Vincenzo?"

She grabs a dish and starts dicing the vegetables to make a meat broth, like they do for women who have just given birth. "Uncle Ignazio took him out so he wouldn't get in Donna Mariuccia's way while she was working." Her voice becomes gentler. "Go to Auntie. She shouldn't be left alone, poor thing, or she'll think it's her fault."

Is it my fault, then? Paolo thinks. *My fault, because I didn't even notice she was unwell?*

On the threshold of the bedroom, he looks at his wife with painful regret. If he'd known, he wouldn't have insisted the night before.

He approaches gingerly. "You could have told me." No reproach, just bitterness. He's devastated. Now that his eyes are filled with her pain, he's devoured by guilt. "Why didn't you tell me?" he asks.

Teardrops pool out from his wife's eyelids and run down her cheeks, following a set path. He sits next to her on the bed. "Now, don't cry. Maybe it would have been another boy. It obviously wasn't meant."

Giuseppina is motionless, staring at the wall. Not a word about forgiveness, not a single apology, unlike Ignazio.

Mariuccia slips out of the room.

La Cala is half-deserted. It's cold. There are just a few porters and sailors bustling around the ships. The wind violently lashes the city walls, slamming window shutters and twisting laundry hung out to dry.

"That boat over there?"

Clinging to his uncle's neck, Vincenzo points at a ship. Ignazio covers him with his cloak to shield him from the *tramontana* wind. The church of Piedigrotta is closed, and there aren't even any beggars outside the entrance. On the Castello a Mare walls, a sentry is doing his rounds, holding on to his hat.

"It's called a skiff. We arrived here on a boat like that, when you were little."

"How little?"

"Very little. You fit in a basket."

Vincenzo wriggles. Ignazio puts him down and he goes to the stone edge of the pier and looks down at the dark, choppy water. The tip of an anchor covered in algae is immersed in the darkness. "How deep is the sea?"

"Very deep," Ignazio replies. He takes him by the hand. Vincenzo has dark, trusting eyes and fair hair like Paolo's. "More than you can imagine. Do you know that beyond the sea, where we can't see, there's another land?"

"Yes, I know. There's Bagnara. Mamma's always telling me."

"No, not Bagnara. Even farther, there's France and England and Spain, and, even beyond them, there's India, China, and Peru. There are countries where much bigger ships than this one go, and they have spices like the ones your papà and I sell, and silks and cloth, and things you can't even imagine."

Wonder fills the child's face. His hand quivers in his uncle's. He wants to run but Ignazio holds it tight: the ground is slippery and Ignazio is afraid he might fall into the water.

"What's silk, Uncle Ignazio?" His *s*'s are still unsure of themselves.

"Silk . . ." he echoes. "It's an expensive fabric for wealthy people."

"Silk . . ." The word takes on a sound of discovery on the child's lips. "I also want to wear silk someday. I want to make a silk dress for Mamma."

Ignazio picks him up again. The child smells his clothes and inhales the scent of spices: a warm, familiar smell that makes him feel safe. Together, they walk toward Via dei Materassai. "Then you'll need to work," Ignazio explains. "These things cost a lot of money." He has no difficulty in speaking like this to the little boy. Vincenzo is intelligent. Very intelligent.

"I will, Uncle Ignazio," he replies after a long pause, in a strange way, softly.

Like a promise.

The door of the spice store keeps making that annoying squeaking sound but there's a new counter, as well as jars for the herbs and spices.

The shutters, too, have been repainted. They carry only the name Florio.

It's February 1803, and the Paolo Barbaro and Paolo Florio company hasn't existed for a month.

After the row at customs, there were others. The last one, a few weeks ago, was about a consignment of buffed ivory and cinnamon.

Paolo went to La Cala because he'd heard from Michele that his brother-in-law had arrived and yet not gone to the store, as usual. He found him talking to a storekeeper, a man called Curatolo. He'd made a deal with him and just sold him the consignment for a ridiculous price.

Curatolo left without saying goodbye, embarrassment written all over his face. Paolo could do nothing but watch his spices leave with him. But shortly afterward, he attacked Barbaro. "What the hell are you doing? All our ivory to him, our competitor?" He could not believe it. "And what are we supposed to do now?"

"Ours? Is there such a thing as 'ours'?"

"It was our consignment. What did you do that for?"

"Isn't that what you do?" Barbaro replied in a nasty voice. "You don't give a damn about what I need and I don't give a damn about what you need." He jangled the coins in his pocket. "And I'm keeping these."

Paolo turned away from him and went home, his pride shattered. He told Ignazio and Giuseppina everything. He forbade her from having anything to do with the Barbaros, Mattia included.

Their company died before a notary. They sold the skiff and part of the goods still in the warehouses, and split the money between them. A sheet of paper, two or three signatures without even looking each other in the face, as Paolo bought the *aromateria* and Barbaro left him Via dei Materassai to look for another place in Via dei Lattarini, next to the warehouses of other Bagnara people.

It was a war, and they still bore its wounds. He still carried the icy anger that had taken the place of rage.

Vincenzo walks behind his mother, and stops to look around. Absorbed, he is sucking a licorice stick. Of course, now that he can walk and run by himself, the world looks huge.

He's about to step into a puddle when Giuseppina yanks him. "Careful! Can't you look where you walk? You're four, not a baby anymore."

He looks at her guiltily. She melts into a sigh. Vincenzo is still the one and only love of her life.

There are different accents around them. A peasant is trying to sell his load of citrus fruit to a British trader in a cloth tailcoat and boots. The cart is blocking passersby, and people are complaining.

"No, I won't buy these . . . *arance*. They are rotten."

"What are you on about? They're all good. See how good they smell!" He picks one and shows it to the Englishman but the latter keeps protesting, pointing at a host of feasting fruit flies.

Seeing the scene, a Neapolitan sailor raises his hands to the sky. "You think people are stupid? There's too many fruit flies . . ."

People from many countries, new languages. Ever since the French started scampering about the Tyrrhenian Sea, peace had ended. The British declared war on the French again, and Napoleon resumed hostilities, attacking ships sailing across the Mediterranean. Merchant ships were no longer safe and the British, who used to be masters of the sea, were pushed into a corner. Palermo and Sicily turned into a free port, removed from French influence and, above all, at the center of the Mediterranean. This has turned Palermo into a city bursting with merchants and sailors from all over Europe. French spices come from ports in northern Italy, British ones from Malta, but that's not all. Goods are arriving from Turkey, Egypt, Tunisia, and Spain.

Giuseppina doesn't know and understands little of all this. It's not a woman's business, as she often tells Vittoria, who, even so, insists on knowing and tortures Ignazio with questions.

Giuseppina arrives at the *aromateria*. Through the window, she sees Paolo behind the counter, with a man dressed in velvet. A little farther, almost outside the church, stands a sedan painted in green and gold.

Mother and son walk in. Paolo sees them and signals to Vincenzo to keep quiet and continues to talk to the customer.

"Our bark is very pure, Baron. It comes straight from Peru and we supply most of the apothecaries in Palermo . . . Smell the aroma." He takes a handful of bark. It's dark and crumbly. Chips fall on the worktop.

The man wrinkles his nose. "What a strong smell."

"That's because we store it correctly." Paolo drops his voice. "Would you like me to mix you some with iron, am I right?"

"Yes, please. You know what it's like . . . My spirit is young but my body, alas, won't keep up with me. I don't fire as powerfully as I once did and you can imagine how unpleasant it can be to retire in certain circumstances," he concludes with a note of embarrassment.

"In this case, the iron will restore your vigor. We'll add a few fennel seeds and lemon peel, to protect you from fevers. Shall I add this to last week's bill?"

"No, not at all." Embarrassment, followed by pride. "Here's payment for the recent purchases. This way we won't have anything outstanding anymore." Coins shine in his hand. "Here you are. I know I can rely on your discretion. I came here instead of going to some of your better-qualified colleagues because I've been told you keep things to yourself."

"Just think of me as your confessor."

Paolo is polite but not servile. Palermo nobility are a strange breed. Attached to their privileges like nails to flesh, in debt down to their pants, and yet clad in velvet and jewels. They sell houses and property they are no longer able to maintain, exchanging them like packs of rigged cards.

Vincenzo picks this moment to disengage himself from his mother. "Papà! Papà!" he calls, clutching at the edge of the counter. He reaches out with his hand.

Paolo turns to his son, looking annoyed. "Not now, Vincenzo."

The child's fingers slide off the wood. He goes behind the worktop and slips into the back room, where he knows he will find Ignazio. He finds him hunched over the accounts books.

"Uncle!"

"What are you doing here?" He sits him on the table, moves the inkwell away, and resumes writing, running the tip of his finger down stacks of bills. "Did you come with Mamma?"

"H-hm." The child sucks on his licorice, swinging his legs. "It smells good. Is it carnations?" he adds, sniffing the air.

"Cloves, yes. They arrived yesterday. Keep still." Ignazio puts a hand on his knee and the gesture becomes a caress. "Where's Mamma gone to?"

"They brought a paper. It was a sailor. She got all upset when she saw it."

"A paper? You mean an envelope?"

"H-hm."

At this point, Ignazio looks up. A strange agitation runs up his back. "Who did she take it to? I mean to read it."

"To one of the Palazzo Fitalia maids, the one who knows all her mistress's business and is always telling her and Aunt Mariuccia."

Ignazio puffs. "Right. She's all we need." He holds his breath and his thoughts in a single sigh. Giuseppina had her miscarriage more than two years ago, and ever since he's watched her and his brother drift apart. They live together but their lives barely touch, not belonging to each other and not seeking each other. An existence of strangers sharing a house.

Giuseppina has slowly resigned herself. She's grown fond of Mariuccia, who has become the nearest thing she can have to a friend. Then two other Calabrian girls arrived, among them Rosa, the maid Vincenzo mentioned. He and Paolo think she's a big gossip. As a matter of fact, Paolo can't stand her.

"So what happened?"

The child lets go of his licorice. He takes on a serious, reproachful expression. "She started crying. Then she dragged me all the way here so she could talk to my father."

Ignazio pauses. The quill hangs in midair for a moment before he puts it back into the inkwell.

It's not like Giuseppina to cry for no reason.

He listens and hears Paolo saying goodbye to the customer, then, straight afterward, his sister-in-law's voice. He signals to his nephew to be quiet. He approaches the entrance, keeping in the shadow of the door.

"So what's the matter?" Paolo says.

Giuseppina takes out an envelope and hands it to him. "It's from Mattia. She's desperate. She's asking us to help her husband. He's in town, sick and alone, with no one to look after him. We're here in Palermo . . ."

The store plunges into silence.

Giuseppina's hand remains outstretched for a long time before Paolo takes the letter.

He tears it into pieces.

"But you . . . you didn't even read it," she stutters, aggrieved more than surprised. "She's your sister!"

Paolo turns his back to her. "She *was* my sister. She chose to take the side of that crook she decided to marry."

Giuseppina opens her arms. "*Decided* to marry? She had no choice! She was fourteen when your father married her off to get rid of her. No woman has a choice when she gets married. Could I rebel when you dragged me here?"

Paolo does not expect this accusation. "Are you still throwing that back at me? Our lives have improved, or are you too blind to notice? Did you want to stay in Bagnara and be a peasant? And here? Can't you see I'm making good money? Where do you think your new clothes or the new chest I had made for you come from?"

"Of course! And we're still living in a pigsty. The house is—"

"We'll get a new one soon!"

"When? I feel like a servant in my own home!"

"Watch what you say or I swear to God—I've never laid a finger on you but—"

Giuseppina clenches her fists against her hips. "Mattia has nothing to do with the row you had with Barbaro and, whether you like it or not, Paolo Barbaro is still your brother-in-law. You've worked with him, shared bread and sweat . . . and now? Damn it! Can't you two try to forgive each other? Your sister—"

Paolo darts her a look that freezes her. His posture, his gestures, his face, everything shows unyielding resentment. Even Ignazio senses his rage. "His own fault. If you betray my trust even once, it's once too many. You know what he wants from me? Money. *My* money, that I bring home after breaking my back, while he wants to act the master. There's my sweat and blood on these coins, mine and my brother's. You don't remember what he did, do you?" The venom rises as he raises his voice with every sentence. "He made us fall out with suppliers. He told other merchants we were accountable to him. That *I* had to be accountable to him. *I*, who turned this place into what it is now."

Giuseppina is afraid now. She steps back against the shelves. "But your sister . . ."

"How dare you ask me to read a letter from a woman who's betrayed her own blood? As far as I'm concerned, they're dead, all of them."

By now, she is trapped between her husband and the shelves.

"Wait . . . your grandmother was a Barbaro. What? Have they come to ask for your help? I'd forbidden you from having anything to do with them."

"Paolo, that's enough." Ignazio comes into the store and puts a hand on his shoulder. He knows how to calm him down.

He cannot forgive Barbaro either. Not so much because of how he vexed him or because of the insinuations that threatened to ruin the business, but because of the rift he caused between them and Mattia.

Giuseppina's bewildered eyes drift from her husband to Ignazio. She runs to Vincenzo and picks him up. The last thing they see of her is the hem of her cloak slapping against the door.

"Why did you have to pick on your wife? She and Mattia love each other."

"Love!" Paolo gives an embittered laugh. "But she doesn't care about what they said and did to her husband." He runs his fingers through his hair, concealing his bitterness.

Ignazio wishes he could hug his brother. Placate him. But he knows it's no use: Paolo is clinging to his resentment.

He bends down to collect the shreds of Mattia's letter. He sees her name on one of the fragments, and Paolo's on another. His family has fallen to pieces just like these sheets of paper, and he was unable to prevent it.

Giuseppina returns home, holding her son's hand tight. He doesn't say anything and watches her silently, the licorice stick once again tight between his teeth.

When they walk in, Vittoria runs toward him, takes him into her arms, tickles him, and covers his neck with kisses.

Giuseppina, however, collapses into a chair. "Nothing." She mimes Paolo's gesture. "He tore it up right in front of me. He doesn't even care about your aunt." She puts her hands over her mouth to restrain herself because a woman mustn't talk ill of her husband, especially not in front of his relatives, even though, as God is her witness, she could scream like a madwoman.

Vittoria frowns. She puts Vincenzo down and he runs to the bedroom. "There's nothing you can do about it, Auntie." She brushes a lock away from Giuseppina's tired face. "That's Uncle Paolo's way. Besides, Uncle Barbaro injured him: he's right to have acted like that, it's too serious an injury."

Giuseppina does not reply. What can Vittoria possibly know about having nobody you can trust anymore? How can she know about how Mattia welcomed her and helped her?

The carriage standing outside the Florios' spice store is blocking the traffic in Via dei Materassai. You can hardly walk through the narrow gap. In the air, the first swallows and a fresh smell, full of hay and a few timid flowers.

Inside, Michele is serving a man, an artisan who's come to buy lacquer and red lead. Meanwhile, Ignazio is taking care of another customer.

A noblewoman.

The lady before him is an attractive woman wrapped in a cloak with fox fur trimming to shield herself from the chill of this inclement March. Her skin reveals a few too many years expertly concealed with makeup. Ignazio gives a half smile and continues to crush wormwood with star aniseed and dittany.

He is now seldom seen behind the counter. Ever since the Florios parted with the Barbaros, in 1803, the business has taken off. They have contacts among many merchants, both Neapolitan and British; as a matter of fact, the latter have become excellent suppliers. They're dependable, and it's entirely in their interest to maintain a good relationship with Sicilians, given the French dominance in the rest of Italy. A few months ago, Napoleon conquered the Kingdom of Naples, and the Bourbons fled to Sicily with their tail between their legs, seeking British protection. Therefore, Palermo is one of the last harbors left that are free from Napoleon's influence, an important place of exchange for the anti-French coalition.

Ignazio deals mainly with administration and accounts. Still, he returns to the counter for a few special clients.

"Coming to your store is always so . . . so *exotic*. There are so many scents from faraway lands. By the way, where is Don Paolo?"

"My brother will be back soon. As soon as he saw your ladyship's carriage, he thought you might be interested in an item he mentioned last time you visited us."

The woman's eyes become attentive. "It's the amber, isn't it?"

Ignazio nods while still crushing herbs in the mortar. "Baltic amber, very pure. It comes from the steppes of Asia, and is already in beads."

There's a squeaking of hinges.

"Signora." Paolo Florio greets the lady with a bow. He puts a wood-and-ivory casket on the counter. "Forgive my lateness but I was working for you."

The lady stretches her neck impatiently. "So?"

"To start with, the box is a jewel in itself, but that's nothing in comparison with what it contains." A golden glow spreads over the counter. "Look. Isn't it beautiful? And it's just the right thing for you: did you know that amber relieves stomach trouble and preserves energy in the body?"

"Really?" She touches the beads then pulls her hand away. "It's warm," she exclaims, surprised.

"Because it's not a stone but a resin. They say there's a spark of life in its glow. But allow me . . ." Paolo leans forward and proffers the string of beads. "Here, try it on."

Her dress lights up with the shimmer. The woman runs her fingers lightly on the beads and admires them. Her wonder is followed by desire. She has already decided. "How much?"

Paolo furrows his brow and feigns reticence. Finally, he mutters the price.

Her mouth shrivels. "That's madness. My husband will chide me for days." Even so, she's still fingering the necklace. She drops her voice and says, bitterly and spitefully, "He squanders my dowry at the gambling table and I'm not even allowed a whim."

"Yes, but you're not spending money on a whim. You're buying a remedy for your health, just like the tonic my brother is now preparing for you. By the way, how is the swelling in your stomach?"

"Much better. You were right, it was nothing serious."

"I'm glad. This is an ancient remedy, something for just a select few customers. If it were anything more complex, I'd be the first to send you to Don Trombetta in Porta Carini. He's an excellent apothecary, as well as our customer." *And one of those who stopped buying supplies from Canzoneri and moved to our spices,* he thinks.

But the lady isn't listening to him. Her eyes are filled with the light from the amber. She gives a deep sigh. "So be it. I will leave you a deposit and a letter of intent. My husband will come by and settle the rest."

Ignazio conceals his disappointment in a cough.

More letters of intent, payments in installments. Some Sicilians are wealthy only in name and their titles aren't even worth the stone on which their coats of arms are carved.

His brother, however, doesn't bat an eyelid. "And I will be here to attend to him."

Paolo goes into the back room to get paper and inkwell. Ignazio, meanwhile, pours the ground herbs into a bottle with some alcohol, then stirs the mixture with a little glass rod. He calls the lady's maid.

"Now listen carefully. The tonic has to stand for eight days. You must give your mistress a small glass every evening after filtering it. Do you understand?"

The girl mumbles, "*Caciettu,*" an assent that reveals her rural origins. "I understand."

Ignazio seals the cap and covers the bottle with a dark cloth. He hands it to the maid while her mistress signs the letter of intent.

Paolo escorts the noblewoman to the door. At last, the carriage frees Via dei Materassai of its bulky presence.

Paolo smooths his waistcoat. "Nice having customers who don't ask for discounts."

Ignazio is wearing a very similar garment, over a white shirt with sleeves rolled up to his elbows. "Let's just hope Cavalier Albertini doesn't make a fuss. Whenever his wife comes to buy things, he then complains that she's cleaning him out." He reads the letter of intent the lady signed. "He could say he never authorized his wife to incur this expense. You know that, don't you?"

"He won't. Albertini is related to notaries, judges, and owns a *fondaco* in Bagheria. He'll pay in the end, because he doesn't want to be embarrassed." Then he looks at his brother. "You should roll down your sleeves. We're not laborers."

And yet this is still how they are viewed. Neither admits it openly. Perhaps this is the reason they are so particularly attentive to the store decor and their clothes.

Ignazio knows that's what people call them, and it stings him.

Some memories are like open wounds salt is rubbed into.

He remembers. It was two weeks ago.

At the Steri customs, at the accounts office, where the spices are recorded and the accounts of goods coming in and going out are kept. A large, rectangular room that opens onto the square ground-floor courtyard.

He was waiting to pass recently disembarked goods through customs then go to the master notary's office to pay the taxes. In the meantime, he had stopped to talk to a young Englishman, Ben Ingham, recently arrived in Palermo.

"I think it's a very lively city but . . . how can I put it? . . . really chaotic . . . Do you see what I mean?"

Ignazio smiled slightly. "It's not easy to live here, I grant you that. It's an ungrateful city, worse than a woman. It flatters you, then . . ." He opened his index finger and thumb and waved them. "Promises a lot and gives nothing."

"Yes, I noticed that. That's why I realized one has to be careful and . . . What's the expression?"

"*Taliàrisi u' cappotto?*"

The Englishman frowned, trying to understand the sentence. He sensed its meaning and tried to repeat it. Then he burst out into a raucous laugh because he couldn't quite pronounce it. *Watching your back.*

Suddenly, Carmelo Saguto's voice filled the room. Ignazio had seen him jump the queue and go straight to the master notary, who had greeted him with great reverence.

Some people had grumbled but no one really protested, only muttered: Saguto was Canzoneri's son-in-law and nobody stood up to him.

Shortly afterward, it was Ignazio's turn.

As soon as Saguto came out of the manager's office, he started picking on Ignazio. "Oh, look who's here, Don Florio. The little one." He made a mocking hand gesture and sought the staff's complicity with his eyes. "How's business? Doing well?"

"Quite well, thank you."

"That's right, you people are doing well." Saguto approached the desk and saw the figure. "Oh, my, all this money!"

The employee heard. "The Florios work hard. You should tell your father-in-law to watch his back."

"They'll have to eat a lot of bread and onion before they get as far as the Canzoneris. No disrespect, of course," another scribe added. "An honorable family. I can still remember your father-in-law's father. A hard worker . . ."

They talked as though Ignazio wasn't there. As though nothing about him, his work, his money, his very existence, was of any worth.

Ignazio nearly snatched the receipt from the scribe's hand. "If you've finished . . ."

But Saguto had no intention of letting him go. On the contrary. He raised his voice and stood in Ignazio's way, preventing him from leaving. "But tell me something, how's your brother-in-law? I mean that Bagnara man in Via dei Lattarini who had to sell everything off. Oh, don't you have anything to say?" He started to laugh. A dry laugh, like a file rubbing against iron. "Even animals don't behave like that."

Ignazio had to call on all the saints to remain calm. "We're all fine, thank you. And don't meddle in our business; after all, I'm not telling you how to act with your relatives."

The volume of the conversations around them had dropped. Saguto took a few steps then turned back. "Are you still trying to teach me how a real family behaves, you mangy dog? You don't hold on to your money when it's a matter of blood ties. Do you know how much money is here?" He waved a stack of receipts.

"Actually, it doesn't look much more than I have. And at least it's just me and my brother. How many of you are there? Four? Five? How many have to split that? Besides, you're Don Canzoneri's secretary, not an apothecary like his sons. You're a paper pusher."

The color drained from Carmelo Saguto's face, but then he turned scarlet. "Fuck, I may be a messenger but you and your brother are just two laborers, I can still remember your brother clearing rubbish from your store."

It was as though frost had just fallen on the customs office.

Behind him, somebody whispered, "True, these Bagnara people used to be laborers," and another, "God only knows how they made their money."

By the door, merchants, sailors, and other employees looked like stray dogs waiting for a bone, frothing at the mouth, ready to pick up the story and spread it throughout the entire Castellammare district, trimming it with more violence and spicing it up with details.

Ignazio felt a hand on his arm. "Have you finished? Because if so, it's my turn." He turned and saw the young Englishman, Ben Ingham.

"I owe you a favor," Ignazio said as they went out.

"You'll pay me back," the Englishman replied. "Although you would have done the same thing. Making a spectacle of yourself is never a good idea, especially in front of such an audience."

Ignazio still quivers at remembering this. The scene is branded in his memory and will not go away. At the same time, he's still grateful to Ingham for his words, which stopped him from smashing Saguto's face in front of everybody.

Ignazio removes his apron and puts on his jacket and cloak. "I don't like working with my cuffs down: they get stained and dusty. In any case, when that lady came in she already wanted the amber. The tonic was just an excuse."

Paolo laughs. "I'd described it in such a seductive way that it must have made an impression."

There's the sound of pestles in stone mortars coming from the back room: an uneven rhythm that punctuates their days. They now have two store boys in addition to Michele, and they're in charge of preparing the powders. And Ignazio has Maurizio Reggio, a bookkeeper who helps him with the invoices.

Ignazio is about to leave but turns back. "But there wasn't just the string of amber in the casket, right?"

Paolo caresses the casket, which is still on the counter. He opens it. "No." He takes out a pair of earrings. Coral beads and pearls. "I asked Captain Pantero to find a present in Naples for Giuseppina, for the Feast of Saint Joseph. He found these. I hope she likes them."

Giuseppina is still hard but lately she seems to have softened somewhat. Perhaps it's the sign of a weary peace she shares with Paolo, dictated by the habit of living with a man she does not love and yet has grown fond of.

At that moment, a customer walks in, a servant in livery. Ignazio takes advantage to slip away and go to their bookkeeper.

For some time now, the Florios have been renting a warehouse at the back of the customs offices, within the large Palazzo Steri property. Cool, well-guarded rooms down a long corridor that ends in the service courtyard, behind the accounts office; there, they keep spices in transit to other ports or waiting to be sold to other merchants. The import tariff is paid only when the goods actually enter Palermo, and not before. It's common practice among wholesalers: better pay rent on one room than incur more taxes. There are spices from India obtained through the British, and those from French colonies, sold in Livorno and throughout the Tyrrhenian Sea, purchased by Italian sailors and sold in Palermo. They have top-quality goods from all over the Mediterranean. They can't claim to be as rich as the Canzoneris, that's true. But they've come ahead in leaps and bounds.

In any case, the stockroom in Via dei Materassai became too small.

When he arrives at the accounts office, he discovers that Maurizio has done almost everything already.

"I've cleared the incoming packages and organized the dispatch of the bark to Messina and Patti. The sacks will be leaving by tomorrow evening." He shows the receipts and indicates a cart being watched by one of the *aromateria* workers.

"In that case, go to the store and record all the transfers. Tell my brother I'll be back soon."

Left alone, Ignazio indulges in the luxury of a stroll to La Cala. The horizon is a clear blue line. The light is growing bright and the wind is no longer as biting as in the previous weeks. Spring is a fragrance in the air.

It's a snap decision.

He finds himself walking down Vicolo della Neve, escorted by a coolness that sweeps away the smells of humanity crammed in the alleys. He walks past the little door where the snow that comes from the Madonie Mountains is sold; somewhere above he hears the sound of a violin and the voice of a tutor correcting his pupil. In the streets, in the *fondaci*, and in the stores, there's a mixture of voices and accents: Genoese, Tuscan, some English and Neapolitan, all together.

He continues down Via Alloro without looking at the wealthy Palermo *palazzi*; he reaches Strada dei Zagarellai, full of women carrying conical baskets or dragging screaming children behind. They pause outside the stores, evaluate, buy.

Ignazio approaches a counter beneath a stone arch. There are all kinds of ribbons on it: silk, lace, embroidered, velvet.

His eye is caught by a gold ribbon. He pictures it on the green twill bodice Paolo bought his wife some time ago.

The woman behind the counter helps him out of his hesitation. "What would you like, signore? This ribbon?"

"Yes." He clears his throat. "It's a present. How much would I need for a bodice?"

There are perplexed looks around him. "That depends. Who is it for? Your wife?" She indicates his mother's wedding band on Ignazio's finger. He raises his hand and gestures, no, he's not married.

"It's for my sister," he says, improvising. He doesn't know why, he's blushing like a child.

The woman looks at him, skeptical. "How much do you want?"

Panic.

"How much do I need?"

"It depends on what she's like."

He tries to reply. He has no idea. How did he get himself into this mess?

"Does she have a full bust? Does she like things to be plain or very ornate?"

"Will she be wearing it as a bow or on the seams?" another woman asks, while fiddling with lace.

A chorus of women is suddenly engaging with him.

For heaven's sake, he doesn't know. Ignazio tries. "She's a little . . . like you." He indicates a girl trying out a cord. She laughs, revealing a mouth full of decaying teeth.

"Cristina, just give him two bolts, this way at least he'll have enough." It's an elderly woman speaking, sitting in a corner, her face like bark. She's probably the owner. "And take a clasp, too."

So Cristina, the worker he's been talking to up to now, takes out clasps made of bone. The old woman is right: some are very beautiful. He chooses one decorated with a mermaid.

Shortly afterward, Ignazio is walking back home with a package concealed under his cloak. It's not far to Via dei Materassai. He's walked the long way around and is now in Vicolo dei Chiavettieri, attacked by the smell of iron being filed and the screeching sound of the lathes.

It's for the Feast of Saint Joseph, he tells himself. *Giuseppina has worked so hard for our family, she deserves this and much more, we forced her to come all the way here and she's always been very respectful toward me and—*

The package under his cloak suddenly feels cumbersome.

He can't give her a present like this. He's not really her brother . . . or, actually, what does it matter? They're brother- and sister-in-law, and she's known him forever.

They're family, right?

It's the Feast of Saint Joseph. Giuseppina receives Paolo's gift with a smile of surprise that turns into thanks. She takes the earrings, holds them up high to stop Vincenzo from snatching them from her hand, and puts them in.

Her husband keeps smiling as she looks at herself in the mirror in disbelief, happy.

The package with the ribbon and the clasp remains in Ignazio's hands, behind his back. He, too, just smiles and feels foolish, out of place, out of time.

He goes away. Shortly afterward, he goes back to his room. He hides the package in a trunk at the foot of his bed.

That's where Giuseppina will find it after his death.

Vincenzo is sprinting through the alleys, heedless of splashing mud on his pants. He reaches Via della Tavola Tonda, and knocks hard on a door. "Peppino, come down! The brig's arrived, *iamuninni*! Let's go!"

A little boy appears on the doorstep. He must be seven or eight, the same age as Vincenzo. His eyes are alert, his hair tousled, his feet dirty. They laugh and run, one barefoot, the other in leather shoes, their eyes reflecting their pleasure at being in each other's company.

"Where did your father say it was coming from?"

"Marseille. The French give the spices to Neapolitan sailors who then resell them to my father. Then he sells them at the store."

They go through the customs door, clinging to a cart. When the driver notices them, he threatens them with a stick and they run away giggling.

They reach the dock all sweaty and red in the face.

Vincenzo's hair is glossy in the September sun. He sees his uncle on the deck, examining the shipment as it is gradually pulled out of the hold. Reggio follows him, holding the papers, counting out loud.

Other traders wait their turn on the dock, but it's the Florios who have the lion's share. Vincenzo knows this because he heard his father announce it with pride the night before. He knows that, if the sale goes well, they'll be able to move house. That's what his mother said.

Followed by Vincenzo, Peppino climbs on a coil of rope. "Oh, look! Your uncle has boots like a gentleman."

"My uncle says it's important. He says people can tell what you're like from the way you talk to them but they won't listen to you unless you're well dressed." He shields his eyes from the sun with his hand. The smell of spices that wafts toward him is stronger than the smell of salt from the sea. He recognizes cloves and cinnamon, and whiffs of vanilla scent.

Ignazio notices him when he turns to speak to Reggio. He also recognizes the little boy with him: Giuseppe Pastore, the son of a Bagnara sailor married to a woman from Palermo.

If his brother knew that Vincenzo frequents this urchin, he would lose his temper and with good reason. Francesco Pastore, Peppino's father, lives by his wits; it's his wife who brings home the money by working as a kitchen maid. But he doesn't agree with his brother; on the contrary, Vincenzo should have contact with all kinds of people and be able to keep his dignity no matter what. Besides—what the hell!—they, too, used to play barefoot in the streets of Bagnara.

Reggio comes up to him. "We've finished, Don Ignazio. Shall I have everything sent to customs?"

"Everything except for the package of indigo and the saffron. Take those to the warehouse in Via dei Materassai."

A kind of murmur rises from the dock, which Ignazio interprets as a sigh of relief. It's no sin to have the largest shipment, he thinks. *Let them come to terms with it.* But, judging by the aggressive looks as he steps down on the land, it's not envy.

It's ill will.

"So you've finished, have you?"

It's Mimmo Russello, one of the storekeepers in Via dei Lattarini, speaking: one of those who used to sell spices of dubious quality and scrape a living in the shadow of Canzoneri and Gulì. "I'm so sorry to have kept you waiting. Do go through." He accompanies his words with a simulated bow.

A few people laugh, some cough in their hands.

"Once upon a time it was only the Canzoneris who laid down the law here. Now that you're here, too, one can't work anymore. What is it—are you two in cahoots?" Russello mumbles.

"Us? With the Canzoneris?" Ignazio's laugh is genuine. "Not even in a dream!"

"You folks laugh while people who have to work starve. As soon as you and Saguto get to customs, everything gets paralyzed. You set the price and take the best packages. So now you're acting like masters over here, too."

Ignazio isn't laughing anymore, though. "This is my work. It's not my fault if customers don't come to you any longer, *Master* Russello." He stresses the word *master* so that those around see the difference between them. "If our prices are higher it's because the quality is the best in Palermo and people know it. You want more spices? Different things? Come to our office and we can discuss it."

"That's right. This way, you and Canzoneri can fleece us between you."

"Then don't complain." Sarcasm has been replaced by coldness. "Nobody's stealing anything from you. This is all our work," he adds in a Palermo dialect that has almost lost all Calabrian inflection.

Russello winces. "*Caciettu*," he hisses. "I understand." He studies Ignazio's clothes, looks down at his boots and indicates them with his chin. "Don't you find them tight? They say when you walk around barefoot for a long time, you find it hard to wear closed shoes."

All around, silence concentrates into surprised, uneasy looks. Only the sailors keep shouting and calling out to one another, heedless of what's happening.

The response comes once Russello is already halfway up the gangplank. "No, my feet don't hurt. I can afford soft leather. But I can tell you your pocket's going to hurt so much you'll cry, if you dare touch our money."

He uses the calm tone of someone merely making an observation, but the traders around him step back, confused. The mild-mannered Ignazio Florio has never used threats.

Ignazio walks away without looking anybody in the face. He feels rage burning inside him: corrosive and unfair. In Palermo, working and breaking your back is not enough. You always have to raise your voice and impose your power, true or pretended, and fight those who speak too much or out of turn. Appearances are very important. The shared lie, the papier mâché backdrop against which you play your part.

Nobody forgives you reality, the true wealth.

His eyes meet those of Vincenzo, still up on the coil of ropes.

His nephew's little face darkens, afraid. Before he can say anything, Ignazio grabs him by the arm. "Who told you to come here? And with him at that! What will people think of us?" he says, indicating Peppino. His resentment is pushing him for an escape route. "If your father knew you roamed the streets like this, he'd give you the stick."

The child mutters an apology. What has he done wrong?

Behind him, Peppino comes down from the coil of ropes and takes a few steps away from them. Vincenzo keeps turning toward his friend while being dragged away. He looks at Ignazio, then at Peppino.

He doesn't understand.

~

Fits of dry coughing. Again.

Paolo roams around the house, a hand over his mouth to avoid waking up Ignazio, Vincenzo and Vittoria, and Giuseppina.

He shivers under the blanket he has pulled over himself. He's sweating. He goes into the dining room: there's a table and a dresser and he leans against them in order to catch his breath. There are two arras on the walls.

He goes to the window searching for fresh air but stops: it's too cold.

Below, white in the moonlight, the flagstones are shiny from the humidity. The fruit seller's baskets stand empty against the door of their old home.

The new home is beautiful. It's on the second floor and has windows, real doors, and a kitchen with a cooking brazier that works.

Another coughing fit. Paolo massages his chest. After every fit he feels it being crushed. He must have caught a chill that won't go away. How did it happen? He's always out in the sun, the wind, and the rain . . .

Footsteps behind him.

He turns. A face in the darkness. The nightshirt hardly covers his barc fcct on the brick floor.

His son is looking at him.

As an adult, this will be Vincenzo's immediate image of his father. Not his voice or gestures or an emotion. His ruthless memory will present him with a hunched-over man looking at him with feverish eyes and with the mark of illness on him.

He will be revisited by the anguish he felt when he had the confused gut feeling that his life was about to change.

He will feel his thin, childish voice in his throat, and also in his throat that smell of disease he has already learned to hate.

"What's wrong, Papà?"

Vincenzo is big now: he's seven and has eyes that give nothing away. Paolo senses a nameless fear in his son's voice.

"It's just a little cough, Vincenzo. Go back to bed."

But the little boy shakes his head. He takes a chair from a corner so he can look out the window next to him. They stand, leaning against each other. Their breaths synchronize and their eyes hover over the same stones.

Vincenzo takes his father's hand. "Can I come to the *aromateria* tomorrow?"

"And what about your teacher? What will we tell the teacher when he comes?"

The boy insists. "Afterward?"

"No."

Ever since his father has decided that he must study, Vincenzo's days of freedom between La Cala and the harbor alleys with Peppino and other Bagnara children are over. However, he doesn't give up. Whenever he can, he runs away to La Cala or to his friends. He spins tops *u' piriu* with them on the *balate* of Piazza Sant'Oliva, the large, smooth stones that form the cobbles in the square. That's where his mother grabs him by the ear and takes him back home, where, every day, Antonino Gagliano, a young man about to become a priest, makes him study.

Writing, counting, reading. He does enjoy studying but he prefers even more to stand behind the counter and listen to his uncle talking to suppliers and ships' captains, learning the names of places and to distinguish the shapes of the ships in the harbor. He can recognize the spice smells: bark, cloves, arnica, even asafetida.

His father seems to read his thoughts. "You must be patient. Patient and persevering: if you don't study you'll never be able to do my work."

"But you never studied."

"That's true." He sighs. "That's why I had to work much harder and even be swindled. But if you know things, then it's less likely to happen. The more you know, the less people walk all over you."

Vincenzo is not convinced. "You have to see things, Papà, not just study them."

"When you're older." He tries to pick him up but can't. A dizzy spell forces him to lean against the jamb. "Come on, let's go back to bed. I'm tired."

Instead, Vincenzo hugs him. He holds him tight against his chest, hides his face in the crook of his father's neck, and breathes in his smell, a scent of medicinal herbs and sweat. Concealed in these smells, he senses something new, unpleasant and sour, that doesn't belong there.

He will remember this hug all his life.

The year 1806 is nearly over but Paolo's cough won't go away. It has become deep and insistent. He doesn't want to be seen by a physician even though Ignazio has repeatedly urged him. Paolo is always tired and can spend only a little time in the store.

Maurizio Reggio looks after the accounts and Ignazio runs the business. It's him customers find behind the counter and him retailers turn to for their orders. His delicate features have been erased over the years of hard work. He's a young man with a calm voice devoid of emotion. His face does not give away either the worry about the business or the fear that the chest cold Paolo suffers from could be something serious.

But it is.

He realizes it when Orsola, the maid Paolo has employed for his wife, arrives at the store, breathless. "Come quickly, Don Ignazio!" She pants and rubs her hands on her dress. "Your brother's sick."

Even though it's winter and nearing Christmas, he doesn't stop to pick up his cloak. He runs, climbs the steps two at a time, and stops by the bedroom door. Sunk in a chair in the corner, Vittoria, fingers on her lips, is rocking to and fro. She mutters, "Blessed Virgin, what a misfortune," and can say nothing else.

Giuseppina is standing up. She is holding a bowl full of soiled handkerchiefs, and looks like someone who knows but can't admit she understands.

Slowly, Ignazio comes in and removes the bowl from her hands. Giuseppina's fingers are trembling. He covers them with his for a moment. "Go to the kitchen. Tell Orsola to call Caruso the physician immediately, then go and wash yourself and the child. You, too, Vittoria. Wash all the laundry in boiling water and lye."

The women leave the room. Only then does Ignazio pluck up the courage to look at his brother.

Paolo is slumped on the pillows. His lips and mustache are stained in red. He attempts a smile that's more of a smirk. "That's what it is. I knew it wasn't a chill."

Ignazio hesitates a moment before sitting on the bed. He hugs him tight. It's his brother, he doesn't care how ill Paolo is. "I'll take care of everything, you hear?" He presses his forehead against Paolo's, just as Paolo did years earlier. "I won't leave you on your own." He gives the back of his neck a squeeze. "I'll get some echinacea made up for you straightaway. Then I'll find a house outside the city, maybe in Noce or San Lorenzo. There you'll have warm weather and clean air. You'll get well, I swear."

In the kitchen, Vittoria and the maid are preparing cauldrons of water to soak sheets and clothes. The girl's face is ashen, her lips tight, like a wound.

Giuseppina can't stop her hands from shaking. Wrapped in towels,

Vincenzo is sitting on the kitchen table. There's a steaming tub at his feet. He sees his mother is distressed but doesn't exactly know why.

Ignazio comes in. He suddenly looks older. "We must all get ourselves checked." He's tense, his voice has lost its warmth.

Giuseppina wishes she could say something, but it's as though there's a stone in her throat. Behind her, her son senses something serious is happening. The way children sense things: with an illumination that is already a certainty.

"Is Papà ill?"

Giuseppina and Ignazio turn around at the same time.

Vincenzo understands.

Giuseppina tries to approach but Ignazio stops her. He speaks to him the way one speaks to a man. "Yes, Vincenzo."

The light goes out of the child's dark eyes. He slides off the table and walks across to his room. There's a slate on his bed and, on it, the homework left by his tutor. He sits down and begins to write.

Nobody sleeps that night.

Not Paolo, the lost soul who keeps coughing. Not Vincenzo, who cannot imagine what will happen to his father and stifles his crying with his pillow. Not Vittoria, who sees the ghost of a new solitude drawing closer.

Not Giuseppina, who, her back turned to her husband, stares into the darkness and keeps her fear locked inside.

Not Ignazio, who's walking barefoot, his shirt outside his trousers, his waistcoat unbuttoned. He takes pleasure in the coldness of the floor.

Paolo's illness changes everything.

He already knows that the news will soon spread across Palermo and that some—the Canzoneris first and foremost—will try to take advantage of the situation.

The business is entirely on his shoulders. He's going to need to take on another worker; he'll need to make sure Vincenzo keeps studying without distraction. He'll have to take care of Giuseppina.

And this makes him tremble inside.

He cannot imagine what the next few months will bring him. How advanced the illness is and what its consequences will be.

He remembers a fall morning when his brother, still an adolescent, dragged him to Mattia and Paolo Barbaro's house to protect him from their stepmother's resentment and their father's indifference. He saved his life. He realizes it now.

Mattia.

Mattia and her children have moved to Marsala. Since Barbaro's illness had left him unable to work, he found an inexpensive house for himself and his family there. Sometimes, Ignazio sends her money to pay for Raffaele's studies or simply help her make ends meet.

Or perhaps, he admits, ashamed, he's been sending it to soothe his conscience.

He must tell his sister. Paolo doesn't know it but his wife has disobeyed his order to sever her relations with Mattia. Giuseppina has been asking him, timidly at first, then regularly, to write letters, and Ignazio has agreed.

This way, he has kept this piece of family, this piece of life close to him. It's a secret he shares with his sister-in-law, one of the unspoken things that always formed a bond between them.

The opportunity to contact Mattia arrives a few days later. Paolo has been moved to the country and Giuseppina has gone with him to find a maid to look after him day and night.

Ignazio and Vincenzo are staying in town, however.

It's early afternoon. The store clerks have gone home for lunch.

"May I come in?"

Vincenzo is doing division at the counter. He raises his head and calls out, "Uncle, there's someone's here for you."

Ignazio looks out of the backroom door. It's one of their freight forwarders who sails on a felucca, come to pick up some aniseed. "Master Salvatore, please come in."

"*Assabbinirìca*—God be with you, Don Florio. You're looking well. And how's your brother? They told me at the harbor that he's not very well . . ." Words softly spoken, respectful, followed by sidelong glances at the child.

"Thank you, we need all the blessings we can get . . . My brother's . . . He's . . . He's got a chest cold but he's certainly not at death's door. He's being treated outside the city and waiting for God's will."

"Oh, I heard some nasty things. Tongues wag."

"They've clearly got nothing else to do. Come in . . ." He pushes him gently into the backroom office and smells the scent of salt and sun that brings back memories of his adolescence.

He wonders if his brother still thinks about the sea and the days spent on board the *San Francesco* between Naples and Messina.

While he signs the freight receipts, he asks the man where he'll be stopping off during the journey.

"I'm returning from Messina, so I was thinking of going to Mazara del Vallo then to Gela . . . Why?"

Ignazio looks at him from below, his chin propped up on his closed hands. "If I asked you to stop off in Marsala to deliver a letter, would you do it?"

"*Caciettu*. Is it important?"

He takes an envelope from the desk drawer. "Very important. You must hand it to Mattia Florio, Barbaro's wife, and to her only. See, I've written down their most recent address on the paper. If they're not there anymore, they won't have gone far."

The sailor nods. He frowns. He remembers something, some gossip about a brother-in-law of the Florios, whom they ousted from their business, heedless of his bankruptcy. Without looking each other in the eye, like strangers.

He slips the letter into his jacket pocket. He asks and wants to know nothing: it's none of his business.

Ignazio follows him to the door.

"May God help you and may the Blessed Virgin be with you, Don Florio. And my greetings to your brother: I'll pray to Saint Francis of Paola to watch over him."

"You, too, Master Salvatore. You, too."

He watches him walk away, swaying on the *balate* as though he were on the deck of a ship. He's somewhat sorry he asked him to deliver the message, but he has no choice. He doesn't know how much time he has.

Giuseppina's forehead is pressed against her hand, her eyes fixed on the rectangle of sky she sees through the window. It's a bright blue, making spring look like a willful, angry little girl.

Paolo is much worse. The cough sometimes prevents him from breathing. She's sent Orsola to tell Ignazio, who now runs the *aromateria* full-time.

A hand touches her shoulder. She grabs it and kisses it. With a swish of fabric, Mattia Barbaro sits in front of her.

The two women look at each other without speaking.

Mattia arrived two days ago from Marsala with her son, Raffaele, the trip paid for by Ignazio. Their lives are increasingly hard but returning to Bagnara is out of the question: Paolo is too proud to show everybody how low he's sunk and, above all, he can't bear people in Bagnara constantly talking about how successful the Florios are.

Mattia had to face a blazing row with her husband—the first after years of submission—because he wouldn't let her go, protesting that they had no money and that Paolo did not deserve this sacrifice.

But she is a Florio and the Florios do not forsake their own blood.

Mattia's face is a mask of resignation and weariness that makes her features droop. Time and sorrows have bleached her hair white and made her eyelids heavy.

Children's voices arrive from the other side of the room: Vincenzo is showing his cousin Raffaele, just a few years his senior, his books. Vittoria is with them, minding them and every so often trying to catch snippets of her aunts' conversation. She, too, was very struck by how crumpled by time and hard work Mattia's face had become.

Giuseppina looks at them, dejected. "He doesn't realize his father's dying." She says this with anxiety and a drop of resentment. "Sometimes I see him standing still outside the bedroom, he doesn't dare go in even when Paolo gestures at him to approach. It's as though he doesn't want to see him like this anymore and doesn't realize it upsets the wretched man."

"He's a child: right now he's scared of what's happening. But you mustn't give in. This is the time for being brave and asking God's help."

"God cares nothing about me. If we'd stayed in Bagnara, I know this wouldn't have happened."

"You can't say that. Perhaps our husbands would have gotten shipwrecked or there would have been another earthquake. How can we know what's around the corner?" She is all too familiar with this bitterness, and that's precisely why she is aware of the harm it can do. "You must stop thinking about what was and could have been. I didn't want to come to Marsala either, but I had to because my husband got ill. Because of my husband I had to forget my family; as far as my brother was concerned, I no longer existed. And look at us now. Here we are, together again."

Giuseppina tries to tidy her hair but it's no use. A lock keeps falling over her forehead. "You still have a husband and you have Ignazio. He's your blood. I don't have anybody anymore, my relatives are all dead . . ." Words with bile, her shawl hanging gracelessly off one shoulder, and powerlessness burning her throat. "What have I got? Tell me."

During the ensuing silence, Mattia closes her eyes. "You have your beautiful son." She smiles sadly. "And you also have Ignazio. Have you never noticed?"

When Giuseppina told Ignazio that Paolo had gotten worse, he called Caruso, the physician.

The latter assured him that he would go to see him as soon as he could get a cart to go to Noce. "It could be phlegm or an accumulation of humors. Let me hear his lungs and I'll be able to tell you."

So Ignazio hired a buggy and went to pick him up from home. He'll take him to see his brother, and tell him Mattia's coming. It'll give him something to hope for, he thinks while riding through the Noce olive groves with the physician.

There *must* be a hope.

It's late evening by the time he returns.

His footsteps are heavy, his eyes bloodshot. Vincenzo and Raffaele are already asleep, overwhelmed by the day's emotions. Vittoria has swept the rooms and gone to bed.

The two sisters-in-law, though, are waiting in the kitchen.

Giuseppina sees despondency in his face. She goes to him and stops, her hands holding the corners of her shawl tight. "So?"

Mattia is with her. He shakes his head. "Nothing. He doesn't want to see you."

She clasps her hand over her mouth to stifle her sobs, and rocks back and forth. "What do you mean? Not even when he's ill? His heart won't soften even now?" Giuseppina hugs her but she pushes her away. "No heart and no conscience. Don't I even deserve forgiveness?"

Ignazio holds her to his chest. "I'm sorry. He started shouting and blood gushed out of his mouth. I had to give him laudanum to calm him down." He seeks reassurance in Giuseppina's face, as she stands behind Mattia, clenching her fists, her eyes shiny.

He won't tell them how angry his brother was, nor of the rage he spewed out. Of how hurt he was when Paolo said that Mattia was dead to him, that if she'd come for the money, she could go away and drop dead because he'd already made out his will and neither she nor that dog her husband would get anything.

He doesn't need to tell Giuseppina. She already knows.

And he cannot tell her about how upset the physician was after he'd listened to Paolo's chest. At least not now.

Mattia pulls away from her brother. "I will take many sins before God but not this grudge." She beats her chest. "He's my brother and I love him, and I pray God forgives him, because he shouldn't have done this to me. I fell out with my husband so I could come here and now my brother sends me away like a leper?"

More sobbing. Giuseppina leads her to the bedroom. "Calm yourself, dear heart," she mutters. "Come to bed."

They're sisters even though they don't have the same blood, Ignazio thinks.

Giuseppina turns to him. "I've put a plate of macaroni and broccoli aside for you. It must still be warm. Why don't you eat and rest, as well?"

He nods, but he isn't hungry.

But Mattia stops outside the bedroom. "The harm done comes back," she says. "There are things you pay for, generation after generation. He's hurting not just me but all of us: he will have to remember this, forever."

Giuseppina shivers and Ignazio also shudders.

Because these words sound like a *magària*, a curse, and once you say certain things, you can't take them back.

They fall through time, go from one generation to another, until they come true.

Giuseppina waits for Mattia to fall asleep before she goes to tidy up the kitchen.

"I don't deserve this," Mattia kept repeating. "I fed him like a mother, I washed his clothes. I protected him. And now he rejects me like this?" More tears, which Giuseppina wiped away as anger rose inside her.

What now? What does she want to happen? For the husband she never loved to recover and come home?

For a woman, a man is safety, the only safety she has. It's a plate on the table, a bucket of coal for the *cufune*, the engraved copper brazier.

She huddles in her shawl. No, that's not what frightens her most. It's something else, that concerns her alone, that's just beyond her thoughts.

A shadow in the dark kitchen startles her.

It's Ignazio, head on the table, his shoulders shaking.

He's crying.

The restrained, stifled sobs of a man unable to keep his sorrow inside because it's too great, but who's afraid of making a sound.

She takes a step back, and returns to the bedroom.

That night, Ignazio sleeps fitfully. He had hoped to get some relief from his tears but that's not the case. On the contrary, he's afraid he won't be able to do his duty. That he'll fail.

But that's something he cannot even let himself think, let alone tell anyone else.

He gets up and dresses carefully so nobody can say that the Florios have troubles. Never mind that it's early, so early that dawn is only slightly more than an impression. The *aromateria* awaits him.

When he goes to the kitchen, though, he finds Giuseppina there. "And Mattia?" he asks.

"The poor wretch is still asleep. She had nightmares last night."

He watches her serve him a cup of warm milk. "What about you? Did you manage to sleep?"

"A little."

She takes the broom and starts sweeping while he dips bread into his cup.

She suddenly freezes. She speaks without looking at him. "Tell me the truth."

He understands, like he's always understood her. The milk in his mouth turns to poison. "He's deteriorated. No point in hiding it from you."

"Did the physician tell you that?"

"Yes."

"Is he dying?"

Ignazio does not reply.

A void forms in front of him. No sound, no warmth. Giuseppina seems to have dissolved, leaving a statue in her place.

Then a sob. And another. The broom comes crashing down. Despair explodes and pours out of her face and her body, from her wide-open mouth.

Ignazio has realized some time ago that when people live together, they end up bonding. You love not the person but your concept of him, the feelings he arouses, even your hatred toward him. You even grow fond of your demons. "Please . . . Don't do this . . ." he begs her, and can do nothing but clasp her against his chest because she looks as though she's falling apart, so violent are her sobs.

He muffles her crying against his neck. He realizes he's also crying, and so they weep together, in each other's arms. However, once the tears have stopped, he feels her tensing up. Giuseppina lifts her head and they almost brush against each other.

The ghost he carries within turns into a body of flesh and blood that is his at the moment.

Not his brother's, not his nephew's. *His own.*

He's always been right behind her. He's never touched her in any way that wasn't respectful.

He can do it now that Paolo is far away, confined to a bed.

She also looks confused. But when he stares into her eyes, her bewilderment melts away. She puts a hand on his cheek and touches his lips.

For a moment, Ignazio imagines what would have happened if it had been him instead of Paolo.

If Giuseppina had been his woman and Vincenzo his son, and this their home. He imagines the days and nights, the children they could have had in Bagnara or here in Palermo. A small, modest life together that would have made them happy, or at least contented.

But that's not the life he has.

Giuseppina is his brother's wife and he is a traitor. That's what he is: a wicked man.

He closes his eyes. For a moment longer, he holds the life he's dreamed of. He holds her tight before letting go of her, then leaves before temptation can grab hold of him again.

A few days later, Mattia returns to Marsala on Master Salvatore's skiff. Ignazio gave her some money, Giuseppina a long hug. Mattia leaves with a heavy heart, and nothing can ease her grief, not even Vittoria's tenderness or Vincenzo saying goodbye with a shy, toothless smile. She knows she will never see her brother Paolo again. She knows there are wounds that cannot be healed, that the time for that is over.

In the bedroom, the illness is a suffocating stench against which the scent of orange blossoms wafting in from outside is powerless. A lemon tree stretches its branches to the window. The sun has the sound of the first crickets chirping in the branches.

By the door, Giuseppina watches Paolo's chest rise and fall with difficulty. She bites her lips. Everything is coming to a head.

A hand touches her arm. "Here I am. I came as quickly as I could." Ignazio is next to her, speaking into her ear. "I've made all the arrangements at the store. Maurizio will stand in for me for . . . for as long as need be." But Giuseppina isn't listening, Ignazio can see it in her bewildered eyes. "I've brought Vincenzo with me. He's playing under the trees. Go and spend some time with him."

She receives the suggestion with relief.

She wants to cry but can't. She is suffering for this husband she's never loved and, at the same time, suffering for herself because she will miss him. It'll be a void she will have to come to terms with in the years to come.

She's lived with Paolo with no love, hatred at times. She will not be able to ask forgiveness for the harm they have done to each other. Paolo is reaching a border beyond which they will not be able to speak to each other. They already can't. The sense of guilt she carries inside her will be her share of purgatory on earth.

Ignazio comes in and dismisses the maid who's watching in the corner. Hearing his voice, Paolo turns his head. His eyes are glistening with fever.

His brother sits on the bed. He no longer asks him how he's feeling: they've done away with this last hypocritical formality ever since the physician went to the store, a few days earlier, and told him the insidious disease had devoured his lungs. "It's a matter of days," he said, "a couple of weeks at most."

Ignazio thanked him, paid his fee, and carried on working.

Instead, Paolo has resisted much longer than a couple of weeks. It's the strong constitution and the Florio stubbornness that's kept him alive.

He grabs Ignazio by the hand. "Today, the maid made me sit under the lemon tree. I started coughing and spat out so much blood, they had to change all my clothes." He struggles to talk. "The Lord giveth and the Lord taketh away, they say." He attempts an embittered smile. "He's certainly taking everything away from me." He coughs. A long, painful fit. He starts speaking again and his voice is like iron scraping stone. "Did Leone, the notary, tell you I've made my will?"

Under the handkerchief, Ignazio's lips are parched. "Yes."

He struggles for air. Ignazio lifts his head and helps him drink. "Nobody will bother Vincenzo while I live. I found a tutor to teach him Latin and other things instead of Antonino Gagliano, who's going to be ordained soon . . ."

Paolo's gesture interrupts him. "All right, all right." Paolo squeezes his arm and Ignazio feels how little strength he has left. "Listen to me, rather. You have to be what I can no longer be."

Ignazio covers his brother's hand with his. "You know I couldn't love him any more if he were my own son."

"No. More. Do you understand? You have to bring him up for me. You'll be his father. Do you understand? His father." He looks at him as though trying to get into his head.

Ignazio can't bear it. He gets up. Outside, Vincenzo and Giuseppina are playing under the lemon tree. He speaks, weighing every word. He doesn't want to upset Paolo. "I met one of Barbaro's cousins at the harbor. He gave me a message from our brother-in-law, Paolo."

Paolo slams his hand on the bed. "Oh, God! I've been thinking so much about him and Mattia." He's weeping now. "I've realized this is the punishment the Lord has sent me. When he was ill, I could have helped him. It would have been a charitable deed. When our sister came here, I could have seen her, poor wretch, but I . . . Instead, I did nothing. I even rejected her." He dries his eyes. "You'll tell Mattia I forgive her, won't you? And that she must forgive me? I didn't, I did nothing! The devil had grabbed me by the soul, damn me."

Ignazio looks at him. He wants to say something, comfort him, but his voice refuses to come out of his throat, and his heart seems to have clamped and tightened like a child's fist. His brother is terrified, he can see it in his face. He must feel death coming closer if he's asking for forgiveness like this, if he's finally repenting for his harshness.

Paolo lifts his head from the pillow. His hair, matted with sweat, sticks to his forehead. "So? What's Barbaro's message?"

Ignazio forces himself to reply. His voice, a prisoner at first, is freed with a sigh. "He says he's praying for you and hopes you recover soon." He doesn't know why he finds these words ridiculous. He starts to laugh and, a moment later, his brother follows.

They laugh together, as though life were a huge joke, as though Paolo's consumption is nothing but a trick played by the Creator, as though they could go back and put everything right. And yet it's not, and that's what's funny: that it's all true and there will be no peace, that everything will remain unresolved, interrupted, shattered.

Paolo's laughter turns into a coughing fit. Ignazio runs to hand him a bowl and his brother spits blood clots and phlegm.

Ignazio hugs him. Paolo is thin. The illness has eaten away at him, leaving just skin and bones, the container of an indomitable spirit that won't give in. Not yet.

When Vincenzo opens the door a few days later he finds a man in a black cassock and a purple stole standing before him. It's Don Sorce, the Olivuzza priest. His face is weary from the heat. "Your mother sent for me," he says. "Where is he?"

The maid arrives. "Quickly, this way."

The little boy sees them disappear around the corner. A scent of summer and heat wafts in from the garden outside the door.

Vincenzo runs out. He doesn't want to know, he doesn't want to hear.

By the time Ignazio arrives, it's all over.

He finds Giuseppina sitting at the foot of the bed. She does not speak or cry. She's biting her knuckles. She looks far away. Maybe she is.

She stares at the body. "We need his good clothes," she mutters, clutching her rosary beads.

He mechanically replies yes. "I'll go to Via dei Materassai and organize the funeral. I must tell Maurizio Reggio to close the store for two days." He pauses. "I have to write to Mattia and our relatives in Bagnara. I'll take Vincenzo with me."

Giuseppina clears her throat but all that comes out is a whisper. "Masses. They have to say many Masses to cleanse his soul because in the end he repented for everything he did to his sister. He told me while I was changing his nightshirt, after he'd confessed. Also donations to the orphans, we need those. Tell Vittoria to take care of it."

Ignazio nods. He holds air in his chest. He breathes. He still can.

He approaches Paolo's body. It's still warm: the skin on his face is transparent; his hands, once strong and callused, are bony. His hair and beard have turned white.

Ignazio reaches out with his hand and caresses him. Then he suddenly leans down, kisses his forehead, and stays like this, his lips pressed against the skin and grief constricting his throat.

He will carry this moment inside him for the rest of his life. The kiss is the seal of a promise, an oath that comes out of his mouth and that only he and Paolo can hear.

He straightens up and leaves the room. He goes to the lemon tree, where the little boy is waiting.

"Did you say goodbye to your father?"

Vincenzo doesn't look at him. He's playing with a piece of wood, splintering it into many pieces. "Yes."

"Would you like to see him again?"

"No."

Ignazio proffers his hand and Vincenzo grabs it. They walk to the buggy that's waiting in the alley.

There is a small crowd—mainly Calabrians—outside the store. Maurizio Reggio is on the threshold. He hugs Ignazio and receives his instructions. A few minutes later, the wooden doors are shut and marked with the black bow of mourning.

Ignazio cannot escape people's eyes. Some cross themselves, others offer words of comfort. He just walks straight ahead, holding his nephew's hand tight. On the doorstep, Vittoria is quietly crying. She pulls her cousin to her, kisses him, and holds him close. "Now you, too, are without protection," she says, "like me."

Vincenzo remains still. Speechless.

At home, they find Giuseppe Barbaro, one of Emiddio's relatives, offering his help to organize the funeral. "May God rest his soul," he says.

"Amen," Ignazio replies.

Everything is silent in the apartment. Orsola takes Vincenzo into the bedroom to dress him in mourning clothes. You can hear the chest in his parents' bedroom being turned inside out.

The rustling of fabrics is accompanied by snippets of conversation. Vittoria, Ignazio, Emiddio.

"The consumption was too advanced."

"Good God . . ."

"We'll have to sort out the coffin," the girl suddenly says.

"It will have to be decorated by a painter. Mass will have to be sung by the friars. He wasn't . . . He was no ordinary man. My brother was *Don* Paolo Florio. Our *aromateria* has prestige here in Palermo, and it was his work that made it so prominent."

All of a sudden, Vincenzo *really* understands.

The texture of his father's hand on his shoulder. Its grip. His beard scratching his face. His stern look. His hands weighing bark on the scales. The smell of spices he always had.

Vincenzo staggers to his parents' bedroom.

His father is never coming back. And, just as this reality takes hold of him, he meets Ignazio's eyes and sees in them the same painful void as his.

Suddenly, the absence spreads to the point of knocking him over.

Vincenzo runs away, his eyes full of tears, his feet slipping on the flagstones. He runs away from that house, deluding himself that he can leave that crushing suffering behind him.

"Vincenzo!"

Ignazio calls him, as the child seems to fly over the cobbles. He suddenly loses sight of him in Via San Sebastiano.

He stops, his hands on his knees. "That's all we need, Vincenzo . . ." he mutters. He catches his breath and starts looking for the child in the midst of the crowded harbor. He avoids acquaintances who stop to convey their condolences, wading through goods ready for shipping.

He reaches the center of La Cala and sweeps it with his eyes, from the church of Piedigrotta to the lazaretto. The Castello a Mare casts its shadow over the harbor. Tens of masts and sails blur his eyesight.

At last, he finds him.

He's sitting at the very edge of the pier, his legs dangling.

He's crying.

He approaches carefully and calls out. The child doesn't turn around but straightens his shoulders.

Ignazio wants to chide him, and that would be entirely fair: after all that's happened, his escape was nothing but bravado. Besides, he's a boy and boys don't cry. But he doesn't tell him off.

Vincenzo sits next to him. They stay silent for a while, next to each other. He wants to comfort the boy, tell him how he felt when his own mother died, after the earthquake. He was about the same age, and he remembers only too well the feeling of abandonment, of a void.

The desolation.

But losing a father?

He can't picture it: his own father, Mastro Vincenzo Florio, Bagnara blacksmith, is just a faint memory. He'd been together with Paolo, on the other hand, ever since they began working at sea.

He is now afraid of what awaits him, terribly afraid, but he can't tell anyone, let alone a child.

Vincenzo speaks first. "What will I do without him?"

"That was your father's lot. It's God's will." In these words, Ignazio seeks an explanation that would suit him, too. "We all have our destinies written in our bones the moment we come into this world. There's nothing we can do about it."

The silence fills with the lapping of the sea against the pier.

"No," Vincenzo says, holding back his tears. "If this is God's will then I don't want it."

"What on earth are you saying, Vincenzo?"

It's a violent sentence, blasphemous, too strong for an eight-year-old child.

"I don't want to have children if I then have to die like this. Mamma is crying, and you're also upset, I can see that." His tone is fierce. He lifts his head. "Now I have to live without him and I don't know what to do."

Ignazio stares into the black water. Above them, seagulls are circling in the afternoon air.

"I don't know what to do either. The rug's been pulled from under my feet, Vincenzo. He's always been there and now . . ." He takes a deep breath. "Now I'm alone."

"*We* are alone." He leans against his uncle's shoulder and hugs him.

Everything's changed now, Ignazio thinks. He can no longer afford the luxury of being a son and a brother. He's the head now. Their work is his now. Everything is his responsibility.

That is his only certainty.

PART TWO

Silk

Summer 1810 to January 1820

U' putiàru soccu ave abbanìa.

The seller praises whatever he sells.

—SICILIAN PROVERB

After Joseph Bonaparte becomes king of Spain, Napoleon replaces him with his own brother-in-law, Joachim Murat, who is crowned king of the Two Sicilies on August 1, 1808.

In 1812, a revolt breaks out in Sicily because of income tax imposed by Ferdinand IV. The Sicilian government promulgates a constitution—drafted according to the Westminster system—that practically divests the Bourbon king of power and stipulates the abolition of fiefdoms and the reform of government apparatuses. The aim is to modernize the island's society as well as to establish an even closer link with the British, who have an interest in keeping Sicily independent.

That same year, Napoleon undertakes his disastrous campaign against Russia. After the Leipzig defeat (October 19, 1813), Murat becomes allied with Austria in the hope of keeping the throne. He returns to Napoleon in 1815 but the Austrians defeat him once and for all at the Battle of Tolentino (May 2, 1815). The Treaty of Casalanza (May 20, 1815) therefore sanctions the return to Naples of Ferdinand IV, who installs his son Francesco in Palermo as lieutenant-general of the realm.

On December 8, 1816, the king stages a coup to unite the kingdoms of Naples and Sicily under the same banner and takes on the name Ferdinand I, King of the Two Sicilies. The 1812 constitution is annulled. The island is treated like a colony and subjected to a harsh tax regime.

SILK DOESN'T BELONG TO PALERMO.

It belongs to Messina.

Or rather, it did.

From the strait to the Plain of Catania, farming families would breed silkworms in the shade of century-old mulberry trees, whose leaves were used to feed the larvae. They were taken care of mainly by women, who were paid for this smelly, thankless task. They enjoyed more freedom and independence than peasant women or servant girls in aristocratic households. They could keep their earnings. Valuable, hard-earned money they would spend on their trousseau or on furniture for their future homes.

Then came the discovery that more silk was being produced in the Far East and at much cheaper prices.

The British consequently start to ship their fabrics, buying yarns from their colonies, then processing them back home, or else importing textiles with exotic patterns. It's the end of European-printed stripes and dull colors. After the long years of wars against Napoleon, people want imagination and brightness.

Sicily's exports to Italy begin to decrease, then practically grind to a halt. The mulberry trees fall into neglect.

The obsession with chinoiserie starts: furniture, porcelain, carved ivory.

And, naturally, fabrics.

Even the Bourbons pick up on the trend, so much so that King Ferdinand decides that his hunting lodge—and *garçonnière*—should be "a little Chinese building."

All wealthy people have at least one room covered in silk.

All wealthy people wear silk.

ↄ—

The door opens. The glass doors no longer rattle, the well-oiled hinges slide without a sound.

His hand runs over the counter. A marble surface on mahogany feather, smooth as velvet. His eyes linger on the floor tiles, then look up at the walnut chest of drawers with the names of the spices carved in them. There's a smell of fresh timber and paint in the air.

Ignazio stands in the middle of the room. He's alone but wouldn't have it any other way.

He's been picturing this moment for two years, ever since Vincenzo Romano, the former owner, agreed to give him the store. When the grief of Paolo's death was still a scar that wouldn't heal.

It was summer then, too.

ↄ—

"What are you saying?" The face of Vincenzo Romano, the owner of the building in Via dei Materassai, had become a full moon.

Sitting at his desk, Ignazio looked him up and down.

After calling him into his office—because he was the one to call people in now—he hadn't asked him to sit down. He'd left him standing like a supplicant in order to confuse him and make him feel uncomfortable. He'd made him wait while he was signing papers. Because the Florios had a lot of business now.

Then he had made his request.

"Are you crazy?" Romano gripped the edge of the desk. "Over my dead body! I'm not selling."

Ignazio was aware of Romano's fondness for money and had expected to come up against a wall but was ready to pull it down. He led his attack not aggressively but firmly. As ever, his weapons of choice were patience and politeness. "Try to see it from my point of view. These rooms and the mezzanine need to be refurbished, heavily refurbished. *Vuautri u' sapiti*—you must understand: Casa Florio can't stay in a place with mold stains and creaking doors."

"So? Just give it a coat of paint and a drop of oil—"

"That's not the issue. It's the water that comes in spurts, it's the damaged floor . . . There's much work to be done, and urgently. I doubt you'd find tenants as good as us and, besides, if we leave, you'd have to fix the place up anyway."

Vincenzo Romano had meant to refuse. But only for a moment. He knew Florio was right.

There it was, the doubt. A crack in the wall of refusal. It was written in his bemused eyes and half-open mouth.

So Ignazio pressed him. "I have a suggestion, if you care to hear it. A compromise that would suit us both."

"What is it?"

Only then did he motion at Romano to sit down.

"An emphyteusis."

"Wonderful. I'll still be the owner but you'll have all the rights. I'll be proprietor only in name, but without public recognition to do anything at all." Romano swore under his breath. "It's not a dog, just the muzzle of a dog—big difference."

"Think about it. The emphyteusis would keep you, at least in the eyes of others, as the owner of the store. I, and my company, would take care of the refurbishment. But of course if you don't want to sell . . ." He opened his hand with an eloquent gesture. "It's entirely up to you. Just as we're free to move somewhere else."

Ignazio spoke with absolute determination. He'd concealed his fears because in actual fact he was taking a big risk. If Romano refused, he would have to find a new building for the store and warehouses in a different area.

It would mean leaving the place where it had all begun with Paolo.

However, they could no longer stay in a store with mold in the back room and chipped doors. It did not befit what Casa Florio had become.

Romano had come to collect the rent and been presented with an unexpected offer. He paced up and down the room before asking, astonished rather than sarcastic, "Are you jealous of the Canzoneris and the Gulìs for having their own store, their *putìa*?"

"Not at all. It's just that I'd like to have some certainties. To know that *u' maruni unni jecca sangu è suo*: if you sweat blood and tears then it has to be yours, without someone else coming to lay down the law. I'm not about to spend money on a store you might one day decide to sell to somebody else. Do you understand?"

Yes, he understood.

Romano left, saying, "I'll think about it."

And he did not think about it for as long as Ignazio had feared. He accepted the offer.

First came the emphyteusis, then the work: the well-sinker, the carpenter, the tiles, and the new windows. After just a few months, Ignazio redeemed the rent. He became the absolute owner of the spice store.

Remembering these six months of work makes his heart leap with joy.

The shelves are crammed with new majolica jars and pots with *Florio* painted on the bottom. In the Via dei Materassai warehouses, in Piano San Giacomo and at customs, sacks of Peruvian cinchona bark are waiting, ready to be ground in order for quinine powder to be extracted.

Aromateria Florio has become what he had always pictured. A real apothecary store.

There's only one thing Ignazio has kept from the old store: the weighing scales his brother had used ever since he'd started to work.

He needs them to remind him who he is and where he comes from.

Outside the door, there's a hubbub of onlookers and aristocrats' servants peering inside, waiting for the store to reopen. It's just to see what's happening in that scruffy little store, they say, the *putiedda* managed by that Bagnara fellow, but their faces betray them, and Ignazio enjoys seeing them so torn between curiosity and suspicion. Never would they admit that they're being stung by envy and wonder, driven by them to stand there waiting.

As for him, he's lying in wait for the one who, until now, has tried to stand in his way. A new game is under way, not only against Canzoneri and Saguto, but against all Palermo's *aromatari*, who are already whispering, wondering, afraid.

Because the Florios are no longer ordinary storekeepers. They are merchants now and can say it with their heads high.

The door opens. Someone comes in.

Ignazio turns.

It's Giuseppina.

"But—but it's beautiful!" Her mouth is half-open in awe. The line between her eyebrows relaxes. She smooths her dark dress with her gloved hand. "I really didn't think it could change so much."

She, too, has changed.

Prosperity has brought maids, outfits made by a dressmaker and no longer darned by candlelight, new shoes and coats. There's more food on the table for her, Vincenzo, and Vittoria, who still lives with them even though she often expresses the wish for a family of her own. However, it's not just a matter of more elegant clothes or hands that are no longer cracked.

There's a new light in Giuseppina's eyes. She seems tranquil.

Ignazio watches her walking around the store, touching the drawers, opening one and inhaling the spices.

She lifts her head and smiles at him.

He can't take his eyes off her.

"Excellent work, truly," she murmurs to herself.

He wishes he could touch her cheek and feel its warmth. Instead, he crosses his arms, taking care not to crease the jacket he had made specially for the reopening. Whoever comes into the store has to see right away that they're no longer dealing with a store boy in shirtsleeves.

At that very moment, Vincenzo arrives. "Mamma! Uncle! Didn't you wait for me?"

The boy is tall for his age. He looks like an adolescent even though he's only just turned eleven.

Ignazio runs his fingers through the child's hair. "We haven't gone anywhere. Besides, what you need to see is in the back. The paint is still drying."

He leads the way down the long corridor to the countinghouse. On the desks, also brand-new, there are inkwells, reams of paper, and blotters.

Ignazio indicates a long, painted wooden sign lying on the floor at the back of the room. The colors are bright, still fresh. Low down, the slender signature of the painter, Salvatore Burgarello, well known in Castellammare. "He finished it this morning and said it should dry away from the sun, otherwise the paint will crack."

Giuseppina's hands are over her lips, as though to stifle a cry.

Vincenzo's eyes, however, dash from the painting to his uncle. He points at the writing.

IGNAZIO AND VINCENZO FLORIO'S
APOTHECARY STORE

"You added my name, too! Why?"

Ignazio puts an arm around his shoulder. "Because you're my nephew and your father's heir."

And because, he thinks with a tenderness that warms him inside, *you're my son in my heart if not in flesh.*

A forest is painted on the sign. At the bottom, a stream flows out from the roots of a tree, and a lion is drinking from it.

It's a cinchona tree.

"Goodbye, Donna Margherita. It's always a pleasure to serve you."

Holding on to Vincenzo's arm, the old lady sways from the counter to the exit. The boy is a tall, angular adolescent a whole head taller than her. She nods and makes a vague gesture of blessing. "Good boy! I've watched you grow. Even when you were a little lad, one could tell you were a levelheaded child. Now you're grown up, you're always respectful. Well done . . . The Lord will reward you."

Vincenzo continues to smile until the door closes. No sooner has the customer left than he puts his hands over his face. "Holy Mother, she did go on and on!"

The store clerks giggle. Everybody finds Margherita Conticello, that antique from the Tribunali district, hard to bear. Delegating her to Vincenzo, since he's an apprentice, is a game from which he always comes out a loser.

There's chatter coming from the countinghouse.

Ignazio appears with a man whose face is darkened by the sun: Vincenzo Mazza, the umpteenth Bagnara man transplanted to Palermo. "Very well, I'll let you know," he says with a heavy Calabrian accent. He shakes Ignazio's hand and gives Vincenzo a pat on the back. "Hey, Vincenzo, look how tall you've grown! What do they feed you?"

"Bread, olives, and onion."

"And your mother waters your feet so you've grown taller by morning, right?"

More laughter.

After saying goodbye, Ignazio returns. The boy stops him. "Uncle, may I have a word?"

Ignazio sighs. He can already imagine why he wants to talk to him. "Come in." He sits down and rubs his temples. He's working himself into the ground, but Vincenzo doesn't fully realize this: he's fifteen and has the typical selfishness of someone who's only just venturing out into the world but thinks he already knows everything. Ignazio motions him to a chair. "So?"

Vincenzo collapses into it like an empty sack. "Donna Conticello was here. Again." He covers his face with his hands. "I know more about her gout than her physician. She wants to be served only by me or you, says she wants to speak with the owners and not the clerks."

Ignazio rubs his lips. "So what's wrong? The poor creature needs someone to talk to and she's taken a liking to you. Just say yes to everything and she'll go away happy. And that's no way to sit. Back straight, eyes ahead, and hands on your lap. How many times do I have to tell you?"

Vincenzo pulls himself up but doesn't take his hands away from his face. Instead, he gives his uncle a pleading look. "Do I really have to be at the counter? I can't bear people who complain: I feel like drowning them in La Cala. I'd be much more helpful to you in the office with Signor Reggio, you know I'm good at accounts. Please!"

Ignazio nails him to the chair with a look. "No. And I've already explained why."

"Because this way I can learn to read people and guess what they really want. Because this way I'll learn discipline and build up resistance to tiredness. Because this way I will respect other people's work." Vincenzo lists the reasons on his fingertips and huffs. "Have I left something out?"

"Yes." Ignazio indicates the room. "Your father and I earned everything you see here starting from a *putìa* that was little more than a storage shed. I want you to realize what this place means to us, the Florios."

The boy hangs his head, his breath quickens. He says nothing.

"Now go back to work," Ignazio commands.

Only after he disappears behind the door do Ignazio's features soften. His nephew is like his brother Paolo, true, but at the same time he couldn't be more different. He has a sunny disposition, likes to laugh, and has no fear of life.

Vincenzo is his pride and joy. He's learning fast but that's not enough. He must also learn to keep his feet on the ground.

Ignazio is still lost in thought when the door opens again. "Can you at least tell me what Signor Mazza wanted?"

Ignazio rolls his eyes. "So that's what's on your mind, right?" He shows Vincenzo a pamphlet. "Here, read."

Vincenzo doesn't wait to be told twice. He grabs the papers and glances through them. "An insurance policy?"

"That's right. Mazza and I want to insure a large quantity of sumac. In practice, by paying a sum of money, we'll protect ourselves against the loss of the shipment."

"So that what happened to Captain Olsen's ship, when you had to pay a ransom for the spice packages, doesn't happen again?"

Ignazio points at a section on the document. "Exactly. If you remember, we had to fork out a lot of money to retrieve the goods."

"Nobody here in Palermo does this but it sounds like a good idea . . ." Vincenzo concludes, returning the papers. He's almost as tall as his uncle, uncommonly so for an adolescent.

"It is. The insurance won't leave you destitute, while the loss of a shipment could, but not everyone understands that," Ignazio explains patiently. "What persuaded me is the fact that Abraham Gibbs is in charge of the company. The British know how to earn respect, they have a fleet that defends them against the French, which is something we don't have. We have to protect our interests and learn from their example. They've rented warehouses and *fondaci* that allow them to trade with the whole Mediterranean; Palermo and Malta are two safe landings for them. They know how to protect merchant ships: they've been insuring shipments for decades, and Gibbs is experienced at this. Moreover, he's not just a trader but also the British consul, and this gives us a further guarantee. Actually, now that I think about it . . ." He looks for a document among the papers and hands it to Vincenzo. "Since you're so eager to get away from the counter, you won't mind being an errand boy. This is for Ingham. Make sure he reads it in person."

"For Benjamin?" His eyes light up. Vincenzo is intrigued by this man who speaks with a heavy foreign accent and manages people and things with a simple hand gesture. He has a lot of money, really a lot if he can afford to rent a whole ship to send the goods he buys in Sicily to Great Britain. Among the British merchants, like John Woodhouse, James Hopps, and even Gibbs, he's the best known. Maybe not the wealthiest—*Not yet*, the boy thinks—but definitely the shrewdest. The most determined.

"*Signor* Ingham to you. Remember, Vincenzo, show respect if you want respect. Just because he's our neighbor doesn't give you the right to become inappropriately familiar. Now run along."

The boy vanishes through the door.

Ignazio sighs. Sometimes, he feels as though he really is his father and, as a parent, he chides him and loves him.

And yet.

There is a dark side to the boy. He's sensed it only a few times. An underlying restlessness, a rebellious spirit that alarms him and, precisely because he's never had to deal with it, which he doesn't know how to handle.

In Via dei Materassai, spring is bursting out on the narrow balconies, the flowers and pots of herbs, the washing hanging out to dry between buildings, the smell of soap and fresh tomato sauce. Undulating white curtains have taken the place of shutters closed against winter storms.

There's a coming and going of men, especially merchants who dress according to the English fashion, complete with waistcoats and cloth jackets. You can hear the shouts of sellers from Piano San Giacomo, and beyond, toward Via degli Argentieri, the clinking of craftsmen's hammers. A dark-skinned sailor is talking to a man with red hair and sunburned skin in what is a blend of Arabic and Sicilian.

Hands in his pockets, lighthearted, Vincenzo walks the short distance between the store and Benjamin Ingham's house. The Englishman is the richest person on this street. Richer than many Palermo noblemen.

Vincenzo straightens his jacket collar and knocks. A butler in livery lets him into the hall, and Ingham comes to welcome him in person. "It's young Florio! Welcome! Come, let's go and sit down."

"Signore . . ." Vincenzo follows the Englishman into his study, eyes fixed on his back. There are fewer than fifteen years between them and yet the young man has built up a lot of experience—in life and business—that has marked him and made him look much older than he is.

Ben Ingham is wearing a plastron and sober clothes. The lines on his face, mottled by the Sicilian sun, suggest tenacity, rigor, and discipline. Vincenzo clearly sees the power oozed by this man. It's a kind of encircling heat, a breath of wind that forces people to keep at least a span away from him. Something at the same time physical and intangible. Unlike other traders, he never raises his voice or loses his temper. He doesn't need to.

Vincenzo doesn't know, however, couldn't possibly know, how much Ingham has had to struggle in order to acquire this position. Arriving in Palermo after the ship carrying the cloth manufactured by his family in Leeds sank, ruining them, Ingham had found himself alone in an unknown city, with no means of support. When Ignazio met him at the Customs House, he was looking for a way into the cloth trade in Sicily, since cloth, silk, and cotton were all he knew and could talk about. Nevertheless, he learned quickly and can now afford to sell even sulfur, sumac, and hides to other British traders.

"Do you have something for me?"

Vincenzo hands him the letter and he begins to read.

Meanwhile, the boy looks around. He's never been here and finds this place highly fascinating, so different from the *aromateria* and its noise. The silence is muffled, the air steeped in a sweet aroma, perhaps tobacco with mint leaves.

The room is full of light, leather, wood, and books. There are foreign seals on the documents.

A rustling sound of paper and hushed voices comes from the door to his right. A man enters the room, shows Ingham a document, and asks him something in English. Vincenzo knows only a few words of it and can't understand what they're saying. He follows the secretary with his eyes as he disappears as silently as he arrived.

Noticing his curiosity, Ingham frowns. "Is there anything I can do for you?"

Caught and embarrassed, Vincenzo tries to justify himself. "No, I—forgive me—this study is so—" He moves his hand, indicating the walls. "So different."

"A piece of England in Sicily," Ingham says, pleased, and encourages him to come closer. "Order is everything. You see, all the books are organized by year and contain sections for debits and credits. I think Don Ignazio also uses a similar system."

"Yes." Vincenzo reads the writing on the leather spines. "I'd like to visit your country, signore," he blurts out. "It must be very different from mine."

"Why not go? You have shipments from England, too . . . You could ask your uncle to let you travel on a ship that carries your goods. It would be a highly informative experience."

The boy's tone grows wary. "Yes, we have a few things." If there's one rule he has learned, it's never to discuss the family business.

Ingham walks around him until he stands facing him. "More than 'a few things,' if memory serves. You've been selling more than just spices for a long time now."

"Yes, we deal in goods from many harbors, and not just in the Mediterranean."

"I can imagine. You Florios haven't gotten to where you are now by selling just cinnamon and cloves for making cakes." He hands him back the document after scribbling something on it. "Oh, and by the way, tell your uncle there are no problems: the people he mentions are creditworthy."

Curiosity sweeps away Vincenzo's earlier caution. He tries to worm out a reply. "So they're drafts to be discounted, right?"

Ingham lowers his eyelids, concealing his true thoughts. "Among other things. But if your uncle hasn't talked to you about it, then I certainly shan't."

Now he understands why his uncle sent him here, and the thought produces the hint of a smile on his lips.

When Vincenzo returns to the store, he heads back to the counter and resumes his work with the others. He doesn't protest. His head is crammed with thoughts; his eyes are still in Ingham's library; his nose still filled with the aroma of the tobacco. In his chest, there's an unfamiliar yearning for the sea and open skies, which belongs to his roots and his family's past.

In the study, Ignazio reads the English merchant's reply. The last line provokes a slight smile.

Vincenzo is very promising. Sooner or later he will do you out of a job.

It's almost evening by the time Ignazio and Vincenzo finally leave the *aromateria*. The spring sky is shifting from gray to dark blue and the few passersby in the streets are trudging along the basalt after a day's work.

Vincenzo stifles a yawn. "Uncle, do you mind if I take a walk before going home? My head's all foggy."

Ignazio responds with a tap on the back. "As long as you're back by the time the San Domenico bell rings, because we have to have dinner, and you know your mother'll start to rant, otherwise."

"I know. In any case, I still have some studying to do because Don Salpietra is coming tomorrow—"

"Then go."

Ignazio watches him walk away, a veil of indulgence over his eyes. Then he covers the few yards between the *aromateria* and the house, and slowly opens the door. A smell of meat stew tickles his nostrils and reminds him he's skipped lunch.

Giuseppina is sitting in the kitchen, holding a rosary in her hand, her head resting on a closed fist, her face softened by sleep. The table in front of her is lavishly set. She has dozed off while waiting.

He stands motionless and hesitates between giving her a shake or letting her slumber and this way allow himself to watch her, to look at the hair that has escaped from her braid, framing her face, on which the first wrinkles have started to appear. Giuseppina opens her eyes and her placid expression is erased by a feeling of guilt. "Good God, I fell asleep while saying my prayers . . ."

Ignazio puts his overcoat over the back of the chair. She recites a short prayer, mutters "Amen," and kisses the rosary. When she looks up at her brother-in-law's face again, she sees the gentleness that makes her heart quiver and forces her to avert her eyes.

Ignazio approaches. "Are you tired? Olimpia isn't helping you enough. Would you like another servant girl in the house? We can afford it, you know," he adds attentively.

She shakes her head and wraps the shawl around her, clutching it over her chest. "No, I don't need one. I know it's not like it was before, and now—and that's just why I was thinking about the past and about Paolo. About how we were and everything we've been through. I started praying for him."

Paolo.

His brother has been dead seven years. Giuseppina continues to pray for his soul and to wear mourning clothes, though not out of grief. No. There is in her a relentless desire to atone for sins nobody attributes to her—a need to punish herself for the harm she and Paolo did to each other.

"I wasn't—no, I wasn't happy with him," she says all of a sudden, as though responding to Ignazio's thoughts. "But he was the husband my family and God had given me and I accepted him. And perhaps if he'd lived, I would have learned to love him, because he wasn't a bad man. He was reliable, hardworking, and couldn't do without work. And if we sometimes argued it was because we were the same, he and I."

"You quarreled because you wanted different things," Ignazio replies, shocked. "Because you'd say white and he'd say black, because you couldn't stand him and he forced you to do things you didn't want to do, and that upset you." He can't stop. He loved his brother more than himself and keeps the memory of him, but he can't allow Giuseppina to turn him into a saint and take faults upon herself that weren't hers.

She raises her hand and is about to reply, then nods. "Yes, it's true. But you know, one shouldn't speak ill of the dead."

Once again, Ignazio feels hope rising. But he knows it's a weed and, as usual, he tears it out with force. He clenches his fists and watches Giuseppina move about the room but can't stifle the sense of injustice squeezing his insides. "Paolo's dead," he whispers. "He's at peace, and you should give yourself some peace, too."

Her hands on the skillets, Giuseppina stops, shrugs, and silently curses herself. "I can't," she finally says. "I just can't." Into these words she pours the pain and anger she carries within, as well as the remorse, the loneliness, and the inability to forgive and be forgiven.

When he comes home, Vincenzo finds each of them locked in a silence he can't decipher. They eat the stew and exchange only a few words about what they did today.

Ignazio is the first one to retire. He taps his nephew on the back, then approaches his sister-in-law, almost touching her. Her hands full as she is carrying the dishes, Giuseppina stops by the kitchen door.

"Good night," he says, his breath tickling her hair. She feels something stirring in her chest: the echo of a memory never lived, of a life she has never even had the courage to dream of.

And, as Giuseppina leans forward, he turns his face away and leaves.

Vincenzo watches the scene without understanding it. *Perhaps*, he thinks, *they had a disagreement*. Or perhaps his mother got upset by something his uncle said . . . *Who knows?* He's always seen those two together and never questioned it. They have been—and still are—his family. They've each brought him up in his and her own way, and it's right it should be so.

Except that this evening, for the first time, he feels that's not the case. In a muddled but unequivocal way, he senses that these two people are not separate but *are* a couple. And that they've created a family around him, sacrificing—perhaps—themselves in the process. Because although they love each other with a feeling that has nothing to do with marriage, it is no less strong or durable. Even though there's a ghost standing between them: that of his father, Paolo.

That's when he understands that there are love affairs not called that, but which are nonetheless deep, and as worth experiencing, however painful.

The church of the *aromatari*, Sant'Andrea degli Amalfitani, is heaving. The men wear dark suits and the few women have black veils. You can hear the voices and smells of the Vucciria market nearby.

Outside the front entrance stands a funeral carriage with horses in dark harnesses and black plumes. The following of orphans is ready behind it. Two mourners are beating their bosoms, peeping toward the door, about to raise the volume of their lament as soon as the coffin comes out.

It's the funeral of Salvatore Leone, an elderly Palermo spice seller as well as one of Casa Florio's best customers.

The coffin parades down the nave, followed by the priest and the altar boys with thuribles. Then, right behind, come the tearful widow and her two daughters, dressed in black silk and crepe.

Vincenzo is in one of the back rows, behind his uncle. He's sweating. It's a muggy September still impregnated with summer.

"A first-class funeral," Vincenzo whispers. "The orphans, the choir of altar boys . . . The hearse alone must have cost him an arm and a leg." He slips two fingers under his collar, where his stubble itches and bothers him. His seventeenth year has brought him the gift of bristly hairs, and he's still learning to manage.

Ignazio nods. "And to think that his family was in a position to hold this kind of ceremony despite the current crisis. In any case, there should be as much dignity in death as in life."

The boy and his uncle go up to the family of the deceased and offer their condolences. The three women, devastated, shake hands and weep.

As the mourners resume their lamentations, representatives of the College of Aromatari, with their banner, gather around the relatives. They watch them and chatter.

"See that?" the boy asks.

Ignazio nods.

"Do you suppose they've heard about the Sumatra pepper deal with Ben's brother-in-law, Joseph Whitaker?"

"It's possible. It's not our problem, Vincenzo. We're going to be paying a high price for this pepper, but at least we found it—not them."

Following a loud cry from the mourners, the widow breaks down into sobs. The hearse starts with a jolt and the procession behind it breaks up. The two Florios keep their distance from the other traders.

"Gentlemen . . . I was just looking for you." A tall, strapping man smelling of sandalwood, Giuseppe Pajno has come up behind them without their noticing. He's one of the wholesalers the Florios buy from and sell to. They know and respect one another. They have done business together on several occasions, including buying colonial produce plundered by Sicilian privateers, then sold in Palermo.

They shake hands. "How are you?"

"Better than Don Leone, that's for sure." Pajno wedges himself between them and speaks softly. "Poor man . . . after a lifetime of working . . . He was a customer of yours, wasn't he?"

"One of our best, even though lately he had trouble keeping up with his payments."

"Like everyone else, these days."

An alarm bell rings in Ignazio's head. "If I'm not mistaken, he was also one of your buyers."

"That's right. Did you know Leone sold his store to Don Nicchi, a few days ago?"

No, he didn't know, but Ignazio doesn't show it. "I'd heard something," he says. "I was planning to go and see Don Leone's relatives in a few days' time. In the circumstances, it didn't seem appropriate to talk business."

Pajno slows down imperceptibly. "You're a gentleman, Don Ignazio. Not like some." He juts his chin at the banner of the College.

Vincenzo understands. "Ah . . . Now, what did they say? All they do is gossip and make trouble. It's like the other time at the accounts office—"

Pajno puts a hand on his arm. "Unfortunately, not everybody respects you. The higher you climb, the more obstacles you encounter, and it's often people who talk too much who cause damage. You see," he adds, addressing both, "I'm a merchant, just like you. All I'm interested in is people who work and people who pay me. Given our relationship, it seemed only fair that I should warn you that nasty things are being said about your work."

Ignazio keeps walking, his eyes glued to the hearse, his face impassive. "What kind of things?"

"They're saying that you don't have a penny in the till and that the business about the pepper is just a rumor to encourage people to buy goods. Since the British left, Palermo has been like a mortuary. We all thought that once the French were defeated, business would pick up.

Instead, everything is still even, though they've sent Napoleon into exile in the middle of nowhere. Since the crisis flared up, it's become extremely hard to find imported spices, it's no longer safe to travel by sea, and you don't know with whom to trade anymore. And you suddenly show off about getting pepper straight from Sumatra." He drops his voice. "You must admit it does sound odd."

"But it's true! We—"

A glance from his uncle stabs him like a knife. Vincenzo falls silent.

"I'll bet the entire contents of the warehouses at customs that I know who is spreading this news." Ignazio's voice is like a razor blade. "It's Saguto, isn't it?"

Slowly, Pajno nods. "He says you're on the brink of bankruptcy. A little while ago, I heard him say you're up to your necks in debt and won't make it to the end of the year. That man's a viper. I don't know why he's got it in for you, but he's the kind who uses the weapon of cowards: gossip. And he knows how to ensnare people, believe me."

Ignazio speaks calmly, concealing his anger in the fists in his pockets. "The contract with Whitaker was signed by proxy by Ingham, who is his brother-in-law as well as his representative in Palermo. Are you doubting his word?"

"I know better than that." Pajno looks at the tips of his shoes. "But Ingham is a foreigner, and many people don't trust foreigners entirely, even when they're wealthy."

"Carmelo Saguto is a louse, but he bites and stings so much that people listen to him. What about you, Pajno? Do you believe him?"

The man puts his hands behind his back. "You owe me for some supplies you received two months ago, and for which you haven't paid me yet."

Ignazio doesn't reply immediately. "I understand," he says, finally. "If I remember correctly, the deal I've signed has a three-month deadline."

"That's true. Let's put it this way: this little chat of ours is by way of warning you to watch your back. You're a trustworthy store owner, Don Florio, and a reliable person."

"Then why did you come to us? *U' niuro s'un tingi, mascarìa*—if black doesn't stain, it nevertheless soils."

Behind him, Vincenzo intervenes harshly. "If you have so much respect for us you could simply have come out and asked us outright if we have the money to pay you. There was no need for this performance."

"Vincenzo! Your manners!"

Pajno smiles and his brief laugh carries an admission of guilt. "Ah, the joy of being young!" He confesses his lack of trust casually, in an apologetic tone attempting to be complicit. "You, too, would be careful if you were afraid of losing money."

At that moment, the funeral cortège pauses for a blessing. More weeping and praying.

Ignazio lingers behind with Pajno. "You'll get your money as agreed, Pajno, crisis or no crisis. The Florios always settle their debts. And if my signature isn't good enough, then you have my word."

Ignazio proffers his hand. Pajno takes it. "This I do trust. I'll be waiting."

On their way back, Vincenzo sees his uncle walking with his head down. He sees the indignation and anger.

"Why?" he suddenly asks, genuinely astonished. "Why do some people hate us so much? And I don't just mean Canzoneri, Uncle, and that snake of a son-in-law. I'm going to smash their faces one of these days . . ."

Ignazio slows down. "I don't know. I've been wondering myself for a long time now. At first I thought it was because we were strangers in the city: they'd accuse us of charging low prices to do them out of business. Then we began to make money and they never forgave us. We've tried to do things our way without asking anyone for help. There are people who would happily set our store on fire if they could."

"But we're all foreigners here. Even Ingham, but nobody's picking on him."

"Because he came with the British and that gave him an advantage: nobody refused the king's allies. But now, after the war with Napoleon, he's facing the same difficulties as us. As a matter of fact, it's surprising he decided to stay after his countrymen left."

Piano San Giacomo welcomes them with a sunny, refreshing embrace. Vincenzo breathes in deeply. "Or perhaps it's because this has become home for him, too."

His words rekindle in Ignazio the memory of his arrival in Palermo, when he was hoping to find somewhere he would belong. He remembers the moment they left Bagnara, when the skiff navigated by his brother Paolo left the dock. The *San Francesco di Paola* seemed reluctant to leave. It struggled as far as the entrance to the harbor, its lateen flapping against the mast in search of a breath of wind.

Ignazio then thought perhaps Bagnara didn't want to let them go. But no sooner had they passed the promontory than a powerful gust penetrated the rigging and made it creak. The lateen swelled and the jib spread open like a wing. The change in speed was immediate.

He recalls Paolo holding the helm tight, taking the boat into the open sea. He thinks again about the promises the city made him upon his arrival, seducing him with its wealth of people, colors, and life. Even though it was very tough in the beginning, even though they had to work so hard, even though he was the first to sacrifice himself in order to guarantee Vincenzo, Giuseppina, and Vittoria a certain standard of living, he, Ignazio, was happy. He worked so hard and did so gladly.

However, Palermo turned out to be treacherous. She gave him so much but also took so much away. She was bound not to play fair.

Giuseppina is standing by the door to her son's bedroom. She watches Vincenzo searching the street with his eyes. He seems to be waiting for someone.

She's almost forty and has never loved anybody as much as her child.

He's her flesh and blood. That's how she knows.

He is in love.

For the first time, Giuseppina feels her age. She has accepted her first wrinkles and shrugged at the first threads of white in her hair. But not this. A woman who'll take her son away from her? She can't bear to think about it. It would mean that a piece of soul she put inside him wouldn't belong to her anymore. She would be left alone.

It must and will happen, that she knows, it's a law of nature. But not yet. It's still too soon.

She turns back, her footsteps muffled by the rug. She takes refuge in the kitchen, where Marianna, the cook, is making dinner.

She sighs. She has no one to confide in. She misses Vittoria, who decided to marry a distant relative and is now living in Mistretta. His name is Pietro Spoliti. He's a tradesman who, like the Florios, had a boat on which he would travel back and forth between Tyrrhenian ports. He was always bringing news from Bagnara, about who'd gotten married, who'd died or left. Giuseppina needed to keep contact with her village and the world of her memories, so she would invite him to stay and eat in order to hear his stories and that familiar accent.

One day, however, he took Vittoria aside and asked her to marry him. He knew he couldn't keep her in the same comfort as her relatives, but promised her a dignified, free life. She would no longer be a servant in somebody else's house but the mistress of her own.

Vittoria's thoughts were confused and her heart disoriented. But she was a practical young woman: she was nearing twenty-five and spent her days, here in Palermo, doing house chores with her aunt and embroidering. She felt like a household nun, like one of those old maids who pay for their room and board with housework, making themselves invisible in the eyes of the world so as not to disturb anybody, and allowing the years to pass.

When Pietro returned, she accepted him. Together, they told Ignazio and Giuseppina. Her uncle was generous: he gave her a large dowry and held her in his arms for a long time, telling her she'd made the right decision. Giuseppina, on the other hand, gave her a nasty look, as though she'd been betrayed. "Why do you want to leave?" she asked in earnest. "Have we ever deprived you of anything?"

"No, Auntie, you haven't. You've been like a mother to me," Vittoria replied, her head down. "But now I want a home of my own and to be able to decide what to do with my life. And that's something I can't do here. Here I am just your niece, and I don't have a roof of my own or an income. I don't want to be the family old maid for the rest of my life. I'm lucky: Pietro is an honest man and I think he'll treat me with respect."

Giuseppina had nothing to say to this. It was straightforward: Vittoria had more lucidity than she, as well as more courage. She was choosing to live in a household with smaller means, far from Palermo, but to be the mistress of her own fate.

She looks around and dismisses these sad thoughts. Their home can't be considered luxurious but they do have a daily maid, as well as one hired by the hour for heavy work. There's only the *corriola*, the trunk with her trousseau, left from the furniture brought from Bagnara. Everything, even the linen, is new.

They live in a comfort she wouldn't even have dared imagine twenty years ago. And yet she still misses Bagnara. She misses her newborn son clinging to her breast.

She feels alone on this island, far from the land where she belongs.

She would gladly give all this up if she could go back. To Bagnara. To Vincenzo as a child.

She could even love Paolo. Who knows?

She can no longer remember her husband's voice. She still sees before her his stern face, rough movements, and harsh reproaches. Vincenzo has inherited his coloring, his penetrating look, and that determination that borders on inflexibility.

But when Giuseppina thinks about warmth, affectionate gestures, and silent encouragement, then another face comes to mind: one for which she still has—and always will have—a timid feeling and at the same time the attachment of a wild animal.

Giuseppe Pajno is not the only one to have heard the rumors concerning the Florios. The afternoon following the funeral, Guglielmo Li Vigni, secretary to Nicolò Raffo, another wholesaler, comes to the *aromateria*. He wants to know if they have sumac in stock, and at the same time, almost by chance, asks if they are going to settle the bill for last month's supply of sugar. This is how they discover that Saguto has been to Raffo's office intending to buy their credit agreements. In that petty way of his, all insinuations and allusions, Saguto said he was certain that the Florios wouldn't pay their debts and therefore tried to persuade Raffo to give him the documents. "It would have been advantageous for me, Don Ignazio," Guglielmo says with a sigh. "He had the money ready in hand . . . but I wasn't going to do you this wrong. Besides, I still don't know why he hates you so much . . . You're an honorable man."

"I'm grateful for your esteem, Don Li Vigni. Carmelo Saguto feeds on envy and rage, and his jealousy is certainly not provoked by me or my nephew. It's something he harbors inside him because he wishes he was heaven knows what and instead he's just Don Canzoneri's secretary and nothing else. These are hard times for everyone, but I swear on my honor that you'll get your money to the last penny."

After Li Vigni has left the office, Vincenzo asks, with a hint of fear, "Are we really in difficulty, Uncle?"

Ignazio shuts the door and goes to the walk-in safe. "We have little money in the till, but that's not the same thing."

"But we have the bills of exchange . . ."

Ignazio leans against the desk. "It's pure and simple, Vincenzo: people aren't paying, and if they don't pay, we don't have any money.

You can't eat bits of paper." His tongue feels furry. "We need to ask for a loan. We need the cash."

Vincenzo feels his stomach tightening. Until now his uncle has shielded him from all concerns, and now . . . "But everybody'll find out! That idiot Saguto will tell the world and his wife!"

"I know that, damn it!" Ignazio hits the desk, jolting the inkwell. "When there's no choice one has to swallow one's pride. 'The reed must bow its head until the full moon is over,' old people say. And that's what we'll do." He rubs the top of his nose. "You go home. I'm going to try to talk to a couple of people. Please don't say anything to your mother . . ."

Vincenzo's cheeks are burning. He mutters, "Yes, Uncle," grabs his jacket, and slips out of the room. All his other thoughts are wiped out by this worry. Even the image of a pair of dark eyes that, for some weeks now, have made him blush and stammer like a child.

But it's not easy.

It's not just a matter of pride. Finding someone you can trust when it comes to business is not easy. It won't be easy to find someone who will lend them money and not start blabbing around.

It's only when Vincenzo is as old as his uncle is now, however, that he will *truly* understand what this decision has cost him.

It's late evening when the sound of jangling keys comes from the hallway.

Ignazio.

Giuseppina helps him take off his coat. He, too, has locks of white hair on his temples, and his eyes have grown heavy.

"Do you get enough sleep?" she suddenly asks.

He's taken aback. "I have all eternity to rest. I don't have time now, especially since the war against the French, last year." He puts a hand on her face. "Thanks for your concern, anyway."

She evades the caress.

A lump of bitterness in his throat, Ignazio drops his hand. "Where's Vincenzo?"

"In his room. I wanted to talk to you about him."

His silence is full of questions.

He follows her into the kitchen. Marianna is preparing tuna, desalinating it: she changes the water and covers it completely. It's the only way of removing excess salt. A thick scent of sauce with potatoes stimulates his appetite.

Giuseppina gives the cook a sign and the woman leaves, closing the door behind her. "He's acting oddly. Have you noticed it, too?"

Ignazio dips a crust of bread into the pan and tries the sauce. "Absolutely! He spent all day with his face glued to the store window. I think he was expecting somebody." He licks his fingers. "This sauce is delicious."

The color drains from Giuseppina's face. "Who?"

"I have my suspicions. Don't make a drama out of it. He's just a young man chasing after a skirt." Ignazio is reluctant to say any more because he doesn't want to betray his nephew.

But Giuseppina is a mother and a bloodhound. "Who is she?"

"The daughter of Baron Pillitteri. I noticed he always sits behind her in church, and he's forbidden one of the store clerks to serve her so he can take care of her himself. Normally, he hates being behind the counter but he literally pushed the other boy away in order to speak to her."

"Isabella Pillitteri? That little thing that's all skin and bones? The daughter of aristocracy that lost everything on card tables?"

"Yes, but she looks levelheaded to me. She speaks softly and is always understated—"

"So I should hope! After the way her father and brother have acted—they had to sell their shirts to pay off their debts—she shouldn't even leave the house. She should shut herself away in a convent, except that they wouldn't have her there either, without a dowry." She paces up and down the kitchen nervously, and stops in front of him. "Are you sure it's her?"

"No, but it probably is. Besides, she lives right at the back here, in Piazzetta di Sant'Eligio." Ignazio omits to say that on at least two occasions, Vincenzo had offered to run errands to that area.

Giuseppina walks around the kitchen, clasping her forehead. "Hadn't we better find him a girl from Bagnara and marry him off immediately?"

"Please don't mention Bagnara and arranged marriages!" Ignazio snaps back. "Vincenzo is almost grown up and he's a boy: you can't keep him tied to your apron strings forever, and he's no longer a baby. He's nearly eighteen, do you realize that? And while we're on the subject, let me tell you something I've been thinking about for a while: he's leaving for England with Ingham and his secretary in a few weeks' time. He's asked to go several times, and Ingham has agreed to let him stay with him and take him with him. The change of air will do him good and he'll get this fancy out of his head."

"What do you mean—England?" She collapses onto the chair, a hand on her chest. "My son is going away and you don't tell me anything? This is why he's learning English with that merchant's secretary, isn't it?"

"Yes. Vincenzo needs to see the world and learn as much as possible. And you'll see, once he's been to England, he'll have forgotten all about the young baroness."

Giuseppina shakes her head. The fact that her son, *her* Vincenzo, has looked at this kind of girl upsets her even more than the journey she imagines to be filled with dangers. "He has to get that girl out of his mind!"

Ignazio raises his voice. "Enough! We don't even know for sure if that's the case, and even if it is, we'll make him see sense. And the trip won't do him any harm. Now serve the meal because I still have work to do after dinner."

~

Dinnertime is silent.

Vincenzo is puzzled. He eats, glances at his mother, sees her frowning, and can't think why.

Once the table is cleared, he sits down with his uncle to go through the books.

Ignazio separates the invoices from the promissory notes, while Vincenzo does the accounts.

"There are too many people not paying," he says at one point. "And thank goodness we have the *aromateria* sales, because at present, as suppliers we might as well be giving the goods away. Between wars, debts, and the cold weather, everything's going downhill."

As though in response to his words, the maid comes in to add coals to the brazier that is heating the room. It is a year with no warmth, 1817.

Ignazio waits for her to leave, shudders, and grimaces. "After the loan, it'll be a miracle if we don't wind up with a loss."

"We won't be the only ones," Vincenzo replies. "Everybody is having a rough time. Even Saguto has asked for an extension to payments on behalf of his father-in-law . . . assuming the old man still has a say in anything. Since his apoplectic fit, it's his eldest son who's been running the business."

"Saguto is a lackey. They keep him happy because he brought money into the family when he married the old man's daughter, but he's just a pawn. A dog who barks at corpses and licks wealthy men's boots."

"He's a dog, yes, but he doesn't have much to bark about. The Canzoneris are also in debt now. They've stopped teasing."

"Half of Palermo's in debt, Vincenzo, and the other half has debts it can't collect."

His nephew does not answer. He continues to count and brood. This morning, he went to La Cala. On the way, he saw nothing but desert. Now it's only closed store windows and bolted doors where the British warehouses used to be. In Via San Sebastiano, he saw the landlord of a wine canteen for merchants sweeping the floor of his empty premises.

Since Napoleon's defeat, the Mediterranean has been liberated from the French plague and the British no longer have their main reason for being in Sicily: now they can trade anywhere, with anyone, and however they please. The island has lost its strategic importance. The harbors are empty.

Palermo seemed dead.

On his way back, he walked past Gulì's *aromateria*. He was curious.

The *putìa*, with its walnut shutters and alabaster vases, was deserted. Gulì himself was leaning on the counter, looking out with a desolate expression. Then he saw the young man and spat on the floor.

He can spit all he likes, Vincenzo now thinks. He rummages through a stack of promissory notes and smiles when he finds a sheet of paper with Gulì's signature, black on white.

Ignazio opens the window slightly to let the smoke from the brazier out. "I've never seen so many stores close down in such a short space of time. Even Ingham said he's had far fewer orders than before—"

"Well, what did he expect? Commerce died after his fellow countrymen left. They excused themselves and left us the problems with the Neapolitans."

Vincenzo shakes his head. The changes over recent years have been too many and too quick.

Nobody was able to stand up against the return of the Bourbons: Sicilians were divided. Palermo hated Messina; Trapani, an ally of Messina, hated Palermo; and Catania looked out for herself. They could boast the oldest parliament in the world but didn't know what to do with it, as they had amply proved. They were united on just one thing: a loathing for everything "beyond the lighthouse," beyond the Strait of Messina.

Then disaster struck. The Bourbons returned to Naples.

Since December 1816, state offices and customs have been administered by Neapolitans, and Neapolitans are also military commanders.

Palermo has no longer any power or independence. Heavier taxes, restrictions, and new constraints regarding trade have dealt the final blow.

And the already limping economy has come to a complete halt.

Vincenzo closes the accounts book abruptly. "This month we've paid out more than we've earned, but there are letters of credit about to expire." He lowers his head, stretches out his arms, and emits a loud yawn.

Ignazio gives him a disapproving look. Vincenzo mutters an apology and straightens up. His uncle points at the accounts sheet. "We're not a charitable association." He picks up the promissory notes. "No more extensions."

They continue to work in silence, shoulder to shoulder. At times, when he's lost in thought, Ignazio thinks it's still his brother sitting next to him, and addresses him in Calabrian. Then his nephew looks up and Ignazio realizes his mistake.

That's when memory grabs him by the stomach and turns to regret.

When Vincenzo wakes up the following morning, he finds his uncle ready.

Ignazio is playing with his mother's ring and watches it shine in the light of day. Then he studies Vincenzo.

He wonders what Rosa Bellantoni would have thought of her grandson.

He hears him cursing softly, and finds him tackling a shaving cup and razor, using a towel to dab the bleeding cut under his lip.

"What's the matter with you? Why are you already so tense first thing in the morning? Come, let me help you."

Vincenzo sits down and puffs.

Ignazio's hand is fast and steady. He speaks softly so Giuseppina won't hear him. "What's the matter, Vincenzo?" He rinses the razor and the metal clangs against the ceramic. "You've been acting odd lately. Even your mother's noticed."

The young man pulls away. "I have things on my mind, Uncle."

"Keep still or I'll hurt you," Ignazio says. He lifts Vincenzo's chin with his fingers. "Is it something serious? Money problems you haven't told me about?"

"No, not at all."

One more swipe. The razor glides on the skin under the soap.

"Is it a girl?"

A moment of hesitation. Then an almost imperceptible nod.

"Ah."

Vincenzo blushes.

"Mind who you go after, Vincenzo." The blade delicately skids along his jaw. "And mind what you do and with whom. It's easy to do something stupid, especially if it's your blood ruling your head."

The young man's eyes are a blend of embarrassment and impatience. "You know, I'm not a child anymore, Uncle."

"True. But a woman can turn a man stupid. And you're not stupid." He's finished. He hands him back the razor. "I'll wait for you at the store. Hurry up."

Isabella Pillitteri is sixteen, with black hair, shiny eyes, and a neck like a swan's. She is refined, with a grace that's a blend of the shyness of a novice and exuberant sensuality.

She is beautiful. Very beautiful.

She's turned many heads in Palermo. She is penniless, however, because her father—*recamatierna*, peace be with him—had a passion for cards. Everything had been seized by the creditors, from their palace in Bagheria to her mother's jewels. Then, one day, he was found dead in his bed.

Isabella knows he took poison but it's not something you can say out loud. Suicides are not blessed in church.

Her brother, on the other hand, is being ruined by the women he frequents. There are constant arguments with their mother.

Nobody gives them credit anymore. The only one who accepts their promises is that young man in the *aromateria*.

Isabella knows he's pining after her. She's not surprised when she sees him, morning and evening, outside her windows in Piazzetta di Sant'Eligio, where she lives in a house her maternal uncle gave her mother more out of pity than affection.

He's a little older than her, polite, and his family has some money—at least that's what she hears. But she's not interested in this kind of match. She is a baron's daughter. Her family has no land and is in debt until the next generation, but they still have a china dinner set, even though there's nothing on their dishes but broccoli and onions. This young man is only a jumped-up store boy.

Still.

There he is, like every morning.

Isabella withdraws behind the curtain. "There's that young man again, Mother," she announces.

Baroness Pillitteri rushes to her. "Oh, he's such a nuisance," she says, pulling Isabella away from the window. "Don't encourage him. We don't need his sort. You're the only one in a position to ensure we get a little comfort. You must find a good match, get married, and do it quickly."

But Isabella resists, gives Vincenzo another glance, nods, and he responds with a greeting.

Her mother drags her away. "Shame on you!" She closes the curtains and shakes her. "Are you trying to spoil everything? You can't behave like this with a boor who soils his hands with work. These are contemptible people with no manners."

Isabella gives in and obeys. She knows that aristocrats mix only with one another and that hers is the kind of beauty they seek. She also knows that beauty doesn't last long.

Even so, she cannot ignore Vincenzo Florio's glances. They are not like those of other suitors: they penetrate deep inside her, make her laugh with embarrassment, fascinate her, extinguish her smile, and make her ache.

The following Sunday, at the evening Mass in San Domenico, Vincenzo manages to sit behind Isabella Pillitteri.

He got out of escorting his mother to Santa Maria La Nova this morning. Giuseppina has become oppressive and is constantly asking him what he's doing and where he's going. Vincenzo prefers to be with Ignazio, who is content to watch him with his stern eyes. Never mind. For the sake of one glance from Isabella's feline eyes he can tolerate his mother's invasiveness and his uncle's silent disapproval.

Isabella has white skin, like marble against her black hair. He can almost feel her warmth and the fragrance of her face powder. The attraction is so powerful that he can feel the pulse of the blue vein on her neck, concealed by her collar, throbbing under his fingers.

He dreams of seeing her dressed in silk: in a sumptuous outfit with a neckline that hints at her milky breasts. He imagines touching the silk and feeling her body against his. Then going lower down . . .

He covers his face with his hands.

She's the kind of woman, this he knows, who can drive a man to distraction.

After Mass, Vincenzo lunges forward so as to find himself right in front of her. Since she is petite, Isabella has to look up at him. She raises her eyebrows slightly in a silent inquiry.

It's an instant that's as long as a thousand.

Vincenzo coughs and stands aside to let her through. "After you," he murmurs in a deep voice that comes from he doesn't know where. The girl bursts out laughing and he thinks it's the best sound in the world.

Isabella is about to thank him when her mother pushes her. "What are you doing? Let's go."

Still focused on the girl, who keeps turning around, Vincenzo hasn't noticed the look of contempt her mother has given him.

But, standing next to his nephew, Ignazio has seen it, and returns an equally frosty look.

"Still after her?" Giuseppina spits out her words, which seem to fall on the dining table and roll onto the floor.

Ignazio chooses to ignore her. He picks up his fork and starts to eat. After a morning spent answering questions from Neapolitan officials ready to tax him on his shoes if they could, he's tired and hungry.

Giuseppina goes to the window, sits back down, then gets up again. She ignores the dish of pasta and tomato sauce in front of her. "Don't you have anything to say?"

He carries on eating. "He should know for himself that she's not suitable for him and—"

"And what if he does something stupid? What if we then have to deal with her, her debts, and her bastard?"

"Stop that now." Ignazio raises his eyebrows and motions her to the seat at the table. "Then, and only then, will we handle the situation. Not before. And I'll be the one to do it. You're his mother but I'm a man, so I know how he thinks. Besides, if she acts all flighty, that's not Vincenzo's fault. He's a grown man, so it's normal"—he clears his throat—"that he should go after what all other men go after."

Giuseppina blushes under the weight of Ignazio's eyes. She sometimes forgets that her brother-in-law, too, is a man, and probably also has *needs*.

Keys turn in the lock. Vincenzo arrives, out of breath. "Excuse me for being late. I—"

"I won't excuse you. Where have you been?"

"Mamma, what do you—"

"Now, you keep quiet and listen to me. I don't want to see that Pillitteri girl here, do you understand? She has a brother who squanders money in brothels, and her mother is hoping that some rich man will be foolish enough to marry her. And, judging from the way you're behaving, it seems you're the perfect candidate."

"Oh, by Saint Francis of Paola!" Ignazio covers his face with his hand. "You couldn't wait for me to talk to him, could you?"

The young man walks away from the table. "You can't talk to me this way. Isabella is—"

"Isabella? On first-name terms already, are you?"

"Damn it, her name is Isabella! Yes, I went to stand outside her house. So?" Vincenzo, too, has now raised his voice. "What makes you think she isn't—isn't an honest woman?"

"You just have to look at the way she moves to know the kind of woman she is." When Giuseppina is this angry, there's no power, human or divine, that can bring her back to reason.

And Ignazio suddenly sees it: the concealed side of Vincenzo, the one he's always suspected. Destructive, fueled by determination, nurtured by anger. It's there, throbbing and glowing.

"Calm down, Vincenzo." Ignazio approaches him and tries to placate him, but the young man isn't even listening, and pushes him away. It's as though he doesn't recognize his own mother anymore: he doesn't know the shrew who's spitting insults at him. What hurts him most is the contempt in her face.

"What gives you the right to think you're better than her?" he tells her. "You've always been judgmental, always shut in your own world and never wanted to see outside it! You just enjoy tormenting other people, that's all!"

"I'm your mother!"

"No—" His anger sticks in his throat, preventing him from speaking. He backs away to the door. "Why don't you look at yourself in the mirror and see who you really are before you go insulting people?"

He leaves and slams the door behind him.

He strides the short distance to the *aromateria* at full speed. The store is empty, thank God. Everybody's home for lunch.

He tries to calm himself down by going through a list of herbs and their use.

Witch hazel for soothing.

Cloves for nausea and indigestion.

Tormentil for gut infections.

Horse chestnut root for varicose veins.

Cinchona bark for fevers . . .

Ignazio has quickly finished eating his pasta, now cold, while Giuseppina has been yelling and shouting.

He'll never say it out loud, but he knows his sister-in-law's fears are not unfounded: a bastard is the last thing they need. He therefore leaves without saying goodbye and heads to the *aromateria.* He finds his nephew alone in the office, hunched over the ledgers. He puts a hand on his back. "Do you trust me?"

The young man nods.

"What's going on between the young baroness and you, Vincenzo?"

"Nothing, Uncle, I swear."

Ignazio sees again in Vincenzo's eyes that dark side he's always feared existed. Now it has surfaced, there's no way of pushing it back.

"It's not as my mother says: she just says that because . . ." He runs his fingers through his thick, wavy hair. "I don't know why she says that."

"You're her son. She's scared you'll brush her aside." *And she's jealous,* he thinks. *Because your mother doesn't love you like her child but like a part of herself, with a love that leaves no room for anything else.*

Vincenzo rests his elbows on the table. "In any case, I think she likes me, too—Isabella, I mean."

"What gives you that impression?"

"The other day she was standing behind the curtain and when I walked past her house she greeted me. Now she openly smiles at me even when she's with her mother, who then chides her. That old woman snubs me like a leper."

"Her mother also wants what's best for her."

"And I'm not good enough, right?"

Ignazio doesn't reply. It's true that the Florios are well off but Vincenzo isn't the heir of an aristocratic family, and for that kind of person, blood is everything. He strokes his hair. "Listen. You're going to England next month and you'll be staying there for a few months. If you still want her when you're back, I'll try to talk to your mother and persuade her. But not before. Right now, if your mother was standing in front of the young baroness, she'd strangle her."

Vincenzo can't help laughing. However, his expression darkens. "You know something, Uncle, I've been thinking about this trip. I'm not sure it's a good idea for me to go."

Ignazio freezes. "What do you mean?"

"I'm not sure I want to go."

"You must, Vincenzo." His voice is calm, as usual, but his blood is boiling.

The young man lets go of his pen and a drop of ink spreads over the paper. "What if Isabella—"

"She's a woman, and right now she's beautiful and makes your blood stir, but some things don't last forever, Vincenzo. What does last is this work!"

"If her mother marries her off to someone else I'll—"

"No." Ignazio raises his voice and shakes him. "You can't do this to me. You can't be this ungrateful after all the sacrifices I've made for you and this business. You, too, have to look after this *putìa* and the people who work here."

You can no longer just look out for yourself.

These words are crowding his mind as he's walking, his head down, fists in his pockets.

Words as heavy as rocks.

He tries to shake off his sense of guilt. It's true: his uncle has devoted himself to work, for his sake and his mother's. He feels stifled, like an animal in a cage.

Never has he been so aware of belonging to a family as now.

He reaches La Cala.

Until a year ago, the harbor was heaving with ships, and chests with British or colonial stamps were being unloaded along the docks. Now the whole district seems to be turned inward, wrapped in a mellow silence where you can even hear the lapping of the water.

The prospect of the trip to England resurfaces more strongly than ever.

Oh, God, it's true that I want to go, he thinks. It's what he's wished for most ever since he met Ingham. On the other hand, Isabella is the desire of a rogue heart persuaded by promises enclosed in a few glances from behind a curtain.

His shoes wear out the cobbles, leading him to Piazzetta Sant'Eligio.

To hell with convention. He needs to know.

It's late afternoon by the time Isabella comes out. The first thing she sees is Vincenzo, leaning against the wall outside the front door.

He walks over to her and takes her hand. "So?" he asks hastily. "Tell me now."

She holds her breath and wants to answer but cannot, although she tries. "I—"

A fan slaps her on the lips and breaks her voice. The baroness quickly slips between them. "So what? What do you want?"

"It's Isabella I want to speak to, not you."

"How dare you call her by name? She's *Baronessina* Pillitteri to you.

Now, on your way before I call my son and he gives a laborer like you the blows he deserves."

The young woman stands behind her mother, extremely pale, not reacting, her fists clenched against her mouth.

Vincenzo feels anger rising in his chest. "Your son, *signora*"—never would he give her the satisfaction of addressing her by her aristocratic title—"is probably drunk in some brothel, squandering the last money you gave him."

The woman's cheeks shrivel. She may have been as beautiful as Isabella when she was young, but life has marked her face, stealing every last spark of grace. "How dare you speak to me like this, you miserable dog?"

"I mean no disrespect to you, but you show me none."

Passersby stop to watch them. There are a few heads peering out the windows. "My forebears would have people like you whipped for as much as raising their eyes or saying a word too many, and you now dare speak to me like this! You and your family of longshoremen can go back to the bilge you came from."

Vincenzo studies her. The lace on her dress is darned, and the frill on the hem so worn, it's threadbare. "Did you choose your outfit before going out? Or was it your maid? Of course, I forget, you no longer have a lady's maid, right? In that case you should have paid more attention: the silk in your skirt is torn, *signora*."

The sound of a slap echoes in the street.

Vincenzo stands petrified.

He can't remember the last time his own mother slapped him across the face.

The color drained from her in shame, Isabella backs away to the front door.

Vincenzo notices and takes a stride past the baroness, forgetting his burning cheek. "Isabella!" he calls out.

At first, she shakes her head, then echoes her refusal in a loud voice, again and again before disappearing in the darkness of the courtyard.

"*No.*"

The baroness approaches Vincenzo and, standing on tiptoe, brings her lips close to his ear. Her words are like blades. "Rather than seeing her touched by someone like you, I'd sooner my daughter were dead or dishonored," she says. "Or even a whore in a brothel." She walks away, then speaks up so everybody can hear her. "You could have all the money in the world but it'll always stink of sweat. You'll never be anything but a laborer. It's blood that counts."

Vincenzo stands motionless in the middle of the street while Palermo rushes past him. The windows close again and laughter fades amid the clanging of wagons. Some look on him with sympathy and compassion. Others do nothing to conceal their contempt.

It's blood that counts.

He leaves the square. Head high, back straight. But he feels as heavy as lead.

Everything inside him is shattered. Only humiliation keeps him in one piece.

Never again, he tells himself.

Never again.

"So, how do you find Yorkshire?"

Benjamin Ingham is sitting opposite him in the carriage. He speaks English to him.

Vincenzo's nose is crushed against the window as he studies the countryside. "It's beautiful, but everything in England looks different from what I'd imagined," he finally replies. "I thought it had many cities and houses." He looks at Ingham. "I've never seen so much rain, especially in August."

"It's brought by the ocean winds," the Englishman explains. "There are no mountains here to stop the clouds, like in Sicily." He then looks at Vincenzo's suit and gives a pleased nod. "My tailor has done an excellent job. What you brought from Palermo wasn't suitable for this climate."

The young man feels the cloth of his jacket: it's warm, thick, and stops the damp from getting through. But what truly surprised him was the cotton used for making shirts. His underwear had a coarse texture, while this is soft, made by the steam looms Ingham has described enthusiastically.

He's been learning more in the past few weeks than over a whole year of studying. Everything about this trip is a discovery: the ocean that has given him an awe-provoking sense of vastness, the cliffs of the French coast, the sun becoming an evanescent presence. And the factories. So many factories!

"Before we go home to Leeds, we'll call at one of the textile mills I own," Ben promised when they arrived. "A textile factory with steam-powered looms. It's wonderful, you'll see."

It's exactly where they're now going.

As soon as Vincenzo steps out of the carriage, he's overwhelmed by the smell of burning coal: a sharp, bitter odor blending with the north wind.

The workers are busying themselves around goods wagons and chests covered with canvas.

He looks at the brick walls in the courtyard. No plaster. No decoration. In the center, there's a building with a large portal and a chimney on a slate roof.

A man comes forward to greet Ingham. It's the foreman: a fat man with a jacket that seems about to burst at the seams. As he walks them to the entrance, he mentions a couple of engine failures.

Benjamin reassures him and says he'll speak to him later. He makes a sign at Vincenzo to follow him.

They go in.

Whistles, thuds, and a constant shrieking that seems to be coming from the roof. The clanging is deafening. Vincenzo plunges into the darkness and heat.

He senses movement. Bodies. He remembers the tercets from Dante's *Inferno*, which he has learned with Don Salpietra, where the poet finds the indolent souls running around and colliding with one another, going after a weathervane, rushing about aimlessly.

Only a few seconds later does he make out men, women, and children of all ages moving around the machines. Many have skin glowing with sweat and wear cloths tied around their heads.

Benjamin tugs at his arm. "There are more than thirty people employed here. The work follows a specific order: over there they produce the yarns, which are then worked in this part of the plant." He indicates a section of the building that seems better lit. Vincenzo sees children sitting and carding the wool. "They used to be shepherds or weavers at home; now they have a steady salary and a roof over their heads."

There's a hiss on his right. He bends over the mechanical spool run ning up and down, as though with a life of its own, weaving the woof and warp. He wants to touch the threads but stops when he sees the fingers of the woman pushing the cloth along the loom. She has two phalanges missing.

He feels sweat gather between his shoulder blades and run down his back. He removes his coat. You can't breathe here. How can people work in these conditions?

Ingham indicates a few black cylinders separated from the work area by a wall. That's where the hissing and clicking is coming from. The closer they get to it, the more stifling the heat. The workers' faces look feverish, and some are laboring with bare torsos. They take almost no notice of the visitors; even so, Vincenzo detects a mixture of resentment and resignation in their furtive glances.

So here it is, the heart of the factory. The steam engine is a monster with a black carapace, shiny with grease. A slab conceals the pistons activated by the heat. Gingerly, almost reverently, he reaches out to one of the tubes. It's hot, and he feels the motion vibrating under the palm of his hand. It seems to be throbbing with a life of its own.

Ingham is right when he says that something like this could never work in Sicily. In Britain, workers don't complain or make mischief, there's no shortage of water, and, above all, no shortage of entrepreneurs.

"People here think differently," he explains in the office after the visit. A maid is serving tea, a blend Vincenzo has never tried and which has a flower scent. He lifts his cup, trying to conform to British etiquette, which is so different from his family's simple rituals.

"Building an enterprise is not just about money. You need ideas and the courage to manage them. Let me give you an example. Who, of all Palermo's *aromatari*, has as much business as you?"

"Not many," Vincenzo admits. "One or two, perhaps. Like Canzoneri and Gulì."

"And why is that? I'm sure you've thought about it."

"They've been familiar with this way of working for generations, so they just carry on." The thoughts he's stumbled over so many times line up in an orderly manner and start to make sense. "They've never believed they could go beyond it. So—"

"They've stopped at what they have. A *putiedda*—a store."

It's strange to hear that word uttered in an English accent.

While Ingham sips his tea, Vincenzo lowers his eyes and ponders. For a moment, his thoughts are polluted by the memory of Isabella. He dismisses it, along with the words spoken by the baroness. "What if these machines were set up in Sicily? Wouldn't it bring our costs down?" he insists.

"Yes and no." Ingham puts down his cup. It's time to resume their journey. "Don't think I haven't considered it. I'd have to import the looms and spare parts, as well as mechanics . . . not to mention the fact that coal is easily available here. Ideally, we would have a factory that produces these machines in Palermo."

"But there aren't any," Vincenzo says, disheartened. "The business would run at a loss."

As they're about to get back into the carriage, Ingham puts a hand on his arm. "In any case, I think we can drop the formalities. Call me Ben."

The sirocco is a wet blanket cast over Palermo.

The aristocracy has relocated to San Lorenzo or Bagheria for the summer, to villas surrounded by gardens. The luckier ones spend their days shut in their houses, wetting the curtains to cool the air, or taking refuge in underground rooms.

Even children don't feel like playing. You can see them in the sea, beyond La Cala, diving into the water and chasing one another on the rocks.

Those forced to work cross the streets, heads down beneath a ruthless sun. Ignazio hates the heat: everything becomes twice as much effort, and leaves him breathless. He goes to the *aromateria* at dawn, and leaves once night has fallen over Palermo.

This is when Palermo's residents reclaim their city. Life resumes in the narrow streets and the tuff and stone alleys that lead to the rear of luxurious aristocratic palaces whose shutters are closed because their owners are in their country villas. Gusts of humidity blow in from the harbor, so those who are able to take their carriages or buggies for a ride by the sea. There are shiny vehicles and wagons painted with paladins and humble traps full of people in search of a little coolness. The great, popular feast of the city's patron saint, Rosalia, took place just recently, and left the city tired and drunk on celebration and color.

Chairs and benches are dragged outside the doors. Women chatter while keeping an eye on their children, and workers fall asleep on straw mattresses thrown on the balconies.

Giuseppina is waiting for him by the window, some darning in her hands. They eat in serene, familiar silence.

Evenings end on the balcony, watching people in the street. She has a fan made of palm, and a glass of water with *zammù*, aniseed water, and Ignazio has a bowl of *semenza*.

One night, Giuseppina suddenly becomes gloomy.

"What's the matter?" he asks more out of habit than true concern.

"Nothing."

"What's wrong?" he repeats.

She shrugs. She looks sad. Then she says softly, "Do you ever think about our house in Pietraliscia?"

Ignazio puts the bowl of seeds on the floor. "I do sometimes. Why?"

"I think about it all the time. I reckon I'd like to go back there, at least to die." She throws her head back, looks for stars but can't find them. "I want to go back to my own home."

Ignazio is taken aback. "What are you saying?"

Giuseppina is hardly listening to him. "You're all settled with your work," she says more to herself than to him, "while I have no idea what I'm doing here. Except for Mariuccia, who's very old now, and a few other acquaintances, I don't have anybody. I could ask Vincenzo to come with me, and he would help you trade from there, organize your work . . ."

Ignazio can't believe what Giuseppina has just suggested. Grasping the railing, in vain he searches for words. "What do you mean? We send ships to Marseille and you're talking about Calabria? Vincenzo, who speaks English and French, to go and live in Bagnara? He's a city boy—from Palermo, as a matter of fact—and you want him to go live in a village with four streets?" He sounds aggressive, incredulous, angry. "We've been in Palermo for almost eighteen years. Even your husband's buried here."

"Yes, your brother was a fine one. Took everything away from me and didn't even give me an ounce of love. Just grabbed my dowry money then put me in a corner."

"Are you still thinking about this? Your dowry belonged to him and now you're staying right here. Where do you think you'll go all alone? And who'd take care of me and your son?"

The lines on Giuseppina's face twist into a vexed smirk. "Typical of this family. I have to be your servant till the end of my days, right? More fool me for asking you, hoping you were different. But you're like the rest, selfish and *malarazza*—a bad sort." She stands up. "You know what I find most hurtful? That my son is growing up to be like you two, with a heart of stone that—"

"What's the matter with you this evening? How can you say this about your son?"

"Never mind. Just something I'm thinking. No point talking about it anymore. After all, you've also forgotten everything. All you care about is money and the business." She vanishes behind the curtain.

Ignazio remains on the balcony, his fist tight on the railing.

This is ingratitude, he thinks. *It's not my fault.*

He could scream like a madman. Giuseppina's accusation is cruel and unfair, and she does not acknowledge even one of the thousand things he's done for her.

He suddenly wonders if it really is worth working himself into the ground like he does, without an ounce of affection in return. He doesn't mean the affection Giuseppina has shown in taking care of him: in this respect she has never held back.

He means something else, something that bites at his flesh and has kept him awake for many—too many—nights.

Enough.

He goes to his sister-in-law's bedroom. She has changed and is wearing a nightdress, plain, with no frills, a leftover from her trousseau. She's in front of the mirror, untangling clips from her hair.

Ignazio can't stop himself. "Why? Don't you know what you are to me? Why do you always have to remember the past?"

Giuseppina drops her arms. "I told you. This wasn't my choice. Being here is a penance for me."

"Don't hold that against me. People have gone forward, made lives for themselves, and many even settled in Sicily . . . Even Vittoria and Pietro Spoliti live in Mistretta. What do you think is left in Bagnara?"

Giuseppina does not answer. She knows Ignazio is right. And yet she has harbored this resentment for so many years, she cannot do without it now. A resentment that's a thorn between her ribs and her stomach. She throws down the clasps and starts brushing her hair. "Please go away." She slams the brush on the dressing table. "Go away!" she cries.

She hears steps walking away.

But not her resentment, no. That doesn't decrease.

"That's what you are," she shouts, "people who take what they want! First your brother and now you have taken my life. You've reduced me to nothing and turned my son into a swine, a dog."

More footsteps.

She is suddenly caught in a painful embrace. Her nightdress opens, revealing her breast.

Ignazio is holding her back tight against his chest. He's trembling.

They look at each other in the mirror.

Giuseppina sees a stranger and is afraid of him. Because the man who has grabbed her like this can't be the mild-mannered, patient Ignazio. It's a desperate man, an individual who will stop at nothing.

"If I were like those of my blood, I would have taken what I wanted years ago," he whispers into her ear, while his hands confirm his words.

Giuseppina is scared. She's never seen him like this, and the expression on his face makes her legs feel heavy.

But she also sees her own desire, which makes her blush and takes her breath away.

It would not take much, and they both know it.

She's the one who crosses that boundary. She turns to Ignazio. Never mind if she regrets it in the morning. Never mind if they both regret it and aren't able to look each other in the eye for several days. Never mind if their hands experience the path so often traveled with their eyes and their desire, and if they deny it for the rest of their lives.

They will bury this night deep in their memory because the regret and awareness of having betrayed someone who isn't here any longer will be too powerful. It will be something that can never be spoken of, not even if it were a dream.

A shame to keep forever in their memory.

Nineteen years.

This sunny April 3, 1818, marks nineteen years since Vincenzo has been alive and that Ignazio has been a father to him. Eighteen years that, together with Giuseppina, they have been a family made of absences and silences.

Today, at closing time, liqueurs and biscuits appeared on the counter. Ignazio had invited the employees of the *aromateria* to have a drink, then they went home, where Giuseppina had prepared a stew for the occasion.

When he returned, in October last year, Ignazio and Giuseppina were waiting on the dock. As soon as he disembarked, she hugged him with the possessive enthusiasm of a mother. Embarrassed, Vincenzo stood still, then sought his uncle with his eyes. Standing aside, the latter had given him a nod. When he approached, they shook hands.

Nothing else.

But his uncle immediately saw that those five months in England had done him good: the brokenhearted young man was no longer there, but replaced by a proud man with a decided mouth, wide shoulders, and a determined expression.

At home, while the porters were carrying the baggage upstairs, they sat talking in the parlor.

"You won't believe what I saw, Uncle. Over there, machines do everything in half the time." And he told him all about steam engines, looms, and locomotives. Every so often, Giuseppina would leave the kitchen, stand close to her son, kiss his hair, and listen to him, bursting with pride.

Ignazio, on the other hand, was studying him very carefully. "This is why the British can afford to trade at such competitive prices," he concluded.

"That's right. And that's where we could come in, by offering them what they need." Vincenzo took an envelope from his pocket and handed it to his uncle without a word.

"The names and addresses of factories and commercial lawyers," Ignazio commented as he read the paper contents. "I'm very pleased. Ingham has been a good teacher."

Vincenzo clasped his hands under his chin with a hint of a smile. "In the last leg of the journey I stayed with him in London. He met commercial representatives, landowners, and a few factory owners. They thought I was just a boy, so they were talking to Ingham without being careful. I listened and that's how I discovered that they don't like having many different suppliers."

Ignazio saw in his nephew the passion that had long animated him. "All right. So?"

"We could be their middlemen in Sicily. Take tannin, for instance: they use it to work hides and leather and to fix colors. We have sumac here in Sicily, right? Let's buy it, grind it, turn it into tannin, and sell it directly to the tanneries."

Ignazio looked at the list of names, then at his nephew. He'd grown a slight beard, which made him look grown up. But it was his attitude that was radically different: serious, stern even. "Ingham is already doing this," he muttered.

"Yes, but he's an Englishman. We're Sicilian, so we can source at lower prices—"

Giuseppina interrupted and called them to eat.

Vincenzo gestured at her to wait. He went to a trunk and pulled out two packages. "This is for you, Uncle. And this is for my mother."

Giuseppina accepted the present with girlish joy. A length of fabric with an Oriental pattern appeared out of the paper wrapping. She picked it up by the edge and took it to her face. "Silk!" she exclaimed. "What did that cost you?"

"China silk, to be precise. Nothing I couldn't afford." Then he looked at his uncle and motioned at him with his chin. "Now open yours."

Dark cloth for a suit and a tie. Ignazio liked the quality of the fabric and its softness.

"It comes from one of Ben's factories. I'll tell you about it while we eat."

And they talked about it in abundance.

And continued to talk about it.

Ignazio is at the desk while his nephew is looking through the previous years' books, reading out figures, comparing the quantities of goods by income and expenditure. Bark is their most important resource. But there's more.

"The sales of sumac have increased since last year." Vincenzo rubs his fingers on the book. "Almost all of it sold on the British market. And then there are the cargoes of China silk. They literally disappeared as soon as they'd gone through customs."

"The French are serious, too. The other day, Gulì sent a large shipment of sumac to Marseille." Ignazio bites his lip and thinks for a second. "You know something, Vincenzo, I was thinking of also offering to sell semifinished hides, as well as tannin. The British use lamb and kid skins, and we have no shortage of those here. What do you think?"

The young man nods. "I think we should try it. As you keep telling me, you and my father started out with a storeroom and now we receive consignments from half of Europe. Shall we start drafting proposals? Now, you were thinking of leather and I was going to talk to you about the French buying sulfur. Were you reading my thoughts? Why don't—"

His uncle silently points at a folder on the desk with a few notes by Maurizio Reggio. "I beat you to it. I asked around among merchants and mine managers about the conditions for selling sulfur." He gives a quick, heavily ironic glance. "You want to teach a grandmother to suck eggs, do you?"

His nephew's laughter warms his heart.

It's January 1820 and bitterly cold. Ignazio has been suffering from rheumatic pain for some time, and has asked for the brazier to be lit in the office at the back of the *aromateria*.

Vincenzo is peeling oranges and throwing the skins into the coals. A pleasant smell of citrus peel wafts through the air.

Over the past three years, Vincenzo has grown up a lot. Watching him, Ignazio realizes that it's not just Vincenzo's body that has changed but also his mind. It has become increasingly cold and calculating.

For example, he made up his mind to import and sell British bark powder even though he knew Palermo apothecaries would not like this novelty. Moreover, a few days earlier, his wish came true when the official physician, the authority in charge of the sale of new drugs in Sicily, granted him authorization, thus shielding him from any complaints. There would certainly be no shortage of buyers for this fine, top-quality bark.

And there will soon be protests, Ignazio thought.

Therefore, when one of the employees knocks on the door and, embarrassed, announces that a delegation of apothecaries has arrived to "ask for an explanation," uncle and nephew have barely the time to exchange a look of understanding. As a matter of fact, the small group of men in black cloaks is already on the doorstep. And at the head of the line stand Carmelo Saguto and his brother-in-law Venanzio Canzoneri.

Ignazio stands up to greet them, invites them into the office, and sits behind his desk, while Vincenzo keeps standing, looking at them menacingly.

"So tell us, then, Florio," Canzoneri starts. He has bushy, gingery whiskers and the tone of someone used to giving orders. "What's this all about, that you're now allowed to sell drugs? We heard the news but it's too preposterous to believe."

"And good morning to you, too, Canzoneri," Ignazio replies, rolling his eyes. "You're looking well, too."

"And I can easily guess who told you." Vincenzo walks around Canzoneri. He stops behind Saguto, leans over him, and speaks almost in his ear. "As usual, you're worse than a gossiping housewife."

"Did someone say something? Was it the boy?" Saguto turns around abruptly and tries to grab him but Vincenzo leaps back and laughs at him.

Ignazio gestures at his nephew to join him behind the desk, and the young man, swallowing his pride, obeys. He doesn't want a brawl in his office. But neither is he willing to be intimidated.

"No more than your—your discreet brother-in-law has already told you, Don Venanzio. By the way, how is your father? I know he was taken ill a few weeks ago and is struggling to recover."

"It's God's will that he should live on." Canzoneri crosses his hands over his belly. He doesn't like talking about his father, who's been reduced to a vegetative state. It makes him feel out of place even though he is now, in effect, the owner of the pharmacy. "Let's return to us. The authorization. You know you can't sell drugs, don't you? Neither you nor your nephew are apothecaries, and as far as I know you don't even employ one."

"We will be doing nothing that's against the law. The chief medical officer has granted us this possibility and we're very grateful. We have a document that sanctions us, an authorization specially issued. Let me ask you now: what are you doing here?"

Canzoneri huffs and fidgets on his chair. Behind him, Pietro Gulì, the old apothecary who mocked Paolo and Ignazio so much when they first arrived in Palermo, dries his lips then says, "The College of Aromatari has specific rules. You don't belong to it. Even worse, you've neither asked permission nor respected the rules of our guild regarding the sale of medicinal herbs."

"That's because there aren't just your rules," Vincenzo answers immediately. "You know what your problem is, Gulì? You think that laws are made especially for you and that you can make them and break them at your leisure."

"But that's the way it is," Canzoneri replies softly, preventing Gulì's angry response. "This meeting is a preventive clarification. Consider it as such."

Vincenzo leans forward. He, too, now feels a slimy, angry feeling rise within him. "Meaning?"

"You're saying that you still think like foreigners, even though you've been living in Palermo for—it's nearly twenty years, isn't it? You've been lucky and you've worked hard, I grant you that. And yet you're still unable to comprehend that, here, some things change not when someone wants to change them or with authorizations. They change when the conditions are favorable."

"And they are. More than half of Palermo's herbalists are our exclusive customers."

Saguto opens his arms in one of his theatrical gestures. "Of course. You have all this because you did the paperwork. But what if the money runs out?"

"I don't care for the way you're speaking, Saguto. There are times—"

"No, Vincenzo." Ignazio puts his hand on his nephew's arm. This is not how the Florios react.

Vincenzo takes a step back but keeps staring at Saguto, who sneers, satisfied.

Ignazio's attention shifts first to Gulì, then to another man, who's been standing aside until now. He knows him well. It's Gaspare Pizzimenti, an apothecary for the courts. He's of an advanced age, distinguished, with a pockmarked face, perhaps because he had the smallpox as a child. "Tell me, Gulì, and you, Pizzimenti, from whom have you bought your bark supplies for the past two years?"

Pizzimenti clears his throat. "From you, but—"

"You've always said that our products were the best on the market, and that you bottled our English bark without needing to refine it," Ignazio says. "Don't be embarrassed: you can admit it here. After all, we're all honorable men here, right?" He lets his words linger in the air for a few seconds. "Come now, nobody will blame you. You're not the only one to do this. And yet judging by your colleagues, you no longer wish to do business with us, and there are many others like you. But I suspect it won't be very easy to sever relations. On the contrary: it will be neither easy nor painless. I mean for you . . ."

Vincenzo understands immediately and knows what to get and where.

He opens a drawer in the bookkeeper's desk, grabs some papers, and hands them to his uncle. In a flash, stacks of promissory notes appear in front of Ignazio, organized by name and amount.

And all their names are there.

He crosses his arms and stares them in the face, waiting for them to understand. "True, there are rules to respect," he finally says. "Just as it's a matter of honor always to settle your debts, right?"

Saguto's smirk fades and turns into a grimace. Pizzimenti steps back into the shadows. Gulì looks down at his shoes.

Canzoneri gives a deep, almost liberating sigh. "Right," he says.

A few seconds later, they've all gone. Canzoneri still keeps his head high and walks without speaking to anybody. Saguto, however, turns around. He sees Ignazio and Vincenzo on their doorstep and bites his thumb at them. He will not forget what's just happened.

PART THREE

Bark

July 1820 to May 1828

U' pisu di l'anni è lu pisu cchiù granni.

It's the weight of years that weighs most heavily.

—SICILIAN PROVERB

Fueled by the Palermo aristocracy and developed through a dense network of secret societies, hatred toward the Bourbons grows, as they are "blamed" for obliterating all Sicilian ambition for independence by uniting the Kingdom of Naples with that of Sicily and revoking the 1812 constitution. On June 15, 1820, a revolt breaks out, forcing Prince Francesco to take refuge in Naples and triggering the creation of the Sicilian Parliament, which restores the constitution. However, revolutionary winds are also blowing on the mainland. On July 7, an insurrection led by General Guglielmo Pepe forces Ferdinand I to accept the same constitution that Ferdinand VII of Spain had promulgated in March.

The independence-seeking spirit of the Sicilian government—aimed at restoring the Kingdom of Sicily—naturally clashes with the Bourbons, who take advantage of the discord among Sicilian cities (especially among Palermo, Messina, and Catania) and easily suppress the revolt through bloodshed. In November, the monarchy is restored and Sicily is back under the control of the Neapolitan government. And, in March 1821, the powers of the Holy Alliance—Prussia, Russia, and Austria—whose help Ferdinand I had requested, inflict defeat on the insurgents once and for all: on March 24, the Austrians march into Naples and place the king back on the throne. They remain there until 1827, when Francesco I of the Two Sicilies, who succeeds his father, Ferdinand, in 1825, finally manages to push them away.

An injured lion drinking at a stream. The roots of a nearby tree reach out into the water, releasing their healing properties.

It is the image that represents the Florio business: from the sign over the *aromateria* to the statue of Benedetto De Lisi standing outside their family tomb in the cemetery of Santa Maria del Gesù in Palermo.

The tree that plunges its roots into the stream is the cinchona, and its bark has probably saved millions of lives. Its powerful febrifuge properties were discovered, first and foremost, by the Indios in Peru and Bolivia, and do not escape the notice of Jesuits who, in the seventeenth century, take this bark back to Spain. Desiccated and stored in sacks, it is then sold in Europe's most important ports.

They call it "bark."

However, when Europeans become aware of its use in pure form, they also see that it's a drug for the select few. Because it is expensive and comes from a long way away, and because the bark needs to be ground by hand. Moreover, even though it takes away the fever, the powder drains the strength from patients, which is something poor people find even more serious than the actual fever.

In the nineteenth century, there is a development: thanks to mechanical grindstones, it becomes possible to obtain vast quantities of refined bark. The price drops. In 1817, Pierre Joseph Pelletier and Joseph Bienaimé Caventou extract quinine from this bark. But it is only at the end of the century that an irrefutable link is proved between malaria and parasites, and only at the beginning of the twentieth century, when fifteen thousand people a year are still dying from malaria, will the Italian government agree to sell quinine in salt and tobacco retail stores.

"Run, run! They say Spanish ships are approaching the harbor!"

"Not at all! They're Neapolitan ships, they're bringing King Ferdinand here because all hell has broken loose in Naples!"

"The king? If he comes here, we'll drown him!"

"It's the soldiers! The soldiers in Naples demanded the constitution, and the king gave it to them!"

"He gave it to them and not to us! One rule for some, another for us?"

"Ferdinand has to give us the constitution back, the one he took away from us in 1816. It's our right. Long live the Kingdom of Sicily!"

"It's the revolution! The revolution has broken out!"

Men, wagons, horses. Palermo has been in revolt since yesterday, on the occasion of the Feast of Saint Rosalia. Streets and squares are teeming with voices.

Ignazio picks up fragments of shouts from the crowds swarming in Piano San Giacomo.

"Watch out!" He shoves Vincenzo out of the way seconds before a carriage traveling at full speed nearly runs him over.

Those who can abandon Palermo. Others, on the other hand, look for an opportunity to prove themselves and fuel the rage of the populace. No one knows what will happen because of the revolt in progress.

Vincenzo brushes a lock of hair from his face. "We must reinforce the doors of the warehouses. If anybody decides to plunder them—"

"If they want to sack the city they won't be stopped by two extra beams of timber. Let's go!"

They walk up Via dei Materassai, going against the flow. Ignazio goes into the *aromateria*. The shutters are closed and only one door is left open, watched by a clerk.

Ignazio looks around and his mind drifts elsewhere, to a faraway place and time. He was still living in Bagnara when riots broke out against the Bourbons, which led to the birth of the Neapolitan Republic. Then, too, there were riots and deaths throughout the kingdom. But that was, above all, an opportunity to settle personal accounts and family feuds. Murder and plunder often had little to do with political motivations: rather, it was a desire to make your enemy pay, whether he be an unpopular relative, a pilfering farmer, a cunning breeder, or a priest who had levied too much of a tithe.

But no, he thinks, *this time it's different.*

In Naples, some army units rebelled. This led to the discovery that many officers had joined the Carbonari and, following their commanders, a large number of soldiers had gone over to the rebels. Soon enough, King Ferdinand was in trouble. A few days earlier, he had been forced to grant a constitutional charter acknowledging the rights of the aristocracy and the people, and went as far as establishing a parliament.

The Sicilians did not stand by and watch, quite the contrary. The insult suffered in 1816, when the king had abolished the Kingdom of Sicily and repealed the 1812 constitution, was impossible to forget. On July 14, 1820, as the city was heaving on the occasion of the Feast of Saint Rosalia, the revolt broke out. Nobody wanted to continue living as a prisoner in their own home, so the nobility, intellectuals, and other people took advantage of the crisis in Naples to declare Sicilian independence.

The real spark, however, came from the aristocrats. In 1799, the fleeing Bourbons had been welcomed and protected, and yet what thanks had they given in return? They had stripped the nobility of its power, its privileges, and the positions they had always occupied, because that was how it had always been and had to continue. Sicilians ruled over Sicilians. The nobility commanded the peasants.

Sicily was a strange country: the king had no allies among the nobility—on the contrary. Rather, Sicilian aristocrats were competing with the Crown because the king was a foreigner who had imposed himself on their home. Whereas *they* had lived in Sicily for generations, some even since the times of the Arabs and Normans. It was they who had created this island with their power, rituals, blood, and marriages, mixing it with salt, soil, and seawater. They were highly skilled at manipulating the peasants and the poor as they pleased. They would light the fire but then get wretched people to handle it and, inevitably, get burned by it.

"*Jamuninni*," Ignazio says to Vincenzo.

"Where?"

"They want to requisition the goods from customs, no one knows why. It's impossible to make any sense of anything anymore. Bastards!"

"So our shipment is—"

"Everything's at a standstill. They've blocked all outgoing ships, damn it!" Ignazio is furious. "They're saying a provisional government is being formed and in the meantime customs is all at sixes and sevens. Ben Ingham's just informed me. Hurry up, he's waiting for us there."

Ignazio walks decisively. Crowds throng the alleys up to the square courtyard of the Customs House, which is invaded by merchants and seamen.

The entrance is manned by soldiers who look like they wish they were anywhere but there, and certainly not now. They keep the crowd at a distance, brandishing rifles and shouting that they will shoot, but nobody seems to be listening to them.

"I insist. You will let us through because it is our right."

Vincenzo would know Benjamin Ingham's voice anywhere.

Ignazio joins him. "Signor Ingham's right. We have a ship about to sail. Our documents are in there." He points at a white building behind the soldier. "If our goods don't leave, you'll be causing us thousands of *oncie*'s worth of damage."

"We can't, signore," a soldier replies. "Besides, it wouldn't do you any good. A military dispatch has forbidden all departures."

Voices are raised.

"What do you mean? And who sent this dispatch?"

"We want to talk to an official!"

"We want to see the documents!"

"Whose decision was it, then?"

The soldiers exchange a terrified glance.

That's when some employees try to escape from the accounts office. They are received with shouts and somebody even hurls dung at them. The customs officers try, in vain, to hide in the crannies along the seventeenth-century walls. The crowd demands answers.

In the end, an employee smelling of sweat and fear steps forward. "There's no point in your staying here!" he cries. "Everything's blocked, nothing can leave. They'll sink your ships with cannonballs!"

"But why?"

Vincenzo looks at Ingham with genuine amazement. It's incredible how he manages to get himself heard in this racket without raising his voice. "That's what they've told us!" a customs officer yells back. "Go home, all of you!" Then he walks away.

"You heard?" a guard says in support, raising his rifle. "Go away!"

A few merchants step back.

Vincenzo does not give up, however. He follows the man and grabs him by the arm. "I'm not taking this bullshit from you," he says. "There was no dispatch." He pulls the man to him. They're inches away from each other and can smell each other's odor of tiredness and anger. "You may trick the others but not me. Nobody can decide anything whatsoever."

The customs officer tries to wriggle free. "Let go of me or I'll call the guards."

"How much?"

The man's pupils dilate. "What? What do you mean?"

Vincenzo's other hand travels to the man's collar and grips it hard. "How much to let the ship sail?"

Ingham has followed him, with Ignazio. He stands by the young man, his eyes fixed to the ground. "I'm joining in with young Florio," he mutters. "How much?"

The man hesitates. "I—"

"For God's sake, hurry up!" Ignazio exclaims in a single breath, as the captain of one of the ships approaches.

The customs officer lifts his chin toward the warehouses. There's panic and greed in his eyes. "Go there in a little while. To the back door, there." He looks at Vincenzo, then Ingham. "Just the three of you."

In the alley at the back of the Customs House, the shade is down to a strip. Minutes turn into hours. The Doganella door is shut, guarded by a handful of soldiers.

The July sun is a ferocious animal. Ingham's face is a fiery red, covered in freckles. Ignazio wipes his forehead with a handkerchief.

One of the doors suddenly opens. The customs officer's face is a white dot in the darkness. "Come in."

The three men exchange glances, slip inside, and take a couple of steps. The shade washes over them like cool water, and they are enveloped by the smell of dampness.

"How much?" the customs officer asks.

Vincenzo suddenly feels pity. The man is nothing more than a terrified wretch.

His thought is immediately confirmed. "I have three small children to feed," he whispers, "and I'm putting my job on the line for you."

Vincenzo goes to the door to make sure nobody is coming. Ingham sets the price. The man haggles. A pouch goes from Ignazio's hands to those of the employee, who checks the coins.

Immediately afterward come the authorizations.

"The documents are dated three days back so there won't be any problems. The ship must sail on the night tide, with its lights out and its sails down to a minimum. The harbor will remain closed, at least for now. I'll make sure there's no soldier in that part of the dock . . . That's provided all hell doesn't break loose."

Ingham's smile is like a knife. "I have no doubt you'll make sure of it."

Ignazio calls Vincenzo to him. "We have the authorizations for us and Ingham. Run to the ship, hand them to the captain, and explain everything to him. Make sure you talk only to him."

Vincenzo slips away, followed by the customs officer. Ingham and Ignazio walk down the corridors and into the deserted courtyard where the doors of the warehouses rented out to the public lead. They are locked and barred.

Everything seems safe. They draw a sigh of relief.

Outside, Palermo lies in heavy torpor. The heat and excitement have left it exhausted, messy, asleep in the late afternoon closeness. The two men follow the wall to Porta Felice, the only gate that is still open.

Ingham walks lazily, his hands in his pockets. "I was very impressed with Vincenzo today. He showed remarkable presence of mind for someone his age. He was very pragmatic but there was no time for subtleties."

"That's right."

The Englishman watches Florio from the corner of his eye. "Aren't you pleased with him?"

"Yes, of course. I'm proud of him, he had the guts to do it. It's just that there are times . . ." He stops. He doesn't know what to say. Vincenzo has an aloofness he cannot entirely understand.

They come to La Cala. The wind from the sea rustles amid the trees and ships. Not far from the entrance to the Doganella there are still traces of the morning's scuffle.

The Englishman pushes a capsized wagon out of the way. "Vincenzo is very . . . very hard, you're right. He's incredibly determined."

Ignazio sees the ship they have chartered. On land, his nephew is speaking to a few sailors. "You think so?"

"Yes." Ingham stares at Vincenzo. "You know, I have many nephews in England, my sister's children, strong, serious young men. But none of them possesses your nephew's rage. Don't get me wrong: it's a healthy rage, the kind that gets you very far."

Ignazio senses admiration in his voice, perhaps even a hint of envy. And yet it does not make him happy.

Vincenzo has been to England again. He has been away all summer and has recently returned, bringing back with him a large wooden chest and a English blacksmith with whom only he can speak. They have shut themselves away in the Piano San Giacomo warehouse for a few days. It is at the end of one of these days, after night has fallen, that Vincenzo goes to Isabella Pillitteri's house. He tells himself it is by chance that he has ended up there against his will. But he knows that's not the case.

The house is empty, the windows shut. He's heard that the two women had to move slightly out of Palermo: the relative who had allowed them to live in that house decided he could not keep them for life and forced them to leave, their few belongings packed in sparse luggage and loaded onto a cart. As for the brother, rumor has it that he enlisted in the Neapolitan army so he could bring home a little money and keep away from brothels.

His eyes fixed on the balconies, the plaster flaking with age and negligence, Vincenzo thinks that there is some kind of slow, twisted divine justice. An unwritten law of fate: if you hurt somebody, sooner or later you will feel the same pain.

It is a thought that provokes a bitter realization: he is so different from the brokenhearted boy who went to England for the first time. Then he was a fool, a babe who'd allowed an old shrew to insult him in public. Now he is a man. And yet he still feels a twinge of anger and regret. Anger because Isabella would not listen to him, because she had run away, because blood had been more important to her; regret because the possibility of having a family with her was stillborn.

Water under the bridge, he thinks. He's twenty-five years old, and sooner or later he will find a girl with whom he'll have a few children. But not now, because he doesn't want any complications with women or family. But he will be rich, oh, yes, rich enough to wipe that self-sufficient, annoyed expression from the faces of people like the Baroness Pillitteri. He will be so rich that he will have no trouble finding a girl from a family with as many titles as mortgages.

A noblewoman who would stoop to a bourgeois like him.

Money doesn't lie, he tells himself. Possessions don't say one thing and mean another. It's people who are two-faced. And what brings him most pleasure, more than a woman's body—he got familiar with them in England—or a bottle of wine, or food, is his work. Its earnings. As for social recognition, he doesn't care how long he'll have to wait: he will get it.

The following evening, Vincenzo came home sweaty, with oil stains, but contented. He asked his uncle to go with him tomorrow morning, and to bring along Reggio as well as another worker with a sack of bark.

When asked for an explanation, he replied, "You'll see."

And now Ignazio cannot believe his eyes.

The machine is an iron carapace that emits a hiss. Inside, two large iron forms make up the grinder, closed with a hermetic lid.

Ignazio reaches his hand out over the lid, then looks at Vincenzo, who is waiting, arms crossed, to see his reaction. Nearby, Maurizio Reggio is stunned and fascinated. Vincenzo motions at the English worker to halt the machine. Ignazio and Maurizio approach. The lid is lifted gently. Both are immediately surrounded by a dark flickering, as the smell of bark spreads across the room. Powder of the same consistency as ash has accumulated under the metal plate.

"You did write to me about this," Ignazio murmurs, astounded, "but I never thought it was this fast. It grinds more bark in half an hour than five workers in an hour." He looks at his nephew. "Is this how they work in England?"

"That's right. Only with these machines. Then they export it to the colonies. Look: the powder is much purer because the dregs stay at the bottom, so it's ready to be sold. You don't even need to sift it. Just collect it in glass jars."

Maurizio Reggio dunks a finger into the powder. "It's impalpable . . . Truly incredible."

Vincenzo bursts into a brief laugh. He closes the lid again so the volatile elements won't be dispersed, then tells the Palermo worker to fetch some jars. "Secure the tops and put our wax seal on them." Then he thanks the blacksmith in English and says to his uncle, "I'll tell him to train our workers to use the machine, so that he can go back with the next shipment to Leeds."

The three men go out into the open. It is one of those days when the sun is still hot but the light is no longer blinding and there's a slightly pungent coolness in the wind, which smells of the sea.

"England does you good. And us, too." Ignazio takes his nephew by the arm. Vincenzo has become a man, with Paolo's tousled hair and his mother's long eyes.

Giuseppina.

His sister-in-law is growing old, just like him, and yet she still has that indomitable expression he's been drawn to ever since he's known her. He has been by her side, taking care of her, for years.

He could not do otherwise.

He rubs his mother's ring. Paolo—*recamatierna*, peace be with him—has been dead for many years. He and Vincenzo manage the business together.

He could find himself another woman: one who gives him love and with whom he could finally start a family. Have a little happiness. Even tenderness, perhaps.

Yet he is still with Giuseppina and Vincenzo.

It is the life he has chosen. He can admit it to himself with the serenity of a man who has settled accounts with his past.

Some might say he is a daydreamer. But Ignazio does not pretend, nor act out of a sense of duty.

What he feels for Giuseppina no longer tastes of passion. It is something reminiscent of the gentleness of fall evenings, an awareness that summer is behind them and that winter is just around the corner.

~

It's nearly noon by the time they reach the *aromateria*.

"When you wrote to me from London, saying you were planning to buy this machine, I was perplexed, but now that I've seen it I have no more doubts." Ignazio is thinking out loud. "If we sell the quinine in sealed jars, our market will no longer be confined to Palermo but will take in the whole of Sicily."

"That's my plan, Uncle."

Maurizio walks ahead and opens the door to the store. The scent of spices blends with the air, steeped in the perfume of the sea, that drifts in from La Cala. "But I don't think it's the right time yet, Vincenzo," he says. "Particularly because we don't have enough people. Besides, you'll see, the apothecaries won't be very happy."

Vincenzo shrugs. "They'll change their minds. It's a matter of time." He speaks with assurance as he flings open the flap that separates the counter from the back of the store. "And we'll show them how to do it."

The customers greet them. Ignazio shakes hands and stops to speak to a sales clerk but cannot dismiss a memory that has crept into his mind. Four years ago. His idea to ask the chief medical officer for the authorization to sell drugs. The concession. And then the apothecaries landing on the *aromateria*, furious and silenced only by the promissory notes flung in their faces . . . *Have times really changed? Do they ever?* he wonders on his way to the office.

Vincenzo is busy with calculations and venturing sales forecasts. "We already have the authorization for medicinal powders, Uncle. Neither apothecaries nor *aromatari* can object. We haven't used it up to now but . . ."

Ignazio runs his fingers through his hair, which has patches of gray in it. "You know how much quinine apothecaries buy from us and at what price. Can you imagine how much profit they make from sales in their own stores? By selling bark, we'll hit them right in their pocketbooks. You can imagine what will happen, can't you?"

His nephew raises his arms and swears through his teeth.

Ignazio keeps still for a moment. "However . . . there is a solution that might bring us some luck." He drums his fingers on the table. "Call Maurizio. We must draft an application to the viceroy."

The days go by. The application is drafted with great care and the waters tested with informal chats.

Finally, Ignazio and Vincenzo turn up in person to see Pietro Ugo, Marquess delle Favare, Viceroy of Sicily.

They spend a long time on brocade couches in a room with a very high ceiling, waiting with other supplicants. The palace clerks give them looks as inquisitive as they are contemptuous. *What do these velvet-clad laborers want? Why do they expect to speak to the viceroy in person?*

Ignazio is impassive. He did not become one of Sicily's most prominent merchants by heeding the opinion of lackeys whose only luck was having a father who was also a palace servant.

Vincenzo, on the other hand, walks up and down the room, his hands on his hips, and gets upset when he sees other people, who arrived after them, being shown in. He puffs demonstratively when a priest in a cape walks past.

Ignazio looks up imperceptibly. "Vincenzo, calm down."

"But, Uncle . . ."

Ignazio raises his hand. "Enough."

Sinking his teeth into his lip, Vincenzo sits back down next to him.

They wait. Outside, the day is going by in Palermo.

It is late afternoon by the time Pietro Ugo receives them.

A valet in livery shows them in, then blends in with the tapestry in the study.

Two large whiskers, and bright eyes beneath a forehead made larger by baldness. Sitting at a desk with tortoise and horn inlays, he looks them up and down and focuses on Ignazio. He examines him for a few seconds before deciding that, yes, these two can take a seat.

Ignazio speaks softly, his back straight, his fingers pointing at the documents. He describes the machine and explains that they already have the authorization to sell drugs.

"In this case, what do you want? If you already have an official document . . ." Pietro Ugo listens attentively. "I mean, quinine is a drug. Isn't it included in the chief medical officer's authorization?"

"Yes and no. Until now, its sale has been the exclusive prerogative of apothecaries." Ignazio crosses his hands in his lap. "It's a delicate matter, Your Excellency. We do not claim medical skills we know we don't possess: our investment is of a purely economical nature. We wouldn't like to find ourselves with a machine we cannot use because of a bureaucratic impediment."

"I understand. So you would like an ad hoc authorization." His fingers massage his chin, covered with a goatee, his eyes already focused on other thoughts. "I'll tell my secretary to examine the matter and—"

Vincenzo puts his palms on the desk and speaks with ardor. "We're only asking you to protect our rights, Your Excellency. We want to practice our work as merchants in peace, and this machine will allow us to do it in an innovative way. We are nobody's servants and are not asking for any favors. We want our right to work to be acknowledged."

The viceroy is taken aback, as though he has only just noticed him. "And who would you be, young man?"

"Vincenzo Florio, Your Excellency."

"He's my nephew."

The two Florios speak in unison: Vincenzo with pride, Ignazio with embarrassment.

The viceroy watches them, a hint of amusement in his eyes. "Fire and water," he mutters, then slowly leans back against the chair, his eyes fixed on the ornate edge of the desk. "You know, I've heard all kinds of supplicants today: people asking for money, assistance, protection, even a priest who wants a particular parish." He looks up and his tone changes. "But nobody asked me for the acknowledgment of the right to work, as you have done."

He stands up.

Ignazio and Vincenzo do the same. The meeting is over.

Then, strangely, the viceroy proffers his hand to them.

When the Florios realize he does not intend for them to kiss it but shake it, they are more surprised than hesitant. The valet sees them to the door. As they are about to go through it, the viceroy adds, "You will soon have news."

~

And the news arrives at the end of 1824.

Shortly before Christmas, a paper bearing the royal seal is delivered to the management of the general accounts office that deals with sales rights.

The news spreads across Palermo, goes into bookkeepers' rooms, through grocery stores, and finally lands in Via dei Materassai.

There is a celebration in the office: they will now be able to sell quinine powder not only in Palermo but also in Licata, Canicattì, Marsala, Alcamo, and Girgenti.

Glasses of wine are passed around. Maurizio Reggio lifts the bottle. "Here's to the Florios and all who work for them!"

Ignazio laughs and drinks. It has been a good year: not only have they obtained the sales license but, a few months ago, they even acquired an ownership share of a schooner, the *Assunta*. "We'll use the *Assunta* for deliveries throughout the whole of Sicily," he announces, holding a glass in one hand, and placing the other on a map of the island spread on his desk. "Packaged quinine in sealed bottles with wax and our seal. Deliveries every month."

Vincenzo proposes another toast.

At that moment, there's the sound of crashing glass from the store.

Immediately afterward, shouts are heard.

"What's the matter?" Ignazio rushes into the *aromateria*, followed by Maurizio and his nephew. Two frightened lady customers are slipping away, leaving already wrapped purchases on the counter.

"Thieves! Scoundrels! Whom did you corrupt to obtain this license?"

Carmelo Saguto is trying to smash the store. Francesco, the head clerk, tries to stop him by pressing his hands against his chest, pushing him away.

Ignazio feels the crunch of broken glass under his feet, and sees golden powder on the shards. The fragments of a jar of cinnamon are scattered around.

"And now you're here, you bastard! You're crooks!" Saguto yells. "What, have you suddenly become experts? You know you have to have studied before you sell drugs, and you never did. You want to sell bark powder? Tell me the truth: did you buy this license?"

Ignazio cautiously approaches. "We obtained the authorization to sell medicinal powders four years ago," he says softly. "Don't you remember? We have a license. So what's new?"

"Powdered quinine! And what's all this about you having a machine? What's this novelty that half-English nephew of yours brought from England?"

"Who wants to know?" Vincenzo comes forward but his uncle stops him.

"Oh, the little dog barking." Saguto laughs and wipes the saliva off with his sleeve. He looks at them both with malice and ferocity. "I don't remember. Do you still have the promissory notes?"

Ignazio does not reply. But then he senses Vincenzo quivering behind him, so he replies, still calm, "It's a grinder, Don Saguto. It does what the workers do with the mortar, only faster and better." He just wants this man to go away.

"Tell that to the idiots you're going to sell it to. A machine has no eyes, so it grinds everything the same way. You know something? Go ahead and do it. Go sell this powder. It will ruin you first of all, because as soon as everyone realizes what swindlers you are, nobody will want your rubbish anymore." He spits on the floor. "Stick to your own work, to what you do best."

Ignazio drops his arms. "You shouldn't have said that," he tells him in an icy tone. He shows him the door. "Get out."

Saguto laughs with contempt.

Francesco pushes him toward the door. "Come on . . ."

"Don't touch me, you dog!" Saguto yells. He smooths his tie, which has become loosened, affecting an elegance he does not possess.

Carmelo Saguto's look travels past Ignazio and stabs Vincenzo in the face. "I'm leaving, yes. You could have all the money in the world, but you'll still always be what you were, and your behavior proves it."

"I said, go away!"

Vincenzo stands next to his uncle, his hands on his hips. "No, wait. What was that you said again? What is it we are?"

"Jumped-up lice. You were born laborers and laborers you've ended up."

An icy atmosphere suddenly falls on the room.

Vincenzo's fist is so quick and unexpected that Saguto has no time to dodge it. It hits him full on, between the base of the nose and the eyes, propelling him to the floor.

Immediately afterward, Vincenzo grabs Saguto by the collar and drags him out of the store, into Via dei Materassai. He beats him up methodically, violently, his teeth clenched, without shouting.

Francesco, Ignazio, and Maurizio Reggio cannot pull them apart. Vincenzo hits Saguto again and the latter punches him in the eye, making him stagger.

But Vincenzo is young and agile. He headbutts Saguto in the stomach and sends him down into the street mud.

"That's enough now!" Ignazio shouts. He stands between the two men, while Maurizio and Francesco finally manage to push Vincenzo against the store door. "You, inside!" he commands his nephew, who is protesting and panting. Then he addresses Saguto, who is down on the ground. His pants are dirty and there is a tear in his jacket, revealing the lining.

Vincenzo has struck with the intention of hurting.

"If I don't finish my nephew's job it's because I have self-respect. You're a coward, Saguto. All our lives, you and Canzoneri have spat venom on us Florios, insulted us, and ridiculed us with your arrogance. But now that's enough. You hear me? Enough! That time is over. You amount to nothing. If we're laborers, then so are you. My family and I have come up in the world, this is what we've worked for . . ." He indicates the store. "And what have you done? What you were, you still are—Canzoneri's paper pusher. And you'll be that forever. Now get out of my sight and don't come back unless you decide to apologize."

He goes back into the *aromateria* without deigning to give Saguto or the knot of onlookers that has gathered another look. He takes a deep breath. His heart is beating fast and his hands are shaking slightly.

He lifts his head, meets the baffled looks of the clerks and Francesco. "Get back to work," he says, panting. Then he goes into the office, from where he hears a series of curses. Maurizio has made Vincenzo sit down and is holding a wet cloth against his cheekbone. "I've sent a boy for some ice in Via dell'Alloro," Maurizio explains. He takes off the cloth and replaces it with a colder one. "What a scoundrel. How dare he come here to insult honest, hardworking people?"

Ignazio keeps standing. He studies his nephew, who is sitting by the desk. "Let me see," he commands. A bruise is emerging between the eye and the jaw.

Vincenzo does not complain or say anything. He is staring into space. In his face, there is darkness: not anger, not rage, but something more obscure and undefinable.

"Go into the store, Maurizio," Ignazio says. "I'll stay here." Maurizio Reggio is startled by his tone, cold as metal. Never has he heard Ignazio speak like this.

He leaves uncle and nephew alone.

Ignazio approaches Vincenzo. His hand opens and closes. He is itching to slap him like he's never slapped him before. Instead, he says in a low, furious voice, "Don't ever do this again—do you hear? You must never show them that you're vulnerable to their insults. Never."

The darkness in Vincenzo's eyes dilates, as though about to burst; then it vanishes, and is replaced by bitterness. "I couldn't stand him. He made me angry and I lost it."

"Do you think I don't know what they call us? That to them we were and always will be laborers?" Ignazio shakes him and raises his voice. He, whose gestures are always so self-possessed, always so measured. "They've been laughing behind my back and making my life difficult for twenty years. What do you know about goods swapped at the last minute, or about officials who make you wait in line while attending to other people first? First, they did that to your father and me because we were a couple of wretches, and afterward because we decided to expand and trade with the nobility. They thought they were dealing with lucky people and not two men who were breaking their backs. Do you really think I don't know that to them we are not much better than mud? But I am not like them and neither are you. It's different now. They've started to spread rumors about us because . . . Listen to me carefully, Vincenzo: it's because of envy. They're angry and afraid of us, and anger eats away at them. So what you need to hit them in the face with is our earnings, because they are the measure of their failure. Not fists, because they definitely are longshoreman behavior. The facts must speak for you. Remember that."

Vincenzo stands up abruptly, but feels dizzy and has to sit back down. Uncle Ignazio has never spoken to him openly about these things. "But then you . . . You . . ."

"Calm, Vincenzo. Self-control. I've ignored it for years but I've never forgotten it." He touches his forehead. "I've noted everything here. I'm not forgetting anything they've done to me. But never show them you're angry, because rage drives you to make the most stupid mistakes. These are people who think with their bellies. But we're not like that. You have to develop a pair of *cuorna ruri*, horns that are as hard as those of a bull, and not hear them but keep walking straight down your path."

They look at each other.

"Do you understand?"

Vincenzo nods.

"Now let's get back to work."

Ignazio returns to his desk. He ignores the pressure and breathlessness in his chest. He picks up papers and a pen, then puts them down. He looks at his nephew again. He is sitting with his face in his arms.

Vincenzo is not his son only because he was not born from his seed. But in all other ways, he's given him his all. And a man wishes he could spare his son suffering and disappointment even when he knows they will help him grow and become stronger and shrewder, and *farisi crisciri i' scagghiuni*, as old Palermo people say, to cut this teeth.

He looks at Vincenzo and his heart is breaking. He wishes he could take away his pain, but that's not possible. It's a law of life, just like the one that regulates the cycle of days and seasons: each one of them carries the mark of its own suffering.

Lying on the bed, Vincenzo is looking up at the ceiling illuminated by the moon. His cheekbone is throbbing, painful.

The wind is blowing; he can hear the sheets hanging out to dry lashing against the balcony grating.

He turns over on the bed.

Laborer. That's what Saguto called him.

It lasts just a second. The last image of Isabella Pillitteri.

That shrew of a mother had called him the same thing: *a laborer*. That's why he lost it with Saguto, he can admit it to himself. He should be thankful to his uncle for getting the man out of his way or he would have slaughtered him.

Isabella.

The memory of her is no longer as painful as it used to be. But the sense of shame persists—that and a desire for revenge. But not on her. She is now a shadow, a ghost lost in the folds of an adolescence when he was too mollycoddled. Some time ago, he read an announcement in the newspaper that she was marrying a marquis twenty years her senior.

It did not happen because it could not and was not supposed to happen.

Ignazio's voice echoes in his ears. He pulls a face and the shadow of the laundry swaying in the wind seems to answer him.

Vincenzo is intimate with anger.

He has been storing it in his chest for years. He's raising it like a daughter. A bolt of lightning cracks the night in two. It's about to rain.

He is not like his uncle, who is patient, self-possessed, and brave.

Vincenzo believes he is brave. But calm? Self-possessed? He touches his bruise. That's something he is still working on.

He is twenty-five years old. A man. He still sleeps in his nursery, in a bed with a painted copper headboard.

He has studied, he has traveled. His clothes are finely tailored. He thought his family was respected, and they probably are, but not by everyone, and not as they should be.

And that's what outrages him. To discover that it's never enough, never sufficient. That no matter what he does, he always carries the original sin for which he is not to blame.

In Via dei Materassai, in the alleys of the Castellammare district, they are the Florios: middlemen, merchants, wholesalers of colonial produce, and persons of esteem one can go to for advice concerning a consignment of goods or a letter of guarantee.

But this is a city inside another city, and Palermo by the sea has little to do with those who live beyond Cassaro, the large road that, at the exquisite Baroque intersection of Quattro Canti and Via Maqueda—the wide, elegant stone street created by the Spanish viceroys—divides the city into four districts: the ancient Kalsa, now the site of the courts of justice; the Albergheria, where the Royal Palace is situated; Monte di Pietà, with its Capo market; and, finally, Castellammare, the old Loggia quarter, where he lives.

He slams his hand on the bed. Outside, a burst of rain pelts the windows.

He can see challenging him, demanding that Saguto lowers his head and gives him the right of way.

Vincenzo usually looks the other way. But he will not do that anymore. He will walk with his head higher and higher, like his uncle, who has turned to stone and no longer needs anybody.

He will make them eat their arrogance: common people like Saguto as well as aristocrats like the Pillitteris. All of them.

He swears it to himself and seals the promise with his anger. He must have patience. Patience and resentment.

In the other room, one door away, Ignazio is standing, watching the thunderstorm.

He hears a knock. He turns and sees Giuseppina in the doorway, her hair down and with puffy eyes.

"If it weren't for you, he'd already have gotten himself in trouble so many times." She speaks softly and her voice is practically lost in the storm. "You brought him up for me as though he was your own." In vain, she tries to swallow her pride and her tears. "Paolo would not have treated him the way you have."

Ignazio is surprised. Something is startled in his resigned chest. He does not want to read in her words something that's not there: Giuseppina is still angry about everything her husband—and fate—put upon her, and perhaps will always be.

And yet.

"I love Vincenzo." *And I love you*, his eyes tell her. *I'm here, a step behind you.*

She nods. She would like to say more, much more, but does not. Because resentment is a stone embankment between your throat and your soul. It's her security, her excuse for justifying her unhappiness.

The spring air is warm. It smells of sea and blood.

Ignazio looks at the tuna being unloaded one after another, victims of the *mattanza*—the slaughter—following the Feast of the Holy Crucifixion that May, in 1828. Their large, shiny eyes almost look astounded. Their silver skin has been ripped open by harpoons.

At the bottom of the black boat, other creatures are waiting to be unloaded. They are going to be dragged into the *tonnara*, where they'll be hung by the tail for two days at least, so that blood and other humors may be drained before they are gutted.

He turns and his eyes search for Ignazio Messina. Florio finds him talking to the *rais* of the *tonnara*.

Ignazio Messina is their secretary, hired after Maurizio Reggio left his position, having confessed that he felt inadequate to the large volume of work; Florio himself knew that Reggio was not up to the task anymore, but did not want to dismiss him after so many years of service and dedication. His resignation came as a relief to all: by now the size of the House of Florio business required people with experience and enthusiasm, something Maurizio no longer had.

Ignazio Messina, on the other hand, is shrewd. Ignazio Florio immediately took a liking to this man, who, although he is of an advanced age, is full of energy. Above all, he has eyes that appear peaceful but which can actually delve deeply.

The secretary joins him. He looks satisfied. "This second netting has gone well, too. I told Alessio to come by the office tomorrow and pick up the money for himself and the crew."

"Good," Ignazio mutters. He shields his eyes from the sun with his hand. The tuna fishers are finishing unloading. Some are carrying pails to wash away the blood, others are collecting the ropes.

From the boat ramp he can see the coast almost all the way to the Madonie Mountains.

Below stand La Cala and Palermo, with its tiled domes and ocher walls. He remembers his arrival there and how thrilled he was to see the city on offer, noisy and full of promises.

Then life changed, the business grew and Vincenzo with it. After all these years, even the pain of losing Paolo has become less burning but has turned into a melancholy feeling, a sadness stuck between his throat and his chest, that makes him sigh.

Sometimes, he misses Paolo, it's true: but above all he feels a powerful regret for what has been and can never return, and remembers his strong body, his hope, his enthusiasm, and even the emotion of a love without hope that used to make him feel alive.

He misses being what he used to be.

He misses the sea.

He knows this by the pang between his stomach and rib cage. He feels a sense of loss when he recalls the boat rolling under his feet and the sense of freedom on the skiff, twenty years ago.

He, a creature of the wind, has been forced to become a man of the land and of money.

The pain that was no more than a lament of the soul suddenly turns into a grip that shortens his breath. His blood pumps in his throat. He closes his eyes and leans on Messina's arm.

It is not the first time.

"Don Ignazio, what's wrong?"

The grip eases and his mind focuses again. "Just tired," he says with a dismissive gesture.

"You work too hard. You give yourself to the business, body and soul, and never rest." The secretary seems genuinely concerned. "Your nephew knows how to deal with customers. You could—"

"This is my concern," he says, interrupting him with more harshness than is necessary.

The other man falls silent.

They slowly walk around the wall of the plant.

"I've always liked this place," Ignazio says softly, his words carried away by the wind. "I took over its management a few years ago, when it wasn't very productive. There wasn't much fishing, the British had gone and there was no more money around. Then, just within a few years . . ." He clicks his fingers. "Everything changed."

The secretary looks around. "The timing wasn't right. But this year, the sea has been generous." He makes motions with his head to the inside of the building, from which they can hear voices, thuds, and chains squeaking. "We can cure it and sell it on the mainland, beyond the lighthouse."

"That's right."

Ignazio leans against the wall. Beneath him, there is black water and cliffs; in front of him, the reflection of the sun. His life has always been like this: an ebb and flow of right and wrong timing to which he has had to adapt. Maybe that is why he has become so good at it, by working hard at being something he was not.

He comes away from the wall. "Let's go back to Via dei Materassai. I have things to finish."

"But, Don Ignazio, it's afternoon already. By the time we get back to town, it'll be time for vespers."

Ignazio walks ahead. "Don't put off till tomorrow what you can do today. Besides, Vincenzo is waiting for me to complete some transactions."

He gets into the buggy. He takes one more look at the sea of the Arenella *tonnara*, his heart heavy with desire and regret.

ᘏ

On May 18, 1828, Ignazio opens his eyes. He sees a light filtering through the shutters of the balcony overlooking Via dei Materassai: a sharp glow that heralds the summer, as does the swallow song in the attic.

He is tired. He's had a bad night. He's had digestive problems for a while, so much so that he sometimes prefers to eat just bread and fruit.

He does not feel like getting up but he must. He props himself up on the mattress, is suddenly dizzy, and falls back down on the pillows. His left arm is hurting, but that's normal since he usually sleeps on that side. He catches his breath and waits.

He dozes off without even noticing.

It is an hour later by the time he wakes up. He calls Olimpia, the maid, and she shuffles into the room. "Here I am, signore."

She flings open the shutters. The sun floods into the bedroom, illuminating the untidy bedding. "What's wrong, Don Ignazio? Sweet Jesus, you're as white as a sheet."

Ignazio stifles a cough and sits up with difficulty. "Nothing. I didn't digest my food properly. Can you make me some water with bay leaf and lemon?" He massages his chest. His stomach seems to be bubbling up.

Olimpia picks up the clothes he dropped higgledy-piggledy the night before, too tired to tidy them away. She presses the pleat of his pants while still chatting away. "Your nephew looked in on you a little while ago. Poor thing, he was worried. He saw you were asleep and left you to it. He's at the store now. Just give me a minute and I'll make you water with bay leaf."

She disappears. He props himself up against the night table to get up. It's easier to breathe standing up.

He drinks the decoction, shaves, and gets dressed.

I'm not a youngster anymore, he thinks, looking at himself in the mirror. His eyelids are swollen, his hair streaked with gray, his hands shaking. Time is a creditor that does not accept promissory notes.

He hears Giuseppina's voice coming from the kitchen. She must have gone to the market early in the morning. She says it's something she enjoys doing. Ignazio knows it's really because she does not trust the maids.

He has barely done up his tie when she appears in the doorway, one hand on the jamb, the other on the knob. "Olimpia says you're unwell. When Vincenzo and I went out, we also thought—"

"I'm all right," he interrupts her, sharply. He puts on his jacket but the movement makes him moan. The stabbing pain in his arm has increased. He suddenly vomits and staggers.

She can barely hold him up before he falls. For the first time in many years, Ignazio and Giuseppina are close. He can smell her perfume; she senses how ill he is.

His heart is thumping under his breastbone. The pain suddenly explodes in his chest.

Ignazio collapses. Giuseppina cannot stop him: he is too heavy, she is dragged down with him, and, in the fall, the bowl of water shatters. Water and shards are scattered on the floor.

"Olimpia!" Giuseppina screams. "Olimpia!"

The maid rushes in and puts her hands on her head. "Don Ignazio! Sweet Mother of God! What happened?"

"Help me put him on the bed."

But Ignazio is practically unconscious and prey to convulsions.

"Call Vincenzo! Run to the store and tell him to come right away."

"Woe!" Olimpia cries. "What a tragedy!" Her screams really seem to presage a disaster.

Giuseppina is on the brink of tears. Ignazio looks waxen and is sweating. She holds him to her bosom and brushes his hair off his face. She unbuttons his collar and pulls off his tie.

What's happening to him? He can't die, he's always been here, he's—

"Ignazio!" she calls, tears in her voice. "My Ignazio!"

She is sobbing now.

She feels a shudder in her brother-in-law's hand.

Ignazio opens his eyes and meets hers. His fingers open and touch her cheek.

For an instant, Giuseppina sees everything in him. What and how much, and how, and for how long. She realizes how wretched she is going to be from this moment on, and how fortunate she has been without knowing it.

Vincenzo rushes into the room. "Uncle!" He throws himself on the floor, next to Ignazio. "Uncle, what's wrong?"

He puts his hands on Ignazio's chest while his mother keeps holding his uncle tight against her and rocking. He practically snatches him out of her arms. "Uncle! *No!*"

Again he yells no, and again he calls him. He can't die like this, not him. How will he manage on his own?

Ignazio seems to look at Vincenzo for a moment. He even has a faint smile.

That is when his heart gives way.

Ignazio Messina is the one who informs the registrar of the death of Ignazio Florio. He also asks Serretta, the notary, to come to Via dei Materassai the day after the funeral to read out the will.

Wearing a mourning tie, Vincenzo waits in the drawing room, crammed with Bagnara folk and staff. In a corner, dressed in black, stands Giuseppina. She seems suddenly aged. She is grieving, and the light has gone out of her eyes. She who was always so hard, such a fighter. For the past two days she has been going into her brother-in-law's bedroom, placing a hand on his bed, sighing bitterly, then leaving. Back and forth.

When Serretta arrives, relatives and employees sit around the table. Everybody except for Vincenzo, who continues to stand by the window and look out. He has his arms crossed over his chest and seems impassive.

The May light is flooding over the walls and spreading over the Flemish tapestries purchased years earlier from captains who traded with the East, and over the ebony and walnut furniture. Vincenzo now realizes everything was picked out by Ignazio.

Thanks to him, in thirty years, everything has changed: he turned their *putìa* into an enterprise and made them into what they are.

The Florios of Palermo.

And he made a man out of Vincenzo.

The notary reads out figures, ownership shares, legacies and bequests to his nephews in Bagnara, a sum of money for Mattia and her children.

Vincenzo has not stirred.

"Don Vincenzo, did you hear what I said?"

Don Vincenzo. All eyes are on him. He is the head of the family now.

Serretta, the notary, is waiting.

"Yes," Vincenzo replies.

He knows what is in his uncle's will. They drafted two similar documents a few years ago, each nominating the other as his heir. But Ignazio recently added another clause. It is a sign, a message. When the notary reads out the codicil, Vincenzo can almost feel Ignazio's steady, gentle presence right there, next to him.

"That the business should continue to operate under the name of Ignazio and Vincenzo Florio."

He signs his acceptance of the inheritance without a word. He shakes the notary's hand. He kisses his weeping mother on the forehead. He goes to Ignazio Messina. "Please take care of the paperwork. I'll see you later in the store."

He goes out.

His feet know where they are going.

His head down, he walks decisively, dodging passersby. He reaches La Cala and goes to the far end of the pier.

He sits on the ground, just as he did so many years ago, when his father died.

He then said to his uncle Ignazio, "We are alone now." *I am alone now*, he thinks.

A tear, just one tear, runs down his cheek.

PART FOUR

Sulfur

April 1830 to February 1837

Addisiari e 'un aviri è pena di muriri.

To desire and not have is sure grief.

—SICILIAN PROVERB

In 1830, twenty-year-old Ferdinand II becomes king of the Two Sicilies, and obviously favors economic and social revival. A political and tax overview is launched and, above all, infrastructures are substantially boosted. The Bourbon reign becomes a time when technology and science are widely exploited: engineering is boosted, as is the creation of railways and the building of military ships with metal hulls. Italy's first pension system is set up, and the first network of electrical street lighting is started. Moreover, there is a drive toward improving the exploitation of solfataras, and this leads to an open conflict with the British and the French, who are determined to purchase sulfur below market prices.

Between 1830 and 1831, revolutionary movements break out in France (with the accession to the throne of Louis-Philippe d'Orléans, a constitutional monarch) and in Belgium (which obtains its independence). In July 1831, in Marseille, Giuseppe Mazzini founds Young Italy, which supports "independence from foreigners," "national unity," and the constitution of the republic; however, the revolutionary movements organized by Mazzini's supporters in 1833 and 1834 all end in bloodshed.

SULFUR. In Sicilian, *u' sùrfaru.*

The devil's gold.

Rocks that light a fire.

The accursed wealth of merchants.

The treasure landowners suddenly found under their feet after cursing it for centuries; its presence made the soil barren and not even suitable for pasture because of the fumes.

But now there are winding corridors being dug underground. Children and men line up like ants and surface with basketfuls of yellow stone that deform their backs.

The clods are weighed and put in sacks, ready to be sold.

Once loaded, the sulfur travels from Sicily to the rest of Europe: to France and especially Britain, which is guaranteed the lion's share of the production; but there are other destinations, too, including northern Italy.

The sulfur is burned in a lead room and, through heat and steam, is turned into oil of vitriol, precious sulfuric acid, used for manufacturing dyes and useful in the transformation processes in the chemical factories that are sprouting all over Europe.

The devil's gold makes you rich. It creates well-being and jobs.

Everywhere. Except in Sicily.

But that is something Sicilians do not realize.

At least, not all of them.

~

The sun has only just risen. It brings the warm, peaceful light that's typical of a spring morning, like on this day in April 1830.

In Via dei Materassai, activity is already under way.

Giuseppina takes a *tricotto* cookie and dunks it in milk. There are crumbs floating. "Will you be home for lunch, son?"

Vincenzo does not reply. Stern, wearing a dark frock coat and highly polished boots, he is absorbed in a note the messenger has just brought him.

"Did you hear what I said?"

He makes a sign for her to be quiet. Then he suddenly screws up the piece of paper and throws it away. "Damn it!"

"What is it?" Giuseppina goes to him. "What's wrong?"

"Nothing. Never mind."

Olimpia picks this moment to come into the dining room. "Have you finished? Can I take the cups away?" she asks in a singsong tone. Her smile wanes when she notices that the master is tense and the mistress is worried, so she picks up the crockery and vanishes without a sound.

Giuseppina insists. "What happened?" Her anxious voice goes after Vincenzo. Her black dress rustles, like sand on the floor.

"Nothing, I said." He takes his coat and gives her a kiss.

"But—"

"Don't worry and mind your own business."

The woman stays behind, clutching her chest. Vincenzo, her own flesh and blood, has not belonged to her for a long time. Nothing and nobody can enter his world made of money, men, and goods.

The only person who cared for her died almost two years ago. She is old now.

Slowly, her heart heavy, she sits back down.

Vincenzo opens the store, just as his uncle used to. A few minutes later, the workers arrive; then Ignazio Messina comes in, having already been to La Cala to get the latest news.

Vincenzo's greeting to everybody is more like a grunt. He calls his secretary, who looks at him for a moment and immediately realizes something is wrong. "What is it, Don Vincenzo?"

He sits at the desk that used to belong to his uncle Ignazio. "The *Anna* is lost."

"Holy Mother of God!" The secretary slaps his forehead. "What do you mean? What happened?"

"Pirates. She had only left Brazil three days earlier. They probably followed her from the coast and attacked as soon as she was en route for Europe."

"Good God!" Messina exclaims. "And now these cowards will ask for a ransom. Any dead? Was anyone hurt?"

"Apparently not, at least that's what this morning's dispatch says." Vincenzo slumps in his chair. "Bastards, that's what they are. It was a European ship without an escort, which had never been that far, so they noticed it right away."

"Yes, that's probably what happened . . . We really didn't need this abduction. It will cause a big loss. But let's look on the bright side. You were right to employ Captain Miloro, he knows what he's doing and is worth holding on to." The secretary leans on his elbows on the desk. "We've gotten all the way to Brazil without knowing the route of the American clippers and without asking for the British to mediate. This is a great achievement. You can shed tears with just one eye, Don Vincenzo."

"Miloro knows all the winds and streams, and he's studied. He's no jumped-up ship boy." He drums his fingers on the table, where a map of the Atlantic is spread out. "I'm not worried about the cargo: it's a big loss but it's insured. What's important is that we now know we can buy coffee and sugar from the colonies without needing to go through the British or the French. This means our own goods, like oil and wine, can also get to America." Vincenzo's smile is embittered, like a grimace. Even though it has turned out like this, the way is now open. He can establish trade relations with the Americans, and that's not all. He can reach America with his ships and his goods, like Ben Ingham has been doing for a long time now. The Englishman already has holdings in the railways that go from the east coast to the west coast of the United States.

Messina instinctively glances toward the corridor, outside, where Palermo is waiting for news that will feed chatter and gossip. "Except that when people find out . . ."

Vincenzo stands up. He strokes his uncle's ring, the one that belonged to Ignazio's mother, and which he removed when his uncle was already in his coffin. He imagines how pleased his uncle would be with the result, how he would look at him, concealing enthusiasm under a layer of dispassion.

"When people find out, fools will be delighted because we've lost a cargo. The cleverer ones will follow our example." He heads for the exit. "Later on, go and make the report to the insurance company. But now come with me."

"Where?" The secretary has barely the time to pick up the folder and documents and run after him down the corridor. Sometimes, he simply cannot keep up with this man.

"To the *tonnara*."

The Ignazio and Vincenzo Florio Company is extremely wealthy for a Palermo business. It trades in spices and colonial goods, has holdings in an insurance company formed by Palermo and foreign merchants, and shares in various steamers and cargo ships. It manages the *tonnare* of San Nicolò l'Arena and Vergine Maria, and, more recently, has taken over that of Isola delle Femmine: investments that have become profitable after lean years.

For Vincenzo, however, "the *tonnara*" is the plant in Arenella. The one and only true passion of Ignazio, who chose to keep renting it even when tuna fishing was in severe crisis.

"It's a matter of love," his uncle would say.

And he, too, has fallen in love with the place without knowing it, and wants it the way you yearn for a woman's body. Like the kind of love that grows inside you until it becomes impossible to stifle it, one that lasts a lifetime.

Ignazio Messina gets out of the carriage, followed by Vincenzo. The secretary leans on a stick and Vincenzo overtakes him, taking quick strides. He walks past the *marfaraggio*, the actual plant, painted the same black as fishing boats.

He reaches the *trizzana*, the dockyard where boats are kept, and where there's hard work going on. Inside, there are the voices of men and the dry smell of the sea and algae. The sailors are getting ready to drop the *tonnara* into the sea.

"Don Florio!" A barefooted worker comes to meet them. "I have a message from His Lordship. He's waiting for you at the slide, where the tent is."

"Thank you." Vincenzo gestures at Ignazio Messina to follow him.

"The baron?" he asks, perplexed.

"Yes, Mercurio Nasca di Montemaggiore." Vincenzo walks past a group of men mending the nets to catch the tuna just as they arrive into the Mediterranean in order to mate. "He's one of the *tonnara* shareholders, together with the Monastery of San Martino delle Scale."

"Yes, I know he's one of the owners . . . But how come he's summoned you to this place? I mean, it's odd that an aristocrat should stoop to ask for a meeting in a *tonnara*."

They go past workers in the process of caulking the boats. Vincenzo, who is more than a span taller than Messina, looks over his shoulder. There's a smell of pitch and tar in the air. "Well, what do you suppose a baron might want from a trader like me?"

"Only one thing."

"Exactly." Vincenzo cocks his head toward his secretary. "Nasca di Montemaggiore sent me a note a few days ago, requesting a meeting. And to act with discretion."

"Oh. So the rumors about him—"

"Are true. He's in dire straits. I discounted some of his promissory notes, and he found out about it. That's why he wants to talk to me: I think he's hoping that one of us common mortals will lend him money."

There's a white tent glowing against the blue of the sea, down the cobble-and-mortar slide.

The baron is sitting at a camp table. He is a middle-aged man in rather threadbare clothes that speak of a taste linked to the past: a shirt with lace trimmings and a tailcoat with embroidered edges. Behind him stands a servant in livery; next to him, a distinguished-looking man, possibly his factotum.

Around them lie shreds of netting and anchors left to rust.

"Signor Florio." His tone is that of a monarch granting an audience, and he proffers his hand to receive the homage of the common man. Vincenzo takes it and gives it a mighty squeeze. The aristocrat pulls it away and clenches it into a fist over his stomach.

Then, not waiting to be invited, Vincenzo sits down and says to the servant, "A chair for my secretary, please."

The man obeys.

The baron's forehead is beaded in sweat, although it's only a warm April day. "So . . ." he says, then stops.

Vincenzo is impassive. "So."

The factotum whispers something into the baron's ear, and the latter nods with evident relief and gestures at him to continue. "His Lordship wishes to ask for your cooperation." He aspirates his consonants, the way people from inland Sicily do. "The baron has had to meet unexpected expenses because of unfavorable economic circumstances, and in addition do some maintenance on the Palace of Montemaggiore. His *fondaco* situation is especially delicate at the moment and he is experiencing a temporary cash crisis—"

"In other words, he's run out of money." Vincenzo addresses the baron directly, while the nobleman keeps his eyes on the sea. "I understand perfectly well. My business as an entrepreneur also exposes me to great risks. You have my full sympathy, signore."

The baron clears his throat. A few words trickle out. "I'll be frank with you, Signor Florio: I need a loan. That's right. This is why I've asked for a preliminary meeting in this place. It did not seem proper to discuss a business deal at my palace."

Vincenzo does not reply.

The silence becomes like salt. Dry and bitter.

"How much?" Messina asks.

The factotum hesitates. "Eight hundred *oncie* at least. His Lordship is willing to offer his share of the *tonnara* as guarantee." He takes some documents from a leather case and hands them to Ignazio Messina, who begins to read them.

"You must give us a few days to estimate the amount of the loan and the guarantees he offers," Messina says once he has finished.

The baron's voice takes on a tone of fear and shame. "I—I have very large expenses and—I'm afraid I have to ask you to reach a decision by tomorrow."

"Tomorrow?" Vincenzo's surprise seems genuine. "I didn't realize you were in this much trouble." He turns to Messina, but the secretary shakes his head, indicating the papers.

It's not enough time.

"You see? Even my secretary says it's not possible. A week is the minimum we need to estimate your guarantees." He does not wait for a sign of discharge and stands up. "You'll know my answer in a week. Good day, gentlemen."

The baron reaches out to him. "Wait." He grabs the factotum by the sleeve and tugs at it. He is practically shouting. "No! For the love of God! It'll be too late by then. Tell him!"

The factotum tries to calm him down while Messina, disconcerted, picks up the documents, gives a vague bow, and walks away without a word.

He catches up with Vincenzo outside the carriage. He chooses not to see the ghost of feeling in his eyes. "But, Don Vincenzo, don't you think—don't you think you might have been a little—" he pants.

"No. If he wants this money then he'll do whatever it takes to have it, and he will have it, but on my terms."

"As a guarantee against the sum, you provide land and sea equipment, the accommodation ladder, the anchors, the body, the *bottacci*, the sea area opposite, and the *tonnara* warehouses . . ."

Michele Tamajo, the notary, reads in a monotonous voice, as though chanting at the deaths registry.

Wearing a dark suit, Vincenzo is lost in a secret thought. He ignores the buzzing fly trapped inside the room, the rustling of the document pages, and the creaking of the chairs.

At an appropriate distance, Baron Mercurio Nasca di Montemaggiore is staring at him with hatred. His cheeks are flushed and his eyelids heavy. If looks could kill, Vincenzo Florio would already have died in great pain.

"And that is all." The notary turns to the baron. "Are you sure you wish to sign this?"

The baron indicates Vincenzo. "This loan shark doesn't give me a choice!" His voice is full of resentment.

Only then does Vincenzo seem to notice him. "Me, a loan shark? Baron, I'm not a charity."

"You are taking advantage of my destitution!" He twists his mouth. "You are forcing me to sell."

"No, signore. Don't lie. I asked for a week to draw up an estimate of your guarantees, and just as well I did because I discovered that the plant equipment was in terrible condition. Consequently, I proposed to buy your share of the *tonnara* to help you out. You responded only by asking for the payment to be in cash to silence your creditors. You got it. And now you have the audacity to say that I didn't give you a choice?"

"You don't have noble blood, and it shows! You're a nasty individual with no respect." His voice becomes a hiss. "*Vous êtes un parvenu insolent!*"

Vincenzo, who has just picked up the quill to sign the contract, freezes. Never mind that so many years have passed or that it should be in French instead of dialect. The insult still—always—stings. "You can pull out if you wish," he mutters icily.

The silence starts weighing heavily on the room, broken only by the buzzing fly. A drop of ink falls on the paper.

Everybody—and the notary is no exception—knows that the baron is ruined. But he also knows that the baron is a man of rare pride. "It is up to you, Baron," he then says to save appearances. "What do you choose to do?"

The temptation is strong. The baron is probably thinking that he can perhaps hold out for a little longer, sell the last of his wife's jewelry or else give up his share of the *tonnara* to the monks of San Martino delle Scale, who already own part of the building. But he knows only too well that the monks hold their purse strings very tight and that his wife's jewelry is little more than junk. He stifles a humiliated sob. "For God's sake, sign. Sign, then get out of my sight."

Vincenzo signs with a flourish below the ink blotch. He gets out of Ignazio Messina's and the baron's factotum's way, so they take care of the paperwork, and withdraws to the other side of the room, arms crossed, his knitted eyebrows making him look like a bird of prey.

At the end, Messina comes up to him. "You could have stayed in the office. I have the power of attorney. There was no need for you to witness this scene."

But Vincenzo keeps staring at Nasca di Montemaggiore. "In future, perhaps. But not today." He holds out his hand. "Give me the bag."

"But—" Messina receives a look that brooks no contradiction.

Vincenzo approaches the baron, who is slumped on the chair, and drops the bag in his lap. He does not have the time to take it, and the coins fall on the floor and scatter all over the rug. Vincenzo Florio leaves the room as Baron Nasca di Montemaggiore is on his knees, picking the money off the floor.

~

"Gently, gently . . . What are you doing, for heaven's sake? Can't you be careful with other people's possessions?"

Giuseppina is getting worked up as she guides the porters along the hallways of her new home.

A large apartment with an upper floor. Still in Via dei Materassai, but at number 53.

Vincenzo bought it from Giuseppe Calabrese, a neighbor of the store. Actually, to be precise, it was an acceptance in lieu of a debt Calabrese was not able to honor in time. Business is business and honor has nothing to do with it.

It is actually two apartments he has joined together by knocking down a few walls. If you look out from the roof, you can see La Cala all the way to the horizon and, at the back, the city and the mountains. And since he likes the view, he will also have a small terrace built, for spending summer afternoons.

Giuseppina lets herself drop on the chair and just points at the room where the furniture should go. The maids will sweep the floors and tidy up later.

Vincenzo appears in the doorway. "So, do you like it, Mamma?"

"Of course I do. It's large . . . and there's so much light."

Her thought is a thief that runs to the hovel in Piano San Giacomo, then to the other place, in Via dei Materassai, where Ignazio died. Rented apartments, suitable for working people.

"It's a beautiful apartment." Giuseppina looks around and nods. Her son has had it refurbished; he has changed the door and window frames, and painted the walls and ceilings with patterns of flowers and blue skies. There is even running water and a carriage house. "Of course, the air here isn't like in Bagnara but—"

"Still?" Her son rolls his eyes. "I wish you'd stop going on about the village. This is our home. No more rent or cottages in Calabria. From now on, this is where we live."

Once again, Giuseppina is forced to lower her head. She has never had the right to have a say on where she lives. Far from it.

When she asked if they could afford such a luxurious apartment, Vincenzo looked up from his papers with a calmness that was as placid as it was annoying. "When did you start telling me how to spend my money, Mamma?" he asked. "Of course we can afford it. We're not storekeepers anymore. Only yesterday we passed the San Rosalia cargo through customs and we'd barely unloaded the goods when the auction for the shipment of cotton began." Over the years, Vincenzo's laugh has become raspy. He's now thirty-three. "We need a home that's worthy of us. You'll never want for anything as long as I'm here."

A worker calls Vincenzo, and he leaves.

Giuseppina stands up again and looks through one of the windows: she can see a large stretch of Via dei Materassai and a part of Piano San Giacomo.

They certainly have come a long way.

Even her rancor had dissolved over the years, until it vanished with Ignazio's death.

She has nothing left but herself and her memories. Her son—her flesh and blood and reason for living—is an island, the same as she has been for such a long time. And now she must be brave because there's something causing her anxiety and stopping her from sleeping at night. At fifty-four she feels old and knows that Vincenzo cannot be left alone. Every man needs a woman for company, to keep his bed warm and take care of him, and to put up with him when he's in a bad mood. To give him children, heirs, because that's something Casa Florio needs now.

What Ignazio and Vincenzo have built cannot be left at the mercy of the wind and the rain. It's an heirloom to be passed on and safeguarded, and for that you need good blood.

They need a woman brought up like a lady. Her son must start a family. Giuseppina clenches her teeth as she thinks this. She must talk to him about it.

And she will have to step aside. Soon.

What is left to her is the knowledge that she's alone—and something else that's more bitter, more subtle, and more painful: that she turned down the love of her life.

That evening, mother and son sit opposite each other, alone, like they used to do in the old house. Light from a lamp is bathing the tablecloth, the crockery, and their hands. Olimpia, too old—and too common—to serve in Casa Florio, has been replaced by a girl with a freckled face and her mother, who cooks and does the heavy work.

Giuseppina starts cautiously. "I wanted to speak to you, Vincenzo."

He looks up from his plate. The furrow between his brows grows deeper. "Problems?"

"No, none. But there could be, so it's better to prevent them ahead of time." She feels a worm eating into her flesh but she must be brave. It's about something that goes beyond her life, so it must be faced. "You're over thirty." She pauses. "You must think about the future, and not just yours."

Vincenzo puts his spoon down. "Are you talking about a wife?" he asks without looking up.

Giuseppina takes a deep breath. "Yes." A woman who will share this house with her, sit at the same table, and sleep in her son's bed . . .

It will not be easy.

Vincenzo picks up his wineglass and takes a sip. The memory of Isabella Pillitteri's neck is a flash. "You know, there was a time when I was hoping to hear you say this. But that moment's gone." His onyx eyes stare into his mother's brown ones. But it's just for a moment. He gets up and kisses her. "You take care of it. Find me a suitable bride to your liking, from a good family and with an adequate dowry. Then let me know." Before walking through the door, he adds, "Don't wait up for me. I have an appointment."

"With whom?"

"You'll see. It's a surprise."

There are a few men on the steps of San Giovanni dei Napoletani. They are mainly merchants of Calabrian and Neapolitan origin, with their children. They share origins, profession, and the place where they live. Prayer is an excuse, and the aim is to look one another in the face, talk about work, and gossip.

There's no politeness in their glances. Vespers appears not to have had any effect on them.

The sacristan mutters, "These people clearly have time to waste," and shuts the church door, bequeathing the echo of a thud.

Vincenzo is deeply absorbed in conversation with a man who has a square jaw and a thick Calabrian accent. They appear to be intimate, and that attracts the curiosity of the other merchants. Unlike Uncle Ignazio—*recamatierna*—who was always affable, Vincenzo Florio has a difficult character. He keeps the world at arm's length.

But, damn it—they all think—*he's a shrewd one.*

Vincenzo hears their voices: background noise, echoes of envy mixed with admiration. His attention is focused on the man in front of him. "As you can see, there are Bagnara folk and Neapolitans galore trading on the coast. But I'm not interested in them. I look farther."

The other man, shorter and stockier, looks around. "You mentioned it in one of your letters. So what did you . . ."

An observant eye would notice that the two men have similar traits. A high forehead, large, powerful hands, and a dark coloring. However, the cut of the new man's clothes and his slightly unsure body language suggest that he is not as well off as Vincenzo Florio.

Vincenzo takes him by the elbow and leads him to Palazzo Steri. "This is the Customs House," he explains. "But it hasn't always been that. It was originally a nobleman's palace, then it became a courthouse, then a prison for heretics, murderers, and thieves." He stops. The palace, a black, stone shadow, weighs over them. "I don't want a Cain in my house. Do you still resent me for what happened when we were children?"

"Perhaps, in the past," the other man replies sincerely. "What I remember about that time is my mother's despair, the hunger, and the humiliation of having to ask relatives for money. We sold the house and moved to Marsala . . . I was angry with your father and your uncle, yes, and partly because everybody was telling us how well you were doing."

"But then you started receiving small sums of money, right?" Vincenzo drops his voice. "It was Uncle Ignazio who sent them without telling anyone. I found the remittances in the books from years ago. I still remember when you and Aunt Mattia came to Palermo. My father was dying. It felt strange to find out that I had a family. I often thought, afterward, about what it would have been like if we'd been closer. But that's not how things turned out . . ."

The other man nods. He understands. "My mother loved you all. She always thought about you and always said a prayer for your father and your uncle."

A feeling rises in Vincenzo and gets caught between his stomach and his throat. He pushes it away. "I am not Uncle Ignazio, remember that. I'm a man who doesn't want to stop at what he has."

"So am I."

In these words and determined tone, Vincenzo finds what he was looking for.

"Come to Via dei Materassai tomorrow. I'll introduce you to Ignazio Messina; he'll show you everything. He is elderly, experienced, and you'll need to be by his side." He puts out his hand. "Then come to the house. My mother doesn't know anything yet but she will be happy to see Mattia's son."

Raffaele Barbaro, the son of Paolo Barbaro and Mattia Florio, finally smiles.

~

The narrow street is calm and quiet even though it's near the city walls and the Customs House. Via della Zecca Regia is made up of narrow houses that partly look out on Via dell'Alloro: peaceful houses for small storekeepers. No connection with the surrounding aristocrat palaces.

In the study of the second-floor apartment, darkness is superseding the light of the setting sun. Fall 1832 is coming in large strides, shortening the days and bringing gusts of *tramontana* wind.

Four men.

"Imagine the desert in black Africa. Arid, desolate, hopeless. There is the odd oasis, with a water hole and two crooked palm trees. It's exactly the same thing here: whenever you find an enterprise, it feels like a miracle."

Vincenzo opens his left hand and counts on his fingers: "There are a few cotton mills, a couple of harquebus factories, and a brass and an iron one. The others are just *putìe*, workshops with a master builder and fifteen workers or so, if they're lucky. Now, my business, Casa Florio, has no factories: it trades. We bring together manufacturers and buyers, either in our own name or on behalf of third parties."

Across the desk, Tommaso Portalupi, a Milan trader arrived in Palermo just a few months ago, listens attentively. The hair on his temples is thinning; he has hazel eyes and a prominent nose, marred by dark veins. Next to him sits Giovanni, his much younger mirror image.

Portalupi puts his elbows on the desk. "I am also a middleman, Signor Florio, and the reason I've come to you is because I specifically asked around for the best supplier in Palermo. My job is to find raw materials to then be processed in Lombardy. I'm interested in wine, oil, tuna in brine, sumac, and sulfur. I don't want to go to British merchants, because they would bring in their own production, and nor am I interested in the low-quality produce some have tried to palm off on me. Which of these goods would you be able to obtain for us and on what terms?"

Vincenzo exchanges a glance with Raffaele, sitting next to him. He leans back against the chair. "Ask away. I can get you everything that is produced in Sicily. Everything."

They are interrupted by the tinkling of glass against metal. The door opens. "May I come in?"

A young woman in a brown dress walks in, carrying a plate of biscuits. A delicate aroma of vanilla spreads across the room. "Mamma told me to bring these in. They're straight out of the oven." She takes a step back and looks at Vincenzo.

Vincenzo, who was accepting a glass of liqueur from Giovanni, turns. He sees her.

She must be one of Portalupi's relatives, he thinks. Perhaps his niece or his daughter. She has the same coloring, the same intonation, and even the same prominent nose. She moves in an understated way, holding back. He does not often fall prey to feminine charm, and yet this girl makes an impression on him: a straight back and a gentle face.

Palermo women do not have that clear, fearless look.

Tommaso Portalupi gives her a pat. "Thank you, sweetheart. Now go."

He waits for the door to be closed before he resumes. "Sulfur, Signor Florio. Wine and sulfur."

Vincenzo crosses his hands on his lap. "Of course. How much sulfur and by when?"

That evening, Vincenzo notices that his mother is particularly attentive. She serves him personally at dinner, pats him, and inquires about his work.

He eyes her with suspicion.

He's tired. He has removed his jacket and tie; his waistcoat is unbuttoned, his hair tousled. After a hectic day he can finally be himself.

Afterward, Giuseppina pushes her plate away. "Listen, son. I've found a young woman who may fit our requirements." Her use of *our* does not escape Vincenzo's notice. It's as though his mother, too, is going to be married. But he needs neither a companion nor a housekeeper: he just wants a woman who will give him strong, healthy heirs. Giuseppina will take care of the rest, as usual. "Yes, Mamma."

"It's a young woman from a good family, brought up by nuns: she's responsible and respectful. It was they who brought her to my attention."

Vincenzo presses his face against his closed fists. "Then what are you worried about? Because I can see you're worried."

Her nervous fingers rub the tablecloth. "Her family is distantly related to the prince of Torrebruna. It would be a prestigious match. They have intimated that they would be happy for you to marry her. Of course, there's the problem of the dowry: they don't have much besides their title, a warehouse near Enna, and a house here in the city." Giuseppina is choosing her words carefully.

Vincenzo's sense of alarm grows. "Nothing that can't be solved. But—?" Because he can feel a *but* hanging between them.

"They state a condition. They would like you to stop running the business directly yourself, to hire a steward and not manage the *aromateria* anymore. They don't consider it decorous given their title." Giuseppina falls silent and waits for a sign or a word.

Vincenzo does not move a muscle. Then he covers his face with his hands. He speaks softly, as though not fully believing what he has just heard. "You would like me to abandon my work . . . for a woman?"

"A woman? She's a girl." She tries to minimize the situation. "You marry her to start with, then we'll see. Once you've got a firm foot in the house there's nothing they can do. You'll be the one holding the purse strings."

But Vincenzo throws his head back, laughs uproariously, and slams his fist on the table. "Now? Now you say this to me?" The coarse bitterness in his voice alarms Giuseppina. "Do you remember what happened when I wasn't even twenty?" He looks up and his eyes are lava rocks. "Do you remember Isabella Pillitteri? Do you remember when you told me I had to forget about her because she was penniless? You do remember, don't you?"

Giuseppina expected everything but this. She leaps to her feet. "What's she got to do with this? That was the daughter and sister of debauchees who were after money."

"And what do you think these people want?" He follows his mother, who has started clearing the table. "Not only are they after my wealth but they're also trying to dictate to me how to live my life!"

"Nobody can dictate anything to you. She's a pious soul, a little girl attached to nuns' petticoats. She'll obey you whatever you say: you're the man of the house and you're in charge. You're the one with the money."

Vincenzo points a finger at her. "My answer is no—to them and to you. I asked you to find me a wife, not to marry me into a family of wretches who feel rich just because they have a title, and who even go stating conditions."

Giuseppina is furious. She thought it was a done deal, and now . . . She abandons the dishes on the table and faces him, hands on her hips. "You can't forgive me for what happened fifteen years ago even though I opened your eyes? You should thank me but no, it's all my fault. And what did I do? You saw how her mother treated you. Yes, son. I know all about it. People told me about that shameful scene in the middle of the street. The truth is you're as vindictive and heartless as your father. It's no use. There are things that you Florios have in your blood." She twists her mouth in a grimace. "You carry on like this and you'll end up alone as a dog."

Vincenzo has to restrain himself from smashing something. Giuseppina sees it in his face and takes a step back but he grabs her by the arms and talks into her face. "Better to be a mangy dog than spend your life going after a woman who doesn't want you."

He lets go of her. She staggers and clutches the chair.

She looks at Vincenzo and does not recognize him anymore. She blinks and fights back her tears. She stays like this even after he has left the room. Never has she wished for Ignazio to be at her side so much as now.

Her awareness of having been cruel to him bites at her rib cage.

She thought she would make her husband's life unbearable, that the hatred she harbored for the Florios would keep her away from them. Moreover, she thought she had an ally in her son. Instead, tonight she has discovered that the mother's milk laced with hatred she fed him has resulted in poison. Hatred has been etched into him.

Handshakes.

The clinking of glasses.

The maid serves liqueurs and cookies.

"Your sulfur is the most competitively priced we've found on the market, in terms of value for money." Giovanni Portalupi is having an animated conversation with Vincenzo. He drums his fingers on the contract. "I heard you own a quarry."

"I've taken over one of Baron Morillo's mines." Vincenzo takes a sip of port. He likes to speak with this straight-talking man. "*His Grace*, the baron, doesn't like to soil his hands with work but he needs the rent money, so . . ."

Giovanni shrugs. "*Pecunia non olet*, the Romans used to say. A maxim that's particularly appropriate to sulfur."

They laugh.

He's about to continue when a middle-aged woman comes in, walks up to Portalupi, and whispers in his ear. She has strong features and a warm expression, a strange blend of strength and gentleness.

"Mamma," Giovanni says, "allow me to introduce Don Vincenzo Florio. We've just signed a contract for sulfur supplies. This is my mother, Antonia."

Vincenzo greets her formally. "Signora." Then his eyes shift slightly to where he has seen the movement of a shadow. He indicates discreetly. "And who is she?"

At first, Giovanni does not appear to understand, then sees his sister standing in the doorway. Nobody pays attention to her, usually. "Oh, that's Giulia."

The young woman turns when she hears her name. Accustomed to a house overrun by businessmen talking about goods and calculations, she soon learned to keep her place.

"Yes, you. Come here." He reaches out with a hand. She joins him. "My elder sister, Giulia." Giovanni cocks his head. "This is Don Vincenzo Florio."

Vincenzo glances at one, then the other. "Really? I would never have thought you were older."

"Just by two years. Not enough to mother him but sufficient to hate him for being a boy and younger."

Giovanni laughs. "It's only that I'm our mother's favorite."

"I have no preferences." Antonia takes her daughter under the arm and gently leads her away from the two men. "Giulia has always been stubborn, and her brother a daredevil. It wasn't easy raising two children like that."

Vincenzo's eyes linger on Giulia. "Yes, but it must have been fun."

The young woman studies her fingertips for a moment. "We've been happy, and that's all I need." She lifts her head and gives him a velvety look. "Memories of a happy childhood are the best gift parents can give their offspring."

After they leave the room, Giulia feels a bittersweet sense of relief. She looks back while her mother precedes her to the kitchen.

"This Florio is an odd sort of man, don't you think?" Antonia says. "So young and already so wealthy. Your father mentioned he has a reputation as something of a rebel. They say he made a fortune buying land from impoverished aristocrats at reduced prices. There's even a rumor that he lends money at exorbitant interest."

"*Mon père* wouldn't do business with a bad man, surely."

"Business is a man's department, my girl. It follows rules we couldn't possibly understand—" A violent coughing fit interrupts her, forcing her to sit down. Winter—although not harsh in Sicily—is the hardest season for those who, like Antonia, suffer from chest complaints.

Giulia is immediately by her side. "Are you unwell?"

Her father rushes in from the parlor, breathless. "Antonia . . ."

She rubs her chest and reassures him. "I'm all right." She strokes her husband's face. "I've been better since we've been in Palermo. The physician was right: the mild climate is beneficial."

Tommaso Portalupi sighs. "I've asked Don Vincenzo to stay for dinner." His voice drops to a whisper. "He has many business contacts, he's wealthy and well known in the city. We need his goodwill. But if you're not feeling well . . ."

Giulia puts a hand on his arm. "I'll take care of everything with Antonietta's help. She hasn't left yet, has she?"

Her father's face expresses regret. "I'm afraid so. You'll have to do everything by yourself." He kisses her on the forehead. "I know you're capable of miracles, so perform one."

Giulia sighs. When will she learn to keep quiet? She has always done her best to be kind to everybody, only her kindness is all too often a nuisance for her.

Her mother has stopped coughing and clings to her daughter's arm in order to stand up. The two women go to the kitchen. Antonia lets herself sink into a chair and sighs.

Giulia puts on an apron and opens the cupboard. What can she make for a dinner worthy of their guest?

What would he like? Something strong-tasting, a new flavor? But what?

She moves swiftly, searching among the jars and bowls in the pantry. She notices the pan with last night's stew.

Her hands stop.

There. Stew, bread crumbs, eggs: there are some. Spices . . . yes. White cabbage leaves instead of savoy . . . Never mind. There's no liver mortadella either but you can't find it here in Palermo, people don't even know what it is. I'll use thinly sliced salami . . .

Antonia watches her preparing meatballs. Her Giulia is skillful. She feels a vague sense of guilt toward her daughter, past twenty and still without a family of her own. Moreover, over the past year, her own chest problems have necessitated constant treatment and attention.

Leaving Milan, economic security, and their nice house near the Navigli has been difficult for everyone. And all because of her. Her consumption had reached a stage where she could no longer tolerate the cold and the fog. She needed light and sunshine in order to survive.

Antonia feels guilty because she forced the entire family to turn their lives upside down and move to this city; beautiful, yes, but also very difficult, where poverty lives side by side with aristocratic pomp worthy of a European court. She, too, misses Milan, its calm atmosphere, its streets full of stores and the solemnity of large buildings in the city center. She misses the smells and flavors, and even the morning mist that blurs the edges of the landscape and muffles the sounds. She was accustomed to a more sober beauty with soft edges, not the opulent, vulgar, and excessive life of Palermo.

However, that's the way things turned out, and her children had to adapt. Naturally, while Giovanni works with his father, Giulia has to stay at home with her and has little opportunity for entertainment. But then, isn't that what happens to girls who don't marry? Isn't it their duty to look after their aging parents?

Besides, business has a little trouble getting started in Palermo: few contacts and much suspicion. It's a closed shop, in the hands of those who know this market well. This is why her husband has invited that man to dinner.

During the meal, Florio turns out to be a pleasant though not very talkative guest. He speaks chiefly about business with Tommaso and Giovanni. Then he suddenly addresses Giulia. "So you did the cooking?"

The young woman is taken aback by such a direct question. "Yes. I hope you like it . . ."

"It's all very good. It can't have been easy to organize a dinner at such short notice. Other women would have been overwhelmed . . ." He laughs softly. "My mother, for instance. Thank goodness we have a cook for these tasks."

Giulia looks down and thanks him with a smile.

Giulia continues to smile. But it is a different smile, one that dissolves in anxiety.

Don Florio watched her the entire evening. Quick, stolen glances, never crossing the line of respect but treading at the very edge of it.

She has always lived in a world of men, and learned ever since she was an adolescent to keep her father's acquaintances and her brother's friends at a distance.

And yet now she's confused, because nobody has ever looked at her this way.

She tosses and turns in her bed.

On the other side of the wall, beyond Giovanni's bedroom, Antonia Portalupi is also struggling to sleep.

She thinks about their guest: his behavior was gentlemanly, his manner polite, and yet he has made her feel uneasy. Even now, suspended between sleep and wakefulness, she can't work out what it is that troubles her about this man. She has shared her anxieties with her husband, but Tommaso merely shrugged his shoulders in return.

"There's nothing strange about it. After all, Giulia is quite pretty, so it's natural that a man should give her a second look. If he starts courting her, then so much the better for us: thanks to her, we could have better supplies. Besides, Giulia knows she has to look after you."

The sea air is a warm breath that filters into the alleys. It advances in slow waves, slipping into the houses through the gaps in the door frames.

It's dawn but Vincenzo is already at work in Via dei Materassai. He's in his office. The room is getting too small: he is going to have to rent an apartment and turn it into the company headquarters, the way Ben Ingham has.

The thought of leaving this place engenders others, which become interwoven with the plan of Baron Morillo's sulfur quarry in front of him.

He remembers standing next to this very same desk, but with Uncle Ignazio sitting behind it. And he remembers a man, his hat in his lap, looking downtrodden, sitting in front of them.

"No point in beating about the bush, Don Florio. I cannot honor the promissory note I signed."

Ignazio sighed. "What can we do, Don Saverio? I've already given you an extension. We cannot carry on like this, you know."

The other man nodded. "I came from Agrigento especially for this. I have a large quantity of sulfur that I can't sell because I have no means of transporting it to the sea and I don't know anyone willing to come and take it away."

"Why not?"

"Because they know I don't have the money to pay them."

"And how did you come by it? I mean, sulfur isn't that easy to find."

The other man opened his arms. "It's from land that belongs to my wife. You practically find it just by digging with your heel. And you can't even have goats grazing there: they all die poisoned."

"Is it good quality?"

"It's pure and clean. To tell you the truth, it looks freshly spat out from hell." He begged, his hands clasped together: "If the promissory note goes in front of the judge, I'll end up in jail. Please."

Uncle and nephew exchanged glances. And they immediately thought of their French associates.

"I'll come and take a look at this sulfur," Vincenzo said. "If it's as good as you say, I'll take it and tear up the promissory note right in front of you."

And that was what happened.

They placed the load in Marseille for three times what the promissory note was worth. After his uncle died, Vincenzo bought that land.

From that moment on, sulfur became an important entry in the Casa Florio balance sheet.

His thoughts wander and get mixed up.

Vincenzo ponders, and turns his uncle Ignazio's ring.

His uncle. His mother. He wonders what Ignazio would have said about Giuseppina's dogged determination to find him a wife among these noble young women—barely older than girls—who come from families where cousins married cousins and uncles married nieces, and who never sparkle with intelligence and often not with beauty either.

Their blood is as rotten as the furniture they sit on . . .

"Vincenzo?"

Lost in thought, he did not notice that his clerks have arrived and that Raffaele has not only come into the office, but is standing right there, by his desk.

Vincenzo rouses himself and looks at his cousin, waiting. He knows he must bring him up to date about the purchase of land where he wants to build a wine cellar.

Raffaele silently lays a map of the Marsala coast over that of the sulfur quarry. Vincenzo studies it for a long time. "I like the fact that it has direct access to the sea," he finally says, "because the roads there are little more than sheep tracks and large wagons can't get through.

We can't spend money on carts and *carritteddi*. I want the barrels to go straight from the plants to the hold on the ships." He points at an area on the map. "Here, between the Ingham and Woodhouse plants . . . This is the most suitable spot."

Raffaele searches through his notes. "So in Contrada Inferno, therefore. Two *tummini* of land behind a natural hill. They're selling it to us for sixty *oncie* but there's a tax to pay a certain Baron Spanò . . ."

"Bullshit. Secure it immediately, and give an advance if necessary. There's too much interest in marsala wine at the moment, and we don't want to miss out on the opportunity to build a cellar. Wait and see, the price of the land will soon soar."

At that moment, a clerk announces a guest.

Giovanni Portalupi.

Raffaele greets him with a handshake. Vincenzo, on the other side of the desk, simply nods and indicates a chair. "So, Portalupi, what can I do for you?"

Giovanni puts his hat on his lap. "Your sulfur is proving highly successful with our buyers. My father and I would like to purchase some more."

Vincenzo rests his chin on his hand. "Let me know the quantity and price and we can discuss it."

Giovanni speaks and Vincenzo lets Raffaele reply. The two men reach a quick agreement.

"So a week from today you'll let me know if you can find this quantity, right?" Giovanni finally asks, looking at Vincenzo.

"Yes, of course." Vincenzo gets up. "Actually, since you're new to the city, I wanted to suggest something. Have you ever been to Teatro Carolino? It's not far from the church of San Cataldo and Santa Caterina, quite close to Quattro Canti . . ."

Disoriented eyes stare at him. "No, I haven't yet, as a matter of fact . . ."

"There's a performance in a few days' time. I have a box and I would be delighted to invite you. You and your sister, naturally."

Giovanni is perplexed but not stupid. He understands immediately. "I am sure Giulia will be very happy to come. I'll let you know as soon as possible."

Once he's left the office, Raffaele exclaims, "You've never invited *me* to the theater!" He says it craftily, laughing.

"I can let you have my box whenever you like. Except that you don't have breasts, Raffaele. Now let's go to the Chamber of Commerce."

Giulia Portalupi is still water that conceals a troubled soul.

After the performance at Teatro Carolino, Vincenzo has tried to see her on other occasions. It wasn't difficult: her brother, Giovanni, combines a practical mentality with a strong inclination for worldly pleasures. Vincenzo has introduced him to the members of the Palermo Chamber of Commerce and indicated a ship's captain to transport their goods—a ship of which he is actually part owner.

Giovanni has also taken Giulia with him when dining in the homes of a few merchants, with the excuse that he doesn't have a wife, highlighting the fact that his sister has no friends or opportunities to socialize outside her family.

Politely but unequivocally, he has described her as a wretched spinster.

Vincenzo's impression is quite different.

He sometimes has the feeling that Giovanni is practically throwing her into his arms. Either way, that young man with a foreign accent is always trying to sit them next to each other. Something Giulia clearly cannot stand.

The thought makes him shake his head and give a cynical laugh. Giovanni thinks he's being clever but he's just a little boy aping grown-ups. Using his sister to lure Vincenzo into the Portalupi circle is a fool's strategy: he is not interested in courting or flirting with Giulia.

Although she certainly is an impressive woman.

She doesn't cast down her eyes when somebody speaks, is not always muttering prayers over everything, and does not distract herself whenever the men are discussing business, like his mother has always done. Instead, she follows their conversation attentively, and that intrigues him. She's a woman who is aware of the value of money and wants to learn how this money is earned. Vincenzo can see when Giulia frowns, wanting to say something but forced to keep quiet.

Something else he sees: he makes her feel uneasy.

So much the better, he thinks.

There have not been any significant women in his life since Isabella, only those who have welcomed him into their arms for passion or money. Bodies without faces, images without memories. And even now that his mother is plotting to find him a wife, Vincenzo never wonders what the selected bride will be like. All he can picture is himself, walking into an aristocratic house, head high. He doesn't care if it's because of a title he's purchased thanks to a wife who has brought it as part of her dowry.

And yet.

And yet Giulia Portalupi attracts him, and not with beauty. As a matter of fact, Giulia is not beautiful. She intrigues him with her tight, embarrassed lips, her clenched fists, and her eyes, which, when they're fixed on you, are never dull but express disdain, incredulity, blame, surprise, or simply interest. She is so transparent, so unlike that fool of a brother of hers who tries to be clever.

Vincenzo toys with these thoughts on his way home, hands in his pockets, his eyes searching for the first evening stars.

As soon as he comes in, the maid takes his hat and jacket, then tells him that dinner will shortly be served next door. In the parlor, his mother is busy darning. "Are you sewing, Mamma?" he asks after kissing her.

"Well, I can't very well let you go around with holes in your shirts, can I? Besides, these girls you hired can't darn properly." Giuseppina moves the fabric away from her face. Her eyes are beginning to play up and she can't see as well as she used to.

"They're maids who've been in service in aristocratic houses, Mamma. They darn perfectly. It's you who always finds something to complain about."

"Of course! Nowadays girls can't do household chores well. They have no idea how to run a household. I used to scrub my brass bed with sand when I was fifteen, and I never complained about my hands chapping, like these girls do."

Vincenzo grants her the final word. He sinks into the armchair, lets his body relax, and closes his eyes.

He pictures small, agile hands making Milanese meatballs that have a strange name and a strong flavor.

Giovanni Portalupi is standing outside the box at Teatro Carolino. Next to him, his sister is fanning herself.

The theater is very crowded: everyone, from the nobility to the common people up in the gallery, is chatting loudly. Some people are eating, a gypsy is offering to read palms, and there's even a water seller.

"You shouldn't have accepted the invitation without asking me first. You're always doing this and I hate it." Giulia covers her nose with a handkerchief. "It's still very hot and there's a terrible stench here. Being indoors is unbearable."

"Oh, heavens, everything annoys you today! The first time you came here with me and Don Florio you were much more obliging." Giovanni keeps peering through the crowd. "I wonder where he is. The performance is about to start."

The young woman clutches her fan. It's not just the heat and the stench of sweat that bother her. "Exactly. And besides, Florio looks at me in an odd way—"

"You should be pleased. He's rich and you're no longer a lily in full bloom. You're twenty-four, and a girl your age is lucky to receive the attentions of a man like him. You should be grateful and, while we're on the subject, encourage him a little. Not too much, of course—but within the limits of decency. He's an excellent middleman and Papà is very happy to be doing business with him."

Anger and humiliation come together in the young woman's reply. "I'm ashamed for you. I'm not a load of sulfur, Giovanni, and I have no intention of supporting your plan. If Father heard this conversation, he'd be furious. As for me, the reason I stayed with our mother is in order to care for her. Or have you forgotten that? Besides, I don't like this new friend of yours. He's venal, he's . . . greedy. He looks at everyone as if they had a price tag, but we're not goods. We're people."

"Are you so sure?" Giovanni points out a woman dressed in China silk, looking out of a box. She wears a mourning locket around her neck. "Look at her. That's Duchess Alessandra Spadafora. Widowed, abandoned by her husband, she found herself penniless overnight. Ingham pawned her family jewels and she has agreed to be his mistress in order to redeem them."

"What . . . What do you mean?"

Giovanni seems amused by her shocked expression. "Everybody has a price, dearest sister. Even you, who wishes you could spend all your time reading French books . . . Even you have a price."

"I apologize for being late."

They turn.

Vincenzo has been standing behind them long enough to hear their conversation.

"Oh, at last." Giovanni's smirk is concealed by the dim light. "I was afraid you might have changed your mind. It would have been embarrassing, particularly since you invited us to your box."

"I was detained longer than necessary by a matter in the store. Come." He leads the way up the stairs, to the box he acquired also *aliud pro alio*—although he will never openly admit it—over a debt, and shows them to their seats. Then he approaches the railing. "The whole of Palermo really is here."

"Indeed. But they're running late. There's been a tiff in the dressing room, and one of the singers is going to play female roles for the rest of his life."

They laugh. Giulia, however, sinks into the chair, sealed by an obstinate silence. Yes, Giovanni is right at least in this: she does wish she were at home, reading, and not here, in this place that's more like a cattle market than a theater.

Giovanni takes a seat to his sister's left, while Vincenzo sits on her right and brushes the knuckles of her gloved hand, resting on the armrest. She pulls it away.

A voice rises from the stage and the curtains quiver. The performance begins.

The opera is not to the audience's liking. The shouts drown out the voices of the singers.

"Too hot and too much wine for too many members of the audience." Giovanni indicates the corridor. "Shall we leave?"

Vincenzo seems to agree. "We could take a stroll, provided your sister isn't tired. I have a carriage waiting in the square outside Martorana Cathedral."

Giulia tries to say, "In truth, I would rather—"

But Giovanni does not listen to her or else chooses to ignore her. "Excellent. Yes, let's go. The air here is unbreathable." He leaves the box.

She did not see the glance the two men exchanged.

A complicit glance, man to man.

"Wait, Giovanni—" She tries to stop him but her brother has already gone.

Vincenzo offers his arm. "I'll escort you, if you will allow me."

Giulia is angry. Because Giovanni has abandoned her and because she doesn't want to be left alone with a man she barely knows, especially not someone like Florio. "I don't understand why my brother has left me alone. It's your carriage, so it was up to you to ask for it to be made ready."

"I'm not a lackey, whatever many people might still think."

"Neither is my brother."

Giulia walks around the armchair ahead of him. She wants to leave and would succeed if only Vincenzo's hands did not stop her at the exit. His fingers, which he puts on her bare shoulders, are rough.

She flounders but cannot speak. She should turn around, slap him, and scream. She should but cannot, and not just because she is afraid of him.

Vincenzo drags her into the darkness, away from prying eyes.

What does Giulia feel when Vincenzo's lips brush her neck? When they forcibly part her lips and his teeth bite her?

"No," she says. "No," she begs.

She puts her hands over his to stop him. But hers is a fragile no. Giulia knows she doesn't really mean it, though she couldn't explain why. And yet she does know, and is ashamed because now she is responding to his kiss and his caress.

He's the one in charge. It's Vincenzo who decides when to let go of her. He opens his arms and she slips out into the corridor.

"Allow me." Vincenzo precedes her on the stairs, while Giulia, flushed, walks down, holding on to the banister. Together they reach the carriage, where Giovanni is waiting.

She walks head down. She feels naked, exposed to the world. She doesn't notice her brother's smile this time either.

The *tramontana* wind sweeps down the street on the seafront. Opposite the Marsala coast, the Aegadian Islands are like lumps of iron against the sky. Sprays of saltwater are soiling the carriage windows.

Before Vincenzo's eyes, workers are erecting walls, standing on scaffolding that shakes with every gust of wind.

He knows what he wants and can even visualize it: not just a house with an inner courtyard, a farm like so many scattered in the Sicilian countryside, but a factory like those British ones, with a large central courtyard and warehouses all around.

"Have they finished the storerooms?"

Raffaele walks ahead of him to the courtyard. "Come see for yourself."

Everywhere there are bricks, tiles, timber, and builders mixing mortar. Wooden beams and mounds of rocks force them to turn off from their path several times; in front of them stands the main house, where the factory administrator is going to live.

Vincenzo confidently walks into the first of the two side buildings. Carpenters are driving into the ground supports for the wine-refinement caskets. The workers stand up and tip their caps. He makes a gesture for them to continue and heads to the middle of the hall.

The light is flooding in through the portals and the dormer windows; above him a very high ceiling is punctuated by tuff arches. The air is impregnated with sea and salt.

This will be the heart of the cellar.

Raffaele joins him. He, too, like the others, has trouble keeping up with Vincenzo. "The purchase of the grape crop has gone much better than hoped. Naturally, Woodhouse and Ingham had already grabbed a large portion of the harvest, but I managed to find some ansonica, grillo, and damaschino must in Alcamo. Oh, and a load of catarratto, too. The wine that's already fermented will be transferred here next week."

"So everything as we expected."

"Yes, we planned well. And you were right: the price of land in these parts has soared dramatically, and that's not all. The farmers are removing grain in order to plant vines. They've worked out that they can make some money from this rocky soil."

"Everybody needs money, Raffaele. In any case, the casks of sherry for refinement are arriving next week. Oh, and I had a memorandum prepared for you, with the names of a few coopers in Palermo. One of them is willing to move his workshop here."

Vincenzo touches the plastered wall. Yes, it's a job well done. He wipes the dust from his hands, then gestures at Raffaele to follow him. Still rushing around. "You have shown remarkable commitment. By September, we can formalize our agreement."

"Agreement?" Raffaele's perplexed question is lost in a gust of *tramontana* wind.

"A partnership. Between Raffaele Barbaro and Ignazio and Vincenzo Florio."

The man freezes, so strong is his surprise.

Vincenzo is also compelled to stop and turn back. "I don't need someone to look after my business and not give a damn about the rest. I need someone involved with its money. Besides, you've already put money aside to buy this land. It's a matter of continuing in the same way: a third for you, two thirds for Casa Florio. How about it?"

Raffaele torments the goatee he has grown in the past few months. He has gotten to know this difficult man, and that makes him anxious about accepting; however, it's a precious offer as well as rare, and it would make him into an important person in the little world of Marsala, whereas in Palermo he's just Don Florio's cousin, one of his factotums. "Very well."

"I knew you'd say yes." Vincenzo taps him on the back. "You know it won't be easy to manage the cellar, don't you?"

"What, with the British here in Marsala acting as if they owned the world? Of course not!" He brushes his hair away from his eyes. "I didn't expect you to offer me this opportunity."

"I did it because I mean it."

They head to the main building.

Vincenzo is here and, at the same time, in the future: the courtyard is full of wagons, barrels stacked up in pyramids, and bottles with the label *FLORIO*. He sees it all and feels that, yes, he will be the one to have made it happen. "Our quality will make us stand out," he explains. "They produce a wine for soldiers and only a few top-quality barrels. Whereas we will focus on quality and target different markets: France, Piedmont . . ." Before walking in, he stops in front of a stack of plating. "One more thing, Raffaele: the workers. Talk to them, look them in the face. This isn't a cellar like the others: it's an honor to work here and they must know it."

The following day, Vincenzo returns to Palermo.

In the solitude of the carriage, he takes a letter out of his pocket. He received it through the intermediary of Giovanni shortly before leaving from Marsala. He recognizes the slender handwriting, the faint signature. He reads calmly.

I cannot accept letters like the one you sent me, it starts, and he imagines her voice: indignant, shuddering with shame. *I cannot because there is no bond between us. You are one of my father's business associates, you have no claim on me. I should not even read what you write to me, and yet I do. Your behavior and your attentions toward me also all too often overstep the limits of decency. It is also partly my fault because I am unable to avoid your demands, to which, I am reluctant to admit, I am not indifferent. Even though I am not a loose young girl—I can assure you I am not!—your proximity is a source of great agitation to me.*

I beg and implore you: if you really have feelings for me, do not write to me anymore the kind of words you did in your last letter. Do not contact me again unless your intentions are honorable. Do not take advantage of my politeness or I shall be forced to speak to my father, and I would rather not. If what you have in mind is a sincere, devoted friendship, then very well—and this is where Vincenzo bursts out laughing—*but do not overstep the limits of acceptability or I shall be forced to give up on our correspondence.* Then, the signature: *Giulia.*

Pressing his elbow on the door, Vincenzo thinks. He has known for some time that Giulia is confused, that she wants him and is afraid of him, and this letter confirms it. Besides, how many men have given her a second look in the past? he wonders. Has anyone ever tried to discover what's concealed beneath that severe pose and those clenched fists?

Giulia has never experienced desire. Neither her own nor that of a man. So Vincenzo decides that he will not spare her in any way when he writes back to her. He will tell her of the craving she triggers inside him; of how he lies awake at night, thinking about her; of how much he wants to touch her, to see her hair cascading down her naked shoulders. He will tell her because he knows perfectly well that she will not report his words to anybody, let alone her father. He will tell her because Giulia cannot resist the dizziness to which he is certain she has fallen prey. It's a feeling he knows only too well: he has it when he finally manages to get his hands on a precious cargo or when a complicated deal is successfully closed. Except that she's not a load of sumac or a cellar . . . A load is sold off and you move on to something else: a deal is signed and then you also move on. But he seems unable to move on from this woman, and he's losing his head over her, as though intoxicated by her.

He's dying to have her in his bed, damn it!

They have met several times, in Portalupi's house or on the street, along the Cassaro; she was with her mother or brother and had darted embarrassed, languid glances at him. There have been few other real meetings since the night at the theater during this winter of 1833.

One afternoon, at dusk, using the excuse of picking up a document, Vincenzo went to the Portalupis'. Tommaso was somewhat surprised, to say the least, when he appeared at the door, but had let him into the parlor and gone to his study to get the receipts for the loads of sulfur. Since Antonietta had already gone home, Giulia was sent to take Vincenzo some lemonade.

When she saw him sitting on the couch in the room plunged in semidarkness, the glass and carafe clinked on the tray she was carrying. Giulia stood still in the doorway, motionless in her severe brown dress, frowning, her lips half-closed on a question. Vincenzo took the tray from her hands, pushed the door, and put his hands on her shoulders, then slid them down her arms and brought his face close to hers.

"I was looking for you."

This time, Giulia did not lower her gaze. In her eyes, he saw clear desire but also a kind of opposition, perhaps because she wanted to push him away but could not. Vincenzo raised his hand, stroked her lips with his thumb, caressed her chin, and even ran his fingers along her throat. He took the top button of her collar between his fingers and unfastened it.

Then he moved to the next one down.

But Giulia stopped him. She held his wrist tightly and pushed him away while swallowing air.

"No." She said it with force and determination.

Tommaso Portalupi arrived a few seconds later and dismissed his daughter. She left with an intense look in her eyes, her hand on her throat, as though trying to keep her buttons fastened.

Remembering that scene, Vincenzo feels his whole body aflame. He shakes his head and, trying for the umpteenth time to find a reason for his desire, tells himself that this is a real woman, and she's not even aware of it. She has a sensuality few people see. And this makes her dangerous, since she has no idea of the effect she can have on a man; she certainly has no idea of what she is doing to him.

He thinks that with spring on its way, now that the days in Palermo are growing longer and the sun is warming the narrow streets of the Castellammare district, Giulia will have more opportunities to go out alone.

Giulia is afraid of him, is resisting him, but at the same time yields to him whenever he takes her time, her eyes, and her lips. She doesn't refuse his passionate letters, although the notes she sends in return are full of words that say one thing but mean another. The Giulia who writes these notes is a girl from a good family, who keeps her eyes averted and says she doesn't welcome his forceful attentiveness, but there's another Giulia transpiring, one who looks him straight in the eye, sighs, and gets his blood all in turmoil. Vincenzo feels she wants him, her sense of guilt, and can smell both her fear and her desire when they are close. Giovanni Portalupi doesn't realize that his sister has become much more than bait. Vincenzo huffs. He's annoyed with Giovanni for using his sister in order to draw him in. Neither he nor Giulia are the kind of people who like being used. Quite the contrary. Vincenzo is taking advantage of the situation and carrying on the relationship because it's the first time he is acting with his flesh and not with his anger or brain. And Giulia feels exactly the same. He knows it.

They both want to.

The day after Vincenzo's return from Marsala, Tommaso Portalupi welcomes him very warmly. Portalupi personally pours him a glass of madeira and invites him to make himself comfortable while he himself sits behind his desk.

"So, tell me about your proposal for the new consignment of sulfur."

"A quarter of the production is reserved for you only." Vincenzo crosses his legs. "I already have sales agents in Naples and Marseille. I like having solid contacts in the northern market, such as in Piedmont and Lombardy."

"There are already many competitors on the market, and not just in sulfur. You have a very, very large business. I hear you're now planning on becoming a wine producer."

Vincenzo is unperturbed. "That's correct."

Portalupi rubs the leather pad on his desk. He's looking for the right words. "May I be frank, Don Florio? I'm surprised by this decision of yours: entering the marsala market at this time seems risky to me. The British practically have the monopoly on both the production and sales fronts."

"You're not the only one to think that." Vincenzo stands up and paces around the room. "But I have my sights on a different market from the one exploited by my respected colleagues Ingham and Woodhouse. I'm thinking of wines fit for aristocratic tables. Even royal tables." He walks to the window and looks at the city walls and, beyond, at the blue of La Cala. "Your clients were very satisfied with the sulfur I supplied. There are very important tanneries in England who buy sumac only from us. It'll be the same for our wine."

"We'll see," Portalupi says, darkly. "It's your money and your decision."

They say goodbye. They bump into Giulia and her mother at the door.

Vincenzo greets both with detached politeness. Antonia is pale, and still in her robe. Giulia is wearing shoes and gloves, a sign she's about to go out.

Vincenzo leaves the Portalupi house but does not go too far. He has goods to pass through customs, and Palazzo Steri is nearby. He could send the *aromateria* manager, since they are spices, or else his secretary, but no, he will go today.

He laughs. He knows the real reason for this exception. And it's not the first time either.

Unlike many Palermo young ladies, Giulia goes out alone. Her mother often stays at home because of her chest, and her daughter takes over the domestic chores. This has raised many eyebrows: to walk around without even a maid . . . Strange foreign attitude.

Therefore, with a bit of luck, he'll see her in the street.

Vincenzo spends only a few minutes at customs.

All he needs is a gesture and an employee comes to serve him. He jumps the line, ignores the grumblings of people who have been waiting a long time—including Saguto's son—and points at the sacks of tobacco to be carried to Piano San Giacomo.

Then he heads to Cassaro, where he's certain he will find Giulia, with her dark blue hat and brisk walk.

Giulia sees him first. She's on her way home, carrying a basket. She tries to avoid him but, at the same time, slows down.

"Good day," Vincenzo says.

"Signore . . ." She looks down and tries to walk past him.

He takes the basket. "Allow me . . ."

She's forced to look up. "Allow you?" she exclaims. "You're practically snatching it out of my hands!" She doesn't let go.

This peculiar pulling back and forth is attracting glances.

Giulia huffs and lets go.

"Good girl," he murmurs.

They resume walking, side by side.

"You're taking too many liberties. I think I've already told you—your being in business with my father does not excuse the way you behave toward me."

"What have I done to you? Have I forced you to do anything you didn't want to?" He nods at a passing acquaintance. "I'm not the one who writes letters and gets my brother to deliver them."

Giulia flushes. He's right. He deprives her of her peace of mind and stirs her blood. She's been weak. "You're—you're dangerous and unfair, Don Vincenzo. If your intentions aren't honorable you must never again do what you did last week, when—"

"When we were interrupted by your father?"

Humiliated, Giulia picks up the pace. Via della Zecca Regia is not far: just a few more minutes and she'll be safe. He won't dare follow her past the front door. "It's not right that you should feel entitled to escort me home." She tries to keep a distance from him.

"Nobody will pay attention to what you do. Besides, you're with me."

"That's the point: it's because I'm with you that I'm afraid."

Behind them, there's a sudden commotion and shouts. A carriage lunges past them at full speed. Vincenzo pushes Giulia against the railings of a courtyard.

However, he keeps squeezing her arm even after the vehicle has gone. "Come with me," he whispers in her ear.

"Don Florio, you're hurting me," she protests. They're near Via dei Chiavettieri. "Please," she begs.

"No." He walks ahead, practically dragging her.

Giulia is ashamed and frightened. She puts her hand on his. "Please . . . Vincenzo."

He suddenly stops and looks at her as though seeing her for the first time. His expression is stark, his voice so deep and full of rage that Giulia is upset. "I can't stand this. You can't tell me what to do or not do. You can't beg me. I am not the marble statue of a saint. This thing . . ." he adds, "this thing between us has to end."

They quickly walk to the Portalupi home. He pushes the half-open front door and they are plunged into the semidarkness of the hallway.

Vincenzo drops the basket and snatches Giulia's hat off. He takes her face and kisses her. She tries to push him away but can only yield. It's a bullying, physical kiss.

He pulls away and looks at her as though she were an enemy.

Disoriented, Giulia takes a step toward the staircase but he pushes her against the wall. "Where do you think you're going?"

Once again, they're crushed against the wall.

He whispers into her ear. "You've gotten under my skin, damn it. I didn't expect this and now I can't help it. It's a matter of desire. To desire and not have is sure grief." He stares into her eyes because he wants her to hear perfectly, so there may not bc any misunderstanding. "You're no good to me as a wife. It would not be an advantageous match for me: you're too old, you're no aristocrat, and I think you realize that, too. But I want you."

Giulia can barely breathe. "What do you mean? What are you saying?" He can't, he can't mean *that.* "You want me to . . ." Her brother has told her that there are women who live with men without being married, women considered on a par with prostitutes, but . . . "Are you suggesting I become . . ." she asks, searching his face for an answer. What she sees in it leaves no room for doubt.

"It's better than being an old maid, isn't it? What have you had in your life until now? All you've done is care for your mother and nothing else. Nothing. Even your brother is using you, and he'd put you in my bed to sign another contract, if only he could. I know you're a decent woman, I can see that for myself, so there's no need to tell me. But you want me, don't deny it, you're scared to admit it. I can feel it because the flesh . . ." He puts a hand on her breast. "The flesh doesn't lie."

"So . . ." Giulia's fingers scratch the wall. "You want me to . . ." Anger, disappointment, desire. "What makes you think I—"

"Don't act the shocked ninny. I know you want me."

She raises a hand to slap him but Vincenzo is too quick. He grabs her by the wrist.

"Leave me," Giulia pants as she tries to push him away. But he's too heavy, she cannot, but then she does not want him to stop—that's the truth. What she's thinking is already a sin. But, while she thinks, she holds him close to her.

He kisses her again, on her neck this time, and tears the lace on her dress. It's more like a bite. Giulia can't fight back because, Vincenzo is right, her flesh betrays her.

She wants him from her very depths.

Vincenzo has left but she stays in the hallway of the building. She's still standing against the wall, catching her breath.

She should go to her father and tell him Vincenzo Florio has been disrespectful toward her.

No. She can't even think she could do it. She would die of shame. Besides, she doesn't want to. Because his words are still echoing in her head.

Giovanni is exploiting her. Her parents have always taken her for granted and never asked her what she wanted. She's a steady presence, silent like a piece of furniture.

The apartment is silent. Her mother's voice drifts from the corridor. "Is that you, Giulia? I'm in bed. Your father and your brother have just gone out. Come and keep me company, will you?"

"I'm coming." She notices her reflection in the mirror. Her eyes are red, her skin flushed. A bruise is forming in the crook of her neck.

Soon.

She covers herself with a shawl so nobody sees the mark. Then she goes to comfort her mother and after that to the kitchen to help Antonietta make dinner before she leaves. When she sits down at the table, she can barely eat a bite.

That night, she touches her neck. The mark he left is there. A brand of possession, a bruise, black like an ink stamp.

A week later, a figure wrapped in a dark cloak walks briskly across Palermo, often looking back. The stores are shut, the owners are bolting the doors.

At Cassaro, the shadow heads for the Castellammare district and walks down alleyways as narrow as veins. It slows down when it reaches Piano San Giacomo. It stops. Then it moves forward decisively toward Via dei Materassai. There's a light filtering through the windows of the Florios' *aromateria.*

A gloved hand knocks insistently on the door.

Vincenzo is alone. He looks up from the receipts he's checking by the dim light of a lamp.

Who can it be? he wonders. The store is closed and it's late. Whoever it is, however, is persisting.

He goes to the door and sees the cloaked form. He opens. "You?" he says after a few seconds.

"Me."

He stands aside, then locks the door and returns to his office, followed by the rustling of a skirt. The hood falls back and Giulia Portalupi's pale face appears in the dark.

"Why are you here?"

"My mother needs a concoction. The cold weather has brought on a violent coughing fit and now she's bringing up blood." She hands him a sheet of paper. "These herbs, here."

"You shouldn't be out so late. Your brother should have come."

She lowers her head. "I wanted to come. Giovanni knows but didn't stop me."

Vincenzo's sarcastic laugh echoes through the office. "Ah, dear old Giovanni . . . I told you, remember?"

"Yes." She keeps her hand outstretched, like an insistent plea.

Vincenzo takes the sheet of paper. Without looking at it, he puts it on the table. "But you've come here for your own sake."

He forces her to look up.

"Yes," she replies. "Yes," she repeats, louder.

She hates herself saying it.

He puts his arms around her as she closes her eyes and holds him tight.

Giulia is afraid. Afraid and ashamed. "What will happen to me?" she whispers. "I'll be ruined." She wants to cry but cannot because her body has taken control and is teaching her what to do. "I'll lose my honor. Who'll want me after this?"

Vincenzo slips off her cloak. "Nobody'll want you. You'll belong to me." He says it in her ear while unbuttoning her dress. Then he unfastens her corset and takes off her skirt.

They fall on the floor and make love.

Because it's true and Vincenzo is right: the flesh does not lie. Blood cannot be subdued.

~

Weeks go by. Then months.

Then everything comes to a head one late October evening.

Giulia and Giovanni have gone for a ride with Vincenzo along the city walls, at the foot of Palazzo Butera. In the carriage, the men are talking about business and mutual friends. Sitting next to Giovanni, Giulia is not even looking at Vincenzo, and yet she can feel his boot against her ankle, under her skirt, and the feeling of it makes her quiver.

Suddenly, Giovanni turns to look at a buggy. "Gee!" he exclaims. "That's Spitaleri, the wool wholesaler on Piazza Magione. I have some business to settle with him." He leans out the window to catch his attention. The man slows down and gestures at Giovanni to join him.

"Go talk to him. We'll wait for you." Vincenzo's suggestion sounds like an order. Giulia shifts uncomfortably in her seat as her brother gets out of the carriage and walks to the merchant.

As soon as he's out of sight, Vincenzo leans forward and holds her. "Oh, God, come here . . ."

She closes her eyes and embraces him. They are like fire and straw. With no doubt as to who is what.

This is how Giovanni finds them when he unexpectedly returns: Giulia, her corset undone, her skirt pulled up to her thighs, Vincenzo panting.

Giovanni looks at his sister as she's trying to cover herself up, sees her strands of hair escaped from her bun, and the shame on her cheeks. And he's horrified by the totally unembarrassed expression on Vincenzo's face.

He covers his eyes with his hands, unable to bear this sight. He wants to scream, insult them, hit them. "You . . ." he mumbles to his sister. "You've allowed him to—what have you both done?"

She puts her hands over her face. "Please, don't shout," she whispers. "Stop it," she begs.

Vincenzo takes control of the situation. "Shut up, boy, and get in. I'll come and speak to your father tomorrow afternoon."

Back home, Giulia is given all the blame at once. She confesses her relationship with Vincenzo and admits to having given in to him. Her brother yells and keeps repeating that he thought she was a pure, respectable young woman, and she has gone and given herself to the first man who turned up.

She musters the strength to reply, weeping, that it is partly his fault, but Giovanni puts a hand on her mouth to silence her. "Don't talk nonsense. He took what you offered."

"Shame on you!" her mother finally says. Then she approaches and, with surprising energy, slaps her before collapsing on the couch, panting and coughing. Tommaso paces up and down the room, ignoring his daughter's tears and his wife's heavy breathing. In a deep, menacing voice, he says he will decide whether to send her back to Milan or shut her up in a convent.

She runs to her room and throws herself on the bed, burying her head under the pillow to stifle her sobs.

Anything. She will accept anything as long as they don't take her away from Vincenzo.

The following afternoon, Vincenzo arrives at the Portalupi home for a meeting with the two men. They shut themselves away in the study.

Waiting in the parlor, Giulia and Antonia stare at each other in silence.

But the young woman can't bear it: those three men are in the process of deciding her future without bothering about what she may want or desire, and she *has* to know. She stands up, goes to the study door, and stares at the timber until the molding showing through the cracked paint is etched in her memory.

She listens.

Vincenzo presents the facts as calmly as insolently, stating that he will not marry her, because he has other plans on that front. However, he wishes to keep her under his *protection* and is relying on their *discretion*. "This is how it is. I like your daughter and, yes, I did seduce her. I take full responsibility, if that's what you want to hear. Since the damage is done," he says with some smugness, "I've asked to see you in order to inform you of my conditions. I will not abandon Giulia to the street, and I don't want you to throw her out of the house."

Tommaso Portalupi's anger, generated by his astonishment, explodes in a cry of rage. "You're without honor! You forced her to give in to you and now you want to make her your whore?"

Giovanni steps forward and threatens to demand compensation for his sister's honor.

Vincenzo freezes him with an abrupt reply. "Don't be such a hypocrite. You were aware of everything."

"I thought you were being kind to her because she was my sister, an old maid—"

Vincenzo's laugh is a slap across the face. "And I think you did it on purpose. You thought that if I became interested in her, I would make you privileged customers for my goods, didn't you? You greenhorn. How many times did you leave us on our own? How many times did you look the other way? I made her my mistress because it was her—and not your money—that I wanted."

"You have allowed . . ."

Her father's emotional tone gives Giulia a pang in the stomach.

Once again, Vincenzo replies calmly. "Think about it, Signor Portalupi: I don't know if he had your approval, and it doesn't matter. But your son often left me alone with Giulia; he'd always find a way to get me to sit next to her, and I'd never asked him to. You know what we say here? *A' pagghia vicino u' foco appigghia*: if you put straw next to a flame it catches fire. And that's what happened."

A chair falls to the floor.

Giulia takes a step back.

Giovanni shouts, "Enough! Never mind what happened. Now you have to make an honest woman out of her!"

Giulia doesn't believe her brother is genuinely indignant, she cannot believe it. He's probably just uneasy about being found out and humiliated by Vincenzo, who has revealed his schemes to his father.

"No." Abruptly.

"In that case I'll shame you in front of everyone. You won't get away with it: I'll make sure your name is dragged through the mud. People need to know that you take advantage of innocent young women—and don't even marry them! Everyone must know what a scoundrel you are."

Vincenzo replies in such a low voice that Giulia can barely hear him. "Are you threatening . . . me?"

"Yes. For God's sake, act like a man!"

There's a long, strange pause.

Giulia pictures Vincenzo staring at Giovanni until the latter casts down his eyes. "Half the traders in Palermo are in my debt," he says, finally, "and I am a guarantor for the promissory notes of all the others. I am a receiver, a member of the Chamber of Commerce. I own shares in the main ships that go through Palermo. A word from me to the right people and you'll be on your knees."

"Nonsense. You don't have this much power," Giovanni says, although his voice is trembling.

"Actually, I do. I have it because of my money. Your father will do nothing of the sort and neither will you. You're foreigners. A wrong word and nobody will do business with you, either in Palermo or anywhere in Sicily."

Silence falls over the room.

Standing behind the door, Giulia no longer knows what to think.

At long last, Tommaso Portalupi speaks. His voice is firm but frosty. "I understand your meaning fully, signore. It appears that what I've heard about you is true: you'd step over the dead bodies of your own relatives to get what you want. You have no moral fiber or any respect for anyone. Your decision puts our backs against the wall. Now let me say my piece: you've wormed your way into our home like a snake. You've ruined my Giulia forever, since no man will sit at a table after another man has already eaten there. At least be honest and tell me: will you take care of her? I can't bear the thought that one day you may abandon her to a fate of poverty. As it is, she's without honor, a woman's only wealth."

"I imagine my word is worth nothing to you," Vincenzo replies in a tone that sounds laced with pity. "But, yes, I will take care of her."

Immediately afterward, the door is thrown open. Giulia sees him right before her.

He takes her face between his hands. "Get your things ready," he says very softly. "A week from now you'll leave this house."

It's the worst week of her life. Her mother barely speaks to her; her father ignores her except when he gives her deeply disappointed looks. Giovanni openly treats her like a good-for-nothing.

She eats alone in her room, swallowing food and tears. It's a welcome release when Vincenzo comes to pick her up.

He's found her a small mezzanine apartment that looks out onto the same courtyard as the Portalupi home. He's had it emptied, whitewashed, and furnished.

Seven days later, Giulia steps into it as the mistress of the house, followed by a maid Vincenzo has put at her disposal.

She feels odd in this apartment. At the same time, guilty and painfully happy.

Vincenzo has been clear: he will never marry her. And yet she loves him. She loves doggedly, with the madness of a first love that's foolish and blind, and the full knowledge of being without hope. And she feels grateful to this love, which has turned her from someone to conceal to a daughter to be ashamed of. She's happy to feel this way.

She was a respected young woman, a shadow whose life's purpose was to wait upon her mother and her family. Now she's the kept woman of one of the city's wealthiest traders. Not of a nobleman, for whom it's socially acceptable to have a mistress. Just of a storekeeper.

In many people's eyes, she is little more than a courtesan and Vincenzo a nouveau riche. Even though people fear him—and the power of his money—nothing can ever shield them from their contempt.

But all this is nothing in comparison to what awaits her.

It is on a spring morning in 1835 that, once again, Giulia's life is divided into before and after.

The young woman is alone. She is looking at herself in the mirror, in her home as a kept woman, Don Florio's mistress.

Her face is drawn, marked by black rings under her eyes as a result of the umpteenth sleepless night. She takes off her nightdress and stands naked. She trembles, and not from the cold.

The shape of her body has changed.

That morning, at number 53 Via dei Materassai, the maids open the windows. The crisp air and daylight fill the dining room.

Vincenzo, in trousers and shirtsleeves, is eating a frugal breakfast, looking through some documents from the board of the Chamber of Commerce, of which he is a member. His usually frowning forehead is relaxed.

He still has Giulia's scent on him.

Giuseppina walks into the room as soon as he gets up from the table. "We must talk."

He grabs a *tricotto* cookie and munches it as he heads to the door. "I haven't got time."

"Yes, you do. You know I have a meeting with the nuns of Santa Caterina? They wish to introduce another girl, the sister of one of their novices. They say she's a lovely little thing. What am I supposed to do—tell them my son keeps a woman?"

"Find out what her relatives want, then let me know."

His mother steps right in front of him. "You spent the night with that woman again."

Vincenzo runs his fingers through his hair. He appeals to the saints for patience to face yet another argument with his mother. "It's none of your business."

"Yes, it is. For as long as you're living under this roof, it's also my business. I told you to forget her. And what if, God forbid, she gives you a bastard? Then you can kiss any marriage goodbye, let alone to aristocrats and princesses."

"Mamma." He takes a deep breath. *Calm down,* he says to himself, once again. "I'm a man, not a monk. And this is, first and foremost, my house."

"You dare throw it back at me? Remember what you did!" No God can save him from the row Giuseppina wants to unleash.

"Are you still going on about Bagnara? When will you stop?"

"Never! You shouldn't have done it. It was my house, and you sold it without saying a word to me." Her voice full of rancor, Giuseppina follows him down the hallway and into the bedroom. "You and your father have snatched everything away from me. And I even have to put up with your going to sleep at that Milanese *whore's* place."

At this, Vincenzo freezes. "Now stop it," he says. His eyes are two slits. He grabs some clothes and hurls them on the bed.

"I will not be quiet. Do you know how unpleasant it is to go to Mass at San Giacomo and see the other women's looks?"

He removes his clothes until he's naked. "What other people think is not my problem."

"What are you doing, stripping like that? Did you learn it from that shameless woman?" Giuseppina turns away, blushing.

"You made me; you know what I look like."

She hears the sound of water in the basin, the same one Ignazio used. "If your uncle was still alive you wouldn't do it—keep a woman right before everybody's eyes . . . You're both living in mortal sin."

The lapping ceases. Vincenzo gets dressed, fastens the mother-of-pearl buttons, and speaks without looking at his mother. "This is the least of the sins I shall bring before God. Besides, if it bothers you that much, find me a wife and I'll sleep at home with her." He picks up his jacket and puts it on with sharp movements. "But I'm telling you, married or not, I will not give Giulia up. Never."

It's almost nighttime by the time Vincenzo walks into the courtyard in Via della Zecca Regia. He looks up at the windows of the Portalupi apartment, then heads to the mezzanine. The one he and Giulia share, "living in mortal sin," as his mother puts it.

Women's and priests' nonsense.

At least half the men he knows have a mistress, if not an actual second family as well as their official one. Ben Ingham is one of them, and treats Duchess Spadafora's children like his own. Less frequent are relationships begun through interest that turn into bonds of love.

But he doesn't dwell on this thought. He doesn't wish to.

He rings. Nobody answers. He unlocks the door with his keys, takes off his jacket, and goes into the parlor.

She's not in. Perhaps she's at her parents'.

After the row that followed her decision to live in the eyes of the world as his kept woman, Giulia spent days racked with guilt. Only recently has she resumed visiting her family. Her father, a pragmatic man, quickly forgave her. But not her mother, who keeps blaming her and making her disappointment weigh heavily upon Giulia.

Vincenzo pours himself some lemonade from a carafe. He'll do some work while he waits for her.

He doesn't realize that hours have gone by until the flame in the lamp starts to quiver, stirred by the evening wind.

He gets up and peers at the Portalupi home through the window and sees a shadow, then another: it looks like Giovanni and Giulia; they are arguing.

A few seconds later, the young woman descends and walks across the courtyard, head down. He opens the door, more worried than he wishes to admit.

Giulia is here, before him. She's so pale, as though made of alabaster. She puts a hand on his face without a word. She looks ill.

She kisses him.

"What?" he mutters.

She puts her fingers over his lips to stop him from asking.

"Come with me."

She takes him by the hand and he follows her to the bedroom, entranced by her directive.

He's awakened by the dawn.

Around them, the white ceiling, the curtains shielding the room from prying eyes, and the mahogany closet.

Outside, the sounds of the city remaking itself. He feels Giulia's breath tickling his temple. It's a rare moment of peace, and so precious. The warm softness of her body is a refuge of peace for him. He doesn't have to prove he's better than others.

She's Giulia, he's Vincenzo. That's all.

But when he turns over, she's awake, watching him with those large, dark eyes, serious but calm. She has a hand under the pillow. "I'm expecting your child."

For a moment, Vincenzo doesn't understand.

A child.

It means that, deep in her flesh, something is growing.

Child. My child.

He snatches the sheet off her and studies her aggressively. Her breasts are swollen, her hips fuller. Her belly is rounder.

Jesus wept! He didn't realize!

Now Giulia is afraid. He can tell by her teeth pressing into her lower lip, and the hand clutching the pillow.

The words fly out of his mouth before he can stop them. "Is it really mine?"

Giulia rolls onto her back. She is almost smiling, perhaps having expected that question. "You were the first and are the only one."

It's true and he knows it.

Vincenzo suddenly realizes he's naked. He grabs the sheet and covers his hips, while Giulia remains as she is, her skin shivering in the cold, a twinge in her heart.

"Since when?"

"I haven't bled for three months." She puts a hand on her belly. "Soon, everybody will notice."

Vincenzo runs his fingers through his hair. When did they conceive it? He has tried to be careful but hasn't always managed. They have been together and making love for a year now.

In the end, a bastard has come along, as his mother had foreseen.

"I won't marry you. I can't. You know that, don't you?" He speaks instinctively, quickly, and, as he talks, he feels overwhelmed, angry, confused. "You're not the one . . . My mother is still looking for a wife for me," he adds. He doesn't want her to get any ideas, he thinks. She must understand that she can't trap him just with a belly and a kid. "Tell your brother and father right now. If this is a way to try to—"

"I know." Giulia sits up in the middle of the bed. Naked. Proud. She's almost glowing in the light. "Before you say it, because I expect you'll do this to me, too, I will not get rid of it. This is my child and I want it."

Vincenzo retreats practically to the edge of the bed.

She grabs him by the wrist, revealing unusual strength. "Listen to me. The day will come when you'll find yourself this woman you and your mother are wearing yourselves out looking for, and marry her. Or else you won't come back simply because you'll get tired of me. At least then I will have something of yours, to remind me of you and of us."

Vincenzo wriggles free. "Aren't this apartment and the money I give you enough? Why do you want a bastard? Do you think I'll give you more? I've already told you, I'll take care of you even if I ever leave you."

He wishes he could run away, erase everything: having woken up, the confusion that's making him breathless, that little thing growing inside his woman, robbing him of her.

He can't even imagine what it means to have a child. He's never thought of being a father.

Now Giulia is crying in earnest. She takes the sheet and covers herself. She curls up in the middle of the bed.

All Vincenzo can do is get dressed and leave. Giulia's sobs follow him to the door.

"You wretch! Now this?" Antonia shouts between coughing fits. She rocks in the armchair, her eyes wide open, finding no relief in tears. "And now a bastard. What are we going to do? Haven't we been through enough already?"

Her dark dress buttoned up to her neck, Giulia tortures a handkerchief until she frays its hem. She's alone, or at least that's how she feels. She has come to her mother for a word of comfort, a hug. Now that she needs help, she can't find it anywhere.

A mother is meant to protect you even from yourself. But not her mother, who's a frail woman focused on her own illness.

Antonia is crying, and her tears never seem to end.

Still, she's not crying anymore by the evening. Sitting next to Giulia on the couch, she looks at Tommaso and Giovanni, who have just returned home, and knows it's her duty as a mother to say out loud what they both thought as soon as they heard the news. She therefore waits for her husband to stop pacing up and down the parlor rug, his hands behind his back and his head down, and for her son to stop cursing Vincenzo.

When silence finally falls, she coughs and mutters that there could be a solution . . . With a small sum, a discreet midwife, an afternoon of pain, all trace of the shame could be erased.

She looks at Giulia. "Are you certain that you don't want to—"

"No." Firmly, eyes downcast.

"In this case you must leave." Antonia stands up, coughs, and falls back on the couch. "You'll return to Milan. You'll go to Aunt Lorena, my mother's sister, who lives outside the city. You'll give birth there, and then we'll see."

Giulia shakes her head. "I don't want to go away."

How can she make them understand that she doesn't care if people insult her, if everybody calls her a whore? She knows very well what she's going against. She wants to stay with Vincenzo; too bad if she's forced to accept his life's leftover crumbs. She'll make do with them. It's what she has always done: to hold on tight to what little others are willing to grant her. But how can she possibly explain this to her mother and Giovanni?

She wants to remain in Palermo, no matter how painful this will be.

"You *will* leave," her mother says. Determined.

"No!"

She bursts into tears. Ever since she's been pregnant, she's been crying frequently, almost as a habit.

Antonia and Giovanni exchange a look.

Giovanni kneels in front of her and takes her hands. "Giulia . . . listen. What do you think will become of you if Florio gets married? Not even the faintest memory. His wife will demand that you vanish from his life. There will be no more room for . . ."

Giulia recalls Vincenzo's words. She knows his mother is still looking for a wife for him. "I don't want to," she repeats obsessively. "No."

She goes on repeating it over the following days, when her mother forces her to pack her bags in secret. Antonia mutters that Vincenzo will not want her anyway now that she's pregnant, that her body is going to lose its shape, and that all he's after is a beautiful woman to enjoy. "I told you he was a scoundrel. And you're a naïve fool who trusted him, that's what you are."

She repeats this when Giovanni outlines his plan. Giulia is in the room but it's as though she's not there. He's going to look for passage on a ship bound for Genoa. He'll escort her and make sure everything goes well until she arrives in Milan. Then he'll return to Palermo.

As for Vincenzo, he has disappeared. No note, no visit, whereas before he would spend his nights holding her tight.

It is this void Giulia cannot stand, and which breaks her.

She gives up her resistance, abandons herself, and endures whatever is happening to her, letting others decide for her.

It will be as though she has never existed; perhaps that's how it's really going to be. And yet . . .

Finding a passage on a ship appears strangely complicated.

Among the captains and ship owners known by the Portalupis, nobody has room on his ship. Some even deny ever having carried passengers. Others claim they sold everything the day before. They say it in a low voice, however, looking away or with a sneer.

One is chance, two bad luck . . . but three refusals are too many to be a coincidence.

Tommaso understands.

Then, one evening, there's a knock on the door.

The Portalupis exchange puzzled glances. They're not expecting anybody.

Sitting at the table, Giulia is pale, remote, the victim of a torpor that came over her a few days ago, making her detached from everything.

Her mother says it's the pregnancy but she knows that's not the case. The maid opens the door.

It's that voice, *his*, to snatch her out of the void into which she has fallen. "Good evening."

Vincenzo Florio looks at them one by one. He deliberately avoids Giulia.

Giovanni is the first to confront him. "What are you doing here? You're not welcome. Leave!"

"Just a few words and I'll go." He grabs a chair and sits between Antonia and Giulia, cross-legged. "A couple of days ago, my good friend Ingham said that you, Signor Portalupi, were looking for passage to Genoa. I wasn't particularly surprised: I thought you needed to travel on business." He looks into Tommaso's face. "Until I discovered it was two places you were looking for."

Portalupi removes his napkin from his collar and pushes his plate away. "I don't have to give you an account of my actions, signore."

"Actually, you do. I promised I would keep Giulia under my protection, and that means she has to stay in Palermo. With me."

She looks up. The color seems to return to her face.

"We must protect our daughter," Antonia says. "Giulia doesn't understand what's best for her, especially in her present condition. She can't live here, unmarried, with a fatherless child."

"That's where you're wrong, madam. Your daughter is a perfectly lucid, highly intelligent woman. And it isn't a ring or a priest that will alter our relationship." Vincenzo doesn't smile. There's no triumph, no satisfaction. "Rather, you have been foolish. You should have known I wouldn't allow you to take her away from me. That's unless . . ."

Only now does he address the young woman.

"Unless she wishes to leave, because if that's the case, I'll respect her decision. But not yours—Giulia's." He proffers his hand to her, palm up.

Stay. He wants to say it but doesn't know how.

But Giulia can read it in his face. She feels anger and resentment for what she has been through: the loneliness, these days of abandonment, the isolation, the nights in the cold bed. For all that he is unaware of and she cannot tell him. Finally, she speaks.

Midnight has chimed.

Giulia is asleep, with Vincenzo next to her.

Once again. At last.

Her body has become buttery, round. Even her smell has changed: it's now wild, determined, suggesting milk and lemon.

Vincenzo is awake. He's listening to the thoughts of a Palermo that feeds on its own entrails, destroyed and rebuilt by its residents. He thinks about his business, about the grape harvest, about the goings-on at the Chamber of Commerce. About the problems he's having with the Vergine Maria *tonnara*, which he doesn't yet own and for which he has a wish that's slowly shaping into a plan. Because he loves that place and would like to turn it into his realm.

He remembers his mother shouting, threatening to throw him out of the house if he went back to Giulia, especially now that everybody, absolutely everybody, knows she's pregnant by him.

And being here. The tranquility.

He listens to his woman breathing. He hears, or imagines he hears, another breath intertwining with hers.

The baby.

He moves his hand from her breast down to her belly. Now he can feel the child. She made him feel it.

As well as affection—he, a father!—he has other emotions. Above all, a mistrust he struggles to shake off. This thing, this unborn child, will steal Giulia from him. She will no longer belong to him alone.

It's an unfamiliar kind of jealousy that exasperates him.

And, at the same time, there's a hope worming its way in.

A boy. An heir.

He turns on his side. Giulia hugs him, her chest against him, her belly pressing against the small of his back. *This is home*, he thinks in the zone between sleep and waking. Vincenzo falls asleep and almost doesn't notice the light taps from a child knocking at the door of life.

~

January in Palermo can be mild and have a light that seems to speak the language of spring. But then the north wind starts to blow, reminding everyone that winter has its time to reign and won't yield it to anybody.

The sea says it. Here at Arenella, the spring sea is clear and deep. But in the winter, the water becomes murky, bubbling from within. In this January 1837, deceivingly bright, two men are now walking beneath the *tonnara* walls, dodging the spray of the waves.

"So the court hasn't decided yet?"

"The prince of Castelforte has opposed it once again. The son of a bitch doesn't want to let go." Vincenzo puts his hands in his pockets and shudders when a gust of wind eddies under his coat. "All I need is his share of ownership and the *tonnara* will be mine. Even the prior of San Martino delle Scale has assured me that he will also sell the warehouses. It's just this damned Paternò who won't give in."

Walking beside him is perhaps the only person he trusts, and who is more than just a colleague. Carlo Giachery, all curly hair and bushy mustache, opens his arms. "It's still the story about the legacy to his wife, right?"

"A wife he's never given a damn about. The truth is he doesn't want to be humiliated by a storekeeper like me."

"Or a laborer, to be exact." Giachery can allow himself to speak frankly.

"Heck."

They've been acquainted for almost two years, since shortly before Angelina, Vincenzo's daughter, was born. They met at a dinner at the duke of Serradifalco's house. A gathering where aristocrats—few of them—and middle-class guests—in large numbers—sat side by side with artists and scholars.

Vincenzo was struck by his quick delivery and Roman accent. "In Rome, funeral architecture is a fast-growing sector. All in all, we must thank Bonaparte for his idea of putting cemeteries outside the city walls."

"There are many things Bonaparte should be thanked for," the duke, an enthusiastic historian, added. "Not least for allowing us to discover the magnificence of Ancient Egypt and Greece. Of course he did annihilate entire armies, but look at how much culture he brought to our knowledge!"

Vincenzo was observing the young architect, who was becoming enthused speaking about commerce and art that can and must adapt to everyday life, using the examples of French and British industry. "So you're abreast of the latest British and French architectural trends," he said, "which demand that a factory should be not only productive but also organized in a rational manner."

Carlo nodded energetically. "Yes. I spent my youth between Paris and the Veneto. I've traveled, so I know what I'm talking about. Operating with a specific purpose doesn't mean erecting four walls and putting machines between them, like some factory owners seem to believe. It's all right if you build a mill in the countryside, but in a city you must work out where and how to build it, and who is going to work in it. Factories are becoming part of our cities, so we'd better start thinking about them in that context. As a matter of fact, my brother Luigi and I are working on this, on how to make mills into places that are both beautiful and functional, and make them part of the place where they are built."

By their second meeting, they were on first-name terms. From then on, they continued their discussions and their arguments. For a month now, Carlo has been lecturing on city architecture at the University of Palermo and working directly with Vincenzo. He's the person Vincenzo trusts the most in business, perhaps because, just like him, Carlo does not entirely belong in Palermo. Giachery has the power of attorney and manages the purchase of property and some business. But he is above all a friend.

Vincenzo throws his head back and embraces the buildings with a yearning eye. He loves this *tonnara* so much. "Do you know why I brought you here?" he asks, resuming his walk.

"As a matter of fact, I've been wondering. We've been walking around it for the past half hour."

"What I want is a villa." He turns and points at the walls. "Right here."

Walls flaking because of the salt air, stockrooms carved out of the tuff, a few tamarisks bent by the wind, and stone.

Carlo looks at the building. "I don't understand."

Vincenzo gestures at him to follow. He follows the perimeter of the plant, explaining.

"Forgive me, Vincenzo, but I still don't understand. Why here? It's a *tonnara*! You could afford a villa anywhere. I mean, the best properties are in Bagheria and San Lorenzo. Besides, barely a month ago, you were saying you wanted to buy the notary Avellone's house. Have you changed your mind?"

"Not at all. That's an investment." He seizes Giachery by the arm, as though trying to make him see through his own eyes. "I don't want the usual villa, with pillars, balconies, and statues. I want something nobody has ever imagined building, and I want it here because I want it to express the way I grew up: it will have to be *different*. I don't want a villa, but a house that will also be my home."

That is when Giachery *sees*.

The horizon, both metaphorical and real, opens up.

"The sea . . ."

"That's right, the sea. And the world beyond it, and the wealth that comes from it. You've traveled throughout Europe, you've lived in

Rome, but you've chosen to come here because you know that Palermo is the place for you. Now you know what I want. Give it to me."

An entire world is enclosed in these words.

In the carriage, they discuss other things: the cotton mills in Marsala—"I haven't found the right land yet"—the management of the cellars by Raffaele Barbaro—"It could be more profitable but he lacks the initiative"—and about the board of directors of the Chamber of Commerce.

"I think it's the only place where some people agree to deal with a storekeeper like me." Vincenzo speaks with a mixture of detachment and pride. "Not many, but some, like the prince of Torrebruna and Baron Battifora, realize they have to get their hands dirty if they don't want to sell everything, including their titles. When all's said and done, there are few tradesmen and storekeepers who really move money around, here in Palermo, and even fewer aristocrats who are willing to do business with us."

"Intelligence is rare goods," Carlo says, sighing. "They don't have the mental capacity to understand that the world is changing." He takes a notebook out of his pocket and reads his reminders. "So shall I continue negotiating with the duke of Cumia over the villa in San Lorenzo? It has good land, you could earn some revenue from it."

Vincenzo is staring at the road. His forehead is furrowed with lines that make him look older. When Giachery calls him he rouses himself. "Sorry, you were saying?"

Carlo puts a hand on his arm. "It's this evening, isn't it?" he asks, even though he knows Vincenzo does not allow intrusions into his personal life. Perhaps that's why he asks. "Why don't you go? After all, she's your daughter."

"I don't know." Vincenzo is torn, much more than he shows. "I won't give her my name." He speaks with irritation and obvious regret. "A girl. Another one. It's not just the damage, it's the mockery of it."

He points at the paper in Giachery's hand. "Let's proceed ahead with Cumia. Avellone doesn't want to sell his estate directly to me, but he won't say no to Cumia."

Carlo agrees. "Especially since he's the chief of police." He thinks. "And no one says no to a police officer."

Why don't you go?

Carlo's question keeps knocking at the door of his conscience. All afternoon, at the *aromateria*, where he calls in to sign some orders, and in the office of Casa Florio.

Via dei Materassai is now shared between him and Ingham. He has much more money and power than he could have imagined when his uncle died.

But what is it all for if he can't decide what to do with his life?

Vincenzo received the news of Giulia's second pregnancy with resigned calm. After their first child, Angela—Angelina, as everybody calls her—was born, their situation stopped creating talk: other, juicier scandals were animating the city salons. Their living together now triggers only indignant—and hollow—reproach.

His mother found it hardest to stomach the news. It's difficult to explain to her that she can't stop him from marrying, even though the law requires that she should grant permission for her son to marry. He's almost forty but . . . No, Giuseppina doesn't want to be reasonable.

One afternoon, she appeared right in front of him. She had run to the office, as pale as the gray dress she was wearing.

"So you've gotten her pregnant again, have you?"

The secretary, standing in the doorway, made a forlorn gesture, as if to say: *I just couldn't stop her.* Then he closed the door.

"And a good afternoon to you, Mother. Yes. Giulia is pregnant again."

She brought her hands to her face. "What a misfortune! Doesn't this woman ever miscarry? Am I the only one to whom it had to happen?" She rocked back and forth on the chair where she had sunk. "Doesn't she understand you won't marry her? And you, don't you know how to—"

"Mamma, don't you even think of finishing that sentence! Is that clear?" he said, hands on his hips. "In any case, if it's a boy this time I'm going to marry her. Let that be clear."

She leaped up, furious. "Rubbish! Marry that chambermaid! Are you out of your mind?"

"I'm being practical. I'm thirty-seven and there's not much else I can do. Frankly, I don't want a wife if she's like the dog-faced widow you suggested to me three months ago."

Giuseppina became the picture of the outraged mother. "You're marrying *her*. Remember, I have to give you my permission, and I won't. That woman never came to see me, never showed me respect, and now you want her to come here and act the mistress in my house?"

"Why, would you have let her in?"

"Never!"

"There you go, so you're even." A weariness came over him, a resignation he felt only when he had to argue with his mother about Giulia and the other way around. There was no emotion more troubling than this unease that made him feel as though he were being pushed and pulled from both sides, and had no choice in the matter.

Vincenzo's thoughts now rush ahead, to the moment he heard news of the labor, to the afternoon of waiting. To the announcement that he was a father again.

Of a girl.

Immediately after the birth, Giulia asked him to marry her. She asked gently at first, then firmly. He refused.

He was sent away.

The unease solidifies. She is hard, inflexible. She wants her honor, her dignity back. Vincenzo thinks of Giulia and realizes he's managed to find a life companion even prouder than he. He keeps toying with his uncle's ring. More than ever, he longs for his advice.

He takes out his pocket watch, grabs his jacket and coat, and goes out.

Giulia's apartment is not far.

In the small parlor of her apartment, Giulia Portalupi is holding a newborn baby in her arms, and there's a priest who's come to christen her. Next to her stands her brother, Giovanni; a few steps behind them, the servant with another little girl. It's been a week since the birth, and it's not appropriate to wait any longer before having a child baptized.

It's been a week since she and Vincenzo had an argument.

The priest paces around the room. He feels uneasy, as though he doesn't know what to do. He puts the chrism on the table and lights the candles while muttering prayers. Preoccupied, Giulia is barely following his acts.

It was like that with Angelina, and the same with her second daughter. She is hers and nobody else's: Vincenzo doesn't want to acknowledge her. Giulia is now struggling to tolerate this state of affairs. The solitude and the growing contempt are heavy burdens.

And now, once again, this furtive ceremony, with a priest come to the house in a rush, without even an altar servant. A clandestine ritual celebrated at home, the way it is with illegitimate children. Even her parents refused to come to the christening.

"Mammaaaa," the little girl calls, agitated.

Giovanni goes and picks her up to keep her quiet. "Shh . . . there's a good girl. Your mamma must have your baby sister baptized. Did you know, your grandma has made some sweets?"

Hearing this, Giulia sighs. She would rather her mother were here and not shut up at home, baking cookies for an occasion nobody considers to be a celebration.

The priest starts to chant in Latin. His sharp voice resounds between the furniture and the ceiling. "What name are you giving this child?"

Giulia uncovers the baby's head. "Giuseppina. Like her grandmother."

The parish priest gives her a sidelong glance. He knows Giulia's mother's name is Antonia, just as he knows who is the father of these two girls. It's the second bastard she's borne that godless man Vincenzo. And barely two years apart. She behaves shamelessly, as though she were his wife and he refuses to take an ounce of responsibility.

At that moment, there's a jangling of keys. The front door creaks then closes with a thud, and a shadow in a dark cloak appears by the door to the parlor.

Vincenzo.

The room plunges into silence. Giulia freezes. She wants to ask him to stand beside her. But she looks at the priest again and gestures at him to continue.

Giovanni has seen him, too. "Shall I tell him to leave?" he murmurs.

"No." He came. That is more than she expected.

The priest anoints the baby's chest with consecrated oil and wets her forehead with holy water. She cries and wriggles. At the end of the ceremony, the priest writes the little girl's name on the baptism certificate.

Giuseppina Portalupi, born of Giulia Portalupi. Godfather: Giovanni Portalupi. The godmother is Lucia, the servant girl.

There's nobody else who can take on that role.

While the priest extinguishes the candles and picks up his things, Vincenzo walks into the room. Giovanni blocks him. "Where are you going?"

"I want to see my daughter."

"She doesn't have your surname, and neither does Angelina. You refused to acknowledge either of them, remember?"

"I don't owe you any explanation." He walks past him with bad grace.

Sitting on the couch, Giulia is dressing Giuseppina again. The baby wriggles and whimpers from the cold.

She greets him with a faint smile.

He kneels beside her. "I heard the name you chose. Thank you." He reaches out to touch the child, who keeps moving, restless, searching for her mother's breast. He pulls away.

"I wish it would help in some way," Giulia says, wrapping the baby in a shawl. "But it won't, will it?"

He sighs impatiently. "No." Giovanni and Angelina are standing behind him. He can feel their eyes on his back. "I want to speak to you. Alone."

Angelina breaks free and runs to her mother. She hides under her arm and, from this shelter, stares at Vincenzo with distrust. To her, this father is a figure with blurred edges.

"All right." Giulia stands up and holds Giuseppina against her breast. "Even though I already know I'll be sorry."

She sees the priest out. Next to her, Giovanni gives him a donation. "For the parish orphans."

The man nods with a serious expression, closes his fingers over the coins, and slips out.

A hand on the doorjamb, Giulia looks at her brother. "I need to speak to Vincenzo. Alone."

"You're out of your mind. Either that or you're stupid. What do you think he's going to say to you?" Giovanni indicates the parlor. "Why debase yourself further? What do you think he's going to tell you? You'll never have anything good from a man like that. No family and no respect. You'll always be . . . what you are."

Giulia knows that's true, that her brother's right, that she should have fled to Milan as soon as she got pregnant with Angelina. And yet she opens the door and indicates the stairs. “Please,” she insists, and her request brooks no refusal.

Giovanni opens his arms. “Your life couldn’t get any worse.” He calls Angelina. “I don’t want her to hear you two arguing, poor child,” he mutters.

Giulia purses her lips.

The little girl, who’s been watching her father askance, runs to her uncle and giggles when he picks her up on the fly. Vincenzo follows her with his eyes as she disappears past the threshold. A moment later, he hears the door close and the sound of Giovanni and the girl laughing.

Angelina has never laughed with him.

Giulia returns to the parlor in her robe, the baby sucking vigorously at her breast.

“Your other daughter barely even looked at me.”

“And I’ll bet you’ve never asked yourself why that is. You should, you know,” she replies sharply, then motions at him to follow her. She goes into the bedroom and sits on the bed so she can nurse the baby. Vincenzo looks at her shyly and keeps watching her for a long time. He had not realized earlier that the pregnancy has softened her features.

“Are you sure you don’t want a wet nurse?” he murmurs. “It’ll ruin your breasts.”

She shakes her head. “Why did you come back? I told you not to until you’d spoken with your mother.”

Vincenzo unfastens his cloak and sits on the edge of the bed. “She refuses. She simply refuses.”

“And you don’t want to choose between me and her. I guess there’s nothing else to add.” Her voice is sharp. “Funny how Don Florio, the tradesman without scruples, famous for his ruthlessness, becomes a scared little boy with his own mamma.”

"She's my mother. And she's old and lonely."

"And I'm the Circe who ensnared you. Have you ever told her what really happened? How you pursued me until I gave in?"

"You accepted."

She clenches a hand over her mouth to restrain herself. "Of course, now it's *my* fault." She speaks with rancor, as though uttering a curse. "I couldn't help it, damn my heart."

Vincenzo becomes restless, stands up, then sits down again. "It's not that simple."

"Not for me either." She takes the baby from her breast and puts her over her shoulder. "I could accept the gossip and even bear the contempt for the sake of your love. But we have two daughters now, Vincenzo. Two creatures who need a father. Your mother should accept it, as should you, and stop all these dreams of glory."

"This can all be arranged. Where there's an advantage, people are happy to overlook anything." He puffs. He hates it that Giulia is able to put him on the spot like this. "In any case, my mother will never permit the marriage, and without her consent I cannot marry: it's the law."

"The law requires that you give her your *notice of intent* since you're over thirty." Giulia feels tears prickling her eyelids. She does not want to cry, she will not cry.

She places Giuseppina in her basket and the baby responds with a gurgle that heralds sleep. "If you don't want to marry me, at least acknowledge the girls. Give them the possibility of having a legitimate father."

Vincenzo bites his lip, and she realizes he will not grant her this either.

"You're a coward." Giulia stands up and indicates the door. "I don't want to see you again."

He stays sitting and grabs her by the wrist. "Don't ask me to choose between you and my mother."

The words flash in her mind like a violent, bitter realization. She doesn't hold back. "It's because they're girls! That's why you won't acknowledge them, admit it! Because they can't be your heirs." She clasps her forehead. "I've been so blind. That's why your mother is against it and you don't stand up to her, it's nothing to do with gratitude!" She picks up his cloak and hurls it at him. "Get out!"

Vincenzo grabs the cloak, his expression dark. "You've become nagging since you discovered you were pregnant with this one. I thought I was perfectly clear two years ago."

He had hoped to find Giulia in a more conciliatory mood but . . .

"*This one* is your daughter and she has a name: Giuseppina." Giulia flings open the apartment door. "Since you prefer your mother, get out and never come back." She says it with her throat ablaze and her fists clenched.

Vincenzo looks at her and his desire flares up. It's true, Giulia is looking tired after the birth and her belly is still swollen, but there's something in her that goes beyond the flesh, he realizes now, which makes it impossible for him to leave her. He wants to stay, to sink into her, but he can't because too little time has passed since the birth and you don't touch a woman who's just given birth.

He clenches his fist and punches the door. The wood cracks and his knuckles get soiled with blood.

Giulia jumps and takes a step back. Vincenzo has a quick temper but has never been violent with her. She is afraid.

"It's not over." Vincenzo's voice is hoarse, tight from anger. "You're mine," he says.

Then he rushes out.

Giulia is left alone. She collapses against the closed door and takes her head in her hands. She weeps. Her physical frailty adds to the loneliness and exhaustion of raising two daughters without a father or the protection of a name. However much money Vincenzo may leave in the dresser drawer in the bedroom, it cannot replace the support a man should give his family.

When she chose—or rather when she decided to follow him—she

couldn't imagine what would have happened. She hadn't considered children. There was nothing except Vincenzo.

But now there are her two girls.

What will he do now? she wonders. Will he find himself another woman? One who will keep him warm at night, accept him and not demand the respect she, Giulia, wants? Or will his mother find him a girl to marry?

Suddenly, the fear of losing him is a wave that floods over her.

Days go by, then weeks. Giulia struggles to recover after the birth, so Angelina spends a lot of time with her grandmother Antonia. Giovanni, however, spends his evenings with his sister and, to entertain her, tells her about the goings-on in the city. One evening, however, he stops in the doorway, embarrassed. He looks at her then hands her a bag. "He sends you this. I told him your family were taking care of you but he gave me one of his looks . . . You know what he's like."

Giulia sighs. The bag has the only way Vincenzo knows of showing her how he feels. She takes the coins. "Tell him to come see the girls, at least," she mutters before closing the door.

The following evening, when the girls are in bed and she's about to retire, there's a knock. A tap so light she wonders if she has imagined it.

She pulls the robe over herself and goes to open the door.

Vincenzo is standing on the threshold.

"You could have used your keys," she says, opening the door.

"You threw me out."

She puffs and opens the door wide. "It's your home. You pay the bills."

He ignores her provocation. He heads to the bedroom, where he knows he'll find the wooden cradle with Giuseppina. He parts the voile and looks at her. "Are you still feeding her?"

"Yes." Giulia stands, arms crossed, looking at him. "Angelina is asleep with Lucia in the next room. You can't see her."

He moves away from the baby. "Are they well?"

A nod.

Vincenzo approaches and brushes a lock of hair from her forehead. He hesitates before saying, "You're as white as a sheet, though. Does she let you sleep? Are you eating enough meat?"

Giulia pushes his hand away and goes into the parlor. "You know, it's not a matter of food," she says, clenching her fists. "There are other things that keep me awake at night. There's only one thing that would make me feel better, and it's knowing that you will provide for me and the girls. Instead . . ."

"I sent you some money with that big baby brother of yours." The first signs of anger are already starting to color his voice.

"Because for you everything begins and ends with money, doesn't it? You have a family now."

"I have a mistress who's given me two bastards. It's not the same thing."

Giulia does not react to these words. She is frozen. Her breath catches in her breastbone.

So that's what she is. That's how he sees her.

"You could change everything, if you wanted to." Her whisper sounds like a lament.

He stands with his arms crossed. "This is all I can give you."

"You can't give me anything else because you're a coward." She covers her face with her fists. "You don't want to because you have these damned notions in your head and because you'd be going against your mother, who treats you like a fifteen-year-old. But sooner or later you'll have to make a choice."

He comes closer and grabs her by the throat with one hand, not squeezing but firm enough to take her breath away. "There's no choice to be made."

It's just a moment, but it's enough.

His hand slides from her throat to the back of her neck, and the grip turns into a caress. They kiss, they want each other. It's been too long since they were together. They can't stay apart for long.

As she clings to him, Giulia hates herself. Because she always forgives him, because she loves him and takes him back after every quarrel, because she feels broken without Vincenzo. Ever since she's known him, she's no longer sufficient for herself.

Vincenzo keeps his eyes closed. Because this is his home. The rest of the world might well be treacherous land, but Giulia is his sea.

Vincenzo slips away when, tired, she falls asleep. He leaves without a word because he does not know what to say to her.

Maybe she's right to call him a coward.

However, Giulia is awake. The last thing she hears is the door clicking shut.

She spends the night with Giuseppina next to her. After the lovemaking, the bed feels huge and cold, more so than the other nights when she was alone. Her tears of anger are more powerful than those of longing, her rage stronger than her regret.

Tomorrow is Sunday.

She dresses very carefully in one of her best outfits; it's still a little tight, but never mind.

She dresses Giuseppina, asks her mother to look after Angelina, and tells her she'll be back soon.

Morning Mass at San Giacomo is attended mainly by working-class men and women who don't have time to go to the afternoon service. Among them, more out of habit than necessity, is Giuseppina Saffiotti Florio.

Giulia sees her come in. Her face is stern, her gray hair gathered in a bonnet. After Mass, Giulia follows her. She waits until Giuseppina is practically at her front door in Via dei Materassai.

"Donna Florio!" she calls. "Donna Florio!"

Giuseppina instinctively turns. She squints and doesn't immediately recognize her. She flares up as soon as she sees the child, turns her back to Giulia, and determinedly heads home. "Shameless woman . . ."

Giulia rushes after her. "Stop!"

Some people look out their windows. A carter watches them; a few women just out of church slow down.

Giulia overtakes her and stands rooted in front of her.

Giuseppina has no choice but to halt.

The young woman's voice is loud, to make sure everybody hears and knows. "Donna Florio, don't you want to see your granddaughter?"

People stare and listen.

The response is like a rasp against wood. "I have no grandchildren."

"Are you sure? This child has your name."

"So what? There are many Giuseppinas."

"Except that this one has your son's eyes."

Despite herself, Giuseppina glances at her. The little girl looks too much like Vincenzo: she has his nose, the eyebrows high on her forehead. She suddenly steps back.

This is not acceptable, not right.

"A bitch can never tell whose puppies she gives birth to. She's mated with too many dogs to know herself."

Giulia holds the baby tight to her chest, as though to protect her. "That's true about bitches without a master. It's a shame mine keeps me on a short leash. I wasn't the one to go after him: he was the one to take me away from my home."

"Some leashes can strangle." Giuseppina's tone is full of hatred. "If you thought you'd settle in nicely, then you miscalculated. There's no room for you here."

Giulia does not manage a reply.

Giuseppina walks past her. *I put her back in her place*, she thinks, satisfied. What did she think she would achieve, coming here like this, acting like a scullery maid? She only showed herself for what she truly is.

Giulia's reply reaches her as she is on the threshold of her house. "I didn't choose this leash for the sake of money. But you've never loved anyone, so how could you possibly know?"

From the dining room window, in his robe, barefoot, Vincenzo has seen everything. He follows Giulia with his eyes until she disappears behind the curve in the street.

He hears Giuseppina's angry approaching footsteps. "You saw, didn't you? What kind of woman is she? Real trash. But I put her back in her place. What is she trying to do? Bring scandal to this house? She should keep away!"

He does not turn around.

For a long time, he's been wondering why, after he had indulged a whim, he continued to be drawn to Giulia. Why he had kept going back to her, even after every quarrel.

Now he finally understands.

His mother asks why he doesn't reply. She watches him go to the bedroom and get dressed in a rush. "What's the matter? Now what are you doing?"

"*Mamà, facitivi a quasetta.*"

That is what he tells her, to go knit, as if she were a crazy old woman who should keep to herself. Her face falls, turning into a heap of wounded pride and indignation. "Are you going to her? She's black poison. She's a devil incarnate that stinks of sulfur. What about me? You're leaving me alone?"

She shouts out the window as Vincenzo walks away down Via dei Materassai before the eyes of women watching this little drama.

Vincenzo practically runs down the alleys, past closed stores.

He sees Giulia at the Cassaro. She walks slowly among people in their Sunday clothes, her head bent over the baby. He knows her well enough to see that she's doing her best not to burst into tears. It must have cost her a lot to humiliate herself like this.

Vincenzo catches up with her and takes her by the arm in front of everybody. Giulia is startled. "But—"

"Let's go home. To our home."

PART FIVE

Lace

July 1837 to May 1849

Unn'è u' piso và a balanza.

The scales go where the load is.

—SICILIAN PROVERB

In June 1837, the cholera epidemic that is sweeping across Europe reaches Sicily. The appalling hygiene conditions in which the majority of people live encourage the spread of the disease, which is eradicated only by early October. Contemporary testimonies mention 23,000 dead in Palermo alone.

The years between 1838 and 1847 are relatively quiet, and yet, from as early as 1847, various protests take place in Sicily, fomented by poverty, the constant surge for independence, and social conflicts. The repressive attitude of Ferdinand II stokes emotions and, on January 12, 1848, in Palermo, Giuseppe La Masa and Rosolino Pilo lead an insurrection against the Bourbons: Palermo is the first large city in Italy to declare its independence from the central power. The head of the revolutionary government is Admiral Ruggero Settimo, who, with the aid of aristocrats and the bourgeoisie, tries to involve the people in the decision-making process. Ferdinand grants the constitution, and almost all the other Italian states follow suit: on March 4, Carlo Alberto concedes the Albertine Statute; on March 17 it is the turn of Venice to rebel, and the following day, of Milan. Soon, this revolutionary momentum crosses the whole of Europe, including the Papal State: on November 24, Pope Pius IX is forced to flee to Gaeta. On February 9, 1849, the Roman Republic is born, ruled by a triumvirate (Carlo Armellini, Giuseppe Mazzini, and Aurelio Saffi).

Once again, however, all revolutionary movements are repressed. The fragmented nature of Sicilian politics soon becomes evident (Messina and Palermo are bitter enemies, for instance), as is the incompatibility of the sides at the root of the rebellion: while the aristocracy and the bourgeoisie wish to become wealthy (by taking over the property of the Church), the people hope for a redistribution of the land. In May 1849, weakened and pursued by Bourbon troops, the revolutionary administration decides to surrender. Ferdinand II shows mercy: he does not sentence the leaders of the revolt to death but, instead, sends them into exile. Moreover, he grants a royal pardon to supporters of the rebellion.

COTTON THREAD, needles, bobbins, pillows.

Lace is an art form.

You need steady hands, patience, and sharp eyesight to obtain even just a few centimeters of fabric, intertwining thread after thread, following a subtle pattern.

The Burano lacemakers, who have supported their small island for centuries with their work, know this. They have exported their skill thanks to Catherine de' Medici, who persuaded a few women to move to France and teach their secret art in convents. In the heart of Europe, lace becomes *dentelle*, and adorns the garments of the kingdom's wealthiest men and women. The most famous lace schools move from Italy to the north: to Valenciennes, to Calais, then to Brussels and Bruges.

Napoleon likes lace and makes it compulsory in court dress.

From the dawn of the Industrial Revolution, lace is machine-made in England, using soft fabrics. Even Queen Victoria gets married in a machine-manufactured tulle veil, and this delicate art seems no longer to have a future.

However, hand-made lace lives on. Bobbins are used that allow the workers to interweave threads more quickly. They try using colored silk. Poor girls are encouraged to learn the trade. But it takes years for this ancient art to reach its peak again in Venice and from there to spread once again throughout Italy.

Handmade lace becomes the prerogative of very few, extremely wealthy families. It is a rare possession, as precious as a jewel.

A treasure.

The heat is unbearable, the sun ruthless.

Palermo is dying. Along Cassaro, carts are drawn by emaciated horses. They carry corpses. The carters shout out, "Any dead?" "Anyone got dead to bury?" Some people wave at them and, shortly afterward, a body is thrown down from a window.

The city pays its daily tribute in victims of cholera, an epidemic that came to the island from the mainland in June 1837. Men have made up for what the disease failed to do. After the spread of the epidemic came the people's rebellion, incited by those who accuse the king of having encouraged the contagion: food and water—so people shout accusingly—were contaminated on purpose to decimate the population.

The tuff façades of Baroque buildings, closed and bolted, look like skulls left to bake in the sun. Abandoned by the aristocracy, houses are looted for food and money. Businesses and stores are set on fire. People die in the streets, begging for a crust of bread; there is no more grain coming from the countryside. Fumigation with chlorine does not halt the contagion but fills the alleys with a pungent smoke that blends with the stench of the bonfires in the squares, burning bedding and furniture. Only a few physicians have stayed in the city, alongside a few monks who go from house to house to administer the last rites. Or to bless the dead.

Even the sea, visible behind Porta Felice, looks unreal, almost unreachable. Only a few ships at La Cala, many bearing quarantine signs.

Vincenzo is walking behind the wall on Via degli Argentieri. He has not left the city yet but soon will. He kicks out of the way a stray dog rummaging through the garbage and covers his face with a handkerchief to shield himself from the stench that rises from the sewer drains. Everything carries an inescapable smell of death.

At the top of Via della Zecca Regia stands a carriage with darkened windows, escorted by two men with rifles. Giulia, wearing a hat with a veil, is standing by the carriage, searching the street for him. As soon as she sees him, she clasps her hands over her chest and runs toward him.

"You're coming with us," she says without even greeting him.

He shakes his head, says he cannot leave yet. "The house is not far from Monreale and is well protected," he says to her. "Giovanni and your parents will join you there tonight. Don't go out, and have as little contact as you can with people you don't know," he orders.

Giuseppina's crying and Angelina's whining voice can be heard from the carriage. Giulia holds on to his hands, overwhelmed with anxiety. "You'll come soon, won't you?"

"Yes, yes, I will. Now, you all be careful, have the bedding boiled and—"

She kisses him as though she will never see him again. "I don't want to go," she says, clutching his wrist. "Let's send the girls away. I'll stay with you . . ." she implores. "Who'll look after you if you get sick?"

He shakes his head, says he doesn't want her to, that she, too, must be safe. He practically pushes her into the carriage, while Angelina climbs onto her lap.

Come soon, her eyes seem to say beneath the veil. *Don't leave me alone.*

Vincenzo is forced to look away. He can't bear to watch them go, knowing the disease could kill them within a day and a night. This could be the last time they see one another. Children are easy prey for this disease.

The day before, he made a similar carriage available for his mother and the servant women, and escorted them to the gates of the city. He sent them to the estate in Marsala, where they will be safe.

He cannot leave yet, however. He still has to make sure the warehouses are protected, take care of the supplies, and tell the French suppliers not to send goods that can't pass through customs, since the city is in disarray and nobody is minding the Customs House.

Suddenly, a man emerges from the alley outside Palazzo Steri, and calls out loud to him: it's Francesco Di Giorgio, who's in charge of trade with the Sicilian provinces. "Don Florio! I've found you! Come! It's a disaster!"

Vincenzo's anxiety turns to fear. "Is it the supplies?"

"The valerian tincture, pepper, cardamom, and mint essential oil . . . Nothing, all gone! The little that was left has been requisitioned. When I left I saw a crowd I didn't like outside the store . . . They're all desperate. Apparently they've set fire to and ransacked a pharmacy in the Tribunali district. In the countryside they're even murdering priests because they say they spread the infection . . . People are going crazy!"

"Damn!"

They run to the *aromateria*. The fountains in Piazza del Garraffello have been pulled out; a black *X* has been painted over some of them. The smell of quicklime, used as disinfectant, wafts in gusts, mixed with the stench of the latrines.

In Via dei Materassai, they come across a wall of people. Carmelo Caratozzolo, the *aromateria* manager, is standing outside the door, his arms raised. "We've run out of everything, I swear! There are no ships coming, so there's no restocking! We have nothing left!"

"What do you mean? Not even laudanum?" A man in front of him begs, his hands joined together. "How will I soothe my wife's pain? She's writhing in bed . . ."

Another young man, barely older than a boy, is desperate. "Not even a small bottle of valerian? It's for my daughter, my little girl!"

Behind them, men and women curse, beg, and press to get into the store.

Vincenzo has to plow through, pushing them away with his elbows. The terror that deforms the faces of these men is more evil than the cholera: he can feel it on his skin and can't get away from it; it's as though his arms and legs were hog-tied.

"I don't believe it!" an old man shouts. He grabs a stone and hurls it at the window. “You’ve accumulated the spices so you can give them to your friends!”

At this, Vincenzo stirs himself and leaps forward. They mustn’t destroy the *aromateria*. Everything he is begins and ends within those wood-paneled walls. He first walked in there at the age of eleven, when his uncle took him there and showed him the sign with the injured lion and, in a way, he never left it. More than anything else at this moment, he wishes he could have Uncle Ignazio next to him, and hear his reassuring voice.

“No!” he cries but his voice cannot rise above the roar of the crowd.

“Let’s take it all ourselves!” someone else shouts.

Vincenzo comes between the human mass and Caratozzolo. “Stop!” he yells with all the breath in his body.

The people freeze. Everyone looks at him with a mixture of hatred and hope.

“Don Florio, for the love of God,” the young man says, falling at his feet. “Help us. At least you help us!”

Vincenzo turns to Caratozzolo, but the latter keeps shaking his head. He has tears in his eyes because he truly wishes he could help these wretched people. “Don Florio stands witness. We really have run out of everything. Believe me!”

Vincenzo shows them the palms of his hands. “It’s true, I swear it. I know many of you: you’re Vito,” he tells the young man. “You work at the fish market, your father, Biagio, is a ship’s carpenter and you have a little girl the same age as my daughter. And you’re Bettina, Giovanni the marble polisher’s wife. Behind you there’s Pietro, the stonecutter. I know you and your families because I live here, too. And if I swear to you there’s nothing left, then you must believe me.”

“Lies! You’ve saved all the spices!” a voice from the far end of the square shouts. “Now get out of our way before we remove you!”

The crowd mutters, waves, stirs, presses.

Vincenzo opens his jacket and unbuttons his waistcoat. He reveals his bare chest, on which the first few white hairs are sprouting. "You want to kill me? Here I am. I'm not pulling back. But if I tell you there's nothing, then you have to believe me. Everything's gone. I don't even have anything left for my own family."

The stonecutter has an outburst of anger. "You're saying that because you're going to sell it to your friends!"

Vincenzo laughs, from rage and despair. He opens his arms. "What did you say? What friends? Can you see any carriages here? Or soldiers? No!" He grabs Caratozzolo's arm. "There's only me and this wretch left in the *aromateria.* I'm here just like all of you, and if I get sick then I'll die like a dog, just like you. If I tell you we have nothing left it's because we have nothing left. The supplies at Palazzo Steri are finished. Until the health restrictions are lifted, nothing can get through."

Bettina, the woman, steps forward and takes him by the sleeve. He can't bear the painful incredulity on her face. "How is it possible? You're the largest trader in Palermo and you don't have anything left? If that's true, then . . ."

"Do you want to see for yourself?" Vincenzo indicates the *aromateria.* "Go in."

Silence falls on the square. For a moment, nobody stirs. Then, slowly, the crowd opens up amid sobs and cries of despair, breaks apart, and disperses.

In the end, only the young man on the ground is left. Vincenzo bends over him, puts a hand on the back of his neck, and says in his ear, "Go home, son, and pray to God. Only He can help Palermo."

Vito bursts into tears. His tears get under Vincenzo's skin, because now a father's weeping sounds different to him. Because he imagines himself there, on the ground, kneeling in the mud, wretched and devastated, searching for medicine for Angelina or Giuseppina or, even worse, for Giulia.

The weeping haunts him even when, the following day, he reaches the house in Monreale, where Giulia and the girls are staying. He locks himself in a surly silence. At night, though, unable to sleep, he goes into the room where his daughters are asleep, their hair spread on the pillows, mouths ajar. He sits next to them and listens to their breathing. They're well, they're alive.

He doesn't know if he can say as much about Vito's girl.

Vincenzo Florio, a Palermo trader and industrialist, owner of schooners, sulfur mines, wine cellars, and *tonnaras*, member of the city's Chamber of Commerce, underwriter as well as finance intermediary, is in slippers and shirtsleeves in the modest kitchen of the mezzanine apartment in Via della Zecca Regia. It is October 1837 and the cholera epidemic is finally over after claiming more than twenty thousand lives in the Palermo region.

They've been lucky. They're all still alive. Entire families have been wiped out.

Vincenzo has dined with his illegitimate family: Giulia and his daughters. Tomorrow, he'll go to his mother's in Via dei Materassai. Life is finally getting back to normal.

The girls are already asleep, watched by a nanny. They are lovely and well brought up. Giulia speaks to them in French, a language she learned in Milan as a child. She reads them bedtime stories.

She is still as simple and pragmatic as when he first met her.

Vincenzo watches her tidy up the room and add coal to the brazier. She soaks the vegetables then struggles to open a can. "Can you help me?" she says, indicating the can of tuna in brine. It comes from the Arenella *tonnara*, which he owns in partnership with a half-Frenchman, Augusto Merle, who had relocated to Palermo.

He takes the can and opens it with a knife. The brine squirts up after the metallic click, and a smell that reminds him of his childhood spreads through the room.

The images blend into one another. He recognizes the kitchen in Piano San Giacomo and a shape, with its back to him, pulling chunks of fish from an earthenware pot sealed with wax.

Is it Paolo, his father, or Uncle Ignazio?

The shape turns to him.

His father.

He sees once again the bushy mustache, the stern expression. He watches his father immerse the fish in hot water to get rid of the salt, and say something to his mother about being able to keep the fish for weeks in olive oil.

Something makes a sound in his head, a click, like a clock.

Oil. Tuna.

He's dragged back into the present, and his memories return to the semidarkness. Giulia thanks him. He watches her rub her hands with lemon to remove the smell.

"I could get you a cook," he says all of a sudden.

She shakes her head. "Your mother would keep saying that I make you squander your money. I already have a maid and a nanny for Angela and Giuseppina. Besides, I enjoy cooking."

He insists. "There's my housekeeper's daughter. She's a good girl, and does heavy work, too. I'll send her over."

The response is an impatient sigh. "Sometimes it feels like being your wife. I talk but you don't listen."

Vincenzo puts his arm around her waist. She hugs him, goes past the English-style beard, and kisses him, standing on her toes. She gestures at him to follow her. "Bring the lamp," she whispers with the intimacy of lovers who want each other precisely because of that, each other and nobody else.

They sleep together like man and wife. However, beyond these walls and beyond the courtyard of Via della Zecca Regia lies Palermo. She, too, is a possessive lover, and Vincenzo knows it: jealous, fickle, and capricious, capable of blooming and self-annihilating in a single night.

But appearances conceal a soul of shadows.

Vincenzo knows this darkness well, and mirrors himself in it. He can't afford to lower his guard because what his woman forgives him, the city does not. Palermo will continue to love him, to love the Florios for as long as they keep bringing it money and comfort. The city is going through a mysterious state of grace at this time: it's sprouting more colors, filling with new construction sites and buildings. And Palermo needs his money, the Casa Florio money.

With his shiny shoes and linen jacket, Carlo Giachery watches Vincenzo think. Because he knows Vincenzo is turning something over in his mind and stopped listening to him a few minutes ago. "Vincenzo?"

"Eh?"

"I've been talking to you for some time. Is it my voice that's inducing you to distraction or is there something you want to tell me?"

Vincenzo makes an apologetic hand gesture. "Both, actually. What were we saying?"

"That the Nuova Badia nuns are complaining about the noise made by the cotton mill looms. It's the monks right next door to it who should be complaining, not them. Who knows what's going through their birdbrains?"

Vincenzo props his chin on his joined hands. "That's Sicily all over. No sooner do you try to do something different than somebody will always start whinging and whining because either you're disturbing them, or they don't want it, or they tell you what to do, or they simply try to piss you—"

"I get it." Carlo sniggers into his mustache. Literally. "I was thinking of putting up some cork cladding to muffle the sound but I don't know how much it would help. The devouts are also complaining about the steam from the machines."

"They're looms. It's steam. Hot water! In England, they were already using it twenty years ago and nobody dared say anything. Let them recite a couple more rosaries and keep their windows shut. Instead, listen . . ." He looks for a piece of paper and reads it again. The furrow between his eyebrows gets deeper. "Read this."

Giachery puts on his spectacles and concentrates. "Sales of tuna have fallen."

"At all *tonnaras*, not just here in Sicily; there's a drop in demand also for sardines and mackerel."

"I see." Vincenzo gestures at him to continue reading. "Why do you think that is? Is it still because they think they cause scurvy?"

"Yes. The British are withdrawing and so are other ship owners. But I know it's not true. My family has been trading in brined fish for years, and eating it, and nobody's lost their teeth."

"Who knows? Of course, a drop like this . . . it's not significant yet but it could become so."

Vincenzo makes a gesture of annoyance. "Fresh meat is preserved with ice from the Madonie Mountains. But tuna has always been salted."

"Perhaps a different method . . ." Carlo is pensive. "Like smoking, but I don't know if it's suitable for tuna. Or else—"

Click.

Vincenzo looks up.

Click.

His father soaking the fish in oil after desalting it because . . . *Click.*

He dives into his papers, looking for the calendar. "When's the next *mattanza* . . . ? The next slaughter in Arenella is in ten days' time. So . . ."

Giachery observes him. Vincenzo is animated with a frenzy that almost makes him look younger.

"Why does meat decompose, Carlo?" he asks, standing up. He doesn't wait for an answer. "Because worms start eating at it. But if the meat is cooked, then it becomes more resistant. And how do you preserve it for a long time to stop it decomposing?" He places himself in front of Carlo and leans toward him. "Say if I want it to keep for six months or a year, or even longer, for example for an ocean voyage, what do I do?"

He whispers the answer in his ear.

In May, with the warmth of spring, the first *tonnaras* are dropped. It's a plentiful catch, and the sailors thank Saint Peter and Saint Francis of Paola for granting such abundance.

In May, cans, some made of tin, others glass, full of tuna in oil, are safely stored in Giachery's pantry, under the puzzled but watchful eye of Carolina, his wife.

They're here, waiting for the correct period of time to pass.

A year.

A year, before the experiment can prove successful. Before cooked tuna, covered in oil, sealed in a container, can survive a sea voyage or in any case be preserved long-term. Vincenzo is really trying. With his stubbornness, with the notion that if he doesn't try something new, nothing can change.

And he wants to be in control of his life.

In June, with blinding sun and laundry drying in the first breath of scirocco wind, Giulia takes Vincenzo's hand and tells him she is pregnant again.

On December 18, 1838, at dawn, somebody knocks at the Florios' door in Via dei Materassai. The knocking soon turns to punching.

Giuseppina hears the noise and stops the servant girl on her way to open the door. "Who is it?"

She sees a breathless maid rush into the house. "I'm looking for Don Vincenzo," she says with the hint of a curtsy. "It's important. My mistress . . . My mistress is in labor."

Giuseppina pushes her out. "So? Out—you and her!"

Vincenzo appears. His eyes are still half-asleep but become alert as soon as he sees the servant. "Ninetta, what is it?"

"Signora Giulia sends me. It's time, Don Florio."

"Oh, heavens, today of all days!" He runs his fingers through his hair. "I have a meeting about the cellars and I can't miss it, she knows that. Tell her I'll be there later. I can't now."

The girl quickly vanishes down the stairs.

Giuseppina shuts the door with an outburst of anger. "She comes to find you even here?"

"I ordered her to."

"She's not even your wife. What does she want? More money?"

Vincenzo gets dressed in a hurry, his mind in the bedroom in Via della Zecca Regia, where, he is certain, Giulia is crying out in pain. At the same time he wonders when his mother had become so cold-hearted. In recent years she has grown thinner and let herself go. Her face, which should have softened with age, looks instead as if covered in a crust of resentment against the whole world.

He, too, is getting old: there are gray locks in his hair. His eyelids are heavier, and his face is furrowed with wrinkles. Vincenzo had shelved the idea of a high-rank marriage some time ago. It's hard enough to find a rosebud to marry a man of forty, let alone a man with three bastards to support.

Besides—he thinks but not without embarrassment—Giulia is much more than a wife. She is a companion and a support. She's the only one who's had the strength to bear the dark side he carries in him. Giulia will always come after Casa Florio; she knows that and loves him in spite of it. She has accepted ambition, anger, and social contempt.

She has given him everything.

Except . . .

He doesn't dare continue.

A beam of light illuminates Ignazio's ring. Vincenzo's fingers linger on the fold in his tie. On his way to the office, he goes to Sant'Agostino, to the Madonna of Parturition. For the first time in ages, he utters a silent prayer.

He prays for a miracle.

He goes to the *aromateria*, leaves a note for Lorenzo Lugaro, the accountant, then joins Francesco Di Giorgio at the warehouse in Piano San Giacomo in order to discuss a contract for a shipment of sumac.

Finally, he meets the owner of some vineyards between Trapani and Paceco who is willing to sell him the futures of his ansonica, catarratto, and damaschino. In large quantities and good for wine-making, at least judging by what Raffaele, who still manages the cellar, has heard.

"They told us you were a gentleman and now we have confirmation. Your cousin is a good sort but you have definite ideas. You know exactly what you want, and that's why I wanted to speak to you, the owner."

The man, tall, with a beard, has callused hands but expensive clothes, the sign of recently acquired wealth. Vincenzo thanks him, escorts him to the office door, and, meanwhile, mulls over his words.

Because—and this is something that's been needling him for a while—the marsala wine cellar worries him. Things are not going as they should with Raffaele. He lacks initiative and courage. He'll have to tackle this as soon as possible and have a word with him.

It's noon by the time he can finally go to Via della Zecca Regia. Even now, Lugaro follows him to tell him about the rumors circulating between the Chamber of Commerce and La Cala. "The French and the British have a monopoly on the transportation of many goods and will never give it up to the Naples steamship company. Nobody wants to go against them."

"This remains to be seen."

He cannot think of ships now. Behind his stone-carved face, he spent all morning picturing Giulia screaming in pain, her face moist with sweat and her body torn.

He has been hoping that a miracle, *that miracle*—the only one that led him to church to ask for grace—could occur.

Vincenzo goes in through the front door. Lugaro follows him uneasily.

There's a bustle on the stairs. He arrives to find Giovanni and Tommaso on the doorstep with a few acquaintances.

Their voices get stuck in their throats. Everybody looks at him as though their eyes are weighed down, as though they could strike him and hurt him.

"What's the matter?" he asks. "Is Giulia all right?"

Nobody answers.

Panic.

Vincenzo throws open the door, walks through the rooms, and bursts into Giulia's bedroom. She is pale, half lying on the bed, and the little girls are prattling next to her.

Her mother and the midwife collect the laundry and buckets of red-stained water.

He grabs the footboard. "Are you all right?"

"What are you doing here?" Antonia says, chiding him. "Go down with the other men. Giulia's not ready yet."

Instead, Giulia sits up. "I'm all right, Mamma. Can you step out, please? I need to speak with Vincenzo."

The mother and the midwife exchange a puzzled look. It's still too soon and a woman must rest after giving birth. The midwife shrugs as if to say: *As long as she's happy . . .* She collects her things and leaves. Antonia hesitates, then grabs an armful of stained towels and pushes Angela and Giuseppina out the door. "Come with Grandma, come on, let's put these things in the wash."

Lugaro shuts the door behind them.

Now they are alone.

Vincenzo's tongue won't ask. It just cannot. In this room his power, money, spices, ships, wine, sulfur, and *tonnaras* are worthless. His voice is like a thin thread. "Are you all right?"

"Yes."

They speak at the same time, and stop.

Suddenly, there's a wail.

Giulia indicates the reed cradle. "Look."

Vincenzo approaches the basket and sees a wrinkled face and mouth making strange grimaces. He bends over the swaddled little body and studies it with a curiosity made of trepidation.

Giulia says nothing, and just savors the moment so she can store it clearly in her memory.

He lightly strokes the shape under the blanket, fascinated. "Is it a boy?"

At last, Giulia nods.

Vincenzo covers his mouth and stifles a sob. "Thank you, God," he says. He says it again, so softly that no one can hear him. "Thank you. Thank you."

His business, his whole life, now has a purpose, the way it was for his uncle Ignazio and even his father, who is now a faint memory. The future is no longer a fog bank off the coast. It has arms, legs, and a head.

He wants to hug his son but is afraid. He never held the girls in his arms just after they were born. Then, on an impulse, he picks him up, one hand under the baby's head, the other holding the body. "My blood," he says to him. "My darling. My heart. Light of my life."

The baby is so light and his skin looks transparent in the December light. He has a ferrous, sweet smell of milk, starch, and lavender.

Giulia tries to ignore the tenderness she feels at seeing father and son together, even though her heart is in her throat and she wants to hug them both. She must force herself to speak now, to ask now. To claim. She knows it's now or never. "I've given you a son. Now I want my honor back. You must acknowledge not just him but also the girls. You owe it to me."

Vincenzo looks at the newborn's face: he has defined features, a high forehead, a powerful jaw.

He's a Florio.

But he has Giulia's elongated eyes.

He sits on the edge of the bed, the little one in his arms. He takes her hand. "They will bear my name. You will bear my name. I swear it before God."

Giulia's sigh carries in it relief and exhaustion. She falls back on the pillows and keeps looking at father and son united in this embrace that looks like a miracle.

She feels tears of liberation running down her cheeks. Because of Vincenzo's words, her life will no longer be concealed, marked by shame.

It has taken four years to have this promise. Years of loneliness, of contempt, of reproach from her family, who—even so—have stood by her although she chose to not really know why.

She remembers arguments, separation, and making peace again with her man, Giuseppina's insults, Antonia's nasty silences. All this to reach this moment.

Giulia continues to hold his hand tight. "Will you call him Paolo, like your father?"

My father? he thinks. *The man who conceived me or the one who raised me? The one who actually allowed me to become what I am today?*

Vincenzo lets go of Giulia's fingers. "No." He strokes his son's face. There's sadness in his eyes. "No. His name will be Ignazio."

She nods. "Ignazio," she repeats.

They will carry forever the memory of what they say to each other without speaking. Until the day when it is Giulia who holds Vincenzo's hand and he has the courage to tell her how much he loved her even without telling her.

The light is streaming in through the windows, flooding the stairs, reaching the ceilings, and dropping down on the sumptuously laid table. It sets the Murano glass ablaze and lingers on the Capodimonte china. The house looks like an explosion of light.

Wearing an evening dress, Giulia is waiting for the guests to arrive.

She checks that nothing is missing, that the servants look tidy, and that there's abundant champagne. She makes sure the table linen is immaculate, the silver gleaming, and that the food in the serving trays is kept warm. There are cigars and liqueurs waiting on a shelf.

It's an important occasion, the first time Giulia is hosting a dinner party: they're celebrating the birth of the company that Vincenzo, "her husband"—it sounds so odd—has been promoting.

It's a dinner for business associates, true, a moment of entirely male conviviality. But the guests are among the most important businessmen in Palermo, and not only that: there are also aristocrats, people with titles as long as your arm. She can't afford to make a mistake.

It's her share of the responsibility: she's a Florio now.

She can't quite get used to it. For her, "home" will always be the mezzanine in Via della Zecca Regia. This is Vincenzo and his mother's apartment, which she came to as a wife only in January 1840, more than a year after Ignazio's birth.

First, Vincenzo acknowledged Ignazio, Angelina, and Giuseppina as his own children. Then, a few weeks later, on January 15, he married Giulia before a public official in a civil ceremony. They went to church on the same day, late in the evening, the way you did for shotgun weddings.

Outside family and the witnesses—Casa Florio employees—nobody attended the ceremony officiated by the priest of Santa Maria della Pietà in Kalsa, the same one who had baptized their children.

The man, now old and full of aches and pains, let out a sigh of relief when Vincenzo signed the marriage certificate. He even muttered a "See, that's all it takes," charged with meaning.

At this thought, Giulia smiles. It took a baby boy for her to become Donna Giulia Florio.

She toys with her diamond-and-pearl bracelet, struggling to control her nervousness.

Afterward, she goes to the children's room and peeks inside. Ignazio's asleep, as is Giuseppina. Angelina, however, is sitting next to the French governess, Mademoiselle Brigitte, who's reading her a story. She greets Angelina with a kiss and shuts the door without making a sound. This another change in her life. It is no longer she who puts her children to bed.

The housekeeper creeps up on her and makes her jump. "I beg your pardon," she says. "I didn't want to frighten you."

"It's all right. What is it?"

The housekeeper's name is Luisa and she's a middle-aged woman who used to serve a noble Neapolitan family. "Signora, your mother-in-law," she says, hesitating, "keeps asking questions, says she's unwell, and won't come down to welcome the guests. Also, she can't digest the dinner you ordered."

Giulia massages her forehead. "I'll go speak to her."

Obviously, Donna Giuseppina can't even leave her alone this evening.

Giulia goes to the internal staircase that separates Giuseppina's living quarters from the rest of the family. Shortly before the wedding, in an attempt to make it easier for his mother and wife to live under the same roof, Vincenzo divided the apartment so the two women wouldn't clash over supremacy in running the household.

It didn't help much.

Giulia finds her mother-in-law sitting at her writing desk. She's dressed for home: with a lace cap and a threadbare, gray cotton dress.

"Donna Giuseppina . . ." she says with a bow. Let it never be said she's not respectful toward her. "Signora Luisa says you're not feeling well."

"That's right. I'm a bit breathless and don't feel like going downstairs. Besides, you're there, aren't you?" She studies Giulia's dress with a fierce precision. She pauses on the neckline. "All that lace . . . it must have cost an arm and a leg. And it's very low cut. Too elegant. It looks like a dress for going to the theater."

"My husband suggested I wear it."

Giuseppina makes an annoyed gesture. "He thinks like a man. He likes certain things." *And you've always let him have them*, her expression seems to say. "Anyway . . ."

Giulia clears her throat. She tries to forget the offense. As far as her mother-in-law is concerned, she is the intruder and she must put up with it. Heavens above, how she hates this woman. "Don't you want to come downstairs? Even just to welcome the guests then retire? There's Prince Trigona and Prince Lanza di Trabia, and Baron Chiaramonte Bordonaro. Also Ingham and Signor Giachery. If you don't come at all, your son will be upset." She approaches and takes on a meek expression, although she feels her stomach contract with humiliation. "You know how hard Vincenzo's worked to bring about this contract, how long it took him to persuade his associates to purchase a steamship. Come now, make this sacrifice for his sake." She indicates the closet. "If I help you, you could change in no time—"

"Stop insisting. I don't feel up to it. Bring me a cup of chicken broth instead." Her calmness sounds like a saucepan cracking. "You, rather, are you ready or do you still have to do your hair? Have you done everything correctly? It's not easy to organize a dinner party like this when you have no experience."

Giulia instinctively touches her bun and glares at Giuseppina with rancor. "I didn't think you had organized many parties or dinners for your son."

"Yes, a few, certainly more than you. It's not easy being a Florio, I should know." She looks at her fingers, marked by time. "They're demanding people. They don't have any regard for anybody; when they want something they go after it and get it. They don't admit failure."

Giulia bows her head, unable to give an appropriate response. She hates herself when she cannot come up with a reply. *I won't fail*, she tells herself. *I won't shame my husband but make him proud of me.* But it's a faint thought, a wisp of smoke in her consciousness.

"Have you made the meat roll?" Giuseppina's tone is harsh. "I hope you're using the silver, the set Vincenzo brought from England—"

"Yes. I've also done the preserves and cold sauces for the roast. And *ghiotta trapanese* tuna."

Giuseppina turns on her chair and takes off her cap.

"What about the French wine? I've never understood this obsession of yours with things foreign. I guess you northerners have your ways. Nothing to do with me and I don't want anything to do with it." Thick gray locks fall on her shoulders. "Go check if everything's in order: servants do it all their own way when there's no one to command them. And tell them to bring me the broth; then send up the maid. She has to help me get ready for the night."

Giulia returns to the main apartment, her cheeks flushed, her hands shaking.

She stops a maid and tells her to take the broth upstairs. *Let that woman fend for herself,* she thinks, shuddering with humiliation. Giuseppina has decided not to come, and the reason is crystal clear: she doesn't want to be blamed in case of failure.

Giulia opens a window and seeks comfort in fresh air. The tightness in her stomach relaxes. She looks at herself in the mirror: silk navy-blue dress, string of pearls. A shawl over the neckline: French lace Vincenzo bought in Marseille, where he went with Augusto Merle, a while ago. A gift worthy of a princess.

And yet it's not enough. After three pregnancies, she no longer has the waistline she used to have. But she carries herself well and has a graceful manner. *But what if I'm not good enough for Vincenzo?* she wonders. *What if Donna Giuseppina is right and I embarrass him?*

Because it's true: it's not easy being Vincenzo's wife. All of a sudden, she's living with a man with an intense public life, who's on first-name terms with the most important men in the realm. And she, who has always been in the shadows, is afraid of making a mistake.

She hears the sound of carriage wheels on the cobblestones in the street, of doors opening, of male voices. There's no more time to be anxious.

ᘐ

Ben Ingham climbs the stairs with Vincenzo. They're both flushed from the heat but their faces show that they are pleased. "This is a historic day, my dear friend. Progress has finally reached Sicily! It's taken a few years but still . . ."

Giulia is on the doorstep. "Welcome. I hope you had a fruitful meeting."

Ingham is not surprised by her directness, unusual for a woman. "All signed and sealed. The shares have been paid. The Sicilian Steamship Company is a reality." He's enthusiastic and greets her by kissing her hand. "My dear, you look splendid." Behind him enters a statuesque woman with long black hair streaked with gray, and a diamond necklace: Alessandra Spadafora, Duchess of Santa Rosalia, the woman Giulia saw at Teatro Carolino many years ago now. Ingham's wife since 1837: by marrying her he has become a fully accredited aristocrat.

The duchess greets them with an unaffected smile. She's polite to Vincenzo and warm toward Giulia. Both women share the status of having been mistresses, and this forms a kind of vague bond between them. They have nothing else in common, however: Giulia is still a merchant's daughter, while the duchess was born an aristocrat. Her first husband, with whom she had two children before he died and left her in financial difficulty, belonged to the island's rural nobility.

She thanks them. Vincenzo comes up to her. "Where's my mother?" he murmurs. "She should be here."

"She's barricaded herself in her bedroom. She says she doesn't feel like coming down; she just asked for a cup of broth." They both keep on smiling and welcoming their guests, who arrive straight from the office of Caldara, the notary, where they've signed the document creating the new company.

"Did you try to persuade her?"

Giulia responds by raising her eyebrows.

More footsteps and loud voices.

"This is a truly beautiful house, Florio. I should have come here much sooner." Gabriele Chiaramonte Bordonaro comes in and his attention is immediately drawn to a cabinet made of carved ebony. "Superb! Chinese, right? Is it an antique?"

"It's from Ceylon. Baron, may I introduce my wife?"

Chiaramonte Bordonaro turns. He hadn't noticed Giulia. "Oh, good evening, Donna Florio." Then he heads to the drawing room.

Giulia and Vincenzo remain by the door, awaiting latecomers. "Is that really a baron?"

"He bought the land and the title at the same time. Before that he was the steward of that very land and made a fortune lending money." Vincenzo coughs into his hand. "If people call me a mangy dog, you can imagine what they say about him. But now he has a coat of arms on his front door, so . . ."

The arrival of more guests prevents him from continuing.

Giulia feels a pang of nervousness.

"Don Florio . . . and you must be Donna Giulia." Bowing, kissing hands. Giuseppe Lanza di Trabia, followed by Romualdo Trigona, Prince of Sant'Elia.

The wives, just a step behind them, greet them with a polite nod. Vincenzo kisses their hands and introduces Giulia. "Donna Giulia, thank you for inviting us. This is a very special occasion." Lanza di Trabia, an educated, broad-minded prince, the owner of Palermo's most elegant homes, seems to be evaluating with a single glance the prestige of the place he is in. But nothing could be further from the truth. His wife is a Branciforte. Ancient nobility, one of those who founded the city. Giulia feels her eyes on her and tries to muster a smile, something to soften the severity of their judgment of her.

Stefania Branciforte is a matron dressed in an amaranth-colored outfit. She is of an advanced age, wearing jewels that have probably been in her family for generations. She keeps her eyes downcast, her hands clasped over her stomach. She looks around as though afraid of touching the walls and furniture, and the disapproving looks her husband is giving her serve no purpose.

Giulia suddenly feels poor and wretched. The lace on her shawl seems to lose all its value and her dress all trace of elegance. She instinctively turns to the wife of Prince Trigona, Laura Naselli. She is younger than the princess of Trabia, and has long hair braided in a splendid style. She reads the same distaste in her eyes.

They look at her without seeing her, as though she were transparent.

There's the kept woman who got to be a wife, they say without opening their mouths. *The bourgeoise who spread her legs so she could become rich . . . but still a bourgeoise.*

She bows, as etiquette requires: they are princesses, and she's a nobody's daughter with a far-from-irreproachable past. The two women stare at the air next to her head and nod at the greeting that is owed to them, then walk into the salon, looking around.

"There's a certain pretense at elegance, don't you think?" Princess Laura asks. "The clothes, the furniture . . ."

The other lady shakes her hand and opens her fan. "As you say, pretense."

Giulia feels a lump in her throat. Her face burns and sweat trickles down between her breasts. So was all she has done for nothing? she wonders. In any case, it's not enough, she knows it now, just as she knows that all Vincenzo's money will not be enough for these people to accept him.

She goes to stand closer to her husband, swallowing anger and humiliation.

Trigona greets her with an understated "*Enchanté, madame*," then gives the ceiling a lazy look. "An extraordinary house in so many ways, Don Florio."

He exchanges a glance with the prince of Trabia, who suppresses a smile. "Times change, my friend. Times and people."

Vincenzo indicates the guests. "Come. The other partners are already in the salon."

The wives approach their husbands, deep in conversation. They do not even give her the possibility of speaking to them.

Vincenzo has seen and heard everything.

Only Giulia has noticed the sudden tension in his back. He, too, understands.

Chandeliers glow beneath the decorated ceiling of the parlor. The Capodimonte china is laid out on a tablecloth of linen and Flanders lace. The Murano crystal glasses are waiting to be filled with the French wines kept chilled in silver pails.

Giulia follows Vincenzo, converses with the guests, and feels more than a shudder of uncertainty. Will she do something wrong? Will she be able to estimate the correct timing for the various courses? She hesitates; her eyes ask her husband for help but he's absorbed in conversation with Ingham.

It's the thought of those ladies, as noble as they are arrogant, that gives her the courage to act. She throws her shoulders back and looks at the waiters. One of them pulls out a chair and she sits down. At the other end of the table, Vincenzo follows her example. It's the signal for dinner to begin.

The diners take their seats. With a nod, Giulia prompts the serving staff to present the dishes to the guests so they may choose. Appetizers, meats in jelly and soups, then first and second courses, both meat and fish.

A valet serves the wine while another pours water from a crystal carafe. The servants approach the guests. One after the other, they appear with silver trays and dishes of meat roll, *ghiotta trapanese* tuna, potatoes, vegetables, and lamb.

The princess of Trabia's attention lingers on Giulia, her hand clasping a fork with which she has speared a piece of lamb. She seems astonished, annoyed even. Alessandra Spadafora, on the other hand, has met her eyes and, with a furtive gesture, lifts her glass of wine to her.

Giulia thanks her with a smile concealed by her napkin.

Standing by the dining room door, the housekeeper is keeping a watchful eye on the procession of waiters. In the kitchen, two scullery maids are up to their elbows in tubs, washing dishes and silver so that the diners may have clean tableware.

Giulia is tense and hardly touches her food. She has just a sip of water. What she does try, however, is cooked well, served at the right temperature, with first-class ingredients.

She is so nervous that she doesn't notice the fleeting glances of her husband, seated at the head of the table opposite her.

She allows herself to breathe freely only once the pyramid of fresh and candied fruit and the *semifreddi* are served. Nobody has made any comment and, above all, everybody has eaten heartily, including the two noblewomen, who have sat stiffly on their chairs throughout dinner.

Giulia then gives the order that liqueurs and cigars be brought, in the English fashion, and is about to withdraw with the women to the adjacent parlor when she notices movement among the ladies. It all happens very quickly: the housekeeper approaches and mutters something; she stands up, goes to Vincenzo, and whispers a few words; he squeezes her wrist; she nods and leaves, closing the dining room door.

Without moving, she watches the scene from a distance: the two princesses are preparing to leave. They sighed and said they're tired, partly because the dinner was long and demanding. Once they're back home they'll instruct the coachmen to return to pick up their husbands.

But Giulia does not believe this comedy even for a second. Those two came with their husbands because it was a matter of business, of money. Now, though, they would have to engage in conversation with her. And the very thought horrifies them.

Go ahead, run off, she thinks. *And go gossip. Nothing'll change the fact that Vincenzo is proud of me. Anyone who came here tonight can only say that the Florios keep a table worthy of princes and kings.*

Alessandra Spadafora puts a hand on her arm. "I must go, too, my dear. It's very late and I no longer have the energy I had when I was twenty and able to stay up and revel all night. But may I compliment you on this evening?" She draws closer. "You will come to see me, won't you? After all, we're neighbors and have much in common."

Giulia puts her hand over hers. "I will come very gladly," she replies with sincerity.

The princess of Trabia takes her leave with a regal nod. Trigona's wife, on the other hand, shakes her hand. "A very pleasant evening," she says in a hiss, as though unable to utter the compliment out loud.

Giulia's eyes are shining. She feels she has passed an exam and, most important, that she has not disappointed her husband. She has played her part. Now, relieved, she can retire to her bedroom, and leave the men to their chatter and their liqueurs.

The women have just left when Caldara, the notary, and Carlo Giachery arrive. "Have I missed anything?" the latter asks Vincenzo, who is standing on the doorstep.

"You mean besides dinner? Not much: only Chiaramonte Bordonaro's ramblings. He's severely testing the patience of the prince of Trabia and his noble detachment by telling him about his collection of antiquities." Vincenzo accompanies him to the bar and asks for a brandy.

"He can't help himself." Carlo takes a glass of madeira. "Shame about Baron Riso. It would have been interesting to have him as one of the partners."

"I think the old rogue is counting all his sins so he can give a detailed account to his Maker. They say he's got one foot in the grave."

Ingham approaches and indicates the bottle of port to a valet, who immediately serves him a glass. "Poor man. I can't picture him dying in a bed. Maybe it's all the curses the Turks put on him when he was a privateer. Were he ten years younger, he would have taken the helm of a ship, for all the baronetcy he bought himself. I'll have the pastor say prayers for him."

"It's not a ship. It's a steamship. The *Palermo*."

"What are you talking about? Steam?" Gabriele Chiaramonte Bordonaro intervenes in the group and confuses the conversation. He grabs a bottle of marsala and pours himself a drink. "The problem, as I was just saying to the illustrious prince of Trabia, is that we don't know how to repair it if it breaks down. I'm not telling you this just as a partner but as a treasurer. Do you know any British mechanics who are familiar with these engines, Ingham? Will they send them to you with the steamship? Because all you'll find here are ship carpenters."

"Of course I do." Ingham is not perturbed. "They'll come and teach those who live here how to repair the engines and even how to build them. If you don't pluck up the courage with both hands and take no risks, nothing will ever change in Sicily. Besides, Don Florio and I are not worried, and yet we own the largest share of the company, so why should you be?"

"It's we traders who are always interested in this kind of issue. We don't have our backs covered by an important name or family." Chiaramonte takes a gulp of liqueur.

His head down, staring at his own glass, Vincenzo nods.

The prince of Trigona joins them. "Come now, Chiaramonte. Don't be unfair." His tone is lighthearted but he seems annoyed. "If we are also committing to this business it's because we know that the future waits for no man. Tradition and being cautious are all very well but we must learn to look to the present."

"And to the future." Vincenzo raises his glass. "Gentlemen, a toast. To our enterprise!"

Glasses clink as the men all shake hands.

These words remain entangled in Vincenzo's memory before falling into the void of his consciousness. *Engines. Work store. Mechanics.*

A seed that's going to sprout roots.

At the end, when voices drop and the guests start to feel tired, dark bottles appear on the table, some still with a thin layer of dust on them. Vincenzo proudly picks up a bottle and uncorks it. It's the marsala wine from his cellars. A special reserve, which, he explains, he has been saving for an occasion like this. The guests approach to sample it. The small, tulip-shaped glasses are filled.

It's a good wine, with a sweet, round, but not sickly flavor. You can smell the sea, honey, and the grapes left to ferment. And there's even a hit of sharpness from the salt pans.

A cigar in his mouth, Ben Ingham waits for a few guests to walk away before he speaks. "May I be frank?"

Vincenzo narrows his eyes. It's not like Ingham to ask permission to speak. And neither is that strange, complicit air on his face. He nods at him to continue.

"When I heard you were going to marry Giulia, I was puzzled. I mean, for such a long time she'd been—"

"What Duchess Spadafora was for you?"

The Englishman laughs. "*Touché.* In any case, unlike the duchess, you'll agree that your lady doesn't have very much experience of social life."

"I agree," Vincenzo replies dryly, abruptly.

Ben bows his head. An indulgent smile appears on his strict face, marked by years. "I think you made the best choice. I remember your frenzy in trying to find a woman with a title . . . and all that time you had a treasure right next to you. This woman is a pearl, Vincenzo."

He nods, eyes fixed on his marsala.

The forced choice turned out to be the best choice.

"And something else." The Englishman laughs out loud, and that is also unusual, for he is always self-controlled. Maybe it's the drink or the euphoria over the recently signed contract. "You know, when you started building your cellar in Marsala, I thought you would never exceed my or Woodhouse's production." He takes a sip. He laughs. "There, too, I was wrong. As God is my witness, you are my biggest error of evaluation."

Shoulder to shoulder, Vincenzo answers him in a low voice. "When we began, me, you, my uncle . . . there was nothing here. No factories, no companies, no insurance firms. We didn't have obstacles or competitors, and everything we did seemed like folly." He indicates the crowded room in front of him. "And now . . ."

"Everything's changed now."

"Some things. Not everything."

Ingham also looks at the men in the room: aristocrats from some of Sicily's oldest families, and aristocrats who had purchased their lands and titles at bankruptcy auctions. "The old and the new," he says almost to himself. "There's something I never told you. Years ago, when I acquired the Scala estate, I was told I could take the title of baron. Me, a baron!" He laughs, but it is a terse, harsh laugh. "Your uncle Ignazio was still alive. One day I met him and he addressed me by the title. And I told him that if I was a baron then he was a prince, because of the two of us his certainly was the more noble behavior."

"My uncle was a gentleman." A bitter regret.

"Much more so than some people in this room." His tone grows softer but only for a moment. "As for me, I can't forget how I got here. I was a young man following the British army, sent here by a family who traded in cloth, and who had lost everything in a shipwreck. I wagered on this land and stayed here even when my fellow countrymen left. There were times when the only thing that held me together was the thought that I would still be working the next day. I can thank God for that, and for being still alive . . . As a matter of fact, I thank Him every night before I put my head on the pillow. I know this place and your people, and I have learned to love and despise them in equal measure. I don't need a manor to be Ben Ingham, who sails as far as America and invests in New World railways."

Vincenzo does not reply. Because he knows it's not about money, it's not about power: it's about something more subtle, about taking a step back and bowing your head in deference.

He thinks it but doesn't say it, that these are notions attached to these people's bones. Wealth is not enough, nor is experience.

It's not enough if you don't have the title.

The palace.

The blood.

~

"This one. This one's perfect."

Carlo Giachery watches Vincenzo hunched over the plan of the villa he's building for him. Bright, unusual, full of greenery.

The architect draws a sigh of relief. It's not easy to please the illustrious Don Florio. He lights a cigar and offers him one but the other man declines. Then he calmly sits in an armchair at the corner of the worktable. "So you're happy?"

Vincenzo sits opposite him. "Happy enough. Although I haven't come here only to talk about this project."

Giachery stretches his legs. "It's about the Favignana *tonnara*, isn't it? Last year, when you rented it from the Pallavicinis in Genoa, I did wonder if you were biting off more than you could chew. I mean, you already had Arenella, Sant'Elia, and Solanto . . ."

"Favignana and Formica get a bigger catch than the three of them put together. That's why I picked them."

They look at each other. Vincenzo nods. "I've ordered olive oil and barrels. They're already on their way to the Aegadian Islands. I'm about to go there myself and I want you to come with me."

The next day, they're already traveling by sea. Nobody knows where they're going. They skirt around the Gulf of Castellammare, sail past the Cape of San Vito. Immediately afterward, the Aegadian Islands appear on the horizon.

When they arrive, a crowd of fishermen gathers to see the steamship with the metal hull that has invaded the harbor. Their faces are dark from the sun and salt, and their clothes are very loose. Nearby, there are women followed by half-naked, barefoot children. The island is bare, the houses little more than hovels. Poverty has a face and a body here.

A man comes away from the group: he has a body like the trunk of an oak, curly hair, and a beard that comes halfway down his chest. "I'm Vito Cordova, the overseer—*u' rais.*" He bows his head. "*Assabbinirìca*," he says, using the traditional greeting.

Vincenzo studies him. He proffers his right hand. "Don Vincenzo Florio. I'm the new lessee of the *tonnara*."

"You?"

"Yes."

The fisherman half closes his eyes, which are already narrow, imprisoned in a network of veins and wrinkles. He wipes his callused hand, full of scars, on his pants, and shakes Vincenzo's gingerly. "Nobody from the Genoa lot ever came here. Are you from these parts?"

"I'm from Palermo. The Pallavicinis have leased me the *tonnara* for nine years."

Surprise flashes on Cordova's barklike face. The Genoese owners have always sent their stewards and never come here themselves. "What do you want to see? The *marfaraggio*? The boats?"

"Possibly. What do you think?"

Cordova points at the buildings and starts walking a few steps ahead of Vincenzo and Carlo. Behind them, like a procession, comes the entire village. Their footsteps raise the sand and dust while gusts of wind spin a host of dry Neptune grass.

The *tonnara* stands in the most sheltered part of the bay. Reed roofs, cracked walls, and heaps of rope in the sun suggest neglect.

Vincenzo purses his lips and speaks softly to Carlo. "Pallavicini charges more than three thousand *oncie* in rent for a *tonnara* that's one of the richest in Sicily . . . and look at what he gets away with."

"He doesn't give a damn."

The voice that reaches Vincenzo is that of an old man standing at the entrance of the building, perched on a stool. "He only cares about the money."

They exchange looks. The old man's expresses resignation and bitterness; Vincenzo's, curiosity.

Followed by Carlo, he walks into the building. There's sand and dust around them: the tuff is flaking and the bricks are corroded by salt air. The smell of the sea and algae envelops them, along with the more persistent odor of dried salt. There are dogs loitering in the courtyard and the boat ramps, children flocking around them then running to their mothers for shelter.

However, no sooner have they walked through the courtyard barrier than they're overwhelmed by an unbearable stench that reminds Vincenzo of the one lingering over Palermo during the cholera epidemic.

"What's this place? A cemetery?"

"Kind of," Cordova explains. "There's a *bosco* down there, and dead animals, so the blood drains. Over here we have the *muciari*—the small boats."

"Yes, I know what *muciari* are. My father and my uncle were seamen. And what's over there?"

Carlo watches them, slightly puzzled, trying to keep up with the thick Sicilian accent. "What are you saying?"

"He's explaining the reason for this terrible smell: over there, in that area they call the *bosco*—the wood—they leave the tuna to bleed white and the carcasses to rot, while right here in front they have the *muciari*—the fishing boats . . ."

A man suddenly comes out of the building. He wears a crumpled suit and a straw hat over his flushed forehead. "What are you doing here? Get out! Out!"

The small crowd takes a step back but doesn't scatter. The man pushes them away, stops in front of Cordova, and speaks to him rudely. "Don Vito, why didn't you call for me? I would have welcomed our guest."

The fisherman's eyes turn opaque. "He arrived just like that, without telling anybody. Just showed up."

Vincenzo slowly turns. Carlo knows this expression, crosses his arms, and waits.

"He's right, nobody knew I was coming. And who would you be?"

"Saro Ernandez, at your service. I'm the bookkeeper. You must be Don Florio. My respects." The man takes a deferential bow. "Did you come just like that? I mean . . . without anybody except your secretary?"

"Why? Is that a problem? Besides, he's not my secretary. This is Signor Carlo Giachery, an architect."

The man is disconcerted. "No . . . I really didn't expect a visit so soon. They told us that . . . Well, I was just expecting you a few days later. Also, I didn't think you'd come alone."

"And yet here I am. Come, I need to speak to you."

The office is a room filled with sun rays, shielded from the nauseating smell from the plant. Ernandez shows him the books.

"So, in this particular *mattanza* we've caught three thousand tuna so far," Vincenzo comments. "It's May, the *tonnara* has only just been lowered into the sea, so there'll be others . . ."

"Yes, we expect many more. We've seen shoals that—"

Vincenzo does not let him finish. He turns his back to him and looks at the *rais*, who is still standing by the door. "And what do you think, Master Cordova?"

The man nods. "At least as many more. And a lot of sardines."

The bookkeeper nervously picks up a few receipts. "We also have the salt from your associate D'Alì. Salt from the Trapani pans, you know, of excellent quality and—"

"I'm not interested," Vincenzo says abruptly. "From now on we'll use a different system." He walks up to the *rais*. They're almost the same height, perhaps the same age, although the fisherman looks much older. "Let's change the tune."

Saro Ernandez clutches the papers. "Change the tune? What do you mean? I don't understand."

"We're not going to have just salted tuna," Vincenzo explains without looking at him. "You know they say it causes scurvy, don't you? That's why much of it is unsold, because shipping companies and sailors are wary. So we're going to do something new." He stares into the onyx eyes of the *rais* and finally detects a spark of wonder. "They're unloading several gallons of oil from our steamboat as we speak. The tuna is going to be cut and boiled, then preserved in oil in airtight barrels."

"But—but it'll rot! And even if it doesn't, it'll have to be eaten quickly."

"Not at all. I've been trying this method of preservation for several years now, using tuna from Arenella and San Nicolò l'Arena, with Mr. Giachery's help." Ernandez mutters something in protest but Vincenzo freezes him with a look. "We've been working on this project for longer than three years. It works perfectly well. We'll alter the *marfaraggio* by setting up an area with boilers for cooking the fish and accommodation for seasonal workers. We'll employ families and not just fishermen."

"But nobody's ever done this!" One final protestation. "People here can't do what you think they can! They're just miserable wretches."

"Very well, then. We'll start by ourselves and they'll learn. All the families. Together." Vincenzo turns to the *rais*. "And not only that:

we'll do it the way people used to in the old days: use the tuna fat to make lamp oil, and the dry bones for the soil."

A hint of a smile finally appears on the fisherman's cracked lips. "The families?"

"Yes. They can all work."

Seagulls crying, wind rustling, the heat of the sun.

When the carriage stops, Vincenzo hears the lapping of the Arenella sea. His *tonnara*. An ancestral memory, a call that stirs inside him and mysteriously belongs to him.

Giulia sits next to him, impatient. "Are we there yet?"

He helps her down. There's another vehicle behind them, with their children, Giuseppina, who is now sixty-five, and the nanny.

Vincenzo turns and lets the sea air fill his lungs and soul with satisfaction. Before him stands the villa designed by Giachery, next to the Arenella *tonnara*, a place that captured his heart.

I've always loved you, he thinks. *I've loved you from the very beginning.*

Terra-cotta-colored walls. A wooden front door opens before him, with Carlo Giachery waiting on the threshold. He hands Vincenzo a bunch of keys. "Welcome home."

He walks in, followed by Giulia and the children.

The *tonnara* courtyard has become a front garden with a trellis and trees. Potted plants break up the gray of the cobblestones. The low building has been raised and turned into a house, with large windows and a terrace overlooking the boat ramp. Nearer the sea, there is a square turret.

It looks covered in lace.

Four vertices, four cornerstones, four *pizzi*—peaks. Gothic lines worthy of an English castle, with mullioned windows opening to the sky. An inlay made from tuff, like lace, with sinuous lines carved in stone.

Vincenzo feels Giulia shiver next to him. "But it's—"

"Splendid. Yes, I know. That's why I didn't want to show it to you earlier." He takes her by the hand. "Come." Then he says to the nanny and his mother, "Wait here."

Carlo watches them go inside. He does not accompany them because he knows this is a private moment: Giulia doesn't yet know the secret of the tower room, the one Vincenzo has dreamed of from the moment he realized he could be its sole lord.

Footsteps echo through the deserted rooms. A maid precedes them, opening windows. The sun floods in, spreading over the checkered tiles. The sound of the sea muffles the rustling of skirts and their subdued voices.

Mahogany and walnut furniture reveal their forms: tables, closets, couches, consoles. There are no ornaments but Giulia will take care of that. When he tells her, her face lights up with joy.

Vincenzo walks across a hallway that overlooks the sea, and stops outside a door. He puts a hand on the knob. "Look."

Giulia goes in.

Above her, a rib vault, tall, slender, like in a church. The ribs, painted in red and gold, chase one another then blend into the window frames.

Beyond the yellow of the gold lies the sea. The Gulf of Arenella and the whole of Palermo.

Her breath catches in her chest. She turns around, throws her head back, and laughs like a little girl.

He hugs her from behind. "Do you like it? No one else in Palermo has something like this."

She is speechless from happiness.

The children burst into the room at that very moment. There are exclamations of surprise, noses pointing upward, laughter.

Giulia picks up Ignazio, who is four, and points at the patterns.

Even Giuseppina, the last one to come into the room, looks around, marveling, pleased.

Standing aside, Vincenzo observes them. It's what he wanted: a house worthy of his name and his family. He leaves the room and goes to the small salon. There, Carlo Giachery is lighting a cigar. "They're all delighted."

"Well, it's what you wanted, isn't it? To leave everybody speechless." Carlo leans against the window. He indicates the boat sheds. "You're crazy and I was crazy to listen to you. I never would have thought I could pull off such a building at the back of a *tonnara*. It took you to make me. And in Palermo, of all places."

"It took *me* for many things to be done. And you'll see that when I manage to trade in tuna in oil on a large scale. We've been canning it and selling it for years, and the demand keeps growing." Vincenzo says this without arrogance but mere awareness. "This is what I will reply to whoever calls me a 'visionary.' Facts. It'll be the same with the Oretea foundry I bought from the Sgroi brothers. Everybody told me that a workshop here in Palermo was preposterous, that only *putìe* survive here. But I know that's not the case, and that if somebody doesn't start to think big, this island will always stay in one place while the rest of the world will go forth. You know what they say in Palermo? *Dunami tempo, dissi u' surci a' nuci, ca ti percio.*"

Carlo laughs. "You and your proverbs. You're more Palermo than some seventh-generation Palermo folk. What does it mean?"

"'Give me time,' the mouse says to the nut. 'Give me time and I'll crunch through you.' I'm not the type to give up, you know that, Carlo. As a matter of fact, talking of the foundry, I'd like you to go to the construction site in Porta San Giorgio because the works for the new head office have slowed down. People think I'm crazy, but wait till the ships are made of metal and have steam engines . . . Then having a foundry of your own, which works only for your ships, will lower the cost of spare parts and of so much else." And Vincenzo remembers the grinder for the bark and the insults the Florios attracted when they had the audacity to sell quinine powder and changed the rules.

"Crazy, yes. And don't forget also a *laborer*."

"Better laugh." His laugh is more of a grimace. Some things never change. "Especially when I think of the people who hurled these insults at me and what they said . . ."

"I suspect they'll keep calling you that till the day you die." Carlo is now serious. "You should be used to it by now."

"I am." Vincenzo paces around the room, his hands behind his back. "But I can't resign myself, I just can't. What's insane is hearing people like Filangeri call me a 'laborer' and send his broker to ask me for a loan in the same breath. It's this arrogance, this lack of dignity that makes me angry." Vincenzo seeks out his anger, which he always keeps beside him, and nurses like a newborn baby.

Carlo Filangeri, Prince of Satriano, is in financial dire straits. Misguided investments, some say; luxury and excesses, others claim. For a long time his creditors have wanted to request that he be declared bankrupt. He's in over his head. He is going to have to sink or swim. And Vincenzo possesses the rope that can pull him safely to shore.

Evening comes. They have dinner together in their new home according to tradition: pasta with sauce, fried fish. Potatoes and other vegetables are given as an offering to the house *patruneddi* to ask for their benevolence and their joyful welcome. Giulia follows the proceedings with a raised eyebrow. As a northerner, therefore naturally skeptical, she finds this attempt to ingratiate oneself with spirits somewhat ridiculous, but so be it.

Late in the evening, the couple take their children to their bedrooms. The girls share one room, while Ignazio has another. Giuseppina's room is not far from there. At the bottom of the hallway, overlooking the gulf, is Giulia and Vincenzo's bedroom.

It is not easy to fall asleep: everybody is excited. Even the maids keep walking around on tiptoe, trying not to make noise. Angelina and Giuseppina start jumping on the bed. They are eight and six years old: still children. Ignazio runs, hides, and there's nothing Mademoiselle Brigitte can do to calm him down. It takes a stern telling-off from Vincenzo before they get under the blankets, from where, however, there comes a cascade of stifled laughter.

Vincenzo then looks in on his mother. She's sitting on the edge of the bed, eyes closed, holding a rosary, still wearing her cap. "Aren't you going to sleep, Mother?"

"Prayers first."

For some time now, Donna Giuseppina has become very religious. It's not clear whether this is a true change in her, old age, or fear of the unknown after a life with little happiness.

Vincenzo bends over her. "Do you like this house?"

She nods and mutters a prayer in broken Latin. Then she cocks her head. "This place stole Ignazio's heart and now it's taken yours." She smooths the bedspread with her hand. "Do you want to move here forever? I wouldn't mind. The air is clearer here. It reminds me of Bagnara."

She doesn't mention Calabria much anymore. The resentful regret she once had has gone: Bagnara is a place in her memory where the dreams and wishes that have gone forever are stored.

"No. We'll live here only in the spring and summer, and be in Palermo the rest of the year. Besides, I'll have to go there often because of the office. Although I've had a study set up, so I can work both here and there."

"I know."

Vincenzo says good night to his mother and leaves.

Giulia is waiting in their bedroom. He finds her alone, her hair down, an expectant smile on her face. She hugs him.

He kisses her on the lips with warmth and tenderness.

"I'm not sleepy," he says. "I'm going to take a walk in the yard."

"I'll wait up," she says, getting into bed.

As he walks down the hallway, Vincenzo takes a peek into his children's rooms; they're finally asleep. He goes across the salon and down the stairs.

The courtyard. He reaches the front door and goes out.

Everything is quiet. Above him, the sky is starry. Before him, the gulf. Beyond it, the lights of Palermo.

He touches the water. It's very warm for April.

He walks, his hands in his pockets, his mind free of worries. A wave laps against his shoe.

When was the last time he had a swim?

What on earth are you thinking? he says to himself. *As if you were still a boy!* His laughter stops, and turns into a lump in his throat.

He remembers the first time he swam underwater: his eyes open, the salt stinging his eyelids, the silence in his ears. The chill of the water. The longing for air contrasting with the desire to stay down, weightless, immersed in green.

Oh, my God. Freedom. What a wonderful feeling.

His desire turns to need. Vincenzo wants that feeling again, even if just for a brief moment.

His hands rush to his buttons. Off with the waistcoat, the pants, the shirt, and off with the shoes. The wind is cool, and he can barely feel it.

He looks at his wide chest: he's just over forty years old, has acquired something of a belly, and his arms are no longer as strong as in his youth, but he still has all his teeth and doesn't get breathless climbing stairs.

One foot in front of the other. The sea embraces him, welcomes him. He gets goose bumps when his stomach gets wet.

All of a sudden, his uncle Ignazio appears before him. The memory becomes a presence: he can almost hear his voice and the strong yet gentle grip of his hands. He sees him young, with stubble and the melancholy smile he'd had since Paolo's death. "Easy does it, Vincenzo, don't rush: the sea is like a mother. It will always welcome you."

The memory becomes alive, colorful.

Malta. The year after his father's death. Ignazio had taken him along: he had visited the island, met merchants, and smelled unfamiliar spices.

That was when his uncle realized that he couldn't swim—shame on him, the child of sailors—and decided to teach him.

They found a beach and dived in: Vincenzo naked, Ignazio with a cloth around his hips. They bathed in a blindingly blue sea. He could remember the laughter, Ignazio's arms ready to welcome him; he could still feel the saltwater going up his nose and the subsequent coughing.

And so, after much drinking and choking and laughing and persevering, he learned. And, in the end, he succeeded.

But he has never swum by night. Never.

All right. It's time to try this, too.

He dives in. The water runs through his hair and wraps around his arms. The sea is welcoming, it's true.

He resurfaces, breathes. It's cold outside, but so what? He feels free, light, and wants to shout because, for an instant, his darkness, which he has carried inside him all his life, has vanished. Or at least it's within the bounds of his consciousness.

This is the moment for lightness, for an unfamiliar joy that explodes within him and makes him laugh and cry.

If this is happiness, it's strange because he never thought it could be at once so beautiful and so painful.

He goes underwater again, comes back up, shouts: with happiness, liberation, life. He feels he is where he had to come, that everything that has happened in his life has led him here, and it's right, and he couldn't care less about insults and envy, because he is what he has chosen to be. It's his path.

He does a few strokes then turns on his back. He can now see the *tonnara* from the sea, and house lights reflected in the gulf. One in particular.

The bedroom where Giulia is waiting for him.

Casa Florio. Giulia. His home. His life.

He lies on the surface, spits out a mouthful of saltwater, and laughs. When was the last time he felt so free? Has he *ever* felt so free?

This October light is soft. It has shades of topaz, the mellowness of brass. It bounces off the tuff houses in Arenella and spreads over the sea, which has lost its brilliant summer color and taken on autumnal hues. Even the sand looks dull and no longer has that gleam that forces you to squint.

Almost six years old, Ignazio is leaning against the jamb, unsure whether to go to the beach or go back into the courtyard. He is drawn by the whisper of the sea, by a voice he cannot yet fully understand. All he knows is that it's more than the chatter of his sisters, Giuseppina and Angelina, who are embroidering under the trellis, with the nanny and their mother.

He takes a step forward. The sea is calling to him.

Giulia looks up, searching for him. "Ignazio? Where are you going?" she shouts with a mixture of chiding and tenderness.

And, hearing this voice, he can't resist and turns back.

Giulia puts her embroidery in her lap and hugs him. "Have you finished the homework the teacher gave you?"

He nods. "I've also done a drawing. A ship."

Of course, Giulia thinks. *What else would he draw?* She smooths down his hair and the little boy moves his cheek close to her hand.

Ignazio thinks there's no woman more beautiful than his mother. Not even *Madmwazel* Brigitte, with her strange *r*'s and blond hair.

Giulia knows that no man has ever looked at her—or ever will—with eyes as full of love as those of her son.

A sound of tinkling, followed by the snorting of horses, makes them turn toward the front door. The custodian opens it wide and a dark carriage drives in and heads to the corner opposite the trellis. The vehicle has not even stopped when Vincenzo jumps off and strides nervously to the entrance.

Giulia goes toward him. "Vincenzo," she calls. But he makes an abrupt gesture to keep her away or perhaps just to silence her. "We didn't expect you so early," she says, as her daughters and the nanny stand up and mutter a greeting, their heads bowed.

"It's nothing, Giulia. Don't you go butting in as well." He disappears through the door leading to the stairs, leaving in his wake the sound of heels clicking on the stone steps.

Ignazio sees his mother clasp her hands to her chest and drop her head.

How many times has he seen this kind of scene? How many times has he felt anger toward his father—an anger even stronger than the fear that man instills in him? His father is forever frowning, his face is always stern. He is often brusque with his mother. Why? Ignazio doesn't understand.

He goes to his mother, silently, and looks at her with tenderness. Giulia says softly, "Your father is an important man, Ignazio. He's not a bad man. It's just the way he is. It's his manner."

"But he makes you cry." He reaches out with his little hand, as if he wants to collect the tear stuck in his mother's eyelashes.

Vincenzo's furious voice, then the sound of doors slamming, is heard from upstairs. Strangely, Giulia smiles. "I've shed so many tears over him that one more makes no difference. I know your father, I really do." She huddles in her shawl and looks up at the square tower. "I'm going to see what's happening. You stay here with your sisters." And, as Vincenzo has another angry outburst, Giulia disappears with a swishing of fabric, swallowed up by the darkness of the corridor.

Ignazio looks around. His sisters and the nanny have resumed their embroidering. He hears his parents' voices grow distant.

The whisper of the sea comes again, carried by a light Gregale wind.

The child sneaks to the front door, and goes through it. Before him lies the Arenella sea.

Nobody notices him.

He goes out. For the past few days, his parents have forbidden him to go to the cliffs at the foot of the tower and climb the nearby stack. They're too slippery, they said. And yet he spent the summer skipping around there and never fell. He even went for a swim on a couple of occasions. However, he didn't have the courage to do like the fishermen's children, who dive from the Balata, the large stack beyond the point of the bay. Besides, his father promised he would teach him to dive off there next summer, because the Florios have to be able to swim, because they have seawater and blood mixed in their veins.

Ignazio lets go of the ocher wall, walks across the beach, and edges his way through the rocks. A crab appears from a spur covered in dry algae. He sees it, reaches out to grab it, but the crustacean is faster, flattens itself, and scurries into a crack.

"No!" he exclaims, leaning forward. His leather sole slips on the dry seagrass, he loses his balance, sways, and falls into a puddle of stagnant water.

Ignazio whimpers softly. He looks at his hands: his palms are grazed. He struggles back to his feet. His injuries are throbbing and stinging from the salt but that's not what worries him. His clothes and shoes are dirty. His mother will be angry.

Stupid crab, he thinks, annoyed. How can he remedy this mess?

He cautiously approaches the water. He knows the sea is deep in this spot because in the summer the Arenella kids dive there and resurface with bags full of urchins they then eat on the beach.

He bends down and, cupping his hand, gathers a little water to clean his shoes. The salt seems to sting even more. Biting his lip from the pain, Ignazio leans over and his stomach tenses up and he has a shudder of panic. The waves are tall and spray him. He clings to the rock, tries to balance himself and gather water with both hands. He staggers.

His heart in his throat, he stares into the sea, which has become very black. There's no fish darting about, nor a dance of the anemone, or algae clinging to the cliffs. There are increasingly tall waves that end up soaking him wet.

Mamma'll be so angry, he thinks. *And Papà . . .*

Better not think about that.

He must go back. He feels something behind his breastbone but can't give it a name.

Holding on to a cliff, he tries to turn around and lift his feet, which seem trapped in the puddle.

The wind grabs him, makes him lose his balance, and drags him down. The impact with the water is ice cold and empties his lungs as though someone has sat on his chest. He opens his eyes and reaches up with his arms but the sea closes over him in a foam-and-glass embrace. He feels something seize his legs and drag him down. So he kicks, hitting first the water void, then a submerged cliff. The impact is so strong that one of his shoes flies off.

He's blinded by terror. He opens his mouth to scream but the saltwater floods his trachea. "*Mamma!*" he yells with all the breath he has left, just as a wave carries him up into the air, like a jolt, then sucks him back down. "*Mamma!*" he cries out and swallows more water, coughing.

"*Mamma!*" he pleads desperately, as everything around him turns black.

"So that's what happened, you see? We displayed a steam press at the Exhibition, last summer, the first hydraulic press built in Sicily, for Christ's sake! And so they ask us for a supply of pans and spoons, and we can't do it within a month. And why? Because there isn't enough coal, we need more but we don't have any here, so I have to order it from France. And the ships that should transport it aren't coming, while the foundry has to pay a penalty."

In Vincenzo's office, in the heart of the tower, files are shifted, papers passed from one hand to the other. He finds a folder, opens it, grabs a paper, then puts it down again.

Giulia watches his jerky movements. "You knew it wouldn't be easy to manage a foundry here in Palermo," she murmurs. "Even Ben Ingham pulled out from the business." She approaches him and puts a hand on his arm.

"Nothing's ever easy in this city, but that doesn't mean we can't do anything." Vincenzo stops. Giulia's touch has the power to calm him. He takes a deep breath. "Giachery and I have read the penalties stipulated by the contract in case we fail to deliver. I don't want to pay them. And I had here some documents that—"

But Giulia is not listening to him anymore.

She frowns, her face turned toward the window. She thought she heard . . . She practically runs to the sill and leans out. "Angela! Giuseppina! Where's your brother?"

The two girls and the nanny look up. "He was here with us . . ." Mademoiselle Brigitte replies as she stands up and looks for him. "*Mais oui*, he was wandering around here. Isn't he with you?"

Giulia is startled. Perhaps she's wrong . . . Yes, she must be. And yet she could have sworn she heard her son calling her.

She rushes out of the room and down the stairs. "Ignazio!" she calls.

Nobody answers.

Could he be hiding?

"Ignazio!" she repeats. She walks around the courtyard and calls again. She becomes increasingly anxious.

Still in his office, Vincenzo shrugs. Giulia worries too much. At his son's age he would run away to La Cala, to the harbor alleys, and nobody was concerned for him. Ignazio must be loitering next to the boats between the slide and the *marfaraggio*, or else on the beach, throwing pebbles. What can possibly happen to him?

In the years to come, he will often remember this moment. But he will be unable to say just what prompted him to go to the windows overlooking the cliffs. A gut feeling? Or chance?

That is how, through the foam, against the cliffs beneath the smallest stack, he sees first a hand, then a leg. A body thrashing about, being hurled against the rocks, wrapped with algae that seems to drag him down.

Another thing he will not remember is whether or not he cried out. What he thought, however, will be etched in his mind forever.

This can't be happening to him. Not to my son.

Giulia sees him run past her, across the courtyard, while pulling off his jacket and plastron. When she realizes he's running to the cliffs, she slams her hands over her mouth and follows him. As soon as he reaches the front gates, Vincenzo kicks off his shoes. Then he lunges toward the sea and dives in.

Images get trapped in her eyes and carve their way into her mind as though made of bronze. "Ignazio!" she screams. "Ignazio!" She climbs on the rocks, tears the hem of her dress, reaches out with her arms, and calls her son again. She sees Vincenzo surface, then disappear once again in the dark water. There's a body thrashing amid the algae. Or is it being moved by the waves?

He's still alive, isn't he?

Behind her, Angela, Giuseppina, and Brigitte are crying and frantically clinging to one another. The nanny is sobbing, shouting in a mixture of French and Sicilian that she has no idea how this could have happened, but Giulia is not listening. "Vincenzo!" she cries. "Ignazio!"

It's Ignazio who emerges first. His eyes are closed, he's pale as a sheet, but shuddering and coughing . . . Giulia starts and bursts into tears. *Thank God he's coughing! It means he's alive!*

Vincenzo surfaces immediately afterward. He's shivering from the cold and has scratches on his arms and legs but he doesn't care. He lays the child on the beach and pushes Giulia away when she tries to take her son in her arms.

"Leave him! We must turn him on his side! He has to spit out the water!" He hits him hard on the back.

Ignazio quivers under the blows, moans, and vomits seawater and remnants of food. He opens his eyes for a second and sees only his mother's terrified face. "Mamma . . ." he mutters, his voice hoarse from salt and the screaming. "Mamma . . ."

Giulia starts to cry her eyes out. "My baby . . ." She snatches off her shawl and wraps it around him as he continues to cough and shake. Vincenzo lifts him in his arms and heads to the tower.

"You two!" he orders his daughters. "Get a physician—move!" Then his eyes drift to the nanny. His voice is an angry snarl. "And you, useless woman, get out of my sight. I don't want to see you ever again by tonight. My son nearly died. He got away from your surveillance and you didn't even notice! There's nothing so precious to me as this little one. So get out!"

Upset, still crying, Brigitte moves back then runs to her room.

Giulia is hunched over Ignazio and doesn't completely take in what Vincenzo has said.

But Angelina does hear him. A crease of pain appears on her face that's halfway between a child's and a woman's. "Let's go," she says, tugging at Giuseppina. Then she tells her to stop sniveling, because Ignazio is fine, he's just been a hooligan and is going to get a fever now. She doesn't even know where the anger in her chiding comes from. As she hears the sand, hardened by the salt, squeaking under her shoes, she locks her pain away in her heart, and conceals thoughts that cannot see the light of day. But she knows what her father meant, and will remember it for years to come.

That night, Giulia sleeps in Ignazio's room. The physician has reassured her and said the child is fine, that he has at most caught a chill, and his bruises and scratches will hurt, but that's all. He's given him honey and licorice syrup for his throat, and recommended heat packs on his chest.

But she cannot believe it and doesn't want to leave him. That he is alive, that her husband snatched him from death—to Giulia all this suggests a miracle.

Her husband, Vincenzo, saved him.

During those instants, she didn't see the slightest fear or despair in his face. Only raw willpower and an almost superhuman determination she knows well.

However, Vincenzo hasn't been anywhere near Ignazio since bringing him into his bedroom. He vanished to his office in the tower. It was Giulia who stayed with the child, made him drink hot broth, and changed his clothes.

At one stage, Giuseppina came in, her eyes red and her hands still shaking from the shock. She clasped the little one to her chest, kissed his damp hair, and whispered strange Calabrian words Giulia didn't understand. All she knows is that Ignazio is the only grandchild to whom her mother-in-law shows any affection.

Now, calm at last, mother and son fall asleep. They have their heads on the same pillow, their fingers interlaced. Ignazio fidgets and coughs. Giulia holds him tight. Finally, they both fall into a deep, welcome slumber.

It's the middle of the night when the child wakes up with a start. A sound, a door creaking: maybe somebody's come into the room. He clings to his mother's arms, squints, and peers into the darkness.

His father's here.

He's sitting in the armchair, his face ravaged by tension, his hair untidy. His hands are joined in front of his face and he's looking at Ignazio in a way the boy finds astonishing. It's an expression of relief, panic, and exhaustion. And affection.

He has never looked at him this way.

He immediately understands that his father got frightened, and this notion alone upsets him. Fear for him because—maybe—he loves him.

He wants to reach out to him, tell him to come closer, but cannot. Sleepiness and tiredness have the upper hand. He drifts back to sleep with a gentle feeling of warmth.

He does not see—cannot see in the dark—that his father's eyes are brimming with tears.

In the days following the accident—that is what Giulia insists on calling it—Ignazio stays in bed: the fever, caused by the shock and the cold, has come over him. The child spends his afternoons in his room, alone. Brigitte left in a rush and his sisters are now studying with their mother.

His legs drawn up under him, curled up in a nest of blankets, Ignazio is leafing through a book from his father's library. It's not a book for children but he doesn't care. What's important is not to think, not to remember the terror of dying alone, beneath gallons of water flooding his lungs. That was—he knows and tells himself—the first time he experienced the fear of death. It's a feeling he will carry inside for the rest of his life.

He therefore immerses himself in the book before him, reads aloud a syllable at a time, looks at the illustrations, allows the unfamiliar words to curl in his mouth as he kneads them with his tongue.

Ships. So many of them.

It is how Vincenzo finds him when he returns from the Oretea foundry, after an entire day spent talking to the workers, making sure that the coal, iron, and tin would arrive in time.

He opens the door and stands on the threshold. "What are you doing?" he asks. "What are you looking at?"

Ignazio looks up and Vincenzo can't help noticing the resemblance to Giulia. And yet at the same time there's something that reminds him of the uncle whose name his son carries, the Ignazio who raised him and was always watching over his shoulder. A sort of calmness, an expression that's both placid and determined.

The little boy slips out from under the blanket and gives a little bow. Without saying a word, he hands him the book.

"*Statistical Chorographical Customs Situation of Sicily* by Francesco Arancio." Vincenzo cannot repress a laugh. "Are you reading this book?" There's surprise in the question but not mockery, and Ignazio senses it.

"I like looking at the maps and the steamers," he explains, indicating the pages his father is leafing through. "Look," he adds, pointing at a page. "There's La Cala. Here it tells you how the rivers end up in the sea, past the walls."

Vincenzo nods and looks askance at his son, who is shyly telling him what he saw through this thick network of lines and words.

He has grown before him without his noticing. It's high time he started taking care of him, because Giulia is a woman, after all, and Ignazio can't cling to his mother's skirts forever.

"We're going back to Palermo the day after tomorrow," Vincenzo suddenly says, closing the book and returning it to him. "It's getting cold here."

But that's not the only reason. If he can read an atlas, then he's capable of studying in earnest, so he must start immediately, without wasting any more time.

At eight a.m. on January 12, 1848, the calm of a day like any other is interrupted by a cannon shot.

It's a bang that makes the windowpanes shake and the Casa Florio servant girls, in Via dei Materassai, cry out.

Angelina, who's twelve years old, hugs her sister, Giuseppina, who has started to scream, while Ignazio sits in the middle of his bed, his little face disconcerted, still sleepy.

At the second blast, Ignazio jumps off the bed and runs to his mother. "Mamma! Mamma! What's happening?"

Giulia kneels, takes his face in her hands. "It must have something to do with the king's birthday . . ."

But she's not entirely sure herself, and Ignazio can see her fear and confusion. "Really?"

His sisters come in. They're talking over each other, saying they looked out the window and saw armed people running in the streets.

Another blast. Screams.

They cling to their mother as the walls tremble and the maids yell from terror.

When the noise ceases, they hear other bangs, this time more subtle, more abrupt.

Gunshots.

No, these are not celebrations. Giulia suddenly remembers the notices in Via Toledo, eventually clumsily torn off by Neapolitan soldiers. Notices instigating rebellion.

She mentioned it to her brother, Giovanni, who a few days earlier had brought her news of their mother, bedridden because of a fever. She asked what he thought of these bills that had appeared all over the city during the night. Should they worry?

"It's the fire smoldering beneath the ashes," he said. "Remember the rebellion in 1837, the year of the cholera? The issue has been escalating since then. First the leaders of the rebellion were deported and sentenced to death. Then King Ferdinand gave the order that all the city administrators should be Neapolitans, and this did not go down well with Sicilians. You don't realize this because you lead a sheltered life," he added, opening his arms to indicate the luxury of the house in Via dei Materassai, "but there are women out there who suffer abuse at the hands of Neapolitan soldiers, and if their husbands protest they end up in the Vicaria jail. Not to mention the double taxation on grain. The Bourbons don't care about their own people. So it's natural that people try to change this situation, even by resorting to violence. From what I hear, it's not much better in Milan: the Austrians keep the city on a leash and the Milanese hate them."

"But this isn't Milan. Palermo and Sicily don't have the circles of thinkers like in Milan. What I mean is—" Giulia quickly waved her hands, as though to dismiss a frightening thought. "The nobility never even doubts its privileges or would ever consider giving away part of their lands. Here everybody does what they can to protect themselves, and poor people stay poor because there's no one to open the peasants' or factory workers' eyes . . ."

"That's what you think." Giovanni leaned forward, keeping an eye on the door. He knew Vincenzo didn't like that kind of talk and saw no point in it. "There are those who want to change things in Palermo, too. There are intellectuals among the nobility as well as the middle classes, who hope to be able to lead the people of this land, who want to take their destinies into their own hands. But they are few, too few of them."

"But then . . ." Giulia's eyes were open wide, more from surprise than fear.

Giovanni sighed. "Trust me, Giulia, I don't know what's going to happen but there are a lot of persistent rumors around. The proclamations posted in the city, urging people to take up arms, are just the final signal. Of course, the royal guards tear them down, trample them in the mud, and have a good laugh. They say that if Palermo folk rise up, they'll greet them with rifle shots and, if there aren't enough gallows, hang them from the navy frigates. But this time it's different, you can feel it in the air. People look at soldiers and defy them, they spit on the ground when they pass by. Palermo is tired of taxes and tyranny. The Bourbons have pushed too far."

Giulia covers her mouth with her hands because she now realizes that Giovanni was right, and that the time for rebellion has come. It's January 12, 1848, the king's official birthday . . . "Shut the windows!" she cries. Then she looks at her children and her fear rises. "Get dressed!" she commands in a trembling voice. "Get dressed and ready to leave."

Vincenzo has been at work since dawn in the office overlooking Piano San Giacomo—a building he has recently acquired and where he has set up the finance headquarters of the company. He looks up from his papers at the first shot. Giovanni Caruso, his secretary, is in front of him. "What was that?"

Another bang.

Caruso opens his arms. "I don't know. Celebrations for the king's birthday, perhaps. Isn't it today?"

"Yes, but . . ." There's an explosion, this time followed by a volley of shots. "What—with rifles?" Vincenzo goes to the window. In the square, a crowd is marching toward Porta Carbone, to the harbor. Some of the men are armed.

"There were bills posted in Cassaro a few days ago mentioning an insurrection and calling on people to take part . . ." Caruso says. "But I don't believe it. It's probably the usual handful of lunatics trying to—"

A cannon blast. A battery, this time.

"A handful of lunatics, you say?" Vincenzo slams his open palms on his desk. Screams drown out the shots. "That's the batteries at Castello a Mare. They're firing at the city from the sea!"

Caruso goes to the window. Yes, the sounds are coming from La Cala. Are they knocking down the walls? "*Minchia*, it's true." Vincenzo grabs his jacket. There's no time to waste. If there's a revolt, there will also be commotion and looting. Better ensure everything is safe. "Make sure everything is shut and go home, you and the employees. I'm going to the *aromateria*. I'll send you a message to tell you what to do."

"But you're not going there alone, Don Florio? Wait!"

He's out already. He runs to the *aromateria* and bursts in. Employees and clerks are hiding under the counters, like snails in their shells. Vincenzo borrows a cloak so he won't be recognized, then goes out, immersing himself in the alleys. He must reach the Oretea foundry and order the workers to bar the gates and put away the most important tools. If either the rebels or the soldiers decide to target it, it will be a disaster. But no sooner does he reach Via Bambinai than he has to stop. And he's not the only one.

A barricade. On it, men are shooting at the Bourbon troops. Next to it, still partly legible despite being torn, there's a bill.

SICILIANS, THE TIME FOR USELESS PRAYERS
HAS PASSED . . .
TO ARMS, CHILDREN OF SICILY:
THE JOINING OF EVERYBODY'S STRENGTH
IS ALL-POWERFUL.
THE DAWN OF JANUARY 12, 1848, WILL MARK
THE GLORIOUS ERA OF OUR UNIVERSAL
REGENERATION . . .

"If you have a weapon, come help us defend your land!" a rebel shouts, brandishing his rifle. "Or go back and take shelter at home and—" His call becomes a scream of pain: he's been shot in the arm.

Vincenzo is forced to turn back, his head down, his heart in his throat. The Oretea foundry—his foundry, his challenge, created as a workshop but now on its way to becoming a proper factory for processing iron—is not far from the city walls, near Porta San Giorgio. Now, with the ongoing battle, it might as well be on Malta. Four years ago, he had a new plant built; it's crammed with iron and coal, and it is full of flammable material. He doesn't even dare imagine . . .

"They're storming the Royal Palace!"

"They've burned down the barracks! Some soldiers are dead!"

The voices of Palermo residents are all around him, slapping him in the face. They say it all started in Piazza della Fieravecchia, and there are already casualties. "They're going to burn the houses of the aristocrats! They want a republic!"

"To arms, Palermo!"

He follows the crowd, listens to its voices, picks up news he tries to process. He goes to Via Pantelleria and runs to Via della Tavola Tonda. Once there, he's just a stone's throw from home.

He finds his mother sitting in an armchair in the middle of the room, holding her perennial rosary.

"Are you all right, my son?" she exclaims when she sees him.

"Yes, yes. Where are the children?"

"With her. You must take care of them, my darling Ignazio especially."

Giulia has dressed the children in warm clothes and is also wearing a travel outfit. As soon as she sees Vincenzo, her mask of anxiety dissolves into relief. She goes up to him. "Good God, what's happening? I was worried about you . . ."

He hugs Ignazio, the first one who gets close to him, before his daughters also cling to him, scared.

"The city is up in arms against the Bourbons. There's a rumor that the garrison has put down its weapons; others are saying that General De Majo and his troops have barricaded themselves in the Royal Palace, and others that the king is about to yield. It's total chaos . . . Naturally, the soldiers weren't expecting such a well-organized, united revolt. It's not a bunch of youngsters this time . . . Even the rebels from the country are here, and there's probably an entire contingent from Bagheria. I heard accents from the province, and nearly everybody has a weapon." He looks down at the palms of his hands. He doesn't own a weapon and has never wanted to learn to use one. He's always thought he has the most powerful of weapons: money. And that's what he will use if necessary. "There are already some casualties. The soldiers are retreating to the barracks, to Palazzo delle Finanze and the Noviziato. There's fighting in the streets and the Palermo people have taken some of the city gates."

"That's what I thought. I figured something was going on when I heard the shots." Giulia lifts her hands to her lips and mutters, "What are we going to do?"

"We're leaving the city. Take the money, the silver, and the most valuable things. Let's go to the Villa dei Quattro Pizzi. It's outside the city walls, so easier to defend."

Giulia gives instructions, opens closets, and shuts trunks. The maids run around the house. The girls obey without protesting, especially Angelina, who picks up the valuable lace shawls and hides them at the bottom of a bag.

Ignazio follows her around. "Can I bring my wooden horse? And the books?" he repeats incessantly while the housekeeper orders that the windows be closed and barred. The only person still sitting still in her armchair, mumbling, "These people have no fear of God . . ." is Giuseppina.

Vincenzo quickly writes various messages and tells a servant boy to take them to his associates, in particular Carlo Giachery. He takes documents and a purse with coins from his office. He already knows he's going to need them to get past the barricades and roadblocks.

"The carriages are ready," a maid announces.

Running footsteps on the stairs, cases and chests wobbling. Giulia checks that nothing falls out. She then takes the most valuable jewels Vincenzo has given her and conceals them in her petticoat pocket.

Her husband is waiting for her at the front door.

He gets into the first carriage with his mother and the housekeeper. Giulia is in the second one, with the children and the baggage.

Moving forward is torture: the streets are crammed with carts, barrows, and vehicles that force them to slow down and often stop. There are dead bodies on the ground. Giulia feels a knot in her stomach at every stop; all she can do is hug her daughters, who are clinging to her.

Ignazio, on the other hand, looks through the curtains with a suddenly grown-up expression, even though he's only nine years old. There is more curiosity than fear in his eyes. Above all, there is an intense desire to understand what is happening to him, his family, and his city. He pulls down the curtains and looks at his mother: naturally, she is frightened but she is not muttering prayers or breaking down into tears. On the contrary, she chides his sisters when they start to whimper. When his father got into the carriage with his grandmother, he, too, was calm and his face expressed no emotion whatsoever.

If his parents are strong enough not to show their fear—he tells himself—then he, too, will be strong.

Vincenzo is silent. Sitting next to him, his mother is absorbed in her *latinorum* lament.

The carriage comes to a sudden halt. It seems assaulted by a chorus of excited voices.

Vincenzo tries to hear.

"Nobody can get through here, is that clear?"

"Since when? Get out of my way and those coming behind me."

The coachman argues and asks again for the two carriages to be let through. Immediately afterward, there's the sound of a scuffle. Vincenzo opens the door and comes face-to-face with the barrel of a pistol.

"Don Florio—*Assabbinirìca*," says a young man, the light shadow of a beard on his face. One can tell by his clothes that he comes from a good family. He's no wretch, or at least doesn't look like one.

Vincenzo keeps still. He's afraid. "God be with you, too," he finally answers. "Why won't you let us through?"

"Because we can't. This city needs aristocrats and wealthy people."

Vincenzo slowly gets out of the vehicle and is immediately surrounded by a handful of men of all ages who have barred the road to Monte Pellegrino. There are bundles and baggage strewn on the cobbles; somebody has abandoned their possessions in order to run away. "Why can't we go through? Who gave this order?"

"Nobody's going in or out of Palermo until the city is completely in our hands."

"I see. And who might you be, if I might ask?"

"Free Sicilians fighting for the independence of our land."

Frightened voices come from the carriage. A hand protrudes from the passenger compartment and a sharp little voice protests, "Mamma, no!" Then Giulia gets out, composed, and comes to stand next to Vincenzo.

"What do you want?" she says forcefully, with such adversarial body language that the rebel instinctively wants to lower his pistol.

"Go back into the carriage," Vincenzo commands.

She pays him no heed. "There's fighting in the streets of Palermo. We want to take our children to safety. Please let us through."

"What about poor people's children? They also have the right to be protected. We're all children of this city and have to stick together. Come now, signora, go back home."

Indignant, Giulia is about to give an appropriate response when Vincenzo puts a hand on her arm. "I don't suppose a donation to your cause would make a difference."

The young man laughs with anger and contempt. "I understand. You rich people think you can go wherever you please and order everybody about just because you have money." The barrel of the pistol comes closer to Vincenzo's chest. "Go back, I tell you."

There's the clip-clop of horses' hooves.

Everybody turns around. There are other armed men coming. Their faces are tired and dusty. They stop and one of the riders parts from the group. "Michele! What's going on here?" he asks. "Is this how you treat people? Like bandits?"

"Don La Masa . . ." The young man aiming at Vincenzo puts his pistol into his belt. "He wanted to flee the city."

"And you threaten the owner of Casa Florio?" He has wide whiskers and narrow eyes beneath a forehead with a very receding hairline. He proffers Vincenzo his hand. "Don Florio. Signora . . . I'm Giuseppe La Masa, and I'm a patriot. It's a pleasure to make your acquaintance."

Vincenzo hesitates. He's heard of La Masa, and seen his portrait in various newspapers that describe him as a rebel and crowd agitator; he knows he's one of the most famous—and wanted—enemies of the Bourbon government.

Giulia replies to his greeting first. "Signor La Masa . . ." she says with a nod. "I've heard of you. I even had occasion to read your book some time ago. Actually, a manifesto more than a book, but it was very useful."

Vincenzo turns to look at her, eyes agog. He's angry more than surprised. Has she really read that book? The pamphlet of an insurgent? How did that book find its way into his home? It must be that idiot Giovanni Portalupi's doing.

Giulia responds with a fierce glance. They can argue about it later.

Following his wife's example, he proffers his hand. "If you're a patriot, you can explain to me why we're being forbidden from going to our house in Arenella."

"He offered us money!" Michele exclaims with disgust. "He tried to bribe us! What good can come from someone trying to run away?"

La Masa squints, his eyes becoming two narrow slots. It's not indignation that tickles his interest. "Really?"

"I only meant to make a donation to your cause, signore."

"Ah." The man looks toward Palermo. Beyond the road, the coastline is marked by cannon fire and clouds of smoke. "They're breaking down the city walls. It's of no use." Then he turns to Vincenzo again. "Because the city is on our side. People are sick and tired of being abused by these Neapolitans who come to command here, take away our wealth, and lord over us. And if you're not interested in how they oppress us or how much freedom they deprive us of, I trust that—being a merchant—you're aware of how much they tax us." He turns to Giulia and looks at her intently. "Signora, do you know how many young women have been dishonored by Ferdinand's soldiers? Many, and not much older than your daughters, subjected to the vile desires of men without pity. They send us the lowest soldiers, and the king treats us like a colonized land, a land to conquer and exploit, and not like subjects to rule. He speaks with passion, with courage. He indicates the city once again. "We Sicilians deserve a better life. Because it's not just Palermo that's rising up, it's the whole island."

Vincenzo is alarmed by what he reads in La Masa's face. He sees at a glance that nobody has lowered their weapons and men on horseback have surrounded his children's carriage, too.

La Masa presses him, almost talking in his face. "You, Don Florio, who are enlightened, who are one of the few entrepreneurs on this island. Will you collaborate with our cause? Will you help us build our new world? With your resources and your intelligence, we could create a new Sicily. What do you say? Are you with us?"

The May sunset already has a sense of summer. And yet it doesn't linger long enough to be watched, like in the summer: the sun is a fugitive that flees the mountain to dive into the sea. And the world immediately sinks into the night.

During that splinter of time, Palermo is bathed in a soft light that emphasizes even more the destruction caused by the rebellion: the city walls, overlooking the sea, have been shelled and destroyed, and the alleys are blocked with remnants of barricades erected to stop the advance of the Bourbon soldiers. The barracks, like the one in the Noviziato, have been devastated. Porta Felice has been shielded by a huge canvas to block the view of the sea from Cassaro and prevent an exchange of signals between the Royal Palace and the Bourbon ships at sea.

More things happened in those first few months of 1848.

Alone in his study, with the brazier lit and the window half opened, Vincenzo can draw breath after a terrible day.

A sound.

The door opens. Giulia stands before him, in a robe and slippers. "Vincenzo, it's almost midnight!"

He massages his temples. "What's the matter?"

She comes in and shuts the door behind her. "You haven't eaten. You hardly sleep. What's wrong?"

He shakes his head. Nearly fifty, he feels the weight of responsibility, and it's becoming so heavy, his knees are buckling under it. "Go to bed, Giulia. Don't worry, it's not woman's business."

But she doesn't stir. She stares at him, her mouth twisted in a reproachful grimace. "You also thought that when I told you I'd read La Masa's book. Being a woman doesn't mean being stupid, and that book helped me to understand many things, especially the reason he and many others, like Rosolino Pilo and Ruggero Settimo, are trying to set up an independent Sicilian state. Of course, whether or not they succeed is a different matter . . . You may disagree with their opinions, Vincenzo, but you can't deny that they have the passion to carry them forward. As for me, I'm neither your mother nor one of your daughters. Talk to me. What's on your mind? It's got to do with the new government, hasn't it?"

"Yes." Vincenzo starts to pace up and down the room. "I did something today that I may well live to regret. I bought, on behalf of the revolutionary committee, a large consignment of rifles from England. They're proclaiming the Kingdom of Sicily but they haven't found a king who wants the crown: not the son of Carlo Alberto, Duke of Genoa, nor anyone else, partly because the British are against Sicily splitting from the Bourbons. Last March they staged that charade with those parliamentary elections and picked up four noblemen and people with money. They wanted to apply the 1812 constitution again . . . except that we don't have a point of reference. You see? There is no king of Sicily because nobody wants to set foot on this island. It's crazy!" He sinks into the armchair. "As if having the ships requisitioned and practically being forced to give them a loan wasn't enough."

"It's a revolution, Vincenzo. It's chaos and we have to be prudent." She goes to him, caresses his face, and Vincenzo immediately takes her hand and kisses her palm, he, who seldom indulges in gestures of affection. "Everybody has to make sacrifices."

"I know. But I can't stand the fact that they're waging war with my money: it's taken me a lifetime to create . . . this." He indicates the documents strewn on the table. "Trading has dropped by half since the revolt began. The merchant bank, the foundry, the ships. . . . The Sicilian Steamship Company vessel, the *Palermo*, was working at full capacity, then Ruggero Settimo and the revolutionary regime took it for transporting troops. You were right when you talked about passion. Settimo, for example, as president of the Sicilian government, firmly believes in what he's doing but he's willing to reason. He understands that Sicily is not ready for a republican government, that the nobility would never accept it, so he's trying to mediate and find a solution . . . On the other hand, there's that pontificating Pasquale Calvi, even more stubborn than a republican. I've lost count of the damage they've done to me with their proclamations and claiming that we, the middle classes, also have to support the revolution. And now . . ."

"Have they paid you, at least?"

He rolls his eyes. "Oh, yes. With silver from the churches."

In spite of herself, Giulia laughs. "You mean chalices, pyxes, and censers?"

"That's right. It's not funny: unless I have them melted down, which I can't do, I've no way of turning them into coins."

"If your mother knew that you were thinking of melting these things down she'd have you excommunicated."

Vincenzo does not smile, however. He twists one of the ties on his wife's robe around his fingers. "Even if the revolutionary government seems solid in Palermo, there are too many people on the side of the king and the Neapolitans. We're on the edge of an abyss, Giulia. It would take very little for us to fall."

"But people are happy. The new government is doing its best . . ."

He puffs. "People don't care who governs them if there's no food on their tables. Do you want to know the truth? It's in the nobility's interest that Neapolitans don't set foot in Sicily again. This way, their privileges remain intact and they can occupy the most prestigious positions. There are many members from rich families in the government, you know? People who have studied, traveled, of course, and who have high ideals. But poor people can't eat ideals for breakfast. It's them the government should think about, otherwise . . . And since the government has no money, it comes to me or Chiaramonte Bordonaro, and decides to rope me into the Civil Guard."

"You won't solve these problems by staying up all night or skipping dinner." Giulia closes the files on the desk. "The chalices can wait and the loans will still be there tomorrow." She leans down and kisses her husband on the forehead. "Come to bed," she whispers.

He looks at his papers, then shifts his attention to his wife's breast, white under the muslin. It has been so many years since they first met, and yet he still wants her.

He unties the ribbons on her robe. "I'm coming."

Their subdued voices get lost in the silence of the villa.

The Quattro Pizzi tower is before him, plunged in a honey-colored dawn. The windows of the villa are shut, and the front gate is also closed. The village of Arenella seems dead: there is no one in the street or on boats.

Ignazio closes the telescope a sailor has lent him and swallows air. He feels a new fear, different from the one he experienced when he nearly died. He's had to grow up in a hurry. The past year's events forced his family to escape first from the house in Via dei Materassai and then from the Villa dei Quattro Pizzi. At the age of ten, he realizes how fate can snatch away everything you've been taking for granted until then: certainties, comforts, well-being.

It was a complicated year, 1848, that much he understood. The Bourbons were driven out, there was a new government in which his father and some of their acquaintances were involved. During all that time, his father was even more tense and quick-tempered than usual. But 1849 wasn't any more peaceful. Ignazio heard that Taormina, Catania, Siracusa, and Noto surrendered at the beginning of April, and now it was Palermo's turn. He found this news confusing, but nobody bothered explaining these things to a child.

The whole family relocated to *L'Indépendant*, the steamship Vincenzo bought a few months earlier for his new shipping company, Ignazio and Vincenzo Florio, which complemented the Sicilian Steamship Company: a new venture for which he had sole responsibility, collecting its proceeds. They've taken shelter here because it's a safe place. He heard his father reiterate that to his mother for the umpteenth time last night. The cabins are next to one another, the walls thin. "I've already told you, don't worry, *L'Indépendant* is registered as French: I didn't get the flag changed when I bought it, and that's a good thing . . . Nobody, neither the rebels nor the Neapolitans, will attack it for fear of provoking the anger of the French."

In the night silence, Ignazio heard the rustling of his mother's dress. They must have embraced because everything was suddenly silent. A harrowing silence where he'd heard the beating of his own heart mingling with the lapping of the waves against the side of the ship.

Then, a whisper: "Be careful tomorrow. No matter what happens, just make sure you save your own life."

This sort of prayer deeply distressed him, suddenly revealing the fear his mother always managed to conceal so successfully behind her reassuring eyes.

That tomorrow is now today. A launch is taking his father to the shore, and, as he gradually moves further away, Ignazio feels fear gripping him between his stomach and his heart.

The sailors of *L'Indépendant* walk around in respectful silence. They keep glancing at him, that serious little boy whose clothes cost the same as their annual wage. They look at him and think that he doesn't look at all like his father. He doesn't have his hardness or his impetuousness.

Ignazio senses their curiosity, their envy, and their amazement but he doesn't react. He turns to look at his mother, at the prow. She's like a plaster statue wrapped in a cloak. That's when he notices the dark rings under her eyes, the wrinkles around her mouth, and her lined forehead. He'd never seen any of this before. How can she have aged so much? When did it happen? What does life do to human beings, and how can its passage make a mark on their skin?

Too many questions for a child. Questions for which there's just one answer, which he cannot, however, give himself: his mother's face, at this moment and for some time now, is the face of fear.

With the revolution's fate already compromised, a delegation of prominent Palermo citizens met the commander of the Bourbon army, Carlo Filangeri, Prince of Satriano, at Caltanissetta, and handed him the surrender of the city.

Except that . . .

Except that the people did not want to surrender. They rose and erected barricades against the city guard. "No concessions to the Bourbons, never!" they shouted. Not even hunger could overcome their hatred of the Neapolitans.

Except that the people were abandoned to themselves. The heads of the government fled—even Ruggero Settimo and Giuseppe La Masa—and the aristocrats shut themselves away in their country villas and courtyards, as though they were indifferent to the fate of their city. A city that was now in disarray, starving, exhausted, destroyed, and in flames.

Ignazio doesn't know these things but his mother does. And she's never been so afraid for her Vincenzo, who has now gone to Palermo in the hope that the king—as Filangeri promised—might grant a general amnesty.

He goes to her and takes her hand. "Don't worry. Papà will be back soon."

He says it with a child's pure courage.

Giulia stands staring at the boat, squints, and watches as the small vessel heads to the Arenella marina, where she can see their house. "I hope so, Ignazio," she says in one breath. She squeezes his hand and the child has a sense of willpower akin to hope. "Absolutely. That's how it will be."

He hugs her. "Yes, Mamma."

"My little prince," Giulia says, smiling, also hugging him.

She loves her withdrawn son. Vincenzo is brusque and coarse; Ignazio is calm and placid. He has taken much after her. Patience. Those calm eyes. Generosity. From his father, however, he has inherited determination and that indomitable intelligence that leads him first to understand, then want, and finally obtain what it is he wants. Without rush or tantrums. He doesn't need them.

At that moment, Giuseppina's face emerges from below deck. Her hair is pulled back in a tight bun that highlights her pale, angular face; she, too, is wearing a cloak against the humidity. Angelina is still asleep in their cabin, curled up against the wall.

"Has Papà gone?" she asks.

Giulia says yes and gestures at her to come closer. She puts her arms around both children. "We must pray that the king may grant a pardon to your father and all the others."

Giuseppina looks up at her mother. "Papà didn't do anything anyone else didn't," she protests. She has a proud frown, emphasized by a large nose, like her mother's.

Giulia kisses her forehead. "I know, darling. But your father, like Baron Chiaramonte Bordonaro, Baron Riso, and Baron Turrisi, is wealthy and has been"—she hesitates, trying to find the right word to explain what is happening—"forced to finance the revolutionary government. The king, however, needs money, so I wouldn't be surprised if he decided to punish them for collaborating by asking them for compensation or, worse, by expropriating part of their belongings to make up for his losses."

While his sister grumbles something in protest, Ignazio is thinking. He has always heard his parents talk about business. In his mind, he understands that the government, which everyone hates but has to submit to, is not their friend. "You can't say no, right?" he asks.

"Your father would rather get himself killed than see his name compromised. He won't allow anybody to say that the Florios have no honor. He'll do whatever he has to do."

But he won't do it without putting up a fight, Giulia thinks, her eyes fixed on Palermo emerging from a sea of mist. For him, honor is money, it's the factories he owns, the spices, and the ships. And he will not allow anybody to take his wealth away.

When Ignazio goes down below deck, he finds Angelina awake, putting up her hair. He sits on the blanket on the berth. "Papà has gone."

She doesn't answer but keeps securing her braid on the top of her head with hairpins. The little boy gets up and stands next to her, looking at the items on the travel dressing table. He picks up the painted ceramic hairbrush and starts swinging it by its brass handle. His sister snatches it out of his hand. "It's mine!" she hisses, full of rancor. "You always have to take everything for yourself, don't you?"

Ignazio is disconcerted. He takes a step back, his arms hanging down his sides. "Why?"

"Do you really have to ask?" Angelina slams the brush down violently. The ceramic back cracks.

He shakes his head and retreats further.

"If it weren't for you, it's possible we could go back home. But since your father is so concerned about you, we have to stay here." Red blotches have appeared on Angelina's face, a sign of rising anger. "You still don't get it, do you? We're not here because he cares about me or Giuseppina or our mother." She points at his chest.

It is not so much Angelina's words as her clenched fists that shock him. He looks at them and senses in her hands a resentment he doesn't think he deserves, because he's asked for nothing and would like to return to Palermo like the rest of them.

He moves his little hands up to his chest, shaking his head. "I want to go home, too." As he says this, he feels tears pricking his eyes. "It's not my fault. There are soldiers and I don't—"

"Shut up!" Angelina jumps to her feet, grabs and shakes him. "Don't you understand that your father would get himself killed just to protect you? He doesn't care anything about us, you're the only one who counts. You, because you have his name and you'll work with him. Because you're a boy." She lets go of him, practically pushing him against the wall.

Ignazio leans against the doorjamb so he doesn't fall.

"Me, Giuseppina . . . we're girls. And you're a boy." It's her turn to cry. Small, raging tears she wipes away with the back of her hand. "Until you were born, he wouldn't marry our mother. That's right. She stayed with him even though he didn't want to marry her. It's only after you were born that he asked her to be his wife." She goes to the door. "We're nothing to him. We could all die for all he cares," she says before going out.

Ignazio is alone now. He drops on the floor and sits with his knees against his chest. Many things are much clearer to him now. Like some of the servants' remarks. His mother's bitterness and tenacity. Angelina's hard looks and Giuseppina's sad ones. His father's harshness and his grandmother Giuseppina's protective, almost jealous attitude.

At that very moment, an awareness comes over him, which lasts just a second.

He's still too young to understand what it really means. It's a chill that makes him quiver, causing a tightness in his stomach, but which immediately disappears, absorbed in the muddy bottom of his consciousness.

His life does not belong to him.

Vincenzo Florio is waiting in the Via dei Materassai office. Nobody knows he came back just a few hours earlier.

He disembarked in a nearby part of the city. Giovanni Caruso, his secretary, was waiting for him with a carriage and a small escort. They went through the countryside, bribing the guards.

The streets and alleys bear the open wounds of devastation: damaged buildings, front gates pulled out, furniture used as firewood, abandoned weapons, blood. Palermo people feel betrayed, certain that aristocrats and storekeepers had sold the island's independence in order to save their riches.

The truth is, they are right.

Vincenzo shudders. Giovanni Caruso is slumbering on a couch opposite him. He has stayed with him, showing a loyalty that goes beyond professional duty.

Vincenzo is fifty years old and feels the weight of every one of them. He tried not to get too involved but the circumstances were such that he had to take a job with the National Guard after the leaders of the revolution fled and the city collapsed into disarray. He didn't want to, but had no choice, and distanced himself from the revolutionary government's actions as soon as he could. He hadn't taken a single wrong step in managing his business.

At least until now.

He moves quietly about the room.

He goes up to the second floor, where his mother still lives. Giuseppina didn't want to leave. He sees her sitting in the salon, holding her rosary beads, dozing in an armchair. Strands of white hair are escaping her cap. Her hands are skinny, with age spots. He remembers them as strong, red from lye or icy water, or covered in flour. Or soiled with blood.

It's a blurred memory that turns into a feeling of emptiness. He could have had a brother or a sister . . .

He takes a step back. The lines on Giuseppina's face tell a story of bitterness. He knows she misses Ignazio more than his father. He feels sorrow and tenderness for her and her seventy years so full of pain.

He walks across the rooms, past the salon. He goes to his bedroom, lies down on the bed, seeking Giulia's scent but not finding it. The sheets have been changed and smell of soap.

He closes his eyes as the sense of emptiness mutates into tiredness, then anxiety again.

What will happen now? he wonders. *How generous will the king be and how far is his pardon going to reach?*

He turns over, his eyes shut. Frustration gives him a bad taste in his mouth.

The prince of Satriano, he thinks. *He'll get me out of trouble. He owes it to me.*

Six years earlier, Vincenzo saved Carlo Filangeri, Prince of Satriano, the shame of bankruptcy with a loan. He gave it to him even though the man had called him a "laborer." As a matter of fact, that was the reason he lent him the money, so he would remember that a person he considered inferior had saved him from ruin.

Besides, Vincenzo then thought, *it's always useful to have connections at court.*

The prince informed him through an intermediary that he wouldn't have to pay for the consequences of having been "close" to the rebels or that regrettable incident of buying rifles on behalf of the revolutionary government. Naturally, he would have to return the silver taken from the churches but that would probably be all.

And yet.

Vincenzo decided to take away from this revolution the following lesson: to remember never to trust politicians. Use them, manipulate them if necessary, because every man has his price. But never, *ever* trust them blindly.

His tension slowly dissipates. Sunlight heralds the start of the day. He gets up and changes his clothes. He asks one of the manservants to call Caruso so he can freshen up and have breakfast.

When the secretary joins him, Vincenzo indicates the table. "There's coffee and biscuits. Please help yourself."

The man eats slowly and glances at his employer's face, then says,

"The royal messenger must be here by now. He was already expected yesterday evening."

"Yes, I think so." A pause, clenched between his teeth and the tension. "Then let's go to the Palazzo di Città."

To avoid being recognized, the two men wrap up in old cloaks. The silence in the alleys is now replaced with a hubbub that increases as they approach the Palazzo di Città. When the streets start to fill with people, they realize something's happened. Beyond the Quattro Canti, where the gallows stand, there's a sea of people shouting. They change route and slip into the alley parallel to the church and monastery of Santa Caterina. However, after a while they have to fight their way through the crowd, which smells of sweat and anger. "Quickly, let's go in," Vincenzo tells his secretary. "This doesn't bode well."

Lights and voices are bursting out the large lobby windows. A clerk is throwing documents into the fireplace. Slumped in a chair in the corner, Baron Turrisi is panting, his hands joined.

Baron Pietro Riso goes up to Vincenzo, followed by an evidently relieved Gabriele Chiaramonte Bordonaro. "Royal pardon for all of us. Exile for the others. The people are furious but they can't see that it could have been a lot worse. No death sentence . . . though no doubt he will find some other way of punishing us."

Caruso mutters, "Thank God."

Vincenzo just nods, then asks, "Who's being sentenced to exile?"

Riso opens his arms. "The ones who were most at the forefront: Ruggero Settimo, Rosolino Pilo, Giuseppe La Masa, the prince of Butera . . . Forty or so. It's turned out well."

At that moment a man bursts into the room. He looks distraught, his receding hairline flushed. "You!" he says, pointing a finger at the two aristocrats and Vincenzo. "You sold our island for a plateful of lentils."

"It's over, Don Pasquale," Baron Turrisi says, trying to calm him down. "I understand your ideals have been disappointed, but there was nothing else we could do—"

"It's *Signor* Pasquale Calvi to you. My political convictions refuse the titles of nobility. And with you, of course, there's no hope anything could ever change." He stares at them with incendiary rancor in his eyes. "My companions and I dreamed of a free Sicily, an independent land confederated to Italian states. None of you really believed in this ideal. None! We fought for nothing. And now because of your apathy, we will all have to pay for you. My name is on the exile list. I am forced to leave my country—me! Yes, your fear has condemned me and other children of this land to the fate of exiles. If you'd had courage, if you'd agreed to get armed and fight, by now the Neapolitans wouldn't be at the city gates."

Vincenzo doesn't let him continue. "Enough proclamations and rhetoric, Calvi. Thank heavens there isn't a cross next to your name or by now you would be at the Ucciardone fortress, and I would have taken you there myself, I can assure you."

Mors tua vita mea.

Pasquale Calvi takes a step toward him. His despair is as corrosive as acid. "And you have the audacity to speak? When Ruggero Settimo and I begged you to defend the city, you pulled back, just like all the others, starting with those dogs next to you, Chiaramonte Bordonaro. And you surrendered to Filangeri. Cowards!"

"You asked us to get ourselves killed! We have lives, Calvi, and want to keep living them. Don't you understand that by surrendering we avoided a bloodbath?"

But Calvi will not listen. "You, Florio, not only are you a jumped-up louse but you have a black soul. You're a dog. You should have defended the city, not dropped your pants at the first threat for the sake of your interests."

"Do you have any idea how many people I give work to?" Vincenzo roars, drawing closer. "Do you have any idea what Casa Florio is?"

The man pushes him back. "Damn you!" he cries. "I hope you go to hell, you and your money, and your breed—may you weep over it to the last cent! I hope you weep just as I must weep!"

Vincenzo's heart is suddenly wrapped in darkness. He feels it rise to his head and obscure his eyes. "Are you trying to curse me?" His fists frantically open and close. "Because if so, I'm also good at curses, except that mine come true right away."

"Enough, Calvi," Baron Turrisi says, seizing him by the arm. "It's over. How could we possibly resist once Messina and Catania had fallen? With what weapons? With what supplies? What did you have in mind—half a kingdom? A republic within the crumbling walls of a city? There was nothing else to be done. The king's pardon is already a big deal."

Calvi looks at him as though seeing him for the first time: with horror and contempt. "For you, perhaps." Shouts can be heard through the windows, and stones thrown at the palace walls. "Can you hear the people of Palermo? They don't want to surrender!"

A stone lands on the floor, chipping a tile. Pasquale Calvi opens his arms. It's hard to ignore the distress in his face. The distress of a man in love with his land, who believed in the possibility of a different future and devoted himself to an ideal wholeheartedly, sacrificing his own life. The distress of a man forced into exile. "You've condemned our land to slavery. May the memory of what you've done keep you awake at night, and may your sons someday rise against you and blame you for your cowardice." He runs out as the city quivers with shouts and gunshots.

Turrisi would like to look out the window but hesitates and turns back. "We'd better leave. We'll come back when tempers have cooled."

They say goodbye with a nod and slip out amid office employees and clerks. The doors shut behind them.

PART SIX

Tuna

October 1852 to Spring 1854

Nuddu si lassa e nuddu si pigghia si 'un s'assumigghia.
You don't leave or choose somebody unless you resemble them.

—SICILIAN PROVERB

While in the rest of Europe pro-independence movements struggle to regroup after the revolts in 1848, Ferdinand II is trying to restore unity in the Kingdom of the Two Sicilies. For that, however, he makes very unpopular decisions: he imposes a hefty national debt and suspends until further notice the constitution promulgated by the Sicilian Parliament in March 1848. The people and local administrations, weary of the extended period of instability, accept these taxes. The aristocrats equally distance themselves from any attempts at rebellion, which, however, keep arising. These are isolated cases, though, chiefly linked to the countryside, and have no real resonance in the cities.

The pressure applied by the British government to lessen the tax burden and the repressive atmosphere does little good. And so the Bourbon reign becomes the archetype of a reactionary power characterized by deep unease, both in the country and in its international relations. Ferdinand's son, Francesco II, who ascends the throne in 1859, therefore finds himself surrounded by an often reactionary aristocracy that jealously guards its privileges. Unable to move away from his father's political tendencies, Francesco actually prevents the south from making economical and social progress.

Still, the patriotic momentum of the 1848 exiles does not wane but persists in the writings and interventions of many of them, including Giuseppe La Masa, Ruggero Settimo, and a young, combative lawyer from Ribera, near Agrigento: Francesco Crispi.

"THE NETS HAVE BEEN CAST, *the mesh is stretched. The tuna will come into them on a full-moon night.*" This is what Herodotus wrote in the fifth century B.C. This is how it has been for centuries. Until now.

Tuna: a peaceful animal with silvery skin, able to swim for many miles in shoals of hundreds of individuals. Huge masses that stir the seas, filling it with splashes, waves, and sounds. In the spring, when the temperature is mild, they travel from the Atlantic into the Mediterranean in order to reproduce. Their flesh is fatty, their bodies ready to mate.

This is when the *tonnara* is lowered.

Because the *tonnara* is not just a building, a *marfaraggio.*

It's also a contraption of nets with a succession of chambers: a method invented by the Arabs and passed on to the Spaniards, which reaches its climax in Sicily.

The *tonnara* is a ritual.

The *tonnara* is a place where entire families have been living for centuries: the men at sea, the women in the plants. In the winter, maintenance work is done on the ships and the nets are mended. Spring and summer are the time for slaughter and processing the catch.

They call this gentle-eyed monster the "sea pig" because no part of it is ever thrown away: not the tender, red meat, which is processed, salted, and sold in large barrels; not its skin and bones, which are dried, powdered, and used as fertilizer; not its fat, which is used for lamps; and not its eggs, which become expensive roe.

The *tonnara* is alive because tuna exists.

Salt and tuna have been walking hand in hand forever, albeit in a different form, since tuna cannot leave the sea.

Thanks to military achievements after the reconquest of Sicily in 1849, Carlo Filangeri, Lieutenant of the Kingdom of Sicily, Prince of Satriano, Duke of Taormina, is sitting in his elegant office with timber paneling and decorated with the coat of arms of the city of Palermo. Beyond the window, a warm, late October sun is spreading over the Palermo rooftops, forming lace shadows through the cathedral battlements.

In front of him, on the other hand, lies a series of letters: fiery words dripping with venom, a paper duel between Vincenzo Florio and Pietro Rossi.

Two years ago, in 1850, it was actually Filangeri who wanted Vincenzo Florio to be appointed as negotiations manager at the Royal Bank of the "Royal Dominions beyond the Lighthouse"; in other words, Sicily. He was sure that Florio was ready to go beyond his wide circle of commercial activities. A man as shrewd as he could also be useful in the administration of the kingdom.

Filangeri massages his whiskers, smoothing the curls that come halfway down his jaw. This is a real nuisance.

Pietro Rossi is the president of the Royal Bank. A man close to the Crown, powerful, respected, meticulous, and inflexible. He demands maximum correctness from everyone. Such an uncompromising man cannot take to somebody like Florio, who is constantly stopping and starting, who takes on a business then sets it aside for another, and is only interested in getting rich.

"Let that jumped-up laborer be a storekeeper," Rossi once told Filangeri. "Let him go on trading with his boats and leave politics to those with a genuine desire to serve the people."

Then, less than a week later, he provided evidence that Vincenzo had not carried out his task as negotiations manager in an exemplary manner: he had been unexplainably absent from meetings and had not attended registration activities. At the end of the message, Rossi suggested that Florio resign to avoid the embarrassment of his—by now inevitable, he thought—removal.

Filangeri would never do anything like this, however, not without giving Vincenzo a warning. He therefore summoned him and explained the situation, and thereby confirmed the suspicions Florio had been harboring for some time.

"I will ruin this waste of space," Vincenzo hissed. "He's slandering me before the minister and the finance director, here in Sicily and before you."

"Come now, Don Florio . . . You could take part in the Royal Bank's activities a little more. Attend meetings for instance. After all, I believe you have a large number of associates and presumably trusted people capable of standing in for you. Alternatively, step down from this position that brings you neither prestige nor money. Why do you want to make your life harder?"

"Thank you for your concern, but I know how to run Casa Florio, and things progress only if you're at the helm, if you take care of them," Vincenzo had replied with a grim expression. "That someone like Rossi should come and tell me how to behave is a real insult. I work hard, and dozens of families in the city have an income thanks to me. And he thinks I should sit around waiting for stewards to bring payment receipts and bills of lading. In other words, he wants me to be a paper pusher. Try to understand my reasons. Some things have to be managed . . . from the inside. Only those who work here or have friends in this place"—he opened his arms and indicated the building—"perhaps people with money. You're a friend and I am grateful to you, but I don't care about the money earned from the position: what I care about is work." He looked up at Filangeri from below. His eyes were tired but determined. "You must help me, Prince."

Filangeri moistened his lips and rubbed his sweaty hands on his thighs. Vincenzo was not asking him for a favor but had just given him an order. "You know, Don Florio, it's not easy. He accuses you and has involved the director . . . I have to forward the request and—"

"Forward it," Vincenzo interrupted him. "Send it to the director, naturally. I don't wish to put you in an awkward position, I wouldn't dare. But I would like to remind you that I can be grateful to my friends and ruthless to my enemies. And you know well how great my gratitude can be."

Filangeri didn't reply, but just stared at him. Vincenzo Florio had always been his safety net. When his lifestyle had exceeded his limits, and he was about to be crushed by debts or the shadow of bankruptcy was looming over him more than ever, Florio was there to rescue him. Naturally, he had given him a hand after the revolution, but that was nothing in comparison to all the times when . . .

He had no choice, he forwarded Rossi's letter to the director of the Finance Department of the General Lieutenancy of Sicily, but added that his claim was debatable to say the least, and that it would be better to find another solution. That there was no point in being so rigid.

The dismissal request lapsed.

But Rossi did not give up. And neither did Vincenzo.

Filangeri sighs. *Whatever happens, this business will not turn out well.* He collects the papers and sits back down heavily. He will speak to the finance director. This business has been going on far too long now; it runs the risk of paralyzing the activity of the Royal Bank. And he will add that it's in nobody's interest to stand in the way of a man like Florio.

Along the road that leads to Marsala, a carriage escorted by two men on horseback is swaying in the wind. It reaches the Florios' courtyard, goes through the gates, and stops with a creak. The horses emit an exhausted neigh.

The November sky is a colorless blanket. The rough, gray sea is also roaring with a dissent that's hard to interpret. The Aegadian Islands are faint marks on the horizon. Fall 1852 has walked in without knocking, bringing with it days steeped in frost that hardens the soil.

Giovanni Portalupi welcomes his brother-in-law with a handshake. "Welcome."

"Thank you." Vincenzo's greeting is rough. "What a stupid day. Nothing but wind and clouds. If only it would rain." Without adding anything else, he walks past Giovanni and heads to the main house.

A young man gets out of the carriage. He is tall, slightly overweight, wrapped in a cloak that conceals his body. He goes up to Portalupi and shakes his hand. "How are you, signore?"

"I'm well, thank you. And your father?"

"He's not too bad, thank God. He's stayed behind in Palermo, at the Casa Florio office." Vincenzo Caruso, Giovanni's son, fiddles with his bag and takes out some letters. "From your sister. She sends her regards."

"Thank you. How is she?"

"Strong and courteous as ever. The girls keep her busy, and then there's Ignazio."

Meanwhile, Vincenzo has stopped and is calling them impatiently.

They exchange a look. "Bad news?" Portalupi asks in one breath.

The young man nods. "I'll tell you later. Let's not keep him waiting."

Later comes in the late afternoon, once they have finished checking the books, and calculating the advance payments and the sales orders.

In the main house, there's a sweet smell of wood and wine. An aroma reminiscent of honey and warmth, slightly pungent, that echoes fall days when the must ferments and the barrels are half emptied so they can be topped up with new wine.

The three men relocate to the small parlor, where dinner is being served.

"We don't have Ingham's market shares, true, but we're almost on the same level with Woodhouse. And production is on the increase despite the British tax." Caruso sits at the table and places his napkin on his lap.

"Thank heavens for the French market." Portalupi pours wine. "Try this catarratto: it's from our latest purchase. I've kept one barrel to have with meals."

Vincenzo clicks his tongue. "Pleasant. Fragrant."

"Made in the Alcamo winery. It's an excellent region for white wines." Portalupi presses his face against his fists. "I guaranteed you only the best and so it is." He stresses his pride but not as an argument.

Vincenzo looks at him askance. "And you've worked well, I grant you that. After my experience with Raffaele, I was reluctant to hire family members for the business. The first profits are finally coming in."

They do not speak about Giulia. Not after what happened.

And yet it is Giulia who brought peace between them. It was she who persuaded her husband to employ her brother, and asked Giovanni to work hard at managing the marsala production plant.

"And so the forecast for next year is thirteen hundred barrels." Caruso continues with his calculations. "How many permanent workers?"

"Still seventy, plus the children. Thanks to steam presses we have spare manpower. Besides, Woodhouse produces many more barrels than we do and he employs far more workers."

A servant comes to serve the meal, a thick fish soup. Its smell spreads through the room. The men put down their papers and notes, and start eating.

"Their production method is somewhat antiquated. You should draw comparisons with Ingham, with the production system of the Casa Bianca courtyard, with its steam-powered lathes." Vincenzo dabs his lips with his napkin. "Ingham is a friend and an associate but he had no qualms about starting negative rumors about our wine, which means he fears competition. I know this for a fact from our agent in Messina."

Portalupi sighs deeply. "Ingham is a frigate, Vincenzo. We're a brigantine."

"Yes, but brigantines are lighter and faster. Our production output may be smaller but in terms of quality, we're way out of his league."

His brother-in-law's face touches on a smile, the first one that day.

After dinner, once they are full and relaxed, Portalupi hazards a question: "So, how is it going with that Pietro Rossi business?"

"Not well." Vincenzo tosses his scrunched-up napkin on the table. "Son of a bitch. He summoned me to a meeting the day after I left for Marsala, last month. He wants to force me to resign at all cost."

Portalupi joins his fingertips. "But you carried out your appointed duties, didn't you?"

Caruso clears his throat and looks absently into the distance.

Vincenzo toys with a piece of bread, then replies, "They scheduled the days of duty at the cash desk on the departure dates of my steamships and boats. I couldn't go." It's a defense that sounds like a half-uttered admission.

"But you have good people, though." Portalupi raises his glass, indicating Caruso, who thanks him with a kind of toast.

"That's not the problem. I wouldn't have picked you if I didn't trust you."

"You just can't help yourself, can you? Always need to control everything and keep an eye on every single thing. You just can't be otherwise, right?" Portalupi raises his eyebrows. He's referring to the business but also to his life and his family, and Vincenzo knows it.

He shrugs. "It's the way I am." He says it plainly, as though he cannot help it.

Portalupi pours himself more wine and shakes his head. He laughs. "You're crazy."

"Not at all. You have to make others understand that they cannot disrespect you, and for that you can't be intimidated by them. Rossi thinks he can scare me off with his complaints. If they smell fear on you, then they've won." He pauses. "And I'm not afraid, and let him know that today."

Caruso lifts a corner of his mouth and his face softens with a grimace.

"Your brother-in-law has written to the prince of Satriano asking that Rossi pay the salary owed for carrying out the duties, which he refuses to do."

"And I pointed out to him that it's not by chance that the council meetings are scheduled on the dates when my steamships are due to arrive," Vincenzo adds. "Nothing that doesn't sound true, anyway."

"Yes, and I can picture just *how* you must have pointed that out," Portalupi says, snickering.

They all laugh. Portalupi asks the servant to clear the table, and Caruso takes his leave. He's tired and needs rest. Portalupi follows his example. He knows that tomorrow he will need to be up at dawn, to fit in with Vincenzo's habits.

Vincenzo remains alone in the dining room, plunged in a silence disturbed by the wind thumping against the windows.

He is thinking.

About the first time he came to Marsala and saw this untouched land beside the sea. He remembers the first batch of wine, the trepidation he experienced as he watched the ship setting sail, carrying the first cargo of marsala to France.

His bond with Raffaele was strong then. They could call each other friends and not just cousins. And now he doesn't even know exactly where Raffaele lives.

Pride becomes a mixture of bitterness, solitude, and resentment. Everything was different fifteen years ago.

They were here, in this very room. It was decorated plainly—just the basic furniture and a table—and it was daylight.

Raffaele was standing in front of him. "But I—why are you accusing me of not caring about the cellars? I've devoted myself to them wholeheartedly, like you and even more so, and given my all to them. How can you say I'm not doing enough?" He opened his arms. His face, peaceful until now, had an expression of wounded disbelief. His skin, tight over his cheekbones, was pale. "Where did I go wrong, Vincenzo? Tell me, because I really think I've done everything I could have . . . and this is the thanks I get?"

Vincenzo paid little attention to his protestation. "It's not about dedication, Raffaele. I don't doubt yours. I know you've done your best, but it's not enough and it's not what Casa Florio needs." He tried to be polite, even though he could feel a wave of acidity rising in his stomach. Why did the man not just accept his decision and be done with it? Why was he choosing to act like a supplicant?

The cousin, however, insisted. He was being emotional, obtuse even—as though Vincenzo were robbing him of something—not grasping the fact that Vincenzo simply considered the cellars as his own. That he had no interest in sharing them and that he'd brought Raffaele in to run them only to prompt him to give more, something Raffaele had not been able to do.

This added to the unease. Vincenzo tried to be patient, made an effort, but in vain. In the end, he flew off the handle. "Enough, there's nothing more to add. I've made my decision, Raffaele. I was hoping your attitude would be different—I mean more active. I urged you on, wrote to you repeatedly, but you just acted like a country priest handling a parish of shepherds. I've made up my mind, so there's no point discussing this further."

A new emotion then appeared on Raffaele's face. "What do you mean?" he asked, his anger starting to surface.

"I told you to be more enterprising, remember? Don't deny it. No, no point in saying you don't understand: I have on occasion told you off in the hope that you'd open your eyes and cut some teeth. You can't just put one foot in front of the other in this world and be content, and you're always asking for permission . . ." His voice went up a tone, bent down, and became twisted and angry. "I can't stand complaints and begging. I will buy your third share and you can do whatever you like with the money."

But Raffaele started shaking his head. His face turned crimson and his voice high-pitched. "No, that's not the whole truth." He clutched the back of the armchair. "You just don't want relatives you can trust, because I"—he beat his chest—"I've never cheated you. What you want is servants. Slaves." Vincenzo noticed that Raffaele's cheeks seemed to be dropping, as though he had started to melt. "I believe in these cellars. I've put my heart and soul into them and you're now taking them away from me . . . I don't deserve to be treated like this," he concluded, drying his eyes.

It was this gesture that made Vincenzo explode. "Now, don't start sniveling like a kid. We're grown men talking business. You've been running my company and I don't happen to like how you've done it. So I'm buying you out and that's it, back to the way it was."

For a few moments, the room seemed filled with Raffaele's heavy sighs. Then he raised his head. "Sell my share, give me commission on the sales, but at least let me stay on as a steward. I enjoy working in the cellars and I know the workers." His voice became embittered and low. "They were right when they said I shouldn't trust you. You're just like your father."

"Whoever told you this knows nothing about work or business. I can't afford to be as cautious as you: Ingham and Woodhouse are breathing down my neck, they're sharks, and it would be easy for them to take back from me the little I've been able to nibble away from them. And you're always saying *please* and *sorry* . . . You should grab hold of things instead, tear them off with your teeth and your claws without any pity for anybody. There's a time for being careful and a time for taking risks, and you don't see these moments. I always have to watch over you."

"So now I'm a weakling just because I haven't made you take risks? You're holding against me the fact that I've been too reliable? Instead of thanking me for not getting you into debt unnecessarily? Nice reward!"

"You don't have the balls for this job, Raffaele," Vincenzo shouted in his face. "Don't you understand? You're just a secretary and what I need is a partner. You're not capable of doing what I want, you simply don't have it in you. So just accept it."

Raffaele took a step back as though he had been struck across the face. "A man should put his heart into things, and not just his money. Put love and passion into them. But what would you know about it? You're a real dog." He loosened his tie and slowly shook his head. "Give me my share. All of it and right now. I don't want to have anything else to do with you."

And so Raffaele vanished from his life, claiming nothing more than what was owed to him. Even there, he didn't have enough courage. Vincenzo heard through acquaintances that he had started trading as a middleman and managing vineyards. He chose to stay in Marsala. Good for him.

Then, a few months later, Vincenzo sensed a void that was hard to describe. It was an unusual kind of loneliness. After all, something Raffaele had said was correct: you have to be able to trust people, and, in a way, he trusted his cousin. He wasn't enterprising, of course, but he was reliable. And, besides Carlo Giachery and, however oddly, Ben Ingham, he had no friends.

He realized he was increasingly alone.

Aunt Mattia and Paolo Barbaro died many years ago. His mother has asked him many times to take her to her sister-in-law's grave but he keeps postponing. He doesn't like cemeteries. His family, the one that came from Bagnara, has disappeared. No more roots.

Besides . . .

He raises his glass and drinks a silent toast. Human beings end up disappointing him. Always.

For him, his roots are his companies. The trunk is Casa Florio. Money and prestige have increased tenfold but it's still not enough for him.

And yet . . .

There's one person still clinging to him. The only one he truly trusts. For better, for worse, even when she could be no more to the world but a shadow, and a whore to her own family. She resisted, tenacious, when he rejected her. She welcomed him back when he didn't deserve it. She has never abandoned him. Never.

Giulia.

Vincenzo returns to Via dei Materassai just before Sunday, in time to accompany his family to church and meet a few traders who do business with him.

In the evening, after the accounts books have been shut and the offices are deserted, he goes up to the apartment. His mother is ticking off Hail Marys in front of the *cufune*, the copper brazier; the window, half-open to let the smoke from the combustion out, allows in the sound of the rain that fills the gutters with mud.

He kisses her on the forehead. "Are you well?"

She nods. "And you?" She strokes his face with a gesture that has not changed since his childhood, when she had to wash his face in a basin. "You look tired. Does your wife feed you enough?"

"Yes, of course. It's just that I've been working hard. Besides, she doesn't do the cooking: don't you remember? We have maids and a cook."

Giuseppina makes a gesture of annoyance. "A wife must always watch what the servants are doing or they'll cheat her. Not waste her time reading books, especially in those foreign languages she knows. Now, come with me to my bedroom."

Vincenzo ignores the dig at Giulia and helps her stand up. There's no trace of her former strength in this body abused by time. And yet Vincenzo still sees in her the strict woman who would chase him down alleys, and remembers the adoring looks she gave him in his early childhood.

They arrive at her bedroom. The chest is the *corriola* she brought from Bagnara, and the bowl and pitcher are still the ones she had while she was married to Paolo. A coral crucifix hangs on the wall. There's a shawl on the edge of the bed: another recollection from Vincenzo's childhood.

"You still have this?" he exclaims, picking it up. It's much smaller and more threadbare than he remembers.

"There are things I couldn't give up, for all the money that you and . . . and your uncle brought to this house. You want to slow time down when you get old, but time doesn't stop. So you cling to things. For as long as they're around, it means you're around. You can't see, and don't want to see life ebbing away." Giuseppina sits on the edge of the bed and presses the shawl to her chest. There's a regret that gives her a knot in her stomach. "We call them memories but we lie," she says in a whisper. "Things like this shawl and your ring"—she points at Ignazio's mother's wrought-gold wedding ring—"are like anchors to a fleeting life."

When Vincenzo reaches the master bedroom, he finds Giulia asleep. Unlike Giuseppina, the years have been kind to her. She is still beautiful, even though lately, she has had backaches and trouble digesting. He throws his clothes on the chair. Then he curls up against his wife's back and, in her sleep, she squeezes his hand and holds it to her heart.

The steamer slowly pitches and yaws in the Favignana harbor. Beneath the sun, the village houses—small and little more than huts, with walls of drystone and tuff—seem drawn by a child's hand.

A launch comes away from the ship and reaches the pier at Forte di San Leonardo, the old bastion guarding the harbor. A few men and a boy get out. They brush against the village and head to the right, where there are large warehouses overlooking the sea. The doors are like gaping mouths, closed with gates like teeth sinking into the water.

Vincenzo walks briskly, enjoying the heat of the sun. Ignazio, his fourteen-year-old son, is at his side.

It's the first time he's brought him to the Favignana *tonnara*.

Vincenzo has been managing it for ten years now and has turned it into his masterpiece. It hasn't been easy: the rent has been and still is very high. He had to set up a network of entrepreneurs, assume all the risks of a new preservation method. And now tuna in oil has spread all over the Mediterranean.

He smiles to himself. Ignazio looks at him and questions him with his eyes. "I was just remembering something," Vincenzo says. "You'll see in a minute."

The boy often goes to the office with him, and often also to the Marsala cellars. But never before has his father brought him to the island.

If Ignazio is excited, he certainly doesn't show it. He walks at his father's side, in long, supple strides, and squints because of the glare. "What a beautiful place," he says. "Clean air, silence. Totally unlike Palermo."

"That's because of the wind direction. Wait till you get to the plant."

As a matter of fact, no sooner do they go past Forte di San Leonardo and the curve that separates the village from the *tonnara* than a nauseating stench sweeps over them. It smells of rot, of death and decomposition. Some of them, Caruso included, cover their faces with a handkerchief. But not Vincenzo.

Ignazio looks at him and stifles his nausea. He breathes through his mouth and ignores the stench. If his father can, then so can he. He has Vincenzo's build and features. Now that he has grown up, there's an obvious resemblance. But his eyes still have Giulia's softness.

"The leftovers from the process are left in the sun, decompose, and so give off this smell." Vincenzo points at a wide area beyond the warehouses. "There, you see? That's the *bosco*, the tuna cemetery. The workers unload the carcasses there while waiting for them to dry out."

The boy nods. "What about the boats? Where are they?"

"At sea," Caruso replies, approaching. "It's May, so *mattanza* time."

They walk into the building. In the courtyard, past the trees that provide a little shade, there's a stone corridor. The clearing in front of the sea is filled with nets, rigging, and men mending damaged meshes.

While Caruso heads to the offices, followed by an accountant, Vincenzo takes his son's arm. They walk across the courtyard, to the *trizzana*, the boat shelter.

Ignazio accepts this gesture with wariness and surprise. He cannot remember his father ever holding him this close.

Down below, the waves sound like the sea lapping against the walls of a cave.

"The first time I came here—" Vincenzo stops, repressing a smile. "I was with Carlo Giachery. I remember everything was falling apart here, it was a wretched, dirty place. We didn't even spend the night on the island because there wasn't anywhere decent to stay. Then, the next day . . ." Another smile. He turns to look at the building behind him. "I sent a message to Palermo asking for ship carpenters and builders to do the place up. Meanwhile, I started teaching people how to produce tuna in oil. I removed my jacket, rolled up my sleeves . . ." Ignazio watches him as he repeats these same gestures, takes off his jacket and other clothes until he is in shirtsleeves. "I gathered the heads of all the families and their wives to show them I wasn't afraid of getting my hands dirty." He squeezes his shoulder and shakes it affectionately. "When people work for you they must feel that they're a part of something." He stops. The sun hits Ignazio's ring. "I've told you this many times: my uncle, who you were named after, used to make me stay behind the *aromateria* counter. I hated it but now I see how important it was."

"For understanding people."

"Yes, for getting to know them. Because when someone asks you for something, you have to know what they really want: is it a herb to simply make them feel better or to treat a real pain? If they want wine, are they after quality or the prestige attached to it? If they need money, is it for power or because they're in financial difficulties?"

Ignazio understands and thinks about this. He's still pondering it when he arrives at the village, alone while his father is in a meeting with Genoese agents. The small, narrow streets are flooded in white sunlight; the tuna-oil-soaked tuff is no longer crumbling; there are now flagstones in the square outside the main church. His father has arranged for a schoolteacher for those who wish to learn to read and write, just like they do in Britain. All around the village, there are quarries like gorges sinking into the ground.

Favignana is a cliff of tuff, Ignazio thinks. You just have to scratch the surface and you find this thick layer of yellow, dappled with shells. The soil is pebbly and the few gardens and vegetable patches have been established with determination on the floors of tuff quarries, where muddy saltwater seeps through.

Then, once you've gotten used to the smell of tuna processing, you truly notice the sea: it's an angry, living, fierce blue.

The wealth comes from the sea.

This is an island of wind and silence, and Ignazio thinks he would like to live in a place like this: to belong to it and feel it inside him like a piece of flesh or a bone. At once be this island's master and its child.

He doesn't know that this is really going to happen.

The door slams violently and there's the sound of agitated footsteps and shouts. Giulia looks up from her embroidery and raises her eyebrows. "What's the matter?"

Giuseppina shrugs her shoulders. "I suppose it's *mon père.*" They exchange a glance. "And angry, at that."

They put their work aside and go to the rooms where the noise is originating.

Giuseppina is a reedlike sixteen-year-old with large dark eyes. They're the only beautiful feature in her anonymous face. And yet she is gentle and patient.

As she draws nearer, Giulia recognizes her husband's voice. Then she walks into the dining room and finds Angelina sitting in an armchair, frowning, arms folded. Her father is towering over her.

"What's the matter?"

A look from her husband makes her freeze in the doorway.

"What's the matter?" she repeats. "Vincenzo, what is it?"

Angela's reply is a poisoned arrow. "My father is accusing me of not going along with his marriage plans. He says that I should be prepared and is chiding me for not being attractive enough. As though somebody else but you two made me!"

Giulia turns and looks at her daughter. "Don't you dare speak like that," she says. That's how Angelina is: sharp and angry. She's not the kind of girl that lets herself be swayed, and neither is Giuseppina. But this time, Giulia has to reluctantly admit, she has a point. Sadly, fate has not been generous with her daughters as far as the gifts of beauty and grace are concerned.

Giuseppina goes to her sister and gives her an encouraging, comforting hug.

"I had a meeting at the association with Chiaramonte Bordonaro. I put to him the possibility of a union between our families. Angela is eighteen now . . ." The vein on Vincenzo's forehead is throbbing fast. "But no: it seems that our daughters are not . . . interesting. And not doing anything to make themselves so."

Angela looks at him with her eyes half-shut. She bears a striking resemblance to her paternal grandmother. "Neither my sister nor I are ever invited to parties. And why is that? Because we've never had the opportunity to meet anybody outside these four walls, we know very few girls our age, and people look at us as though we were servant girls dressed in our mistresses' clothes. We have practically no friends, while our brother is paraded about, invited to all the gatherings, and goes riding at the Favorita with noblemen's sons. You take him everywhere with you, to meetings with other traders, and introduce him as if he were an only child. And now you're saying you can't find me a husband? Have you ever wondered whose fault that is?"

"Hush, hush, my dearest . . ." Giuseppina caresses her face and tries to distract her. "You can't talk to our father like this . . ."

"Oh, that's right, I can't . . . because he's the master! And what are we, Giuseppina? Less than nothing! Aren't we his daughters, too? But instead, as far as he's concerned, only Ignazio exists. Ignazio! Ignazio! Ignazio!" Giulia sees her daughter's eyes fill with tears in an escalation of rage, jealousy, and sadness.

Vincenzo closes his fist, then opens it and draws closer to her. "What do you mean?"

"Enough now!" Giulia hardly ever raises her voice, and when she does, she silences everybody. She points a finger at her daughters. "You two—to your room." Then, hands on her hips, she addresses her husband. "To your study. Let's go."

She walks in earnest, not waiting to be followed.

There's much more than anger in those footsteps and quick breathing. Once the door is shut, Giulia turns around. "How could you do such a thing without telling me?!" she shouts. Her rage is overwhelming, reddening her time-lined face. "Offering our daughters to the highest bidder among your associates? What are they, sacks of bark?"

Vincenzo is confused. "They're of marrying age. Why not consider an advantageous match?"

Although it's not the first time they've had this argument, Giulia's feelings today are different. Stronger. Acidic. The sense of flesh tearing, of a gash that, she already knows, will not heal painlessly. "They're respectable girls; they may not be a pair of Venuses, but they're affectionate and polite. It's certainly not their upbringing that prevents them from being invited. It's something quite different."

"You, too? Don't go on about it. They're girls, they'll have an excellent dowry, there's nothing else to say, and that's what men look for nowadays." Vincenzo is annoyed. "They can't accept just anybody, not with their name."

"And yet you know that the name and the money aren't enough. Even now."

This is not a doubt but a statement. Vincenzo falls silent because his wife is right.

He goes to the desk, sits down, and buries his face in his fists.

It was just a suspicion at first, which he's carried around for a few months, ever since he began to let it be known that he had two daughters of marriageable age.

Then it became a certainty. It was actually Gabriele Chiaramonte Bordonaro who had thrown it in his face with his typical directness. "You know I'm a straight talker, Don Vincenzo. To be honest, I don't want to marry your daughters to my kin, and it's not because they're not lovely girls or because I don't respect you . . . If that were the case I wouldn't be doing business with you. On the contrary, your money makes you a very desirable fellow father-in-law. But I'm sure I don't need to tell you that business is one thing and family another. And your girls were born in . . . well, particular circumstances."

Vincenzo's mouth has been coated in bile ever since.

He has not felt this ashamed in years. He stands up. Maybe, he thinks while pacing up and down the room and relating the conversation to his wife, he needs to revisit his youth in order to feel the sting of humiliation in all its ferocity once again. "That's right, it's not enough." His voice is low, steeped in rancor and bitterness. "Our daughters aren't enough. Everything I have done, Casa Florio . . . We are not enough." And, as he looks at Palermo, bathing in the October sun, he doesn't notice that Giulia has tears in her eyes.

"You want a match with an aristocratic family for yourself, not for them." She speaks softly, afraid to let out a sob. Traces of her old pain surface. "It's what you were unable to do for yourself, right?"

She sees her husband hesitate, taking a step back into his soul, betrayed by his fingertips curling into his palm.

She remembers, a lump in her throat. Fingers pointing at Angelina and Giuseppina, as illegitimate, baptized in secret without a celebration or even a toast, acknowledged only after Ignazio was born: the boy, the heir to Casa Florio.

Never mind that they now have a dowry that's the envy of heirs to noble families, that they speak French, wear jewels, or that their church veil is made of lace: they are still two bastards. And she is still a kept woman. Some memories leave a sediment, ferment, but never disappear completely, and always find a way to surface again and cause pain.

Because there's a kind of pain that can never end.

But Vincenzo can't even imagine this: he's incapable of accepting that something should be denied him. Anger dominates his horizon and prevents him from seeing Giulia's bitterness. "Try to understand. Back then I was . . ." He stops, asking for her help.

Help she is not willing to give. Not anymore. "You used to make and break, Vincenzo, never taking anybody else into consideration. For years I lived with our children without any rights, in fear that at any moment you would throw me out so you could marry a noblewoman chosen by your mother." Giulia feels her voice growing hoarse but pulls herself together because some things have to be said, things she has carried inside her for years. "You had your life, you followed your path . . ." She swipes the air with her hand and her voice trembles. "No, now you listen to me. I will not tolerate that Angela and Giuseppina go through what I went through, I don't want them to feel as humiliated as I did. They will not marry somebody who despises them just so you can protect your own interests and those of Casa Florio."

Vincenzo slumps on the chair. "I married you, Giulia." He looks at her from below, silently asking for a truce.

"Because you had a son and you had to legitimize your heir. If it had been another girl, I would still be living in Via della Zecca Regia and you would probably have a wife ten years younger, who would have provided you with a legitimate heir to Casa Florio."

These words carry Giulia's old fear of never having been enough for him. Of being his deepest regret. A failure.

Vincenzo stands up and puts his hands on her shoulders. "No," he says, "and yes." He puts his arms around her and speaks into her ear. "Because if I'd found her, I would never have allowed her to talk to me like this."

He holds her tight. Giulia is surprised and almost frightened. She stiffens but, a moment later, leans against his chest, her fingers searching for the heartbeat under his waistcoat. It feels agitated and nervous.

"I want what's best for my family," he says.

She looks up. "You want what's best for Casa Florio, Vincenzo." She doesn't attempt to conceal her exasperation. "And what's best for you is a son-in-law with a title, who brings prestige to the name Florio. But the girls were born out of wedlock and they're your daughters. No aristocrat will ever want them." She strikes to hurt, to remind her husband that for many people he is still a laborer. The grandson of a Bagnara man. She takes his left hand: his wedding band and Ignazio's ring are on his finger. "Angelina's right. They don't get invited to parties with girls their age and often sit apart at balls. They are well brought up but that's not enough."

"They'll have a large dowry," he replies stubbornly, pulling his hand away. "Their money will be their title."

"No. If you want a future for your Casa Florio then it's not them you need to rely on but Ignazio. He's the one who must make a good match. You need to focus on him."

Left alone in his study, he ponders her words for a long time.

Giulia is right.

He examines his library: the leather spines, the golden lines, the shelves, and the glass doors. Everything illustrates his life: from the books in English to the scientific works, as well as the volumes about mechanical engineering. Because for him producing means building.

So has all my work been for nothing? he asks himself. *Was it all pointless? Was it not enough to work, to create a financial empire with the little I had, experimenting, pushing myself to do what nobody else even tried to in Sicily?*

No, it wasn't enough.

"They want a coat of arms. Noble blood. *Respectability.*" He emphasizes this last word and laughs to himself. A cruel laugh that ends in a growl.

He'd forgotten the bitter taste of humiliation.

His fury takes the form of a wave. Vincenzo stifles a cry and sweeps the paper, account books, and even the inkwell from the desk. The walnut surface receives an angry blow.

The ink spreads over the rough draft of a letter addressed to Carlo Filangeri, Prince of Satriano. Only one name stays legible: Pietro Rossi.

More anger is added to his existing anger. Vincenzo almost feels as though somebody is laughing in his face. "That piece of mud!" he shouts, screwing up the sheet of paper. The ink stains his fingers and drips like black blood as he tries to slow down his breathing.

Pietro Rossi, president of the Royal Bank, who has been torturing him with pointless demands and trying to discredit him in every way and drive him to resign; who won't pay him for his work as trade governor; whom he has tried to ignore but who has now exhausted his patience.

A few days ago, Vincenzo went to the Royal Bank: it was his turn to pick up the money delivered by the steamer, record it, cash the letters of credit, and pay whatever was due.

A hour went by, then another. Nobody turned up.

Shortly before lunch, he gave in to his restlessness, grabbed his overcoat and hat, and headed for the stairs.

There he met Pietro Rossi. "Where are you going?" the man asked without even a greeting.

"To Via dei Materassai. I've been here for three hours and have no intention of wasting any more time."

Tall, thin, with a stiff mustache, Rossi stood in front of him. "Not at all. It's your task and your duty. You will stay here until three."

"I've already wasted a morning pandering to your obsessions, Rossi. Not a single creditor came. Rather, you owe me service certificates dating back to March last year. I can't be paid without those."

Rossi opened his eyes wide and laughed in his face. "You want to be paid? And for what, exactly?"

A clerk who was coming down the stairs slowed down, ready to collect every word and turn it into gossip. Vincenzo gave him a dirty look and the man walked away. "As a governor of the Royal Bank, I'm entitled to a salary of six *oncie* a month for services rendered and for helping with registrations," he said in the kind of tone used to explain something simple to an idiot. "And I can only get it if you're kind enough to sign the documents. Is that clear or do I have to draw it for you?"

Standing two steps below him, Rossi walked up to him and said, in his face, "Forget it."

A slash that left Vincenzo speechless.

"You've no idea how to be a governor," Rossi hissed. "You may have all the money in the world but you don't know what it means to work for the government or an institution. All you care about is business, and the government is useful to you only as far as it doesn't impinge on what you do . . . I don't blame you, but then don't persist in trying to do something you can't." He pointed a finger at him. "Let me tell you something: the world doesn't revolve around Via dei Materassai, your steamers, or your loans."

Vincenzo pushed his finger away. "I do it because I can do it. And who the hell are you to tell me what to do? You think I don't realize you deliberately give me shifts on the days when my ships arrive and I should be in the office? Or that you call meetings when I'm in Marsala?"

"You've been using this excuse for years but we both know the truth." Rossi climbed another step and stood sideways, as though about to leave. "You have people watching your back because of your money, whereas I know what I'm doing and take pride in it. Things you're not even aware of."

"I do my job and you have to pay me for it."

Rossi looked at him calmly. "No," he said, then left.

Vincenzo remained silent for the first time in years. He instead started writing the letter that is now scrunched in his hands, but hadn't found the right words to finish it.

Because his sentences either expressed too much or too little, mentioned indignation and demanded recognition when there was only one correct word: *hatred*. Yes, hatred: toward those who still consider him a *parvenu*, a petty, coarse man. He almost enjoys being unpleasant, thus confirming their prejudices. They won't change, anyway.

And how could he describe to a stranger, which, after all, Filangeri is, why he is so upset today? Why the feeling of unease has returned? How could he explain that he has inside him a clot of darkness that pushes him, even now and always, to accumulate, grow, and find new enterprises? Born rich, Filangeri could never understand.

However much he loves her and considers himself her son, Palermo treats him like a stranger. He tried to be accepted, has courted her with wealth, has created jobs and brought comfort.

Maybe that was what she could not forgive him: work. Power. Having his eyes open to the world, while Palermo keeps hers firmly shut.

This is how Ignazio finds him, with his fist pressed against his mouth, face drawn and fierce. He knocks gingerly and waits in the doorway.

"May I come in?"

His father nods, and the young man enters tentatively. He looks at the ink-stained floor, with papers strewn all over it. He bends down to pick them up but his father makes an abrupt gesture without even looking up. "Leave it. Let the maids pick it up."

Ignazio tidies the papers he's still holding and puts them on the table. He goes to the chair in front of the desk and sits down. He looks at his father in silence for a long time. "Mamma wishes to know if you're coming to eat," he finally says.

Vincenzo shrugs. Then he suddenly stares at Ignazio as though only just registering his presence, and remembers Giulia's words. "They don't wrong you," he says. "They don't speak badly of you even though you're my son." His voice loses its angry tone and grows calmer, almost gentle.

Ignazio listened to the row and knows the reason for his mother's fury. He realized some time ago that his peers treat him with a respect and deference nobody affords his sisters, especially Giuseppina. "I'm a boy, Papà," he says cautiously. "Nobody dares."

There's truth in his words, the only truth. He is male, he is the heir to Casa Florio.

The corners of Vincenzo's mouth lift in a part-defiant, part-spiteful smile. He stands up and sits opposite Ignazio. "Once, when you were little, I found you looking through an atlas bigger than yourself. There you were, reading about harbors and the boats mooring in them . . ."

Ignazio nods. It happened shortly after the accident in Arenella, when he had nearly drowned.

"From that moment on, I made sure you learned not just Latin and other stuff priests teach, but also English and French, and also how to act in society. I had you educated like a nobleman's son and not that of a trader."

Ignazio smiles. He remembers the riding lessons, etiquette classes with his sisters, and especially dance lessons with the music master, and remembers how he'd make his mother spin, and how she would laugh, happily. Giulia had never learned to dance well. But his father snatches him away from his reverie and gives his shoulder a squeeze. "I never had all the things you had. None of them. Naturally, I did learn: my uncle Ignazio would drive me crazy with books, as your grandmother can still tell you. But I never learned to ride or dance because I didn't need them for working at the *aromateria.*"

He looks at his ink-stained hands, and leans his elbows on his knees. Even though he's nearly fifty-five, Vincenzo still has strong hands, albeit marked by work. *And yet it's not enough*, he thinks again. *Working yourself into the ground, damning your soul, none of it was enough to get you accepted by those who have true power: political power, the one that counts.*

"You can go where I didn't manage to."

He says this so softly that Ignazio worries he hasn't heard. Vincenzo leans forward so the heads of father and son are almost touching. "Being able to ride and dance will be as useful to you as traveling and seeing the world, because Sicily mustn't be enough for you. It's what aristocrats do, those with a coat of arms on their front door . . . And that's where you need to get to, do you understand? They will open their doors to you because you can buy the lot of them, with all their clothes and palaces. You already have the money, you're not like me, who started off with what my uncle left me. You have the possibility to make Palermo and its residents say that the Florios aren't inferior to anybody."

Ignazio is puzzled. "But Angelina and Giuseppina also have—"

"Forget them," Vincenzo says abruptly. "They're women." He stands up and makes his son do the same. "You know what they used to call me? A laborer. Me!" He laughs, and in that laughter so full of anger and resentment Ignazio senses ten, a hundred stab wounds still bleeding and making his father act like an injured animal. It's a thought that breaks his heart.

"All—*all* those who showed me contempt have come to me cap in hand, sooner or later." He takes his son's head in his hands and stares into his eyes. "You have to take everything they refused to give me. They have to give it to you, and if they don't, you just go and take it. Because power is about having a purse full of money and proving it to those who think they're better than you. People must act with deference when they see you. Do you understand?"

Ignazio is perplexed. He's only fifteen, and these words make him feel uneasy and confused. His father has never spoken to him like this, and never allowed him to see past the wall of his frowning face.

Why are you telling me all this? he wants to ask but all he can do is stutter another question. "But—but isn't it better to be respected? A frightened man can never be loyal—"

"People are honest with those who have the power, Ignazio, because they know they'll be in trouble if they're not. And money is one of the paths to power. That's why I'm telling you: keep all your cards close to your chest, and never ever trust anybody. Keep your own counsel. Just concentrate on saving your own skin, no matter what it takes."

Ignazio hesitates. He doesn't want people to fear him the way they do his father. Whenever Vincenzo Florio walks into a room, there are those who see him and are afraid, and those who look at him with contempt.

He wants to be respected for what he is and not for his money or lands. He tries to explain this to his father but all he gets in return is a heavily bitter laugh.

Vincenzo stands up and goes to the door. "Ah, the result of an easy life! You say this because you've never had to prove anything, my son. Because I built everything you have, and you don't know—you have no idea—what it cost me." He shakes his head and looks around. "If only these walls could speak, there's so much they would tell you . . . But that's enough for now. Let's go eat."

Ignazio notices with some dread that his father's hair is turning gray. He watches him walk away and disappear beyond the door. He runs his hands over the desk.

You don't know—you have no idea—what it cost me.

He can't get these words out of his mind. He clenches them between his teeth and lets them drop into the pit of his stomach.

Ignazio doesn't know what his father was like before he was born. What a man is before he has a son is often a mystery that a father decides to keep deep inside him and never reveal to a living soul. There's a clear, impassable boundary between before and after.

Ignazio has no way of knowing how much having a son can change a man.

"What are we going to do, Your Excellency?" Vincenzo asks, while a cup of coffee is served to him by a servant in livery. "You are aware of what Rossi is putting me through and yet you do nothing."

Minister Vincenzo Cassisi, with broad whiskers on a bony face, looks askance at Carlo Filangeri, as though he is responsible for that outburst, and indulges in an ironic little smile.

Vincenzo has decided to resolve his dispute with Rossi by going to Naples and requesting an audience with Cavalier Cassisi, who has been the minister for Sicilian affairs for a decade. An audience obtained quickly thanks to Filangeri.

The minister shrugs his shoulders. "And what are you doing, Don Florio? If you were more conscientious in fulfilling your duties—"

Vincenzo's laugh is bitter and heavily sarcastic. "Me? What about . . . me?"

"But, Your Excellency," Filangeri softly intervenes, studying the tips of his polished boots, "this is one of the most important businessmen in the realm. We can't expect him to drop everything whenever somebody snaps his fingers—"

"That's the problem, Your Excellency," Vincenzo interrupts. "Not only do I have my governor duties but I'm not exactly a loafer surrounded by stewards who cater to his every whim. You do understand, don't you?" Vincenzo leans forward, almost touching the minister's arm. Uneasy, Cassisi pulls away. "I pay more taxes than anybody else in the country, I guarantee wealth with my imports and supply the army with medicines and sulfur. And you're putting me on the spot like this. You've even confiscated the silver that the revolutionary government had awarded me in lieu of payment in 1848 . . ." He stops, takes a breath, and sips his coffee.

The other two men look bewildered, but neither of them speaks.

"The government owes me *a great deal*," Vincenzo concludes. "*You both* owe me a great deal."

The minister stands up abruptly in an attempt to distance himself from this impudent man. "Now, this is too much . . . Not only did you subsidize the rebels but you have the audacity to demand payment, and in such a tone! Rossi has a point when he demands your resignation."

Vincenzo does not bat an eyelid. "I have the audacity because I know I can." He leans back in his armchair, his fingers interlaced over his chest. "What would become of the Bourbon reign without Casa Florio? Just consider my fleet of ships, the service I render the Crown, and all the times I've acted as intermediary between you officials and the large banks because the king was in a difficult situation and you needed a loan. Now tell me: what has Rossi done for you?"

Minister Cassisi takes another step back.

Filangeri cannot repress a grimace.

Cassisi returns to sit behind his desk, clears his throat but says nothing.

Vincenzo uses the silence as a lever to ease his words into the minds of the men, and lead them where he wishes them to go.

"So?" the minister says at the end.

"I would like to ask for three things." Vincenzo raises his fingers. "First and foremost I want Rossi to leave me alone. Then I want him to give me the service certificates and, finally, pay me. Not because I need the pittance I receive for being a governor, but because I am who I am and he is nothing more than a paper pusher. He is nothing to me, but I must be someone to him."

And so it was.

"Hooray for the bride and groom!"

"Congratulations!"

The small orchestra strikes up a dance, and the cheer drowns it out.

The newlyweds walk close to each other. Luigi De Pace, the son of a wealthy Palermo ship owner and an associate of the Florios, greets people, takes jokes on the chin, and reciprocates. The bride, Angelina, is petite, shy, with a calm expression. She's wearing a satin dress and a long lace veil her father had made in Valenciennes. Her sister, Giuseppina, is at her side. She adjusts her veil and hugs her.

Giulia looks at her eldest daughter. She's happy for her, proud, but also somewhat sad. Angelina has what she herself was not able to have: a real wedding ceremony. A celebration. A dowry. She gave everything up for Vincenzo's sake. And even after they were married, he didn't register anything—not even a pin—in her name. Never mind. What matters now is that her daughter is happy.

"She's so elegant."

"A bridal veil worthy of a queen."

Giulia, both pleased and sad, keeps the compliment to herself.

It was not easy to persuade Vincenzo to agree to the match. It was Luigi's mother who requested a meeting. After tea and chitchat, the stout woman with thick eyebrows and pudgy hands looked at her and said, "May I ask a direct question, Donna Giulia?"

"Of course."

"My husband hears that yours, Don Vincenzo, is trying to get your daughters married. Is that so?"

Giulia grew wary. "Yes."

The other woman folded her hands over her belly and studied Giulia with a slight frown, assessing every possible reaction. "We have a son you may find suitable: Luigi. He's a good boy, serious, respectful, and a hard worker. He'd keep her like a baroness. Would you like to mention it to your husband?"

Giulia discussed it for a long time—but not too long—with Vincenzo.

He could be stubborn but was also practical: the De Pace family are ship owners and have an extensive trade network. They are not as wealthy as the Florios but possess that entrepreneurial spirit he values above all else. And so, after a short space of time, a dowry was agreed upon and a date fixed for the wedding.

Giulia nods to herself. Angela, her little Angelina, has found a man who will take care of her. Luigi is just over thirty and seems kind and patient. As a wedding present, he has given her a parure set in gold and emeralds.

There's only one cloud hanging over this marriage, as far as Giulia is concerned.

A few days earlier, Angelina was taking off her wedding gown with the maid's help after her final fitting with the dressmaker. Giulia was watching her in the mirror, lovingly following all her gestures, trying to store them in her memory. These were her beloved and much-wanted daughter's last days at home with her.

The girl met her gaze. "What is it, Mamma?" she asked, seeing her mother's eyes glistening with tears.

Giulia waved her hand as though to dismiss a thought. "It's nothing. You're beautiful, you're a woman, and—" She swallowed air. "I was thinking of how I've watched you grow up, of how you were after you were just born, a tiny little thing always clinging to me. And now you're getting married."

Angelina grabbed her robe and immediately got dressed, as though embarrassed. "I remember that time. I was always clinging to you because my father wasn't there and, whenever he was, he would push me away. I hardly knew him." She spoke without looking at her. "Giuseppina and I have always been a nuisance for him."

Giulia rushed to hug her. "Of course you weren't. How can you say that? You know your father has a bad temper but he loves you and would give his life for you both."

Angelina put a hand on her arm. "My father loves money, Mamma, and perhaps you. But not Giuseppina and me. There's only one person who's dear to him, and that's Ignazio." There was no regret in her voice but the simple acceptance of a fact that could never be altered. "And if I have to be completely frank," she added with a sigh, "I'm glad I'm getting married because this way at least I can have a family and children of my own who will love me for who I am."

Giulia's smile fades when she remembers this. She knows Angelina has agreed to marry so she can leave this house. She has traded love for the hope of a better life.

And yet . . . She glances at the newlyweds. Luigi is attentive, he gives Angela a glass of champagne and doesn't let go of her hand. She's laughing and seems genuinely at peace. Giulia hopes that there may already be some tenderness between them. Not love: that—if it ever does—will come in time. *They will be good life companions*, she tells herself. At least she hopes so.

She turns and looks around for her husband. He was constantly nervous in the days preceding the ceremony. She finds him in conversation with other men in a corner of the courtyard. Business, no doubt.

She gestures at the housekeeper to invite the guests into the villa, so that the wedding banquet may begin.

Everything has to be impeccable, as always.

Ignazio, fifteen years old with a mass of dark hair, also watches his sister and brother-in-law. He raises his half-filled glass to Angela and she responds with a smile, and sends him a kiss with her fingertips.

He hopes she might be happy, and wishes it with all his heart. Angelina has always been jealous of him, they have been squabbling for years, and she has often accused him of being their father's favorite. She's been angry and unhappy for a very long time. Too long.

May you finally be contented, he wishes her with his eyes. *May your husband be a good business associate of Casa Florio, just as his father has been.*

He takes another sip. French champagne. Crates of it purchased through the mediation of Monsieur Deonne, his father's trusted man in France. There are baskets of lilies, roses, and frangipani—a flower that practically symbolizes Palermo—in the salon and along the row of rooms, giving off a heavily heady scent.

In the salon where the buffet has been laid out, the silver is glowing as though with a life of its own. Everywhere, there are waiters ready to pour wine.

The Florios have spent a lot on this wedding. "I want people to talk about it for months," Vincenzo said while Giulia, tight-lipped, was drawing up the guest list. "The Florio celebrations must become legendary."

And, once again, Ignazio heard the quiver of his father's rancor through his triumphant tone.

He almost doesn't notice Carlo Giachery coming up to greet him. "Hello, Ignazio. Congratulations on the party. For once, your father has spared no expense!"

They shake hands. This man, with a loud voice and penetrating eyes, has been a constant presence in his life, and is probably the only person who can be called a friend of his father's. Because Vincenzo Florio has business associates, but not friends, something Ignazio learned very early on. "You know what he's like: everything has to be perfect or not at all."

They walk across the rooms, chatting about the guests and the new sumac mill Vincenzo had built behind the *tonnara*. Giachery laughs. "Only your father could put a mill right next to a villa! For him, Casa Florio comes before anything else."

It's true that the mill strikes a discordant note on this gulf. A building nobody wanted, starting with the Arenella residents and ending with Giulia, who hates the sumac dust drifting into the house.

But, with a stubbornness edging on anger, his father had it built.

His father is always full of anger. Even now.

He studies him. No, he thinks, correcting himself, biting his lip. He is disappointed—he can see it in his face: the crease between the eyebrows, his lips pursed into a stiff wrinkle . . . Angela married with his blessing, true, and Luigi is a good match. But not the best.

His father has always obtained everything he wanted except what he's been yearning for the most. And it is up to him, Ignazio, to achieve the results the great Vincenzo Florio was not able and never will be able to reach.

He walks away from the window by which he has been standing until now, takes a glass of champagne, and heads toward the sea and the cliffs. He's seeking solitude and silence, away from the guests. Of course, he is a Florio and the bride's brother, but he also wants to keep an ounce of freedom for himself.

He almost fails to hear his sister Giuseppina's footsteps as she comes to search for him. "Ignazio!" she calls, lifting the hem of her embroidered silk dress to avoid soiling it. "Mamma is looking for you. She wants to know what's the matter with you and says the dancing with the newlyweds is about to start."

Her brother doesn't turn around, so she puts a hand on his arm. "What is it? Are you feeling unwell?"

He shakes his head. A curl falls over his forehead. "It's not that, Giuseppina, it's just that . . ." He waves his hand in a weary gesture. "It's too noisy."

Giuseppina, however, does not accept his answer. She looks at him intently. They're almost the same height, and have eyes that mirror and can read each other.

"I sometimes wonder what our lives would have been like if we'd been different," he murmurs. "If we hadn't had all this but had a choice.

Instead, we're forced to live like this, in full view of everybody." He indicates the tower behind him.

Giuseppina sighs and lets go of her dress. The rose fabric gets covered in a film of dust and splashes of seawater. "Then we wouldn't have been the Florios," she replies, also softly. Then she looks down at her bejeweled hands. She's wearing the coral earrings their grandmother gave her a couple of weeks ago, saying her grandfather Paolo had given them to her more than fifty years earlier. They're not expensive but have great value for her. "We would have been poorer. Perhaps our parents wouldn't have met."

"I wonder if that would have been a bad thing. I don't mean for our mother and father. Perhaps today we would be celebrating with an ordinary glass of wine and not French champagne." Ignazio twirls his glass in his hand. Then, as though performing a ritual, he slowly pours his drink into the sea. "Our father chose to do what he wanted, and who he wanted to be. He did it his own way, with a strength that spared no one. While we have been forced to follow the path he traced for us. We've all done it, starting with our mother."

Giuseppina says nothing. She watches her brother empty his glass, examines his handsome face and sees a strange sadness in it, as though Ignazio is looking at a devastating scene in which he is unable to intervene. And the powerless light in his eyes has the taste of all he has not lived. It's a melancholy that turns his unspoken words into sighs.

Vincenzo circulates from guest to guest without a moment's respite. This is a lavish wedding, blessed by a sun that has cast a golden veil over this April 1, 1854.

He greets the Pojeros, his new shipping associates, Augusto Merle and his family, Chiaramonte Bordonaro, and Ingham, who has brought his nephew Joseph Whitaker along. He jokes with all of them, thanks them, and drinks a toast with his fellow father-in-law, Salvatore De Pace. They talk about ships, business, contracts, and taxes.

There's a handful of people standing apart. The servants have been ordered to serve them first, and he has been to welcome them in person. They're not mingling with the others and their expression is one of detachment, opaque. They are not taking part in the excited discussions at the table, unless they are specifically addressed.

Everything about their manner and evasive answers, even the slight cocking of their heads, suggests unease. They examine the vault in the Quattro Pizzi hall, ponder the furnishings, estimate their cost, and are unable to conceal a blend of envy, admiration, and annoyance, even though it's masked by a blasé bearing. And Vincenzo, who has always been a good people reader, sees it all too well.

Today, anger and triumph taste the same.

They can't account for it, he thinks, watching them from the corner of his eye. *They can't understand how I got this far. And how could they possibly understand? They're aristocrats. They have centuries of privilege behind them. Blood nobility who don't deign to mingle with those who have become rich, like me; who try to get into commerce. And yet they cannot see me differently. They don't know that I haven't stopped thinking about my work, about the sea, the ships, tuna, sumac, sulfur, silk, and spices, for a single second. Or about Casa Florio.*

He orders another round of champagne.

For all their titles and coats of arms on their front doors, they don't have what he has.

He doesn't pause to think that they, too, have something he can never have. He doesn't want to. For today, the darkness lurking deep in his soul must keep still and far away.

Only a little later does Prince Giuseppe Lanza di Trabia approach. He's an elderly man now. He has measured gestures, as though he needs to pace himself, and a calm voice. "A truly magnificent wedding, Don Vincenzo. I must congratulate you."

"Only the best for my daughter and son-in-law." He raises his glass while the couple in the middle of the room is dancing awkwardly, a sign of the intimacy that has just begun to form. A few guests immediately follow their example.

"You made a good match," the prince of Trabia says, staring at the wine in his glass. "Adequate. It will be a happy marriage." Words like drops of poison.

"Thank you."

The other man suddenly clears his throat. "How's business at your shipping company?"

"Very good." Vincenzo waits. A man like the prince doesn't ask random questions.

"You've shown foresight by organizing things yourself and setting up your own company. After the stroke of bad luck with the *Palermo*—"

"Luck had little to do with it. It sank because of the clashes with the Neapolitans. If the revolutionary government hadn't commandeered it . . . Oh, well, never mind, what's done is done, and there's nothing one can do about it."

"Yes, but you are actually the only one with a mixed fleet of timber and steam." His glance speaks volumes. "You're not the kind of man who stops at the first hurdle. You purchased a steamship in Glasgow, if I'm not mistaken. The *Corriere Siciliano*, right? I've heard good things about it, and Naples is keeping an eye on you. You have ships crisscrossing the entire Mediterranean and meeting delivery deadlines, which is something Neapolitan steamers are not always able to do. In other words, you're probably the only person who can draw up an agreement with the postal services."

Vincenzo turns around, slowly. "Do you mean a monopoly?" All of a sudden, he wishes he were somewhere else, so he could speak freely, and not in a packed room full of loud conversation.

The prince of Trabia gives a slight nod. "I heard it mentioned at court last time I was in Naples. It's not just a rumor: the king can no longer guarantee service to our island, so . . ." He takes his watch out of his pocket: a refined object, a French craftsman's masterpiece. He looks at it and strokes the enameled flat part. "Please understand, I'm telling you this because, as I mentioned earlier, not many people could undertake such a venture in Sicily, and above all because this kind of contract must not end up in Neapolitan hands. It would be an incalculable loss for Palermo and Sicily; money that would stay in Naples but that could be used here instead, to create jobs. And, above all, we'd be dealing with a service that would place the island in an even more marginal position. The consequences would be too many and too negative for us Sicilians. Do you follow me?"

"Perfectly."

"Good." The prince of Trabia lifts his head and admires the painted vault. "You managed to create your palace in the end, Don Vincenzo. You may not be a nobleman, but this is a house fit for a king." He squeezes his arm. "Think about what I've said. Take the necessary steps."

The prince of Trabia walks away amid the dancing couples, past those sitting against the wall.

Vincenzo puts a hand over his lips and goes to the window. The rumor about the postal service monopoly has been circulating for a while. And that's all it seemed to be: just a rumor.

And yet . . .

He watches the prince go to his carriage and leave. He thinks feverishly, while music plays around him and glasses are raised for more toasts. Above him, the painted vault of the Quattro Pizzi room gathers voices and moods.

An exclusive postal service by means of his ships could mean a direct relationship with the Sicilian Crown. Not to mention money. *A lot* of money.

In other words, an exclusivity that means power.

PART SEVEN

Sand

May 1860 to April 1866

Cent'anni d'amuri, un minutu di sdigno.

A hundred years of love, one minute of anger.

—SICILIAN PROVERB

Sicilian revolutionary unrest is smoldering beneath the surface, rekindled by vibrant clandestine publicity and a few—failed—attempts at a popular uprising. The wiser nobility and intellectual middle classes, on the other hand, are inclined to involve the king of Sardinia, Victor Emmanuel II, in the process of freeing the island from Bourbon subjection. Francesco Crispi's determination will bring these elements together: he suggests to General Giuseppe Garibaldi the possibility of an "external" insurrection, which, by supporting Sicilian rebels, would ultimately aim to unite Italy. In order to persuade him, Crispi tells Garibaldi that an insurrection has already begun in Palermo (the Gancia revolt, steered by Crispi, from April 4 to 18, 1860). Without the king's explicit support, Garibaldi and his Expedition of the Thousand, volunteer fighters wearing red shirts, sail from Quarto on May 5, land in Marsala (May 11), and finally enter Salemi (May 14), where Garibaldi proclaims himself dictator of Sicily in the name of Victor Emmanuel II. They march on Palermo on May 28 and are welcomed as liberators, then reach Naples on September 7. The meeting between Garibaldi and Victor Emmanuel II, on October 26, in Teano, marks the beginning of the Kingdom of Italy.

However, after the unification, Kingdom of Sardinia officials extend their legislative, economic, fiscal, and trading system to southern Italy and Sicily without adapting it, refusing any compromise. Discontent spreads among the nobility: they have been unable to keep their privileges intact, and have been stripped of their cultural identity. The people continue to suffer because of an economy that has to operate in difficult circumstances and does not seem to have any possibility of improvement.

And so Sicily is, once again, a conquered land.

THE WEST COAST OF SICILY is an alternation of cliffs and sandy beaches. A varied ecosystem with changeable morphology and a very rich landscape.

It is only around Marsala that the beaches become a steady presence: fine, powdery sand brought in by the sea through the San Teodoro Passage of Isola Lunga, a place of breathtaking beauty. Near Marsala, we have Stagnone, one of the richest lagoons on the island: an old Phoenician harbor, a Greek shelter, and a Roman emporium.

Thanks to the presence of salt pans—a system of basins used for refining sea salt through the evaporation of water—the climate in Stagnone is almost always constant and the salinity does not fluctuate.

It is no wonder that marsala cellars sprout near these low, sandy beaches. It is no wonder that the sand comes into courtyards, invades warehouses, and collects on barrels.

The sea, the limestone in the sand, and the constant temperature have made this wine so dense—a wine created by chance, and which became the flavor of an era.

Because the sand that comes to rest on the terra-cotta tiles covering the salt is the same that eddies between the bottles laid to rest in the entrails of the cellars. It's a sand that carries grains of salt and the scent of the sea.

It's this salt that gives the dry taste, the confusing uncertainty, and the flavor with a hint of the sea to a wine that, in other circumstances, would be a sweet wine like any other.

Facing each other, Ignazio and Vincenzo look at each other in silence. The father is sitting at his desk while the son is standing. It's still dark outside.

Giulia is near them.

"It could be a good idea, Ignazio," she says in a conciliatory tone. "You could go away for a few weeks . . . Your sister Giuseppina would be happy for you to stay with her. Besides, I remember how excited you were after visiting Marseille."

But Ignazio looks down and shakes his head. "Giuseppina and her husband are very generous, *Maman*, but I shan't leave. I'm going to stay in Palermo with you and Father. It's my duty and Casa Florio needs me now more than ever."

Only then does Vincenzo seem to stir from his stillness. He is sixty-one and weighed down by age. The bags under his eyes, the legacy of sleepless nights, make him look older. "So be it," he says. "We'll stay right here." He reaches out to Giulia, and she takes his hand and holds it between hers.

She can only accept. Something she has learned at her expense: that if a Florio makes up his mind, then nothing and no one can make him change it. They are too proud, and even more stubborn.

Ignazio leaves them alone. Lost in thought, Vincenzo rubs his beard, which has flecks of gray in it.

The truth? He lacks the courage to admit he is afraid. Not for himself, of course, but for his son.

Time is coiling on itself and hurtling into a future nobody can understand. There's a strange anxiety swelling the air, making everybody suspicious, uncertain, and frightened.

It all started a month ago, in early April 1860. For too long spirits had been inflamed by Bourbon policies, made up of abuse of power, heavy taxes, arbitrary arrests, and show trials. There had been many signs, many small tremors heralding disaster. First, there was a revolt in Boccadifalco; then, two days later, the rebellion in Gancia, the large Franciscan monastery in the heart of Palermo. The monks had actually given sanctuary to the rebels but then a cowardly friar had snitched and soldiers surrounded the church and the monastery, blocking any escape route for the rebels. Thirteen of them were arrested and more than twenty killed. The bells the monks had rung to call the city to an uprising turned into a death knell. Only two men managed to escape and hide for days among dead bodies in the crypt. In the end, they left through a slit in the church wall, helped by local women who distracted the soldiers' attention by staging an argument.

Was this the last of many small rebellions or the advance guard of something bigger? Nobody knew. In the city, some people were putting their belongings in safekeeping and sending their families far away, while others simply waited.

One thing was certain: nobody could bear the Bourbons any longer.

Vincenzo stands up and goes to his wife. He doesn't need to say what he feels because she can read his soul.

"I'd be much happier if he left," Giulia says, her voice tense with worry.

"I know." Vincenzo slowly shakes his head. "I keep thinking about that boy. The one they killed after the uprising. He came to a bad end."

Giulia squeezes his arm. "You mean Sebastiano Camarrone? The one who survived the firing squad?"

He nods.

It happened a few days after the failed uprising. To make the risk of defying the Bourbons very clear to everybody, the prisoners—a little older than boys and not yet men—were shot in the square, in front of their families. But Sebastiano Camarrone miraculously survived. He was wounded, of course, but alive.

Vincenzo was told that the boy's mother approached, and asked out loud for the king to pardon her son. Because that was the law: anyone who survives the firing squad must be spared.

Instead, they shot him in the face.

In the end, the soldiers crammed the bodies into four coffins. The city streets were still stained with the blood that dripped from the cart used to transport the bodies to the mass grave. Nobody wanted to wash away the dark strip.

"I can't bear to think about it," Vincenzo says in a whisper. "He was like our son, intelligent; he had even studied. And these sons of bitches killed him without conscience or mercy."

Vincenzo is not easily outraged, yet this time his sense of revulsion makes a breach in his indifference.

Giulia covers her face with her hands. "Dogs. I keep picturing that poor mother's distress. That's why I wanted Ignazio to go away, because you never know what could happen." She turns and looks at the door. "We've lived our lives, but he . . ."

Her husband puts an arm around her shoulders and kisses her forehead. "Yes, I know, but it's his decision."

She huffs. "The fact that Ignazio is as hardheaded as you is not something I find reassuring."

He disengages himself from Giulia's embrace and goes to his room to finish getting ready. He sends for his son, tells him to hurry, and asks the stable boy to make sure their vehicle has an escort of armed servants.

At dawn, the carriage that's taking them to Palermo exits the Villa dei Quattro Pizzi. Once again, Vincenzo has decided to relocate there instead of staying in Via dei Materassai. With its walls and access to the sea, the villa is easier to defend.

The cold spirals out of the sea and slithers through the two men's coats, making them shiver.

Vincenzo sits opposite his son. He observes him in the half-light inside the carriage. With his high forehead and determined jaw, Ignazio looks very much like Vincenzo's father, Paolo, but doesn't have his personality. Of course, he is polite and *charmant*. He's been admitted to the casino of ladies and gentlemen, he, the only Florio to be accepted by the city's most exclusive aristocratic circle. He's an intelligent young man, with savoir faire and a natural grace he has inherited from Giulia. But what his father admires most is his disarming coldness.

"Your mother's worried and she's right to be." With two fingers, he pushes aside the curtain over the window. "You were a child, twelve years ago, when the revolt broke out, and I got caught up right in the middle of it. It would be better if you went to Marseille. I'd feel better knowing you're far away from here, where anything could happen."

"I'd rather stay." Ignazio's face is determined. "You need help running the business and I know many people who'll give me firsthand news of what's going to happen in the forthcoming hours."

"Very commendable." His father sits back, relaxing, and interlaces his fingers over his crossed legs. "You're twenty-one years old and you already know how to act. I thought you'd welcome the prospect of going to France for a while, especially now, but you . . . And I also thought you could find yourself an attractive Frenchwoman you could pass the time with there, while things blow over here. Besides, I can't imagine someone like you just sitting and staring into the eyes of your sisters' female friends."

Ignazio suddenly blushes. His father doesn't notice his lips pursing and quivering, or his restrained breath swelling his chest.

Only he knows what it cost him to decline the offer to go to France. Because he would like to return there more than anything else. But he cannot and must not.

For a moment, he lets that painful memory sweep over him. A memory as sharp as a piece of glass you can't help admiring for its beauty, glow, and reflection. Blond curls, a gloved hand, a head bending down to hide the tears of his departure. Then the letters, so many letters.

Nobody must know what happened in Marseille. Especially not his father.

His father, who needs him now more than ever. His father, who is increasingly overweight, increasingly tired, increasingly old.

Ignazio could never fail in his duties or disappoint him. That's not what's expected from the heir to Casa Florio. Vincenzo notices his son's blushing but mistakes it for embarrassment. Ignazio is always very reserved about his female friendships. "Ah, son. I know you're a ladies' man." He raises his eyebrows, complicit.

Ignazio forces himself to nod.

"All right, let's forget about women and think of ourselves. Now listen, this is what we have to do."

The son leaves his memories in a corner, the way he always does. He looks at his father and listens.

"We went through a lengthy slump in 1848. There was almost no trading and the taxes inflicted on us by the Neapolitans were destroying the economy. The interests involved now are much more complicated. As a matter of fact, there have been emissaries from the Savoys circulating among noble and tradesmen's families. They've also tried contacting me but I chose not to meet with them, at least not yet . . . I want to work out what's happening first. There's too much chaos, and with Bourbon troops gathering at Porta Carini, there's not much we can do. I think the Bourbons are expecting Garibaldi's men to enter through there but nobody's actually said that. The city is under siege. We have to keep our ear to the ground, see in which direction the wind is blowing, and be ready to take advantage of whatever situations present themselves. It's no longer up to the Sicilians now. The Savoys want to get their hands on Sicily and the whole realm, and this time they'll find a way because they'll get help here. They already have Tuscany and Emilia, but they have no idea what awaits them here . . . Too many uncertainties, too many interests in play."

Ignazio looks out the window again. "We'll do what it takes to protect our Casa Florio."

That is all Vincenzo needs to hear.

Back at the villa with the servants and her mother-in-law, Giulia is anxious and restless. A handkerchief in one hand and keys in the other, she walks through the rooms to Giuseppina's bedroom. There's a maid sitting outside the door.

"Is she up?" she asks.

The maid, young but of strong build, leaves her sewing. She has an accent from the Madonie and red skin from spending long days in the sun. "Yes, signora. She ate without a fuss and now she's sitting in the armchair, as usual."

Giulia walks in. The scent of fresh roses in the room cannot completely conceal the sickly sweet smell of old age.

Giuseppina is in the armchair. Her mouth half-open, she's singing a song, incomprehensible words in thick Calabrian. For weeks now, she's been alternating between moments of lucidity and days when the world capsizes and ghosts from over eighty years become real again.

One of her eyes is vacant, as though a veil no physician could treat has blotted the light from it. There is no cure for old age.

Giulia swallows a clot of saliva and panic. Her anxiety multiplies. She reaches out to caress Giuseppina but pulls her hand away. She is overwhelmed, paralyzed with pity. "Donna Giuseppina . . . would you care to go out?"

Giuseppina gets up with difficulty, her body hunched over by arthritis. The maid puts a shawl over her shoulders while Giulia takes her by the arm.

They walk along the villa's hallways. Giulia has been thinking for some time now that it's not death that erases all guilt and purifies the memory, but illness. In a way, seeing her mother-in-law grow old has been compensation for all the harm she received, and has taught her compassion. She no longer harbors even a shadow of desire for revenge.

They say there's a mysterious justice in the order of things, a balance that follows unknown laws.

They go down into the courtyard, where Vincenzo has arranged a table and a few armchairs. The sea provides a gentle backdrop.

Giulia often writes to her daughter Giuseppina, who lives in Marseille with her husband, Francesco, the son of Augusto Merle, Vincenzo's long-standing business associate. Like Angela's, hers is a peaceful, wealthy marriage. Angelina already has three children, while Giuseppina had given birth to her second just a few weeks ago. Although her daughter's letters betray her homesickness for Palermo and her family, Giulia knows that she is a contented wife.

She's more worried for Ignazio, who seems so controlled, so hard. She wonders what has become of her "little prince," that inquisitive boy enthusiastic about everything. He has become a young man with disarming politeness and a rigid soul, perhaps even more so than his father's. As though he needs to obey a self-imposed rule, Ignazio is above all rigorous with himself. And that's what Giulia fears. This rigidity.

The maid resumes her sewing, while Giuseppina slumbers and, every so often, emits strange sounds or utters disjointed sentences.

She suddenly grabs Giulia's hand. Her pen squirts on the paper and produces a blotch of ink. "You must tell Ignazio that I made a mistake, that I had only one life. You have to tell him, all right?" Giulia doesn't know whom she means, her son or that uncle she never met. Then she sees her mother-in-law's eyelashes glisten with tears. "I loved him. He was the one I should have married, I know this now. I loved him but I never told him because he was my husband's brother. And now I want him to understand that you have to marry not for money but for—" She bursts into sobs, shouts, and wrestles. They can't placate her. The cap that holds her hair in falls to the ground and her lips stretch over her teeth.

On an impetus, Giulia hugs her. "He knows," she says into her ear to calm her down. "He knows." She feels tears stinging her eyelids. The stories Vincenzo mentioned, about that strange love between brother- and sister-in-law, are confirmed. She gently gets her to stand up, dries her tears, and leads her back to her room. There, she puts her to bed and gives instructions for a tranquilizer to be given.

Her final thought, as she closes the door behind her, is that she at least knows she made the right choice with Vincenzo. Even though she had to wait for years.

Along the walls, amid the streets overlooking the Cassaro as far as the sea, beyond the bastions breached by cannon fire, time stands still. A scent of dried algae drifts in from the sea, and from the mountains that of orange blossoms.

It's almost as though Palermo is letting everything just happen to her. That she's her own spectator. But, in actual fact, Palermo is only sleeping. Under her sand-and-rock skin there's a pulsating body, a flow of blood and secrets. Thoughts that quiver from one side of town to the other.

And these thoughts now have a name: Garibaldi. In the name of Victor Emmanuel II he has claimed the dictatorship of Italy, called the people of the island to arms, and already occupied Alcamo and Partinico . . .

But the injury of the Gancia still stings. Moreover, news has spread that Rosolino Pilo, who rushed to Garibaldi's aid, has died fighting at San Martino delle Scale, just a dozen miles from Palermo.

Vincenzo Florio has no way of knowing what's going to happen but he walks into the offices of the Royal Bank with a bag and a decision. He has left Ignazio in Via dei Materassai. He doesn't want him involved.

A flight of stairs.

As a trade governor, he controls, compares data, and obtains information. He orders all the money in cash—all of it—to be transferred into the safe, along with the bank drafts. As soon as the crisis is over, the money will have to be released back into circulation or converted into the kingdom's new currency. In the meantime, it's better to keep it safe.

There isn't much that can be done about the ingots in the treasury, however: soon—it's only a matter of hours—Garibaldi's men will come to requisition the gold supply, which is very substantial.

God only knows where this gold will end up.

It was clever of him to hang on and not give in to Pietro Rossi, who tried to get him to resign.

Even now that the situation is breathing down his neck and everything is collapsing, he knows he's able to do what he's doing. He picks up the papers and stuffs them in his bag: they will be Casa Florio's safe passage to the future.

Palermo is breathing a scirocco, and waiting.

Garibaldi is less than seven miles away by now. The city both awaits him and fears him, uncertain about whether to go and meet the Red Shirts and the *picciotti*—the peasants who joined Garibaldi and helped him during the Battle of Calatafimi—or to barricade themselves in a defense that's most probably futile.

Families are divided. The city is split. Some people have barricaded themselves in their houses, bolting doors and windows, the women are reciting their rosaries and the men quaking behind their closed shutters. Many young men, on the other hand, have picked up rifles and are ready for the assault.

On May 23, Garibaldi's men reach the city gates, not by sea but through the mountains. Palermo's residents watch the dust from the clashes and listen to the bang of the cannons and shots. Four days later, Palermo yields: Porta Termini, the city's most vulnerable entrance, is stormed by a group of brave men. The Bourbons then decide to shell the city from the sea, but it's too late: after a clash in Via Maqueda, the city is conquered once and for all.

The men in red shirts go along Porta Termini and spread through the city. Young people—and not only they—join this crowd that speaks an Italian full of different nuances, new sounds, and various accents. There are hugs and suspicious looks, flags being waved, and, at the same time, family jewels being hidden away. The streets, cluttered with furniture stacked up for barricades, are cleared, revealing the façades of the buildings.

Piedmontese, Venetians, Romans, and Emilians discover the blooming, sensual beauty of a city they had heard about only from the lips of their companions in exile. The cathedral and its Moorish pinnacles, and the Royal Palace with its Norman mosaics, rise next to sumptuous Baroque houses with large, potbelly balconies. Sailors' and fishermen's cottages alternate with imposing buildings like the one belonging to the princes of Butera. What a strange city, they say: at the same time poor, filthy, and regal. They can't take their eyes off the colors, off the ocher walls that seem to reflect the sunlight; they can't understand how the stench of the sewers can coexist with the scent of the orange blossom and jasmine that decorate the courtyards of aristocrats' palaces.

However, while the soldiers are looking around and Garibaldi declares that they can't stop, that they have to keep going and redeem the entire Bourbon kingdom, other men in the city are making contracts and sealing agreements. The provisional government is located in what is now called Palazzo Pretorio, the same Palazzo di Città where the 1848 rebels got together.

Twelve years have passed since then, but a few of those rebels are now back: older, more cynical, perhaps, but no less determined. Many people have unfinished business to take care of or new pacts to make, and this crowded place is not ideal for that. Better somewhere else, somewhere quieter, far away from the crowd and prying eyes.

Along the street of Porta Termini, beyond the Palazzo Ajutamicristo and just before the Magione cloisters, there is an imposing, stern building.

There are unmarked carriages, and a hubbub of voices and people outside the gates and in the courtyard.

Inside, there's a room screened by brocade curtains.

One of the heads of the rebellion is here with Vincenzo and Ignazio Florio. Two guards are watching the door. Anybody walking past it drops his voice.

Father and son are standing still. Their faces don't carry the slightest emotion.

Ignazio watches his father, studying his gestures.

The man seems to be calmly waiting.

"Naturally, the information I am giving you proves my full knowledge of the Royal Bank," Vincenzo says without any emphasis. "I'm exposing myself considerably by offering you this material." He taps the briefcase on his lap, the same one he had with him when he went to the Royal Bank a few days earlier.

Every word is a drop that breaks the silence.

"It's an interesting offer. I shall inform General Garibaldi. He will equally take into account your contribution in producing cannons for the Red Shirts in your Oretea foundry."

"It was my duty as a Sicilian. Besides, as soon as my workers realized they were cannons to be pointed at the Bourbons, they didn't even mind how long they worked."

"You had the foresight to wait and see which way the wind was blowing."

"Yes, the right way."

The man pauses and drums his fingers on the table. He has a strong Palermo intonation, with barely a hint of a foreign accent. "In any case, you've put your business at the service of the revolution, and I'll be the first to take that into account. I've been authorized to negotiate the takeover of the Royal Bank, and your confidential information will give us a comprehensive overview of the situation. Your responsibility stops here."

Vincenzo narrows his eyes.

The man lights a cigar and slowly waves the match to extinguish it. His mustache, yellow from the tobacco, quivers with pleasure as it takes in the warm smoke. He inhales, then shakes off the ashes into a small plate. There's a pistol next to it: the same one he used to threaten the Bourbon guards a few days ago, when leading one of the columns of Garibaldi's *picciotti* who stormed the city. He stares at Vincenzo, reading his thoughts. "As I thought: *Do ut des*," he finally says.

"Exactly."

There's a pause. Ignazio watches, in awe, the perfect stillness of the two men. A duel without aggressiveness.

"What?" the man asks.

"The authorization to create a credit institution for trade requirements in Sicily." Vincenzo crosses his arms over his wide chest. "If the Savoys take possession of the Royal Bank, then we traders need to fund ourselves some other way."

The curtain of smoke becomes a veil through which they observe each other, a net that catches unspoken words.

"You're quite a peculiar man, Don Florio. First you rented out your steamers for the Bourbons to patrol the coast, and now you're here to sell information about the Royal Bank to the Savoys." He moves his hands, and the ash from his cigar falls to the floor and scatters on the tiles. "You certainly don't lack a sense of opportunism."

"Well, at this moment my ships have been requisitioned by your dictator, Garibaldi, so I don't have any left. As for the rest, as I'm sure you can appreciate, I was in no position to refuse anything to the king. In any case, you didn't try to get in touch with me earlier, as you did with others last year."

Another silence, this time made of surprise and wariness. "Ah, Palermo. One would think she was able to keep a secret, but . . ."

"It's a matter of knowing what to ask and of whom," Vincenzo remarks.

The man's large mustache stirs and reveals a slightly contemptuous grimace. "You and your Casa Florio have the possibility to refuse anything to anyone, if you so wish, signore. You obtained the mail monopoly, and one could say you also have a monopoly on the kingdom's sea transport, practically without paying any taxes, thanks to the credits the Crown granted you. You could have helped the rebellion twelve years ago, and yet you backed out, remember? I was there, we both know it, so there's no use denying it. Never mind, it's all water under the bridge. And now you're talking business to me and I'm replying to you. I think it's what we're both interested in."

Ignazio sees his father's hand tighten and recognizes the signs of increasing annoyance. Uncle Ignazio's ring, from which Vincenzo never parts, flashes a glow like an alarm. "I don't like wasting time. I want a yes or a no."

The man smooths a nonexistent crease on his pants. "You'll get your credit institution in exchange for information about the Royal Bank. The only problem could be if Garibaldi is against it, but I don't think he will be. As for the rest . . ." He opens his arms. "My door is always open to you."

Vincenzo gets up and Ignazio comes to stand next to him. "I'll tell you what we need. Help us and we'll be your allies. Give me a guarantee that my business will bear no consequences and that my ships will be returned undamaged. That's all for today. Sometime in the future, we'll discuss the renewal of the mail agreement with . . . *them* in Turin. Can you do that?"

The man proffers his hand. "You have my support besides that other matter," he says, indicating with his head the bag with the documents. "Sicily is always in need of men like you, with broad shoulders, to face the future that awaits her. I'm saying this as secretary of state."

For the first time, Ignazio speaks. "You will be of great assistance to us as a lawyer. You're a man of action." He says it softly, calmly. His is not a request but a certainty. A truth. His voice is hoarse, like his father's, and his tone contains no nuance. "The Florios don't forget those who help them. In Palermo, we can rely on what nobody, Bourbon or Savoy, can. And you know very well what I mean." He gives him his hand.

The man shakes his hand, then Vincenzo's.

They have no way of knowing yet that this man, Francesco Crispi, a former rebel, former Mazzini follower, suspected of political assassination, and, in the future, prime minister, foreign secretary, and minister of the interior of the Kingdom of Italy, will become Casa Florio's lawyer.

It seems a day like any other. Steamers arrive at La Cala and unload spices, fabrics, timber, and sumac; carts full of sulfur and citrus fruit are standing on the dock, waiting to be stowed. From a distance, the peal of church bells calling to Mass, interspersed with the screeching of the first swallows. Beyond this can be heard the sounds of hammers and presses at the Oretea foundry.

Down the streets, between tuff-and-stone walls, the people of Palermo come and go, with their agate eyes, copper hands, red hair, and milky-white skin. Mixed people, welcoming people.

Past Castellammare, where a new city is forming, the villas of the newly rich rise amid vegetable patches and olive groves. Elegant houses are built on the foundations of old *palazzi*, which acquire a new life, surrounded by gardens with exotic plants imported from British and French colonies.

There, Ignazio Florio will create the Palazzo Olivuzza, and there another Ignazio and another Vincenzo will be born, and that's where Villa Whitaker is also to come. But it's too early to tell these stories, or how, also there, art nouveau cottages will be built, which will then be bulldozed in favor of concrete buildings.

No, it's still too early for that.

For now, Palermo seems inebriated, standing motionless on the threshold of a future full of uncertainty, waiting to discover what the new rulers, who arrived as liberators, want from her. And yet the city is distrustful: she has known too many conquests.

Palermo, the mistress slave who seems to sell herself to all, yet belongs to herself only. And this city, where the smell of dung blends with jasmine, receives distressing, unexpected news.

Vincenzo and Ignazio are in the office of the new National Bank. Vincenzo is president of the branch, and Ignazio works with him. Right now, he and his father are talking about the export of marsala wine. The Florio marsala has been awarded a medal at the Florence Exhibition of 1861: it's the most popular after-dinner wine in Italy and is considered a luxury item in France, where it has also won a medal.

Ignazio didn't twiddle his thumbs when his father appointed him manager of the cellars. "And so, Papà, I was thinking of creating a special reserve to put aside for the next world exhibition. Having a medal on the label is worth something—"

Before Ignazio can complete his sentence, a breathless clerk arrives and bows before Vincenzo. His uniform is in disarray and he looks bewildered. "Here, Don Florio. It's a message from Duchess Spadafora."

Vincenzo grabs the envelope; it's thick, good-quality white paper on which a hesitant hand has written his name. "Ben's wife? What could she want?" he mutters.

He looks at the panting man again and hesitates, the envelope suddenly feeling very heavy, as though he already knows that the paper will bring him grief. Then he opens it and reads.

Ben Ingham's house is heaving with people. They're on the steps, on the street, and crushed against the front gates. When Vincenzo arrives, a crowd of employees, sailors, ship owners, and traders parts in order to let him through.

Ignazio watches his father walk to the threshold of the bedroom with increasingly heavy, slower steps. He sees his shoulders drop, his head bow. He puts a hand on Ignazio's shoulder.

Then he, too, looks.

The body has been dressed in English-tailored clothes. Candlesticks have been placed at the foot of the bed, and an Anglican minister is muttering prayers. Nearby, a small group of faithful are on their knees, praying. Ben has always been very religious.

Duchess Spadafora is sitting in an armchair, next to her husband. She looks as though somebody has slapped her: her face is puffy and dazed. She keeps fiddling with her wedding ring; marriage came to her, too, but against the wishes of Ben's favorite nephew.

A little farther away, Joseph Whitaker, his wife, Sophia, and the third of their twelve children greet those who have come to offer their condolences. Gabriele Chiaramonte Bordonaro, hat in hand, is also here, next to the duchess's children.

They're all looking at the bed.

It seems impossible.

Alessandra Spadafora stands up when she sees Vincenzo, staggers, and he goes to hug her. They're both orphans, in their own way.

"How did it happen?" he asks, helping her back to the armchair.

"A sudden malaise last night. He became red in the face and couldn't breathe." She reaches out and strokes Ben's face. His wrinkles have relaxed and he looks peaceful. Then she shows Vincenzo a dark mark on his temple. "The physician said a vein must have burst in his head. He—he—by the time the physician arrived he was already—" She bursts into tears and clings to Vincenzo's arm.

He has a lump in his throat.

He can't look at the body.

Not him, he thinks, stifling his tears.

Ben, who complimented him on choosing to marry Giulia. Ben, who always treated him like an opponent, but never an enemy. Ben, who, with Uncle Ignazio, took him on a steamer about to sail for England.

Ben, who showed him around the English countryside. Ben, who introduced him to his tailor . . .

A brother, a friend, a rival, an associate, a mentor.

To all this, Vincenzo must now say goodbye. He is more and more alone.

ꝏ

The citrus grove of the beautiful villa in the hills of San Lorenzo is stretching before Giulia. It's just been raining. The leaves, glossy from the rain, are glistening in the afternoon sun, and a scent of humidity she finds reassuring is rising from the earth.

This is not a good time. Vincenzo is in a dark mood, angry about the political situation that has arisen since the annexation of Sicily to the Kingdom of the Savoys, who are acting not like sovereigns but like masters. They're imposing their laws and officials, won't listen to those with more experience in dealing with Sicilians, who, granted, may be *malarazza* and distrustful, but who, if you gave them even a little, would lay the world at your feet. But instead, these people would rather come here and lay down the law without listening, without understanding.

Ignazio is distant, absorbed in the business. Giulia no longer has anybody to take care of: Angelina and Giuseppina have their own families, and her mother-in-law is looked after by two maids who attend to her night and day.

She feels deeply the bite of solitude.

But, above all, what worries her is that Vincenzo . . . seems uninterested in her, in what she wants and thinks. The quarrel they've just had is proof of that. The thought of it alone makes her blood boil. How could he have silenced her like that? Why did he say those dreadful things to her?

She goes to the balustrade that separates the veranda from the garden and looks at the trees. There's a sliver of sun between the mountains.

The thunderstorm has cleansed the air of the sand that infiltrates everything.

Giulia doesn't like living here. It's a huge two-story villa with a ballroom, guest quarters, stables, and a farming estate. Vincenzo bought it more than twenty years ago, before marrying her. Of course, it's an elegant abode, worthy of an aristocrat. As a matter of fact, it's next to the prince of Lampedusa's villa and the Bourbon hunting lodge, the Palazzina Cinese. It's a pleasant location, full of citrus groves, with a tree-lined road leading to the sea and Mondello, and cuts the Favorita estate in two.

Vincenzo, and especially Ignazio, now prefers it to the Quattro Pizzi during the summer. But her heart and memories are tangled up in the nets that surround the Arenella *tonnara*. It's part of her life, of her way of being; if only she could, she would pack her bags, leave the two men, and return to that happy place.

She leans against the tuff parapet supported by pillars. A servant appears discreetly behind her. "Donna Giulia, would you like an armchair?" he asks.

"No, thank you, Vittorio."

The man senses her need for solitude and leaves.

Her anger does not subside. On the contrary, it stirs, becomes solid and tinted with rancor.

Giulia hears the French window open behind her and the sound of footsteps.

Soon afterward, Vincenzo's hand appears next to hers.

They stand in silence, too proud to apologize to each other.

Vincenzo is waiting behind the glass door that leads to the citrus grove. He knows he's gone too far, but what on earth got into Giulia? Since when does she want to discuss politics and economics as his equal? It's true that she knows more than a lot of men, but still: she's a woman, after all.

It all began during lunch. He and Ignazio were talking about the issue that had arisen during the frenzied period of Garibaldi's occupation, when the Casa Florio ships had been requisitioned by the Bourbons.

"They've kept three steamers of the five we have. They said they needed them to transport troops. But now, a year later, they're contesting the fact that the mail distribution service has been interrupted, and even want me to pay the fine for the missed services, as it depended on me." He put his fork down so hard that it fell on the floor. "Not only did they sink one of my steamers but they also want money!"

While a diligent servant was bringing a new fork, Ignazio dabbed his lips with his napkin. "The agreement made with the Bourbons was particularly advantageous, Papà. The problem—what they're really complaining about—is the fact that the official forms and stamps didn't arrive in time. Nobody cares about the letters."

"They might as well try sweeping the sea," Vincenzo exclaimed. It's the postal service, we're under a new regime. We're the ones who've suffered harm. What gives them the right to impose fines?"

"You could have chartered other ships. I mean, you made a commitment, didn't you?"

Perplexed more than shocked, the two men turned to look at Giulia. She continued: "When one signs a contract—"

"We didn't think it was worth putting ships and crew at risk. We sent out the sailing ships of the firms that work with us, but not steamers." Ignazio spoke calmly, looking down at his empty plate.

"It's too risky. Palermo and Sicily have been devastated by Garibaldi's transit," Vincenzo added. "The Piedmontese have been worse than the Bourbons, at least until now. They won't hear reason, they just come here, change everything, and impose their way of doing things. You can't put a whole steamship at risk just so you can deliver messages between Uncle Peppino and Donna Marianna. I can understand about the forms, but the rest—"

"The fact is, you did put yourself in the wrong."

Ignazio intervened, preventing his father's reaction. "I'll explain it all to you in the next few days, *Maman.* The situation is much more complex than it appears: it's not just our interests that are at stake but also those of the people who work for us. That's why we set up the mail steamer society, last year." He stood up. "And now, will you excuse me if I go upstairs to work? Papà?"

Vincenzo indicated the upper story, where long reports from the Oretea foundry, now at the service of the steamships, awaited him. "I'll be along later."

Left alone, Vincenzo and Giulia exchanged an annoyed glance. "Our son manages to silence me without showing disrespect. I hate that."

"In case you haven't noticed, Ignazio has much more sense than you." He asked the servant to bring him a digestive liqueur. Lately, food had almost become a torment, and digestion a long, laborious process.

"No. The truth is that you refuse to accept what's happening. You've told me so many times that Sicily couldn't get very far on her own, and that we should become a British protectorate or something, and now—"

"And what do you think the Piedmontese are? They're turning us into nothing but their colony. On top of that, they've seized the Bourbon Crown treasury and taken it up to Piedmont to pay for the expenses of the annexation campaign. Annexation, you hear? It's a farce, a lie staged by Naples and Turin together. And this is only the beginning!"

"You cannot bear anybody telling you what to do. You've always been like this, haven't you? With me, with your children, and with your business: you always have to have it your way. Instead, why don't you try seeing the good that could come from being a single nation, from the Alps to Marsala? Does it mean nothing to you? And what have you got to say about all those who sacrificed their lives for this ideal?"

He stood up abruptly, patience draining from his eyes. He leaned over her, flushed, speaking into her face. "Giulia, the tsar of Russia could be ruling over us and I wouldn't change—do you understand that? Casa Florio doesn't stop at Messina. What I want is for nobody to touch my world, and what they're trying to do is to—" He put a hand over his mouth to stop himself from swearing.

Not with her, he thought.

He straightened up and continued in an icy tone. "They've told me that I have to alter my mail ships to make them faster or they'll hand over my contracts—*my* contracts—to Genoese companies. That's what they want and I'll give it to them, but they have to pay me. They know I'm the only one who can ensure the coverage of the coastline they require. I will not allow them to take away from me what I have conquered. And if I have to deal with a bunch of pompous pomaded buffoons who talk in that singsong tone, then I will. So be it. But I have to protect what I've created. I will never be dependent on anybody or anything. Casa Florio is mine. Mine and my son's. And that's something even you, who's like one of them, should have understood a long time ago."

Very pale, Giulia stood up and, without looking at him, left the room.

What now? Vincenzo wonders.

He approaches her cautiously and calls her. She stiffens. Giulia is stubborn. She has become softer with age, it's true, but there's something inside her that even time can't break down. Because she's like the dracaena that casts shade over the villa porch: green, luminous, but inflexible.

And it's also true that he couldn't do without Giulia, not in this life nor in the thousands to come.

"Don't ever do this again." Giulia articulates every word and her

Milanese accent resurfaces, as it always does when she's angry. "Don't you dare ever again treat me as though I'm stupid."

"And you, don't make me lose my temper."

"We've been together thirty years and you still consider me a foreigner. And what about you? Remember who you are and where you've come from. The son of Calabrians who came to Palermo with patched-up pants, remember that." She shouts and points a finger to his chest. "That's what I can't bear: that you don't realize we're the same, so why do you have to treat me like this?"

They are the same, it's true, and he knows it. But he will never admit it. A man can't apologize to a woman. He stands in silence, his forehead wrinkled and his eyes a blend of resentment and endurance: in thirty years—yes, it's been this long—he's never been able to tame her. This is his way of apologizing. The only way he knows.

He looks up at the sky. He takes her hand; she wriggles it out but he doesn't let go.

Giulia pushes him away. "I should have sent you away when my brother brought you to my house. I've had nothing but misery from you."

"That's not true."

"Yes, it is."

"That's not true," he repeats, grabbing her by the wrists. "Nobody would have given you what I have."

She shakes her head and struggles free. "You've never given me respect, Vincenzo. Never that. And if I hadn't fought tooth and claw for what I needed, you would have silenced me completely."

She walks away, leaving him in the light of the bronze sun setting behind the trees.

"Stoke the *cufune*, Maruzza, it's a cold night."

The maid takes quick steps and fills the brazier with coal. A thread of smoke rises, carried away by the draft coming in through the window. The year 1862 has begun with cold and rain. It's a ruthless February.

Vincenzo thanks the maid and indicates the door. Left alone, he looks at the woman beneath the blankets. His mother's heart is giving way, beat by beat. Years of hardness, anger, regret, and little love are bringing their work to term.

A little earlier, after the final rites the parish priest of San Domenico administered to Giuseppina, Giulia left. She told Vincenzo to call her if the situation deteriorates.

As if it wasn't already at its limits.

The breath struggles to find a way through the body and gradually loses its strength, turning into a mutter. On the sheet, her hand is cast of wax and bones.

His mother is alive, but only for just a little longer. For days now she has been alternating between torpor and difficult wakefulness. She doesn't sleep but keeps slipping into an unconsciousness that is longer every time.

Vincenzo feels a breathlessness weighing on his chest. He wonders why one must suffer so much, why death can't take pity and simply snap the thread and take people away without inflicting this much distress. It's like childbirth: a symmetrical, opposite pain to that of birth: a long torment to go into the arms of the Lord. *Or whoever in His place*, they say.

He slumps in the armchair, leans back, and closes his eyes. He remembers the moment when Uncle Ignazio died. He understands now how merciful fate was to him.

He dozes off without even noticing.

A rustling of fabric wakes him up. "Mamma!" he shouts, leaping to his feet and rushing to her, ignoring the dizziness caused by this abrupt movement.

Giuseppina is groping amid the blankets. He lifts her and sits her up so she can breathe more easily. "How are you? Would you like a little broth?"

Her mouth half-open in a grimace, she motions no. Her body gives off a smell of talcum powder, cologne, urine, and sweat. A smell of old age so pungent that it cancels out that sweet, milky scent he remembers: his mother's true scent.

He must call a maid to change her, he thinks. But not immediately, not now. He wants to stay alone with her a little longer. He smooths her forehead and brushes away the hairs escaped from her plait. "How are you?"

"Everything hurts, as though rabid dogs were biting at me." Tears are smearing her eyelashes.

He dries them. "If you think you can swallow, I'll give you some medicine," he says, indicating a row of little bottles and powders crowding the night table.

But Giuseppina shakes her head. She looks past her son, searching for the sunlight but not finding it.

"Is it nighttime?"

"Yes."

"And Ignazio? Where's my darling Ignazio?"

"Out. He's gone out."

There's no point in telling her that Ignazio, her favorite grandson, is now busy with Casa Florio and managing the marsala cellars, where he spends a lot of time. And that at this moment he's in a meeting with a few Sicilian members of parliament, among whom is their new lawyer, Francesco Crispi.

His mother indicates the bottle of water. He pours some into a glass and helps her drink it. Just a sip to moisten her lips. "Aah, thank you." Giuseppina shuts her eyes, more exhausted than satisfied.

Vincenzo thinks of how little it takes at this point in life to be happy. Clean sheets, a squeeze of her hand, cool water.

"Sit down here," she says, and the son obeys. Right at this moment, he's a child scared of being left alone and who can already sense the anguish of his mother's definitive absence. It's a sorrow he's been carrying around ever since he realized that his father, Paolo, was about to die.

Ben, too, is dead, and that's a loss hard to accept.

And now the hardest loss of all is awaiting me.

Of course, Giulia and Ignazio have been and always will be with him, but his mother is the only family member Vincenzo has had for such a long time. For a second, he wishes he could go back. He would give everything he owns just so he could feel small again, rocked in her arms.

Giuseppina seems to have read his mind. "Don't leave me alone," she says, with fear in her voice, which is now as thin as a thread. He kisses her forehead and hugs her. It's he who rocks her and speaks in her ear all that he has never been able to, and forgives her for the errors that, he now realizes, every mother inevitably commits.

Giuseppina touches his face, now gropingly. "I wonder how things would have been if your father had lived," she says. "If the other child had been born."

But he shrugs. He doesn't know, he whispers. He can barely remember Paolo.

But she isn't listening to him. She looks past the footboard. "I know the Lord will come for me and He knows what's in my heart, and all the wicked thoughts I've harbored. May He forgive me."

"Of course the Lord knows what's in your heart," he says, trying to reassure her. "Don't think about it."

His mother tilts her head. Her skin relaxes and resumes its color. "My flesh and blood," she murmurs. Torpor closes over her like a wave and submerges her. Her body is hot, perhaps feverish. Her breathing slows down even more, and becomes little more than a light breeze.

He lies next to her and closes his eyes.

When he is roused again, a few seconds later, Giuseppina Saffiotti Florio—his mother—isn't there anymore.

Shortly after Christmas 1865, Ignazio walks through the rooms of Via dei Materassai. There's dust and mud on his shoes. The floor reflects the safe flames from the gas lamps he had installed some time ago.

He mentioned to his father the possibility of buying a new house since this one has small, dark rooms, and doesn't become all their family represents. Vincenzo looked at him from below, frowning, his hand suspended over a sheet of paper. "Look for one and let me know what you find."

His father trusts him.

Ignazio, however, still fears him. *No,* he corrects himself as he opens the door to his mother's drawing room. *It's not fear, it's mistrust.* An old split that neither the business nor the trust built over many years of proximity have been able to heal.

Yes, trust. Not when it comes to feelings and words thrown to break silences and say a great deal with very little. Those are reserved for his mother.

And he finds her sitting in a wooden armchair with a lion carved on the back. She's working on a piece of lace, on a pillow, but often has to stop. Her eyesight is not as sharp as it was, and her eyes get easily tired. She's wearing a pair of half-moon glasses with horn frames, and often takes them off to massage the bridge of her nose.

Ignazio approaches and she holds out her hand. "Sit down," she says, indicating a pouf in front of the large table covered in threads and bobbins. He watches in silence as his mother works, as her fingers interweave ecru threads. That's how his mother has always been: reserved, silent, strong.

"I must speak to you, *Maman*."

Giulia nods, closes the stitch, and looks up. White strands cloud over her once-dark hair. "Tell me."

Now that he's here with her, he hesitates. He knows that what he says cannot be unsaid, and he doesn't want to say it, but wishes he could delay this moment, and push it as far away as possible.

But he's no coward. If something needs to be done, then better to do it immediately.

"There's a person I met at the Ladies' Casino, Mamma. A young woman half-related to the Trigonas, aristocrats three generations back.

Her name is Giovanna." He pauses and studies the border of the valuable Qazvin rug his father bought in France a while ago. The final words are the hardest to utter. "She could be a wife for me." He keeps his head down for a handful of seconds. When he lifts it again, he meets his mother's shiny, tense eyes.

"Are you sure, my boy?"

Of course I'm not sure, he wants to say, but instead nods. "She's a graceful, respectable girl. She comes from a very religious family, not very rich but . . . she has a title and knows how to conduct herself in society. Her mother, poor thing, is very fat but if you could see her daughter, she's a real blossom."

Giulia puts her work down. "I know who it is. Giovanna d'Ondes, right?"

"Yes."

Giulia takes his hands and holds them tight. "In that case I'll tell you again, my Ignazio, because I want you really to think about this carefully. Listen to me, I chose dishonor for years just so I could be with your father, and I've never regretted it, never." There are tears pearling her eyelashes, and her face almost looks younger. *She speaks as though she knows about her and me*, Ignazio thinks with a shudder of embarrassment. "If someone is a reason for living for you, then there's nothing you can't tackle. But if you're with someone out of obligation or, even worse, a duty you feel you have to fulfill, then no, you mustn't do it. Because there will be days when you won't be able to speak to each other and will argue, and hate each other to death, and if there's nothing that connects you here"—she touches his chest—"and here," she adds, touching his forehead, "if you can't find anything that truly binds you, you'll never be happy. And I don't mean mutual respect or passionate kisses, but affection, the certainty that there's a hand you can hold every night on the other side of the bed."

Ignazio has said nothing but he's out of breath, as though he's just been running. His body feels heavy, and he's very aware of the scent of rose and lavender emanating from his mother's clothes. He could never have imagined that she could speak so frankly to him.

Giulia puts a hand on his cheek. "Are you sure she's the right woman for you? And I'm not referring to the fact that she would become the mistress of all this," she explains, indicating the surrounding rooms, "but that she'll be your wife."

Ignazio pulls away from his mother's touch. "She's the most suitable woman on many fronts, and considering the importance of a match with a member of the aristocracy."

"For heaven's sake, stop treating marriage as if it were a business matter!" Giulia bursts out. "You sound like your father!" She stands up and walks around the room with her hands on her hips. "By the way, did you tell your father first? You didn't, did you?"

"No."

"I'm glad, because I already know how he would have reacted. I imagine he would have gone to speak to her father on the spot and by now we would already have been celebrating your engagement." She huffs and glances at her son, who responds with an unfathomable look. "Please be honest with yourself even before you are with me. Will you be, if not happy, then at least content with this girl? Because you can't go through marriage while your heart and your memory are elsewhere. You'll end up doing an injustice to yourself as well as two other people. To the one you truly want and to the one who is forced to be with you."

Ignazio freezes.

His mother knows. She knows about *her*, in Marseille. How did she find out? Not from the letters he's always received in Marsala, no, that's impossible.

The answer hits him hard.

Giuseppina. His sister also knew.

He's forced to drop his head because his distress is too intense. Ignazio cannot, is unable to hide his feelings from his mother. "There's no hope, *Maman*. As for me, I have responsibilities toward you, my parents, and to Casa Florio, and—"

"To hell with the money and us parents. Do you know what your grandmother called me when I became your father's mistress?" Giulia's face is flushed; she is agitated and that's not good for her. "I have swallowed much bitterness. And yet I would do it all over again a thousand times. That's why I'm asking you, one last time, and if the answer is yes, then I'll go to the d'Ondes house myself to speak with Giovanna's mother. Are you sure about your decision?"

Nailed to the armchair, Ignazio doesn't know what to say. It's like having heaven within reach, being able to stretch your fingers and pick the apple from the tree of knowledge of good and evil. His mother is on his side, and she would help him. But his father . . . his father would be too upset. His father could never accept that everything he'd worked for was lost because of a whim. He's done so much for Ignazio, who is aware of how much he owes his father. The time has come for him to reciprocate.

To be accepted by the Palermo that counts. To have access to the drawing rooms of the aristocracy. To become the most powerful among the powerful. Or else yield to the thought that has been gnawing at his heart for years: that of waking up every day of his life next to the woman he loves. The way it has already happened.

But it happened in the past, and that's where it must stay.

He closes his eyes tight. Ambition gags the memory with smoky fingers. And yet one image still manages to escape. A kiss tasting of tears and honey, stolen in the garden of a house outside Marseille.

So that's the way it is, Giulia thinks. *You start alone, and you end up alone.*

She walks through the house in Via dei Materassai. She crosses the salon and reaches her mother-in-law's apartment, which has now been refurbished so that she and Vincenzo can live in it. She goes farther up, to the roof, where, a few years ago, Vincenzo had a terrace built.

Palermo spreads before her, enclosed between the mountains and the sea.

She and Vincenzo are alone now.

Just over a week ago, Ignazio married a girl with velvet eyes and an almond-white face. Baroness Giovanna d'Ondes is accomplished as befits a noblewoman, albeit a recent one, with the customary dowry of debts in her retinue.

In the end, her husband has the title he wanted, the aristocratic wife, the blue blood. For his son, for Casa Florio.

As for the young woman, Giulia immediately liked her. Everybody calls her Giovannina because she is delicate, petite, and graceful, if a little too thin. She'll need to use her claws if she wants to earn her son's respect, just as Giulia had to do with Vincenzo, and she will. Behind that saintly expression, Giovannina conceals a mettle of steel, of that she is certain.

I hope she'll be a good daughter-in-law, Giulia thinks, and in her heart prays that her son has made the right choice. That how he felt about *that other woman* now truly belongs to the past. She couldn't bear to think he's unhappy.

She looks into the distance, at the sea: the couple have gone on a brief honeymoon on the mainland. Giovanna will have a chance to get to know Ignazio better. They'll begin to grow together.

She hears footsteps on the stairs and turns.

Her husband is there, behind her.

"The maid told me you're here." He drops heavily on a chair and Giulia feels a pang of worry. Vincenzo is very tired. Very tired.

He notices the worry crease on her forehead and calls her to him with a nod. "I can't remember what it's like to be just the two of us."

Giulia makes a sound that's halfway between a laugh and a bitter sigh. "I do. We were always inside a carriage or hiding somewhere until my brother discovered us."

Her mind flits to her parents, dead for some years now. To her mother, Antonia, who never completely relinquished her mask of reproach and disappointment, and her father, Tommaso Portalupi, who, on the other hand, forgave her. "It hasn't been easy staying with you, you know?"

She almost doesn't realize she's said it until her husband responds. Just a few understated words, almost a confession. "But you did stay."

Giulia looks at their joined hands. Uncle Ignazio's ring is missing from Vincenzo's finger. He gave it to his son on his wedding day after having it strengthened. "Because this ring belongs to another Ignazio, the one who was a father to me," he said as he gave it to him. "It was he who founded Casa Florio. It's right that you should have it now, and that you should hand it on to your sons."

Vincenzo restrained his overwhelming emotion when, without a smile, his son took it from the palm of his hand and put it on his finger, over his wedding band.

Now Vincenzo looks at his wife, his life's companion, for better, for worse.

"Yes," she replies, simply. She leans over and kisses his gray hair and he squeezes her arm and relaxes against her body. Giulia thinks about all their quarrels: about their illegitimate children, about the impulse to run away after she discovered she was pregnant for the first time, about his refusal to marry her, about his mother's contempt, about the animosity she had to bear for years, and society's scorn. "Yes, I stayed."

And she would not have had it any other way.

Epilogue

September 1868

Di cca c'e 'a morti, di dda c'e 'a sorti.

On one hand there's death, on the other destiny.

—SICILIAN PROVERB

THERE'S AN INTENSE FRAGRANCE in the air. A sweet scent of honey, flowers, and fruit, of ripe olives and grapes left to macerate in the sun.

It feels like spring.

And yet it's a very mild September.

The building is immersed in the greenery of a vast estate: the Villa dell'Olivuzza, which will become the Reggia dei Florio. Long Gothic lines rise from the floor, enclosing an arched portal, and part in mullioned windows screened with white curtains. There are bees buzzing beyond the snowy fabric. The sun has lost the harsh light of the summer but is pleasant.

The room—on the second story of the right-hand wing, in the quietest part of the house—is lavishly furnished. The two windows overlook the garden. From below, from the servants' quarters, you can hear the washerwomen rustling as they beat the laundry.

One of them is singing.

Velvet armchairs, Persian rugs, a mahogany dressing table, and a large bed with a carved headboard.

Vincenzo is slumped on the pillows. Although the weather is warm, he's wearing a smoking jacket and has a blanket over his legs. A half-open eye is staring into space, one hand resting on the surface of the sheet while the other is obsessively searching for the edge, pulling it and scratching at it.

Giulia looks at him and her heart sinks.

Her eyes are dry as she sits in the armchair next to him. She cannot cry anymore but she knows the tears will come. She certainly knows that.

Don't go, she thinks. At one stage, she even says it in a whisper he can't hear.

No, she mustn't think about it. *He's still here with me*, she screams inside. *Until death snatches him from my hands, I will defend him.* In her deeply lined face there's a determination generated by despair.

She looks for her work basket and takes a needle and thread, and goes back to embroidering the christening gown she promised her son and daughter-in-law. Their son will be born soon—or will it be a girl? No matter, as long as he or she is healthy—following little Vincenzo, who is just over a year old.

She smiles despite herself. Her son has been a good boy: he produced an heir for the business straightaway and gave him his father's name. So that Casa Florio may always have a Vincenzo and an Ignazio.

And he, her Vincenzo, the love of a lifetime, has seen him. He's held him in his arms. He was able to do it at the end of May, immediately after they moved to this villa that used to belong to the princess of Butera, when his body played that cruel trick on him.

It happened four months ago. They were already in bed, in this very room. She heard him tossing and turning under the blankets. "Giulia, I'm not feeling well," he suddenly said, sounding drowsy. She jumped out of bed and reached out for the electric light switch, that novelty Ignazio had had installed as soon as he'd bought the villa.

She immediately saw his ravaged face. The droopy eye, the twisted mouth.

She understood.

She ran to call the housekeeper. The physician came and administered medicines. The grimace froze, and his voice remained hoarse.

From that moment on, however, something in her husband changed.

He handed the entire business to Ignazio. He would never admit it, but his body was no longer in tandem with him. Not even seventy years old, it had betrayed him, and he couldn't trust a traitor.

Moreover, a few days later, Vincenzo called Quattrocchi, the notary, and drew up a will.

"Why?" Giulia asked with a hint of anxiety after the notary had left. Sitting in the study armchair, he gave her an odd look. Annoyed. Gentle. "The Lord helped me this time, but I don't know about next time. I don't want to leave anything untidy."

She bent and kissed his forehead. "You won't leave anything because you'll get well. You just need rest. You've grown old, Vincenzo, just like me, and we must slow down now."

"Yes . . ." He puckered his lips. "Slow down." Then he added softly, bitterly, "I never thought this time would come for me."

They hugged.

Giulia sensed his fear. It struck her right in the middle of her chest and sapped away her strength because it showed her clearly what the future would be like: something too dreadful to imagine, let alone bear.

Vincenzo was never afraid. Vincenzo was strong. If only he wanted to, he could defeat death.

And yet he's gotten worse over the last few days. Perhaps another blow has struck the parts of him that have already been attacked before. He barely speaks and hardly eats. Not even the prospect of the imminent grandchild can shake him out of it. He simply can't take it anymore. Years of exhaustion, getting up early and working till late, of tension and anger, are now taking their toll.

And she, who loves him like no other woman would have loved him, knows he has stopped fighting. That he's tired, that this is no life for him. That he has decided to go. Vincenzo, always so active, like a stormy sea, can't live confined to a bed.

But Vincenzo is not unconscious. On the contrary. He remembers.

Two years earlier, when his son brought him to see this house, surrounded by this enormous park full of palm trees, dracaena, and roses, he felt a shudder go through him. He asked the coachman to take a path along the main road, semi-concealed by the olive trees.

And there he found a dilapidated house with the branches of a lemon tree grown wild stretching toward a window without frames.

He got out and took a few steps toward the detached door. "Yes, this is it," he said, his voice quivering and a lump in his throat.

Behind him, Ignazio had been watching him, perplexed and even fearful. "What is it, Papà? What is it?"

He swallowed air and turned. For a second, through the trees, he thought he saw the form of his uncle Ignazio giving his hand to a little boy.

"Here. This is where my father, Paolo, died."

Ignazio looked at the ruins with dismay. It must have been a modest house, but was now a hovel, a skeleton.

Vincenzo felt a shudder rise from the earth to his skin, an omen more than a tremor.

He knew there and then that everything would end where it had begun. That everything in life revolved in a circle. And that this circle would come to him, too.

The laughter he emits is a gurgle of saliva and anger. He slams his healthy hand on the sheet. This is what he's reduced to: a piece of flesh that's washed and cleaned, looking at Giulia's expression of distress, since she's never been able to conceal anything. To see compassion in the eyes of his daughter-in-law, who seemed terrified of him at first.

Everybody was terrified of him. And now he is half a man.

He turns his eye to the ceiling, searching for the ivory crucifix. The other eye is blind, and doesn't respond. It's no use. "Christ, let's get it over with," he hisses, but his voice is incomprehensible, little more than a drowsy lament.

Giulia is immediately at his side. Her work basket rolls on the floor, needles and threads strewn over the rug. "Are you unwell?" she asks. "Vincenzo . . ."

He turns with difficulty.

How much has he loved her?

Only then does he realize with total clarity that she's the only woman who could have been at his side. That Giulia was not a punishment or a fallback, but a gift. Without her patience and her love, he would never have succeeded in doing anything.

Nothing, if he hadn't seen the same fire as his in her.

With a huge effort, he drags his hand next to hers. He takes her small, wrinkled fingers. "Did I give you enough?" he asks with difficulty. He struggles to speak clearly but his tongue feels like dead flesh. "Did I give you what you wanted? Did you have everything?"

Giulia understands. She understands the slurred words no one else can make out, and realizes what they mean.

Her eyes mist over with tears because she, too, knows that he will never tell her words of love. It's up to her to do it for both of them.

She sits opposite Vincenzo, the way he did when Ignazio was born. She utters the words she has never dared say to him, while her flesh is being torn apart and her heart is breaking. "Yes, my darling. You have loved me enough."

Just a few hours later, a servant boy arrives from Via dei Materassai and shouts that, yes, another boy is born. They'll call him Ignazio junior. The lineage and future of Casa Florio is assured.

Vincenzo barely grasps the news. The blood in his brain encounters obstacles, returns with little oxygen, and stagnates between his lungs and his heart.

He's immersed in a dream.

He's at Arenella, at the foot of Villa dei Quattro Pizzi. He's young, has the strong body of a thirty-year-old and sharp vision. It looks like nighttime but the darkness is suddenly illuminated, as though he can see his surroundings in the dark.

Maybe this is a memory, the recollection of that nighttime swim when he felt the whole of life flow through him.

He takes his clothes off, dives, and swims into the open sea. Now the sun glares off the water with an intensity that hurts his eyes. He feels light and strong. Pure, as though after a christening.

The lapping of the sea is the only sound he hears. He sees Giulia's bedroom window and knows she is waiting for him. But behind him, in the open sea, there's a small flat-bottomed boat with a lateen flapping against the wind.

It's a skiff.

It gives him a start. His father, Paolo, is at the helm. And at the side of the boat, ready to pick him up, is Uncle Ignazio, gesturing at him to approach. He's laughing, calling him.

Vincenzo turns. Giulia is waiting for him at home. He can't hurt her like this. He can feel that she is suffering.

And yet the outstretched hand is stronger, draws him more than anything else in the world.

"Come, Vincenzo," his uncle calls. He laughs, he's young, like that time they went to Malta together. "Come."

And so he makes his choice.

With large strokes, he swims toward the boat. Giulia knows it. She will understand.

Soon she will join him.

ACKNOWLEDGMENTS

I have always considered novels as one's children. Difficult, at times naughty children who demand absolute dedication. This has certainly been my most demanding child.

Like all children, this novel has godparents. First and foremost, I must thank three people: Francesca Maccani, a wonderful woman who read and reread this story with extraordinary passion and dedication, pointing out errors and inconsistencies; Antonio Vena, the invaluable friend all authors should have because of his ability to see beyond the text; Chiara Messina, who kept my spirits up during dark times and never said no to me. She never stopped "turning on the light."

Huge, infinite thanks to Silvia Donzelli, my fantastic agent, who doesn't miss a trick and whose patience with my anxiety attacks is epic. I don't know what I would have done without you.

Thanks to Corrado Melluso, a friend and adviser for whom I have infinite esteem, who said to me one day in Castellammare, "You can. Of course you can." Thanks for that and for everything else.

Thanks to Gloria, who has always listened.

Thanks to Sara, who knows these books from the inside.

Thank you to Alessandro Accursio Tagano, Angelica and Maria Carmela Sciacca, Antonello Saiz, Arturo Balostro, Teresa Stefanetti, and Stefania Cima, and especially to my dear, my dearest Fabrizio Piazza: booksellers who never stopped encouraging me, as well as being wonderful friends.

Thank you, in no particular order, to those who have helped me in drafting this book. Claudia Casano, for her essential advice on the toponymy of old Palermo; Rosario Lentini, who introduced me to the

Florios in all their complexity and gave me an objective perspective on the history of this extraordinary family; Vito Corte, for his suggestions on architecture; and Ninni Ravazza for the invaluable work he carries out on the world of *tonnaras*.

Thanks to my family, especially my husband and my children, who never lost faith in what I was doing and came with me on my reckless explorations around Palermo and not only there. Thanks to my mother and my sisters, who never asked for updates. Thanks to Teresina, she knows what for.

Thanks to S.C., who, I know, is smiling.

Thanks to Nord, who believed in the project right away and accepted me in an extraordinary way. Thanks to Viviana Vuscovich: I couldn't have wished for a better pair of hands than yours to take this book for a stroll around the world. I will always remember our chat under a half-sunny, half-rainy sky.

Thanks to Giorgia, who has Job's patience and unusual diplomacy with an author who always forgets everything. And thanks to Barbara and Giacomo, who put up with me, support me, and are always there for me, and know how to soothe my anxiety attacks. It is you who make Nord into a home.

And, finally, thanks to my diamond cutter, my *magistra*, Cristina Prasso. Thanks to the woman who has made this book into what you're now holding in your hands: thank you for the passion, commitment, beauty, and love you put into it, thank you for the words and the calm you are able to give me. Thank you for your patience. Thank you for having heard my voice. I hold you in infinite esteem.

One more thing, the most important. The story you have read is the story of the Florios as well as the city of Palermo, a place I love very much, just like I love Favignana. The historical facts that concern the Florios are fully knowable and described in dozens of books, and it is on these facts that my plot hinges. Where knowledge was lacking, inventiveness and workable imagination came in: in other words, the novel came in. The desire to do justice to a family of extraordinary people who, for better or worse, marked an era.

This is "my" story, in the sense that I have written it the way I've pictured it, without an easy hagiography, by slipping between the folds of time, trying to reconstitute not only the life of a family but also the spirit of a city and of an era.

A NOTE FROM THE TRANSLATOR

In addition to the usual challenges involved in translating literature, working on a historical novel presents the extra complication of vocabulary. There is frequent delving into dictionaries and the Internet to look up words for objects, architectural details, and fashion quirks that you may never come across again. There is also the dialogue. Should you echo the period, or make it as accessible to a modern readership as possible? It is not always advisable to translate late 18th-century Italian into 18th-century English, which has undergone more dramatic changes over the centuries than Italian. It takes less concentration for a modern Italian reader to grasp the language of Alessandro Manzoni than a modern Anglophone to focus on Hawthorne or the Brontës.

Then there's the challenge I enjoy the most: translating regional dialects. We must remember that Italy became a united country only in 1871. Prior to that, it was formed of principalities, dukedoms, a republic, and many states, each with its own language or dialect, traditions, laws, and characteristics. In the case of *The Florios*, we are introduced to a family on an island marked by Greeks, Normans, French, Spanish, and Arabs. The vast majority of Italian writers, even nowadays, use a certain amount of regional dialect in their writing. Although the official language throughout the peninsula is Italian, regional variations creep in with the odd phrase, idiom, or even word. Sometimes, the difference is so marked that it is not understood in another part of the country. Translating dialects is an interesting point. Do we translate it into a British dialect or a North American way of speaking? I choose not to. Venetians do not have the same sensitivity, history, or humor as Mancunians, Londoners, or the residents of New Orleans. They don't have the same history, the same body language, the same food, or the same temperament. When I asked the lovely and extremely helpful Stefania Auci to explain a few Sicilian expressions I could not find in any dictionary, it transpired that some expressions simply didn't have an equivalent in English—because English simply didn't have an equivalent mindset.

Personally, I choose to omit rather than disguise. And so, somewhat sadly, much of the regional relief in the dialect has to be sanded into a more standard English. In the case of *The Florios of Sicily*, some Sicilian expressions were too colorful, too onomatopoeic, or had too beautiful a sound to cast aside. So, I decided to keep them in the text, and slipped in an explanation somewhere in the vicinity, hoping this way the reader will enjoy its rich flavor, even if he or she is unable to break it down into specific ingredients. After all, where's the fun in having everything handed on a plate, without the need to be intrigued? Wouldn't we then be deprived of mystery and its child, inquisitiveness?

—Katherine Gregor

Here ends Stefania Auci's
The Florios of Sicily.

The first edition of this book was printed
and bound at LSC Communications in
Harrisonburg, VA, March 2020.

A NOTE ON THE TYPE

The text of this novel was set in Adobe Garamond Pro, a typeface designed in 1989 by Robert Slimbach. It's based on two distinctive examples of the French Renaissance style, a Roman type by Claude Garamond (1499–1561) and an italic type by Robert Granjon (1513–1590), and was developed after Slimbach studied the fifteenth-century equipment at the Plantin-Moretus Museum in Antwerp, Belgium. Adobe Garamond Pro is considered to faithfully capture the original Garamond's grace and clarity, and is used extensively in books for its elegance and readability.

HARPERVIA

An imprint dedicated to publishing international voices,
offering readers a chance to encounter other lives and other
points of view via the language of the imagination.